HELEN
ALL ALONE

by
WILLIAM BUCHAN

LANCER BOOKS · NEW YORK

A LANCER BOOK • 1966

HELEN ALL ALONE

LANCER BOOKS, INC. • 185 MADISON AVENUE • NEW YORK, N.Y. 10016

It was October 13th, 1950 and, at nine in the morning, sunlight the color of pale sherry was filling a cube of a kitchen, high up in a cliff of a house in Cornwall Gardens, S.W.7. Helen, in a blue housecoat, looked out over a sink and an empty window box at staggering chimneys, the topmost rusting leaves of a plane tree and her favorite weather, a perfect London autumn day, and was hollow with fear.

A boiled egg cooled rapidly, untouched, in her landlady's spotted egg cup that went with the rest of an inadequate set of china. The toast turned to leather in its chromium rack. On the bright check oilcloth of the table top, Helen's hands made pleats and cross-pleats in a napkin, while her eyes sought some kind of answer from a sky of perfect, unclouded and absolutely neutral blue.

With a series of intensifying hisses, the coffee machine boiled over, and this brought Helen to her feet, to juggle clumsily with hot metal and an oven-cloth worn too thin. She burned her hands and lost a good deal of the

5

coffee in the sink, but when she was seated again, with a large spotted cup steaming in front of her, her look of terrified concentration had gone. She could eat nothing, but drinking the coffee too quickly, and smoking between mouthfuls, she was—she said it out loud—"more herself" again.

"More myself?" she said in a low voice, and thought, what kind of self will *that* be a month, a year, from today? What are they going to ask of me? Almost furtively, she slid from under the day's newspaper a piece of commercial stationery, a communication from a shop, and—as she looked at it—something of the same horrified concentration came back into her eyes. This time she shook herself, picked up the letter firmly and read what she already knew by heart, right down to the blocked "e" in the typescript. "Hogg & Nimmo, Ltd.," it said with a certain old-fashioned elegance in the lettering and the small cursive decorations around it. "Gentlemen's Outfitters, 334 Strand, W.C.2. and at Cheapside. Over 100 branches throughout the United Kingdom." Telephone numbers, her own address, followed and then the brief, third-person message:

"Mr. H. Tenby Sanders will be pleased to receive Miss Helen Clark at the above address on Monday, 13th October, at 11 A.M."

This letter had arrived the previous Friday morning. Helen now had a little less than two hours before her interview. Even though she had been warned to stand by, as long ago as six months, still, when the letter came, the shock had been profound. Her willingness to accept whatever might be coming to her had not even been put to the question; she had not, of course, expected that it would be. Once having served where she had, in the last war, she was (she had thoroughly understood) never in life to be "discharged." Only, the war had ended five years before, and many things had happened, and rapidly, since, and her wartime self, like everyone else's, had undergone many modifications. Nothing, at twenty-seven,

6

could bring back the single-mindedness of nineteen or twenty-two, the ages at which she had entered and left the particular war work which had been hers. She could not now recapture the devotion, the recklessness, even the physical endurance she had shown in those times. She was older, she knew more of the world and, having more to be afraid of, was more likely to be afraid.

Helen banged her coffee cup gently down into its saucer once, twice, and a curious look came over her face, a look of bitter awareness and resigned amusement and a kind of affection, all at once. She was thinking that, whatever might have happened to alter or distort the personalities of those who once worked for him, one nature would not change, even fractionally, in five years, or fifty: that of Mr. H. Tenby Sanders himself. She picked up the letter again, gazed at it, gazed over it at the mild blue of the sky and wished, childishly, that she could be going to the Zoo instead. Then she banged the cup down so hard that she broke the saucer, kicked back her chair, sprang up and stood straight, fists clenched at her sides. This time her look was furious, but positive. She was no longer questioning the sky. If *they* could have been ranged before her she would have had plenty of questions for them. For example: what the hell did they really think they were playing at? What kind of idiotic claptrap was all this dressing-up, these fantastically detailed pretenses? Did they not know they were mad—demented moles burrowing away from the daylight, misinformed, corrupted, out of date? In a world of swift communications and nuclear threats, what sense could there be in the methods they used? And why couldn't they let her, Helen, alone? Had she not enough troubles to wrestle with already?

She had built a very pretty case against *them*, was already seeing them sitting, like Etruscan nobles, in circular tombs of conceit, gorged with taxpayers' money, and forever fortified against the consequence of their mistakes; she had accused them in her mind of running a department of state on the lines of a schoolboy thriller; when suddenly all the heat and ferment of her feeling

7

was cooled by the recognition that nothing she was thinking could possibly apply to H.T.S. himself. Him she had come to know extremely well; as well as a young and lively intelligence, and an unhampered intuition, could approach to knowing a nature as complex and as deeply instructed as a Hindu sage. More important, what she knew of him she loved and had given her respect to, as she had never supposed she could to a single human being. If H.T.S. wanted her services, this could never be for a frivolous reason, nor to satisfy a momentary whim. That he should have called on her, he who had so many names to call—this could only mean that some work was on hand which, from their wartime relationship, Mr. Sanders thought that only she could do. So from the initial shock, and the careful putting-by of anxiety as time went on, came the debilitating fear which was still at the bottom of her rage this Monday morning.

Helen's taxi edged into the Strand, into a tide of snouting scarlet buses, jay-walkers, and thwarted motorists in newish cars. The pavements were thick with people forging along, jostling and side-stepping one another, grimly determined. All looked weary, none cheerful. The radiant day spent itself above them. No one stopped to look at the weather. No incident, no human explosion—of grief, or rage, or mirth—seemed likely to occur to break the steady seepage to east and west, or to alter the pattern of shuffling march and counter-march past the packed, strident shops.

Five years the war had been over, but still Helen was entranced by shops: great, speckless windows with *things* behind them. With every month the variety grew. She was (and not only from necessity) a devoted window-shopper, swift in appraisal, needle-sharp to detect something new. Nevertheless, of all the shops she had ever gazed in, Gentlemen's Outfitters had had the least of her attention. Their displays had a quality of boredom peculiar to themselves and, Helen guessed, slow to be affected by war or social change. The Strand shops were dullish, anyway, in Helen's opinion. She looked at them now, over the heads of the pavement crowd, with an attentiveness sharpened by anxiety.

Helen looked, then, at her hands—rather red, she thought, and the nails lustreless without varnish. She looked at her gloves, wished they were new, and could not decide whether to wear or carry them. The taxi slowed, waited, then fetched a smart half-turn across the road and the driver said, "Here we are, Miss." Helen's watch showed four minutes to eleven.

Hogg & Nimmo's shop was almost insultingly dull to look at. Two plate-glass windows, framed in brown-colored marble and brooded over by a contraption of wood and iron, which must be a shut-up sunblind, held displays of singular recessiveness. The left-hand window had a number of belted raincoats in various sandy shades. The right-hand one had two white shirts, a kind of chromium trophy of antlers carrying collars, and a great many dark blue and black, minutely pin-spotted or faintly patterned ties. The glass door, thickly framed in brown wood, had "Hogg & Nimmo, Estd. 1864" on it, in white china letters. The second "m" was missing from Nimmo.

In more or less feverish broodings on this visit, Helen had imagined a variety of different scenes, of different receptions which might be accorded her, all more or less bizarre or dramatic. What she had not prepared herself for was solid, conventional ordinariness, a kind of dusty tranquillity in the outfitter's shop. The heavy door muted the noises of the Strand. A soft library light fell from a long glass skylight set into a high ceiling. The vista was of receding showcases and glazed cupboards, all dark brown wood and watery glass. A strip of drugget ran over black linoleum, the full length of the shop, to a door of hammered glass marked "Counting House." There were two men in the shop—one on either side—both quietly at work arranging stock. Halted, a little breathless, just inside the door, Helen took in the scene, noting that one of the men was elderly and bald, the other bald and young. It was to this one, where he bent helpfully forward over some open collar-boxes, that Helen addressed herself.

9

She had to repeat her words, so feeble was her attempt to adapt her voice to the quiet of the shop. "I have come to see Mr. Sanders," she said, too loudly the second time, and looked hard into the face of the bald young man. Nothing altered in his expression, but for a slight intensification of his courteous and receptive look. He had an almost perfectly round pale face, and a thin, very neatly trimmed, smear of a brown moustache. Perfectly round spectacles gave him a schoolboy appearance. He bowed towards Helen.

"I am Mr. Sanders, Madam," he said in a modest and sensible tone. "What can I do for you?"

"You're *not* . . . I mean, perhaps you are, of course. . . . But not *my* Mr. Sanders!" Helen felt sick with discomfiture. To be so strung up, to be so let down. Could there be another branch (one of the hundred) in the Strand? Madness. Impossible. Oh, their tricks! She was suddenly angry again, and said in a high, clear, cold voice:

"I have an appointment with Mr. H. Tenby Sanders for eleven o'clock, and it is eleven o'clock now."

The assistant's face assumed a remote expression. He touched his spectacles, bowed a trifle coldly, and then was round the end of his glass counter and off down the shop with remarkable speed, beckoning Helen to follow. "This way, Madam, *if* you please."

His colleague did not look up as they passed.

The door marked "Counting House" led into a small dark lobby. Another door marked "Counting House" stood opposite. Narrow, steep stairs ran up on either hand. Helen followed the assistant up the right-hand staircase, observing bleakly the worn metal nosing of the stairs, the pea-soup dado, the dirty landing window giving on to a blank brown wall. There was a fairly powerful smell of cats and stewed tea, and new cotton cloth.

Two floors up, the assistant stopped at a door. It had a frosted-glass panel with "Managing Director—Private" on it in black paint. Irritation, and impulse of vague disloyalty, swelled up in Helen. Mr. H. T. Sanders, she said to herself, waspishly, was certainly acting this one out, in depth. The assistant paused and bent his head to the door, listening. Then he tapped three times, paused again and, without a word, whipped the door open a third of its traverse and, with a firm pressure on her back, pushed Helen into the room. She heard the door close behind her, and feet running briskly away downstairs. An unforgotten, dearly-loved voice said, "Helen! It's been *too* long!"

Quite breathless now, and off balance from her violent entry, Helen blinked, stared and, in a throttled voice, made the joke she had been treasuring, the password she knew was expected of her:

"Dashed pretty place you've got here, Colonel Sanders," she said, and burst into tears.

At one time during the war, Colonel Sanders and his "circus" had been stowed away at a country house in Northamptonshire called Owlsey Towers. Its name had been the house's only charm, and none who worked there would surely ever forget its peculiar dreadfulness. All through one sad autumn and bitter winter they had tried to keep their spirits up, to make a joke of the Towers. But something stronger than they, an awe-inspiringly powerful Victorian wrong-headedness which had planned the place, made almost every joke fall flat.

Owlsey Towers was haunted by no ordinary ghosts, but by the odious fantasies of its builder, and these were either at a darkly flaunting maturity, or in a leprous condition of decay. The house itself was vast, sprawling, Italianate, built of yellow stone with towers containing loggias, and tall, narrow windows of sheet glass. Even for the architecturally curious it had nothing of pleasure, being meanly designed for its size, lacking even quaintness in its impropriety to time and place, representing nothing but a senseless expense of labor and material.

Indoors seemed to be either salons or boot-cupboards: there was no human-sized room in the whole place. Miles of corridors led nowhere, or hairpinned back on themselves. Fiddling little after-thoughts of staircases were, often, the only means (short of a half-mile walk) of get-

11

ting from floor to floor. As winter approached, the whole
force huddled closer together, abandoning room after
room, blocking passages with wallboard, attempting to
conserve what little heat could be made. When it rained,
bedroom ceilings dripped, mositure coated mahogany
banisters and streamed down walls of fading silk. They
stuck it as best they could. They wryly recognized that,
seeing what they were engaged in, the place had certain
advantages. For who would ever seek them out, or ever
want to?

That winter merged slowly into a chill, unpromising
spring, a season of high winds and continual cold rain.
When the birds were beginning, in spite of it, to find
their voices, and some fresh green was showing here and
there among the rusty black and verdigris of the evergreens, a young girl, pregnant, had drowned herself in
the lake. After a day's search of the dripping conifers,
someone had found a note on a desk. The Colonel himself had fished her out.

For all of them this occurrence was miserable; its effect
on H.T.S. had startled Helen. Never before or since had
she seen him—whatever the disaster or disappointment—
so upset. He had gone quite wild, refusing to eat or speak,
and spending a whole night stamping about in his office
or sitting collapsed in a chair. Next day, when Helen
found a few snowdrops under a cryptomeria, she brought
them to him. It seemed the obvious thing to do, for they
were the only flowers anyone had yet seen at Owlsey
Towers. Sanders had touched her cheek gently—the sole
familiar gesture he had ever made—and turned sharply
away.

Heaven knew what would have happened to their morale if outside help in the shape of a joke-bearing Major
General had not come swiftly. That very day he arrived,
one of their rare visitors, and a stranger to Owlsey
Towers. Walking after luncheon with Colonel Sanders
along the pasty gravel of a terrace, he had made the remark which Helen now quoted as her password. He had
not meant it as a joke, and they never saw him again.
But it was probably his finest contribution to the war.

12

Now Helen found herself being guided, with kindly pats and soothing words, to a chair of great size and luxury which made her feel better, simply to sit in it. Mr. Sanders, in black coat and striped trousers as bulging, baggy and home-made-looking as his uniforms had always been, was striding about the room collecting bottles and glasses from various cupboards.

"Overwrought, poor girl," he said, with his back to her, "and you've had more than enough to overwreak you, if that's the word I'm looking for. Here," he said, putting a large brandy and soda into her hand, "you drink that up. I never drink in business hours, of course, except when I do," and he mixed an even larger one for himself. Then he sat down behind his immense desk, upon which no paper of any kind was visible, and sipped his drink thoughtfully, looking at Helen from wonderfully bright, light-colored eyes set in velvety, dark brown pouches like a boxer dog's.

Helen took a long swallow of her drink, and the world steadied around her. There was nothing exceptional about this office, but its atmosphere was decidedly pleasant. The carpet was soft and deep; the windows were curtained in an unemphatic but admirable dark damask. The walls carried a number of framed certificates, with important-looking seals. There was a club fender of bright brass with a red morocco top and, above the fireplace which held a small, hot fire, a painting of a boy in eighteenth-century dress riding a rocking-horse.

Mr. Sanders appeared to be in no hurry to begin. He sipped and smoked and gazed unpointedly at Helen, his eyes full of the utmost friendliness but also (she knew) diagnosing, searching, looking for confirmation or rebuttal of certain things he needed to know. Beyond the window, through a gap between tall buildings, Helen could see trees, barges, blue sky above the south bank of the Thames. For the tenth time, her glance went back to the boy on the rocking-horse. Mr. Sanders put down his glass.

"Archibald Nimmo, 1724-1786," he said. "Pretty, isn't it?"

Helen permitted herself an ironical look. "I knew you were thorough," she said, "but this—"

"Saucy as ever!" he said, crossly. "Thorough, be blowed. It's true!"

Still Helen persisted, now revived enough, perhaps tipsy enough, to tease her old master and enjoy it.

"Which are you, then," she said, "Hogg or Nimmo?"

Mr. Sanders' voice was a muted bellow. "Both, you beastly girl, both! Oh heavens, no—look, Helen, you can't. . . . Oh, but I can see you can—you *have* been thinking. . . . Mixing me up with those dreadful people. . . . No, don't interrupt. Common cloak and . . ." His voice took on a terrible note of scorn. "But, Helen, you should have known me better. Oh, I know, *wartime*—but then one has to do all sorts of things in wartime, silly things—war-winning things. . . . But now, really *serious* matters. . . . Oh, look, you've made me out of breath!" He sat back puffing, looking half-hurt and half-amused.

Helen's total bewilderment showed so clearly that Mr. Sanders looked contrite.

"Ah, now, poor duck," he said, "how could you know? Five years is a long time and, well, I suppose, rumors get about. Still and all," he looked cross again, the scornful note came back into his voice, "you should know better. I suppose you stopped your taxi fifteen doors away, or something awful like that?"

"It didn't even occur to me," Helen said stiffly. "Though, come to think of it, I probably ought to have. Anyway, how can you be both? Hogg *and* Nimmo, I mean."

Mr. Sanders leaned forward and looked earnestly at her from his brown-ringed eyes.

"Because my mother was a Miss Nimmo, Helen," he said, "And *her* mother was the only daughter of the last of the Hoggs. This is a family concern, Helen. I simply must just have failed to mention it. We have been haberdashers for many generations. It is a very decent little business."

"Do you really have a hundred branches throughout the United Kingdom?" Helen asked, to placate him.

"We do, we do!" said Mr. Sanders gaily. "And Paris and Brussels and Toronto and Rio de Janeiro, and all sorts of places. Only they're not all called H. and N. The name's a bit old-fashioned and slab-sided for some contemporary tastes. But if you know——, and——" (he mentioned two famous department stores), "those are what might be called branches, in the sense that we own them outright."

"But . . ." Helen sent a puzzled glance round the office.

"Where's all the apparatus of management, you mean? Well, not here, as you've seen for yourself. It's all in an uncomfortable great glass box in Finsbury, if you want to know—horrible place, full of sprinkler systems and downtrodden girls and staff problems. I don't trouble myself too much about admin.—as you see."

In some ways, Helen had early discovered, H.T. Sanders was transparent. At present a slightly guilty look had come into his face, which he turned away from her to look out of the window.

He really is the ugliest man in the whole world, Helen said to herself fondly, looking at the bloodhound profile. And I bet he cuts himself in pieces about his staff problems. I bet that's the best-run, most pampered office on earth!

Mr. Sanders turned back from the window and faced Helen calmly, seriously.

"Helen," he said, "you came through that door just now blue with fright."

Helen sat up straighter in her deep chair, holding tight to her gloves and bag. Here it comes, she thought.

"I know you are a brave person," he shook his head slightly at her instinctive shrug of denial, "—a really brave person; and by that I do not mean a raving psychopath who doesn't understand fear, or a person of dull sensibilities and low imaginative power. I mean someone who has the brains to be afraid when there is reason, but who uses her head to help her heart, and her common sense and wit to control her imagination. Now, you've had a not altogether nice time since we parted. Indeed,

15

meddlesome old thing that I am, not long ago I nearly came pounding in to interfere. Don't look so shocked! I care very much for those I do care for; and, in any case, have you forgotten? You are still, so to speak, 'plotted.' Mere routine, and only for me to interpret. But, in this case, you must believe, I liked to keep an eye . . ." For a second, again, the guilty look came into his face.

Helen knew that her dry throat would not let her speak, so she did not try. She simply sat rigid, gazing at Mr. Sanders with very large eyes from a face quite empty of color. The deep, slightly harsh voice—made comforting by its many small alterations in pace and pitch, the humor threading seriousness like a vein of mica—continued to beat gently on the quiet warm air of the room.

"Let me see, you left school roundabout the outbreak of war. And it was pretty well straight from school that you came to me. Your father . . . as you know, I knew your father. . . . Quite irreplaceable for any of us, and for you—well, I won't dwell on it. But your mother—and I've asked you once or twice not to blame her too much, I'm sure quite in vain . . ." he smiled at Helen, a little sadly, "she is really quite absolutely otherwise occupied." These odd last words came out with perfect finality, and just the suggestion of a grimace.

I know what he's thinking. . . . Her father had got himself killed early on, had been among the very first casualties of the war, regretted by all who knew him, and desperately, mutinously mourned by his child. Her mother had married, in 1944, a handsome, randy, loquacious barrister with political ambitions, who had arranged for himself an interesting and profitable war. He had finished up as a full colonel, and was now nursing a constituency considered safe, even at that time, for the Conservatives. Helen and her mother had never quarrelled. They had simply found it better to stay apart.

The heavy face of Mr. Sanders, with its strong vertical creases, took on a mock-mournful look.

"I cannot, I really cannot go about righting every wrong in the world. I haven't the time or the equipment. And the world wouldn't thank me if I did. Got to have its

16

quota of wrongs to provide the necessary friction. But I can—" here he patted his large clean blotter with both hands, "I can, and I will, go with all four feet into situations that seem to fall within my province. Indeed I am paid for just about that. Now, Helen, don't interrupt. You shall have all the say you want in a minute."

He was looking at her closely now, bending his brilliant eyes, with their shadows of sickness, full into her own. His look was searching, but the girl looking up at him felt no strain, no wish to look away. Her own gaze swam up to his like a fish to a strong light.

"I have left you wondering for six months what I might be wanting of you. I regret very much having to have you warned in that way. It could have been so simply done between us but—I was abroad. I have not long been back. And none of the old lot is with me now, so I had no choice. . . . Also, I wanted you to be warned in good time. You had had a bad knock, and I needed you to get over it a bit before we got on to other things. . . . I've one thing to say about that, by the way, and you must not hate me for saying it. I always admired you, Helen—I think you know—quite apart from being fond of you as yourself, and as your father's child. But I knew, even when you were nineteen, that yours was an unusual temperament. I guessed that you were, in a good sense of the words, 'capable de tout.' Where work was concerned I turned out to be right. I never knew anyone to *abolish* herself in things as you did—dive in head first and stay in to the bitter end. I rather thought that this same quality would show up again, in life—in love; although I couldn't tell how."

He paused, and looked away for a moment. Helen's throat was throbbing, the sick pain was back in her stomach. She had relinquished her bag and gloves and was holding tight to the arms of her chair. She was praying that H.T.S. would stop, and at the same time longing for him to go on.

"After you left me you did some extra secretarial training, and got a job as secretary to a ballet school which promptly went bust. You then became P.A. to that intol-

17

erable fat man who runs a chemical business, and makes speeches about 'Management as a Vocation,' and joins everything in sight. You got fed up with him making pompous passes at you, so you moved off to an advertising agency—a rare basket of snakes, in this instance, if I may say so—and you'd stuck that for a year, being steeplechased after by account executives or whatever they call them, when along came . . ."

Helen bent her head abruptly. Mr. Sanders' tone became gentler, softer, although every word was still clear.

". . . someone who had a particularly rare and special gift, a gift of which you were surely in great need. Please understand me, Helen. I would never have the impertinence to moralize, even if I thought the situation demanded it, which I don't. But you see what I mean about your being 'capable de tout.' You were born to go overboard, one day, in this particular way: just as surely as you were born to survive the experience. You abolished yourself again, and it was right that you should. I would . . . I would have given much to have saved you the suffering afterwards; but the experience, for you, was essential."

Helen raised her head and looked at her old friend with affection, tiredly. She felt as if blood were flowing again into limbs made numb by cramp. Yet, had he not always known how to lighten loads, to bring one back to life?

"What you didn't know, poor Helen," he continued, "was that the particular gift I mention is never, absolutely never accompanied by staying power in any moral or domestic sense. It can't be. This is some dispensation of nature's. Great lovers, and I mean really great ones— not just barroom braggarts and memoirists—are not only extremely rare, they simply, like quicksilver, cannot be kept in one place—with one person. So the end of your wonderful time was a foregone conclusion, through absolutely no fault whatever, mental or physical, of your own. There," he added hastily, "that wasn't meant to be a lecture. It's all, your love affair and everything, part of why you're here today. And one of my several reasons for saying that you are a brave girl. How's your drink?"

For the past few minutes Helen could not have raised a feather, let alone a glass, to her lips. The glass stood half-full on the small table beside her chair. She shook her head, smiling, while Mr. Sanders took a pull at his own drink.

Helen found her voice, a husky, exhausted voice, and said: "You know an awful lot about me—about what I am and what I've done, both."

As much as one human being can ever know about another, and more than most could ever aspire to knowing. He has two kinds of power—his own, in himself, and the powers he controls. He wishes me well. He is not inquisitive; he is not, in any sense, a spy. Yet he cannot know it all. . . .

She found courage to say, quite lightly: "I'm over it, you know; quite settled down again."

"You make it sound like measles. But then, in this country, love and the measles are one. So I expect you are wise." He looked briefly at the ceiling, and then brought his eyes to bear on her again suddenly, full of power.

"One thing I'm now certain of," he said crisply. "This thing has *hurt* you, but it has not *harmed* you—and that is the important point."

He pushed back his chair and walked past her to the farther window and stood for a moment, looking out. Then he turned to a tall cabinet standing between window and fireplace, and began to dig in his pocket for keys.

"Helen," he said, and his tone was now dry, brisk, military, a tone she remembered from most of their encounters in the war. "Helen, come over here. I'm going to stop beating about the bush, and we're going to look at some maps. I remember your passion for maps."

It was an absurd piece of furniture that H.T.S. was now bending over; it might have been an egg-collector's specimen cabinet, but that it had a shallow glass case at the top, and the case was full of various kinds of white collars, all neatly labelled. Turned-down stiff collars for day wear, stick-up collars for evening, curious high-collars with rounded points, even a Gladstone collar with immense spikes. Each label bore its stock name—"The Stanley," "The Roehampton," "The Glenfinnan." H.T.S. had got his key into a lock hidden somewhere at the back. He then took hold of one corner of the cabinet, pulled, and the whole glass case, with about two inches of woodwork, swivelled away revealing a broad screen of milky glass with an arrangement of knobs and switches on one side. The whole thing looked, from above, like a large television set lying on its back.

Something familiar, an old excitement, began to take possession of Helen. This was known, enchanted territory again.

"I remember your passion for gadgets," she said under her breath.

"Impertinence!" said Mr. Sanders. It was unsafe even to whisper in his presence. He had ears like a bat.

"Now," he said, "I want you to pay great attention." He set a small pointer and pressed a switch. The glass screen lit up and was an illuminated small-scale map in color, very sharp and bright in its projection.

"You recognize this country?"

"Yes."

"An independent kingdom till 1940. What is it now?"

"A People's Republic. A satellite of the Soviet Union."

"Are we in diplomatic relations with it?"

"Yes—yes, I think so."

"We are. Of a rather hampered and tenuous kind. You'll hear more about that." He touched the switch and the map disappeared.

"What is the name of the capital?" Mr. Sanders asked.

Helen felt an instant's panic. It seemed so important to answer briefly, unhesitatingly, as she had been trained to do. Sofia? No, that was Bulgaria. S—something. She said, not quite certainly:

"Senj?"

"Correct. Have you ever been there?"

"No."

"Have you ever seen picture of Senj, or of the country in general? Stills or films?"

"I must, I suppose . . . at some time. Some geographical magazine . . . but I have no picture in my mind."

"Good. Here's one." He pressed another switch. A colored picture came on to the screen, evidently taken from high up, at a flat angle. Helen saw wooded hills, with higher hills, snow-capped beyond, and a broad river coming from between low hills, in three great loops, through what looked like cultivated land. She saw a town, a city, compact, rougly circular cut in two by the river. On the right bank (from her viewpoint) were massive buildings of a kind familiar in all central European cities—palaces, ministries, perhaps nineteenth-century apartment houses—great areas of roof tops, balconies, porte-cochères. Low down on the right, she could see, were older buildings, narrower, winding streets, houses leaning in on one another, the high, ribbed back and ornamented steeples of a great church.

"It's charming," Helen said dubiously.

"It was," said Mr. Sanders. He altered his switches once more. Another colored picture came on to the screen, but now this was a close-up of some particular section. Helen could see the leaves on trees, boats tied to a quayside, people walking, children, trams—even a jaunty dog.

To the left of the picture were ancient-looking turrets and the beginning of a parapet, evidently one end of a bridge. Round-headed trees ran up from the bridge, beside the river, edging a broad street with tramlines in it. On the other side of the street was a handsome, stern-looking building, late baroque of Austrian character. Beyond this was, perhaps, the edge of a park; more trees, some low bushes, the conical top of a pavilion which might be a bandstand. Beyond again, and half-hidden by trees, was a square, comfortable-looking house which could have belonged to Bayswater. H.T.S. touched this with his finger.

"The British Legation," he said.

"They look peaceful—ordinary—pleasant enough,

21

these pictures," said Helen. "Were they taken before the war?"

"They were taken last Friday."

Mr. Sanders stood back from the cabinet and looked at Helen, who had put out a hand to steady herself. A sudden weakness had invaded her body. Her head felt muzzy. It was precisely as though she had opened a door and found, not a room, a corridor, but night and wind and the sound of an ocean beating far below. Reality, of a kind, had suddenly come very close.

Helen shook her head, and this made her feel better. H.T.S. without a word handed her a pair of spectacles with black light-guards. Her hands trembled a litle as she put them on. Their lenses blurred the edges of everything and altered colors. She felt as though she were at the oculist's.

"Look straight at the screen."

Another switch clicked and another picture positively sprang at her from the mildly-lit glass.

"Stereoscopic. I *see*," she said.

"Correct. Do you know this man?"

The picture which filled her vision was of a man somewhat, but not perhaps very much, older than herself, wearing a tennis shirt. Only head and shoulders showed, and behind the head were leaves, branches, the edge of a conservatory. An awestruck little voice in Helen's mind said, "Wow!" for this was a startlingly handsome face in the traditional English way. After a second's study, Helen could see that it was better than handsome, even if ruined for the movies because of a forehead too broad, too powerful, and loaded with lines of thought or anxiety. It was, she thought, a tremendously sad face although, in fact, in this picture it was smiling with what was evidently real amusement, not just a social smile. Not an easy face to forget; and there was no reason that she could see why one should want to forget it. A touch of arrogance, impatience, intellectual restlessness— you could attribute these things, but they only made the face more interesting, original, subtly exciting. Some sense

22

that she was slipping, being immensely, discreetly, and imperceptibly pushed towards something unknown made Helen weakly rebellious for a moment. She expressed rebellion by giving a little giggle and saying in a brassy tone of which she was at once ashamed:

"No. What a smasher! Is he married?"

"He was," replied Mr. Sanders, in a way which was neither encouraging nor the reverse.

The switch clicked again, twice, and Helen gave a little gasp of pleasure. Here was another face, glowing up at her in three dimensions; the face of a child, a girl, three or four years old. Its owner must have been standing, in full sunlight, in summer. There was a mote-filled golden mist about her and, for background, some bushes of roses of a very dark crimson.

Helen's response to this face was not purely conventional, but something more complicated, less generalized. Most people have a private category of faces to admire, to trust, to love. Most women have an image, however vague, inside them of the kind of looks they would wish for their child. Helen had never given the question much conscious thought, but now, looking down through the cumbersome spectacles which pinched the bridge of her nose, she forgot where she was, whom she was with, what she might have to fear, in deep pleasure at examining the small face so cunningly presented on the screen. No doubt whose child this is, she mused, noting the broad forehead (calm as milk where the other was scored and bitten), the well-marked eyebrows with odd little peaks at each outer corner, the straight-staring black-blue eyes under thick, dark lashes. The other, the man, had brownish hair which might once have been fair, pushed away a little at the temples. The child stared confidently out from under a smooth, thick fringe the color of wet sand, but bright and sleek as floss.

The picture went out. Helen made a small sound of regret.

"You can take that thing off now," said Mr. Sanders.

Helen sighed and put up her hands to her hair. Strong magic, she thought, for this time of the morning; and pretty well on an empty stomach. Oh, what can all this be leading to? She gave Mr. Sanders a feeble smile.

"It's not so much the box itself, I suppose, as the way it's used," she said, half to herself.

"It's an excellent box!" H.T.S. replied, defensively, beginning to puff. "Why, my good girl, that screen alone isn't just an ordinary bit of glass. It took six months to make and cost—well, a great deal. I ask you, when did you ever see such truth, definition, such life in any reproduction?"

"Well, what else does it do?"

"Hundreds of things! You really are the world's most disbelieving girl."

H.T.S. bent angrily over his switches. "Here," he said, "look at this."

The small-scale map was back again, but this time it was pocked all over with minute triangles in solid black.

"Know what those are? Can you guess?" he asked. Helen shook her head.

"That's today's exact position for all your friends you thought I was mixed up with," said H.T.S. with a touch of malice. "You know, the boys who always take the third taxi on the rank." He chuckled, and then straightened his face rather guiltily. "I shouldn't be disagreeable about them," he said. "They're brave and useful, and they often come to sticky ends. But they're apt to get set in their ways. Now, *here*," and the map disappeared, to be replaced by a large-scale one of the city of Senj, "—here is the situation in one particular place." There were a number of black triangles, Helen noticed, and three red ones, a little larger than the black. "The red triangles are *my* people," said H.T.S. with quiet pride. "So you see, if anyone were to go to Senj—sent by me—they would not exactly be compassed about by a great *cloud*—rather the reverse, what with secret police, and political police and uniformed police in really laughable hats: they're the cloud of witnesses, I suppose—but they would know that they were among friends. . . ."

The broad, heavy face was so unnaturally vague during this speech that Helen thought, so that's it, at last!

24

The faces of the man and the child came into her mind's eye, and with them the faces in the street this morning, and the busyness she thought she could not share, and the wretched little flat she called home. She felt her heart lighten suddenly.

Mr. Sanders closed the cover of his box and there it stood, once again, a dull, odd-looking cabinet for collars and masculine trinkets. He moved away from it, grumbling:

"Despising my box! I don't know what you expect me to do. I can't have a great brass-bound ops. room here, can I, full of maps and teleprinters and God knows what? I'm a respectable haberdasher, I keep telling you, and one liable to visits from other haberdashers at any time." He peered at Helen's coat, and shook his head. "I'm a draper, too, come to think of it, and I say you need a new coat. That line was a stinker. Cleverly designed, but sweated out of ex-Japanese-army stuff some cheapjack export-import artist managed to unload. You wasted your money, Helen. Something must be done about that."

He had moved close to her now and stood looking down at her very seriously.

"Helen," he said, "I owe you an apology. I've taken an age leading up to what I'm going to say, but . . . well, five years and five years. I had to be sure."

"And you're sure now?" Helen's tongue felt too big for her mouth.

"Oh yes, bless you, quite sure. Helen, I want you to go out to Senj, for perhaps quite a long time. Some months, anyway. There is a job to be done, and I believe that only you can even attempt to do it. It is no ordinary job. If you succeed, I cannot say what your reward will be. If you fail, no one—least of all myself—will blame you. Will you go?"

Panic shook Helen for a moment. She stammered: "What sort of a job is it?"

"Your objective will be one person and only one, and you will have every help that we can give you. But the achievement will be your work alone."

25

"Do I—do I have to kill someone?" Helen asked, just louder than a whisper.

"No," said Mr. Sanders. "Cure him."

At a quarter to four in the afternoon of Sunday, October 19th, Helen Clark was on her way in a bus to Campden Hill and the last of her interviews. The fine weather had held all week, and this was just such a brisk and brilliant day as the one on which all this had started. "All this," Helen still called it to herself having, at present, no means of confining her experiences within an exact phrase.

It had certainly been a busy week, and an exhilarating one, and Helen supposed she was a little less mystified by what was happening to her than she had been at midday on Monday. Nevertheless, whole tracts of the future remained dark for her and when lulls in the rapid whirl had allowed her to think, her heart had missed several beats at the thought of how much she was going to have to contrive, to spin out of herself, if her mission was to succeed. She had been grateful for a mass of practical details—sheer "admin."—which had had to be got through, and some of which had been delightful in themselves.

When H.T.S. had finally explained himself to—at least —his own satisfaction, he had proceeded to move in quite an impressive way. To begin with (and Helen had no doubt that her old chief rather enjoyed exhibiting yet another bit of his concealed ops. room) , he had pulled out a huge drawer in his desk, apparently full of colored telephones. Without any of the mundane boredom of dials or intermediaries he had spoken directly, and with marked authority, to a number of people. His last call, on a green telephone, had been brief.

"Charles," he had said, "she's coming down to you now. Get someone out to meet her. A quarter of an hour, yes."

"That's the F.O.," he said. "You're to go there now. Some young chap will talk to you, give you a post-report about Senj and fix your journey. He'll know nothing beyond the story as we've agreed to it. He's not supposed to.

26

Probably be a bit stuffy, so just play your part with becoming modesty. Put yourself in his hands. That's where you belong—on paper. Now, here's your passport, with a brand-new visa which looks like a crossword puzzle."

You were never really in doubt for a moment that I would do what you asked, thought Helen, and, as usual, you were perfectly right. Well, wasn't this just what I was wanting—to get away? On any terms?

Mr. Sanders had written a name and address on a slip of paper. "That's his mother. She's expecting you on Sunday at four. Be punctual. This," and he wrote another name, "is where you are to go for some clothes. They'll be expecting you. Ask for Miss Martineau. And this," he had produced a neat thick packet wrapped in fine white paper and secured by a rubber band, "is some pocket money. The F.O. will take care of your tickets and things. You need not keep accounts."

Helen, dazed, had taken the piece of paper, the solidly comfortable wad of clean notes and put them in her bag.

"Oh, I nearly forgot," said Mr. Sanders, and wrote on another slip of paper two more names and addresses. "You leave for Vienna by train on Monday the 20th; you will arrive the following afternoon. Go to this hotel, where you will be expected. And on Wednesday morning, at 11 o'clock, go to this other address. They have something for you which may interest you; and you may meet someone who will help you. I expect you will leave Vienna for Senj by air on the 23rd. It will be a dreadfully uncomfortable flight, I'm afraid; but, till that, you are to be as comfortable as possible. A little holiday."

He must have pressed a bell somewhere, because the door opened suddenly. No one came in. Mr. Sanders walked round his desk and took both her hands. She could still see the kindness and encouragement in his eyes, gleaming from between their bistred lids, the almost paternal anxiety in the tired, heavy, humorous, irascible face.

"Au revoir, Thésée—bonne chance!" he had murmured, and at once the bald, young, owlish Mr. Sanders

27

(were they all called Sanders?) was rushing her down the dingy stairs and out to a taxi waiting in the Strand.

During the short ride to Downing Street, Helen had lain back in the taxi, looking at the roof. She felt weak, and also elated and inclined to be hilarious. She wanted very much to talk to someone, even to sing. It might be, she reflected, less of a man's world than formerly, but still —it seemed to her—men did most of the talking. She could talk, she now felt, for an hour without stopping, but who was there to listen? Well, her time would come.

This thought put an end to hilarity. "Au revoir, Thésée!" Sanders had said. "Au revoir, Theseus!" What a delicious and wholly typical way of making her feel brave, dedicated, important! But was she not really much more like one of the silly, garlanded girls sent from the kind daylight into the labyrinth to be destroyed by the Minotaur?

There was no time to thrash this out now. The taxi was hovering in Whitehall, preparatory to turning into Downing Street. It plopped into that celebrated cul-de-sac like a water-rat into a pond, and stopped abruptly. Two policemen paid no attention, continued to chat beside a modest, black front door, but Helen came in for some vague interest from a knot of foreign visitors, one of whom took her photograph. Since they all had cameras at the ready, and were generally festooned with expensive optical equipment, Helen supposed them to be Americans. She looked narrowly at the one who had taken her picture, but he had turned quickly back to gazing at the front door of No. 10 and seemed to be waiting, in his raincoat and grey fedora, as patiently as his comrades for something interesting to happen.

Helen allowed the Italian splendors of the Foreign Office to engulf her. It felt more like a great picture gallery, a college, some important cultural monument, than her idea of a government department. A thicket of columns bore coffered vaults and beyond lay a courtyard with pigeons wheeling, looked down on by tall, serious windows. There was not a soul in sight. She turned from the colonnade through a door, climbed a flight of steps and found herself in a vast, quiet hall, which seemed dusky even at midday because of its size and dark colors, even though illuminated by enormous windows of clear glass. August! she said to herself, very august! Now what? From behind a long mahogany counter a burly, red-faced man in the dark blue official uniform ornamented with crowns, was leaning in her direction, interrogating her.

"My name is Helen Clark." She found herself using a confidential tone automatically. "I believe I am expected."

She was given a pink form to fill out. After she had put her own name on it, the form was taken away from her. "That's all right, Miss. I'll do the rest for you. Marsh!" his voice was a kind of whispered shout, "take this young lady up to Mr. Harland."

And into a deeper dusk she had gone, up flights of museumlike stairs, behind a small, fatherly man in blue. Because her senses were extra-sharp that morning, and all her perception at full stretch, Helen was at once impressed and exasperated by the soaring arches, the broad steps, the solid, sober, antique shabbiness of it all. She was impressed and, at some central, feminine, common-sense level of her mind, exasperated by this architectural statement of power, confidence, and orderliness, so enormously—she thought—at variance with the facts.

Very effective, too, in its day, thought Helen. She had been left by her guide to sit on a long, worn red morocco sofa, buttoned all over. She sat on its edge, feeling once again rather lost and lonely, but happier than she could have believed possible to be part of something again.

When Mr. Harland came, he seemed to Helen absurdly young and far from tidy. Her head was still full of tall, sage gentlemen in high collars, braided frock coats and black four-in-hands. Mr. Harland's spiky fair hair looked as if it had been combed with his fingers. His tie was halfway under one wing of a soft collar and his dusty grey suit was creased. One of his shoelaces was coming undone. Helen warmed to him at once. Here was someone of her own time, a man of the present-day Office of blinding overwork, continual anxiety, diplomatic tightrope walking. Britannia no longer ruled the waves, and Mr. Harland was human. He was also intelligent and efficient, filling her hands with duplicated memoranda about the post at Senj, a typed itinerary, tickets for her journey. He was friendly and bothered and as uncomfortable doing business in a passage as she was. Once or twice his manner was touched with the official, which made Helen think of a small boy in his father's hat. "Actually, it's all a bit irregular. . . ." "As a matter of fact, it isn't really our job. . . ." This, Helen recognized, was occupational; as a carpenter would be bound to complain if asked to do something which was more strictly the plumber's affair.

Helen had conducted her side of the interview according to Mr. Sanders' instructions, trying to seem modest, practical, a trifle studious. As far as Mr. Harland was concerned, she was going out to Senj as nursery governess to Victoria, the Minister's small daughter. For reasons of morale, and because the Minister was a widower—"Fearfully sad thing," said Mr. Harland—the F.O. was stretching a point to help Helen get there quickly.

"Well now, you've got your passport? Good—then that's everything." Mr. Harland escorted Helen as far as the stairs. "I do hope you'll enjoy it," he said earnestly. "I'm afraid, though, it'll be a bit grim. These Transcurtainian posts aren't much fun just at present." He looked shyly at her, sideways, to see if she liked his joke. Helen smiled. They parted and Mr. Harland hurried away, back to the room which, he had told her, he shared with three other men. Back to files and telephones, and papers "Passed to—," "X. please see," "Hold for return of Y.," "S. of S. to see." Layer upon layer of authority towered above Mr. Harland, a long ladder to climb.

Somewhere at the centre of this great pile must be a fine room looking, perhaps, on St. James's Park, where the Secretary of State himself, the great S. of S., would be —the ill, intelligent, elephantine man who had been a miner, who, with his shrewd courage and his blunt words had so amazingly endeared himself to a permanent staff not usually inclined to like "politics."

Helen had walked slowly out into Downing Street. The American visitors had gone. One policeman alone remained on guard at No. 10, yawning and scratching his chin.

When Monday came, the fine weather went. Helen drove to Victoria through sheeting rain which blinded the taxi windows. The last of London for her was hissing tires, misted glass, a black-and-brown herd of umbrellas and soaked waterproofs jostling in the station yard. Then, from her corner of a first-class compartment, she watched water, and iron, and smoke-streaked yellow brick move faster away. Long ribbons of slate on low houses, crazy chimney-stacks, eyeless blocks of factories came and went through billowing smoke which the rain pressed down to window-level. It was a few minutes past ten in the morning. She was going abroad for the first time in twelve years. Excitement, sheer pleasure in movement, and a kind of relief, a sense of escape, kept her on the edge of her seat, bright-eyed, noting everything. You'll be tired out before Dover at this rate, she said in her mind, as though to the child Helen off to the seaside.

New luggage lay heavy and secure in the rack above her. New clothes, new shoes made her feel precious, luxurious, feather-light. Mr. Sanders' Miss Martineau had known her business. Nothing about Helen was quite out of character, not even the fur-lined broadcloth coat laid on the seat beside her—"You really *must* have this, Madam, in *that* climate!"—but only the best had been thought good enough, just the same.

It was raining at Dover, with a squally wind whipping up white peaks on a dull grey sea. Helen waited, passport in hand, behind a party of four short men in raincoats and grey fedoras. They reminded her of something, but it was not until they had passed, with remarkable speed, through the passport control, and disappeared in company with a polite young man in a black hat, that she remembered the group she had seen waiting outside No. 10. These could be the same men, but Helen knew now

31

that they were not Americans. Close to, their foreignness, of another kind, was obvious. Something quick and shrugging in their manners, a continuous movement of sharp dark eyes in deep-carved, weather-beaten faces, said Central Europe to Helen, although she could not have told why. Something uneasy, tough, a trifle defiant also made her think of peasants turned bureaucrats. The men looked intelligent, powerful and, like certain animals, only doubtfully tame.

Helen was watching the retreating backs of the four men, the camera and light-metre cases bouncing at their sides, and wondering which, if any, of them had her picture with him, when a voice said, "Your passport, Miss." Did she imagine it, or did the tall man who looked at her passport so quickly, and handed it back with the hint of a bow, look extra hard at her? She went on towards the Customs shed with the feeling that he had been on the edge of saying something unofficial, perhaps of wishing her luck.

The channel boat slammed and squirmed its way through a short sea. Unable to breathe the oily air between decks, Helen tied a scarf round her head and faced, with keen pleasure, the unremitting wet wind and spray. She was free again, moving forward to a future which could mean the end of all the worlds she knew; towards experience which, for good or ill, would color her life forever afterwards.

Before coming on deck Helen had made a survey of the various rooms, looked into the dining salon and bar, hoping to get another sight of her four Middle Europeans. They were not to be found. They must have got a cabin. I wonder if they're hitting it up with vodka . . . or playing poker . . . or just being as sick as dogs! She wondered why they were crossing by this means at all. Airports would be natural to them; they would be at home amongst miles of windy concrete, anonymous bustle, enormous noise. Anyway, here they were, and here was she; and Helen at least was happy with her mode of travel. Mr. Harland had been apologetic: they simply could not guarantee her a seat in an aircraft. Priorities.

Waiting lists. Did she understand? He had seemed relieved to hear that Helen preferred boats and trains. A half-dozen nightmare trips in aircraft in the war, on duty, had put an end to any slight enthusiasm for flying she might once have had.

Now, ruled straight across her vision, just faintly discernible in the grey-white haze, lay the edge of Europe, the threshold of adventure. Beyond that leaded bar there stretched a continent, a vast curving mass of land into which her own island, with all its jewelled history and rich complexities, could fit a thousand times. Beyond France, Austria; beyond Austria, Rumania; beyond Rumania, Russia, where arrangements were being made for the reduction of history and the simplification of all complexities. Between this dancing boat and the Union of Soviet Socialist Republics lay torn, exhausted peoples and cruelly divided minds. What especial grace had she, to set out to redress a balance and make all straight—even in one small corner?

"You can't believe," she had said in horror to Mr. Sanders when, finally, he had let her get a word in, "you can't honestly believe that the influence of a good woman—even supposing I were anything of the sort—could cope with this sort of thing? It's too corny!"

Mr. Sanders had been very cross. "It's got nothing to do with good women, as such! If I thought a good *baboon* could do the trick, I'd send the best I could find. That you happen to be a woman might help: equally, it might wreck everything. But the fact that you're you; and that I know this, is what matters." Helen had had to be content with that.

Calais. It was like seeing the results of a fire, in broad daylight. One had heard so much, had been—on paper—too intimately concerned with devastation, had seen enough and to spare at home. But Helen had not thought how so solidly ugly, so happily remembered a town as Calais, dumped on its straight-edged coast under an immense blank sky, might look when blown to concrete lace and iron cobwebs. There were cranes at work on tiptoe at the dockside, bright steel rails and poles and wires, and the Town Hall's tower, like a gouty thumb, still amazingly upraised. There were also acres of smashed stone and concrete, and black, serrated brick and nothing that had any shape at all. It could be a challenge to reconstruct, or a chilling hint of finality.

Sea gulls mewed in the rigging of the tidy ship. A crane's arm swung slowly over to the forward hold. Helen's spirits, assailed by the size of everything, of Europe as well as evil, wavered between hope and despair. She clutched her new coat about her, and looked down at her proud new luggage as though she had never owned it.

Then, all at once, she was back in her holiday mood. The loosely-packed, mutually hostile group of passengers with whom she was standing, was suddenly twice its size, interpenetrated by soft-shoed French porters. Blue might be the color of the vigor which so shook and swayed the well-fed crowd, pasty with a bad crossing and slowly herding towards the solid ground of France. Blue blouses, blue berets, blue jowls, blue Norman eyes, bobbed and glowered and flashed. A smoke of garlic and small oaths went up and filled the confined space. Helen looked at them with love, and smilingly ceded her luggage to a surly, wall-eyed old man who made off with it like a lizard. They are just as I remember them, she thought. What their town has suffered, they have suffered, and they are just as they were. Just as they mean to be! She paused for a second at the top of the gangway and took a long breath of air, which was damp and salty and touched with the smoke of long-distance trains.

"But I'm not that kind of girl!" Helen struggled awake from a dream of confused pressures, of being pulled and pushed about by a crowd of people, certain that she had spoken these uncharacteristic words aloud. A violet-blue light set high in the wall of her sleeping-compartment, just defined, without illuminating, blankets, the blinded window, dark wooden panels against which her coats swung on their hangers. It also showed a faint, moving

34

gleam as the metal door-knob turned smoothly, quietly—reversed, and turned again.

Helen lay rigid, head half-raised from her pillow, breathing suspended, her eyes on the handle of the door. Nothing happened for a full minute. Then there came to her, clear above the rolling clatter and creak of the train, an extraordinary sound. Somebody in the corridor was saying something, vehemently. The foreign words came jetting out with a furious sibilance, like compressed air. Helen had never heard anything so unmistakably angry spoken in a whisper. There was a sound of rapid movement, two light thuds, a dull scraping, which told her as clearly as if she could see it, that someone had been jerked violently away from her door. Helen lay as she was, watching the door-knob for perhaps five minutes. She was not thinking at all, simply concentrating with all her instincts on whatever was threatening her. At the moment when she was about to relax, fall back to her pillow, breathe deeply again, she heard rapid footsteps in the corridor and a light, but urgent-sounding tap on her door.

"C'est moi, Mademoiselle," came a voice she recognized, "c'est le gardien . . . you have been disturbed?"

Helen leaned over and slid back the bolt. The sleeping-car attendant's face, anxious, respectful, appeared in the gap.

"Excuse me, Mademoiselle. I was absent for a moment from the coach, and I feared—"

Helen looked almost with affection at the long, dark face beaming concernedly down at her. This, at least, was someone she knew. Earlier, he had been friendly and helpful, answering her questions, helping her with a Customs declaration, promising no disturbance until breakfast-time.

"Someone tried my door," Helen said. "It was bolted, anyway. I think there were two people, perhaps more. Did you see them?"

"Not to recognize them, Mademoiselle," the answer came rather hastily. "They were not of *my* coach, I can assure."

"Oh well," Helen said, "I expect it was a mistake."

"Be assured, Mademoiselle, that it shall not occur again. I shall not again leave my seat down there at the end of the corridor."

"Good night, then; and thank you."

The attendant seemed to hesitate, to waver in the doorway. The noise of the train was altering; they were slackening speed. The wheels began to jump and click, the carriage shook sideways and danced, as they met a system of points. Helen looked at her watch, which showed fourteen minutes to three.

The attendant said: "Mademoiselle is traveling to Vienna. Mademoiselle has friends in Vienna?"

"Good friends," Helen answered, thinking of H.T.S. The conductor seemed relieved. "Then I will bid Mademoiselle good night. Mademoiselle will be called for breakfast when we have passed Ulm. And," he ceased to be formal, "please bolt your door again!"

The train was now sliding quietly to a halt. Slips of light showed at the sides of the leather blind. A muted clangor, metallic echoes, the whistle of another train, came from outside. This must be a big station. The train rolled ever more slowly, smoothly, to a standstill and stood hissing gently.

Helen found that her shoulders and neck were aching. She was wide awake, and uncertain of further sleep. Wrapping a rug round her she moved to the end of her narrow bed, lowered the blind and looked out into the sparsely-lit station, at great slices of shadow and patches of yellow light. Strasbourg. Almost exactly half-way. She felt confused; not frightened, but open, now, to a variety of apprehensions. She realized that, concentrated on one aim, one destination, she had forgotten her early training and failed to take account of the unaccountable. Heaven knew, nothing was more likely than that a girl on her own, on the Orient Express, should have some small adventure of a fatally familiar kind. Some confident amorist might have spotted her at the Gare de l'Est, noted her compartment number, resolved to try his luck. Even less "romantic" explanations were possible. Drunks. A commonplace mistake. Only, there had been that furious, fantastic whisper in a language she did not know. There had been something in the attendant's manner which was more than concern for the orderly conduct of his sleeping-car. After all he must, in his time, in his job, have seen enough irregular comings and goings. Her door had been bolted. No harm had been done. Why, then, had he shown so much alarmed concern, such a degree of relief that matters were not (how could they be?) worse? And why had he said, "Mademoiselle has *friends* in Vienna?" with such a particular emphasis on the word "friends"?

Helen realized that she must not rule out the possibility that someone unfriendly might have an interest in her movements. She knew enough of the organization and methods of various undercover agencies to know how much results depended on a minutely-elaborated attention to detail. She knew also what brilliant deductions were often made, and acted on, from wholly wrong premises. If, then, she had become an object of scrutiny, she was going to have to keep her wits about her, neglect no possibility, to be forced to divide her attention at a moment when, she thought with sudden desperate anxiety, she could not afford to divide it at all.

"Oh God," she said aloud, "what a crashing irrelevance!" and realized that this was very much what she had been saying when the turning of the door-handle woke her up.

When the attendant called her with a loud and cheerful knocking, the train was drawing out of Ulm. Helen, abandoning night thoughts, had climbed back into bed at four and had slept dreamlessly.

As she tussled with the over-ingenious washing arrangements of her narrow cabin she was conscious of two immediate wishes. One was for breakfast, for which she had an unaccustomed hunger (she would never see the spotted cups, the plane leaves, the chimney pots again), and the other for a further, a more piercing view of her four foreigners—the "Beggers on Horseback," as she had half-absently christened them. If they were going to mean anything in her life she must find out at once who they were, where they were going, and what part they might be going to play in the happenings of the months ahead.

Helen had a long walk to the dining-car down heaving corridors, past doors still shut, and doors open showing beds being made, or compartments already transformed for the needs of the day, seats strewn with papers and knitting, where the beds had been, and people sitting talking, or quietly staring out. Her own attendant, collarless and with a fringe of black stubble, gave her a gold-filled grin of complicity. Daylight and normal things were working their magic. The train fled on, through fields and allotments, bleakly neat, past crowds on bicycles coming off shift from factories, and busy, grim-looking transport, all testifying to German industry and will to survive. . . .

As she reached the dining-car and paused, clutching a handrail, on the clashing steel plates between two coaches Helen felt a little pain of apprehension in the pit of her stomach. She was truly alert now. Last night's experience had wakened her from a private sleep of long duration, one more exclusive than any physical sleep could be. Helen was working now, as a slight tension in her movements, a lifting of her chin, would have shown anyone as percipient as, for instance, Mr. Sanders. This might be going to be momentous, this entry to the dining-car. Helen was ready and, in the light of morning, prepared to enjoy her part of it to the full.

She was proportionately disappointed when, on entering the warm, food-smelling, plate-clinking atmosphere of the dining-car, she saw no one at all who could be pinned down for her special attention. She got plenty of glances, admiring ones from men, more liverish and critical ones from their women, before she found—with difficulty, and only because someone chose to leave at that moment—a seat at a table for two opposite a man who seemed composed of every possible shade of brown. The four Central Europeans were nowhere in sight.

Helen bowed slightly across the table to the man in brown, who bowed back gravely, giving her what, she felt, he would certainly call the "once-over" very rapidly and inoffensively, with a pair of bright squirrel's eyes.

"Looks like snow," he said, but without any particular air of wishing to start a conversation. Helen looked out over an infinity of dull green roofs and saw the dove-colored sky shading almost to black, with a hint of yellow, where the train was going. The rusting lines of roofs ran only so far, and then merged into a neutral haze at no great distance. She could tell by the steam on the carriage windows that it must be very cold outside.

"Could be," she said, and debated with herself whether to say more. She did not wish to have her attention distracted, but if, and when, her four men showed up, it might be useful to have a companion, for cover.

"It's rather early for snow, isn't it?" she said.

"Well, yes, it is," said the man, not without distaste. "But I've known it to snow in Vienna in September, for the matter of that. And anyway, the weather's like everything else nowadays—cockeyed."

He did not seem to wish to enlarge on the general cock-eyedness of things, however, but returned to his breakfast, eating with small scraping and pouncing movements of his knife and fork, and chewing primly as if testing samples. Helen, who had expected to hear the uncertain weather of Central Europe blamed on the Labor Government, was, on the whole, relieved.

She ordered a substantial breakfast and, while eating it, and enjoying with the holiday side of her mind the differences between this and her daily fare for five years—the thick blue Wagons-Lits crockery, the perfect rolls and the eggs in a scalding hot china dish—she took stock of the other people in the dining-car, and kept an eye on the door through which she had come.

I am being childish. I am really disappointed that those men are not here. And yet, this sort of thing—she remembered Mr. Sanders' scathing remarks about "cloak-and-dagger" operations—might be damned dangerous, and is certainly a ghastly bore. It's got nothing to do with

39

what I'm really after: and yet—I can see how some people might suppose it had. She frowned and broke a roll in half with unnecessary violence, registering a determination not to be sidetracked, to use all her training and native wit to confound anybody who might have got hold of the wrong end of the stick.

Looking up, she found the squirrel's eyes looking at her questioningly.

"Something up, Miss?" the man inquired, in the same unirritating way as before.

Helen was, for an instant, confused.

"No," she said, "no, certainly not. Why?"

"Well, you were going at that roll as if you'd like to wring its neck. Or someone's."

Helen laughed. "I was just thinking," she said, "that what one is doing—important, perhaps, only to oneself— is almost never the same thing as other people think, are determined to think, one *is* doing. If I make myself clear?" Gossiping will be my downfall, Helen thought. It was pleasant, though, to talk to this singularly undemanding man.

Her companion shrugged his shoulders.

"That's an old story. Even in business. You wouldn't believe," here his tone became almost vehement, "I travel a lot and spend half my time, fully half of it, calming people down, getting them into a state of mind to do business with me. You'd hardly credit the ideas they get about what I am, or might be, up to! Trouble with foreigners is they think we British are as smart and cunning as they come. Feel they have to get up very early for us not to diddle them. Whereas we—well, we think we're the biggest simpletons that ever walked, and all the double-dyed cunning's on the other side. And they talk about One World!" His voice had a noticeable edge of bitterness.

"Well," said Helen mildly, "it's a nice idea."

"That's just about what it is—a nice idea!" His tone was scornful. "Take a look at that little lot . . ." and he nodded past Helen's shoulder.

Helen looked sharply round and as sharply back again.

40

Involuntarily, she tucked her legs under her seat, as though someone might drag her from it. Why had she let herself suppose that the dining-car was the last coach of the train? It had seemed an obvious supposition, considering how far she'd had to walk. It was clear, now, that there must be at least one more coach beyond. Her four beggars on horseback had come to breakfast, and through the door behind her head, the door Helen was not watching. They were now settling themselves, with grunts and heaving movements, at the big table directly across the aisle from Helen's seat.

For a moment she clung with her gaze to the sensible, brown, middle-aged face across the table; just for long enough to get her breath, to think rapidly, to prepare to look across the aisle. She knew that she must look: nothing would be more obvious than a rigid refusal to turn her head.

"What . . . what about them?" she asked, hoping that her voice would sound as before.

For answer, the brown man reached down beside his seat, fished up a folded newspaper and handed it across to her. With his other hand he indicated a news item low on the front page. The paper was the *Continental Daily Mail*, published in Paris, and its date was the day before.

The paragraph in question was headed "Return of Iron Curtain Trade Mission. Exploratory Talks 'Successful.'" One glance was enough to pull together all Helen's wandering suspicions and suppositions about her four men. No need, any longer, to tell herself that she had been fancying things; that people who idly took one's photograph, and then happened to be travelling in the same direction, might easily not be connected with people who tried one's compartment door in the small hours of the morning. There were now, worse luck, reasonable grounds for connecting them; and they were decidedly travelling in the same direction. These men— and there was no doubt that her companion knew who they were—were on their way back to Senj.

Helen read the paragraph slowly, but with half her attention. "Attempt to broaden basis of trade . . . cer-

41

tain specific requirements . . . frustrated exports . . . Received by President of the Board of trade . . . visits to factories . . . privately entertained by a group of Members of Parliament." (They'll catch it from Mr. Attlee, thought Helen.) She looked across at her companion, who was looking at her keenly.

"This is . . . these are the same people?" she asked. "Are you sure?"

"I'm perfectly sure. Saw 'em in London myself. Saw 'em at the B.O.T., as a matter of fact. Lovely-looking bunch, aren't they? Only hope they got a flea in their ear. You don't want to believe all that about exploratory talks being successful. You could say that about just about anything. It's the last word, not the first, that counts."

Now she must look. She put down the paper and turned her head, to meet the varying expressions of four pairs of eyes all staring into hers.

The men were squarely established, each with his elbows on the table and one, while still looking at Helen, was clicking his fingers for the steward. Each man wore a suit, tight in itself, which bulged and wrinkled with the movement of heavy shoulders and thick, short arms. All were neatly turned out, although shirts and suits and nondescript greyish ties had a curious lack of individual style, as though it had not been thought necessary to differentiate production much in this department. Helen allowed her gaze to wander coolly, indifferently from face to face, hoping that she disguised the intense concentration with which she was trying to memorize each individual trait. All four men were much of a height; all had large ears and broad heads, flat on the top. All had thick, healthy hair and faces of that ruddy brown which comes from exposure to the weather and is sometimes intensified by heavy drinking. One had hair of a true coal-black; the others were more or less uniformly light brown. There were too few distinguishing marks, Helen thought. Conceivably they might all have been brothers, or at least of one family; but the black-haired man stood

42

out. One of his eyes was black as his hair, the other brilliant blue.

Helen brought her eyes back, without haste, to her own table. By now, she had given the men names in her mind, and attached the meagre distinguishing marks she had noted. One had a broken nose, one a small scar on his right cheek, another a pronounced cleft in his chin. This classification would have to do for the present. She would not look their way, otherwise than very briefly, again. Helen lifted her coffee cup and drank slowly, her eyes on the cloth. There had been something curious about the gaze which the four men had directed at her. They had simply looked, without amusement, or ferocity, or desire, without, in fact, any personal quality at all. They had gazed as people do who, after travelling a long distance, behold the thing they came to see.

"Well," said Helen's companion, "there's the other half of your One World. Sell their own grandmothers for cat's meat, that lot would, and then pinch pussy's dinner and sell it again. What I'd like to know," he went on, directing a brief glare at the four men, who were now talking, their heads close together, "is how they ever came to get to London on a Trade Mission, when we're hardly even on diplomatic terms with them, let alone any kind of commercial ones. I'd like to know where they're going in this train, because it doesn't go to Senj. They'll either have to change at Vienna or go on to Budapest and come back. Or I suppose they might fly—but then, why not fly all the way? I can't see them being very welcome in Vienna, the Yanks are that jumpy. Anyway, you seem to have made a conquest." He looked at Helen with slightly derisive respect.

"Perhaps they've never seen a white woman before," said Helen absently, falling easily into the brown man's generalizing habit.

"Well, don't look now, but they're all staring at you again, as if you were something to eat or something. I don't like it!" he added, with surprising brusqueness.

43

"Don't like what?" Helen was startled away from the web of her own thoughts.

"The way they're looking at you. I've a good mind to sock one of them."

"For goodness' sake, don't," Helen said. What an odd character this was. He did not look the socking type, but then few of that type did. At all events, the brown face was now nearer crimson, and the little man had both fists on the table, tightly clenched. He was a small man, but not feeble, and Helen was afraid that he might really be capable of getting into a fight at this time of the morning. Nothing at any time, least of all the present, would have given her less pleasure. She signalled, not as discreetly as she meant to, for the steward to bring her bill. There were no other passengers, now, in the dining-car. Helen thought it important to leave and get back to her compartment before the four men finished breakfast.

The steward seemed not to see her signals. One of the four men, as though at a private signal of his own, downed his cup of coffee rapidly and began a barging progress from the table. Helen's heart stopped for a moment when she saw him turn and lurch away down the dining-car towards the door through which she herself had come. A phrase from the war came back into her mind, where a forlorn little voice said "Things may be going to be a trifle dicey!" Nevertheless she paid the steward when he came, under protest from her little companion, who wanted to pay for her breakfast himself.

"Well, have another coffee with me, do," he said, "you're better off here." (He may be right about that, thought Helen bleakly.) "I get bored stiff in my sleeper. Stay and talk."

Helen shook her head. The little man in brown would be astonished to know how greatly she would prefer to stay; but she said good-bye and moved off down the dining-car, head high, without looking back.

International trains have their doors at both ends of the carriage, one on either side. These doors open inwards and, outside, there are steel steps and a drop of four feet or so to the ground. Helen traversed the first

44

two carriages after the dining-car without incident, until, coming through one of the dark concertinas with over-lapping, shifting floor-plates which connect the carriages, she found her way blocked by the man who had gone ahead. It was the one, she noted mechanically, with the deeply-cleft chin, the one she had nicknamed Charlie. An instant of pure terror shook Helen. Charlie was standing gravely with his back to the next corridor, as though waiting to greet her; with his back to the corridor and also to the glass door, which he had opened. A great screeching clatter and a blast of bitter air came up through the open doorway. Below, a long way below, the rails streaked by in a blur of speed. Helen turned with a gasp to run back, back to the dining-car and safety, and was caught at once in a paralyzing grip by the man with the black hair. Trying to fight with him, quite use-lessly, and breathing his powerful smell—sweat and charcuterie and rank cigars—Helen saw over his shoul-der the hard, expressionless faces of the other two. The hands which were holding her, hurting her, spun her violently round. She clutched a vertical brass handrail and faced, giddy and sick with fear, the rocketing rails be-low. Charlie glanced over his shoulder, into the corridor, and said one word, urgently. Helen felt the hard body be-hind her withdraw as though for a swift physical effort, a spring. Then, from behind them, like a terrier through a hedge, bellowing with rage and using feet and elbows with amazing force, hurtled the man in brown. Inside a second he had taken in the situation, winded the black-haired man, hooked Helen round the waist, and whisked her to comparative safety by the other door. A moment later, puzzled faces could be seen bobbing and mouth-ing at the glass door behind Charlie's back. With great speed, and without saying a word, the three others bolted back towards the dining-car, the black-haired man bent almost double. Charlie, without exhibiting any feelings whatever and as though he had now had enough fresh air, politely closed the door and set off after them at a dignified pace. The brown man looked once at Helen's face, threw open the door of a lavatory and said:

"In there, and take your time. I'll be here when you come out."

Helen knelt among the clean white tiles and vomited painfully.

"Nothing odd about it at all, to their way of thinking," said the man in brown, whose name, it appeared, was Mr. Hargreaves. "You see, when *we* travel abroad, we pay—we have to pay—some regard to the ways and habits of the people we travel among. Take our shoes off in mosques, take our hats off to funerals, cross the street when it says, and all that. But they carry their way of thinking and doing things with them, because for them—there isn't any other. We're all corrupt and bourgeois and out of date, so they've been brought up to believe. So we've got nothing to teach them, and no rules that matter. Our laws and customs don't mean a thing to them, even that one about not throwing young ladies out of trains."

They were sitting in Helen's compartment with the door closed and a very anxious attendant hovering outside. At first Helen had sat and shivered, her teeth chattering, but the attendant, with whom Mr. Hargreaves seemed to be in some sort of collusion, had quickly found brandy and hot coffee for her. Now she felt better, but exceedingly tired, as though convalescing from a long, black illness.

After a while, during which Mr. Hargreaves rambled gently on, without once asking Helen a direct question, or expressing any astonishment that this should have happened to her, she found strength to talk.

"I still cannot understand," she said, "not so much why they did it. . . . I mean there may have been a why, or they may have thought there was . . . but how it could be *them*. A Trade Mission . . . known about . . . written about. Men of standing, I suppose, not just ordinary thugs?"

"Perfectly ordinary thugs, I do assure you!" Mr. Hargreaves spoke with great decision. "And as to Trade Missions, that's all eyewash. Those monkeys are political police, if ever I saw any, and I've seen plenty, one way and

46

another. As to their being men of standing, well, yes, in a way, they are. For as long as they *do* stand, that is. It's a dicey game, as I suppose they know. Mark you, they're bound to be well briefed. They'll have said their piece about sugar-beets or saxophones or whatever they're pretending to want to export, very nicely. But the question someone's got to answer—and I'm glad it isn't me—is how they got permission to go to London at all in the first place. That's what's got to be known and that, if you'll forgive me, is more important than what happens to you or me."

Helen thought of Mr. Sanders and wondered if he could have foreseen anything at all like this. Was she now, she wondered, one of his red triangles, moving rapidly across the illuminated box? Or was her mission purely a personal hunch, a chancing of his own arm? Was she outside his real system altogether? Looking across at Mr. Hargreaves, who appeared only a little dishevelled after his battle, Helen thought, What can I say to him? How can I thank him? He has saved my life. I have never had my life saved before. Yet he seems to wish to make nothing of it. Indeed Mr. Hargreaves' manner had not altered in the least. He remained as lucid, as remotely friendly and mildly disapproving as he had been at breakfast-time, which now seemed very long ago. Helen leaned forward, smiling into the sharp squirrel's eyes.

"Tell me," she said, "what do you do—when you're not saving people's lives, I mean?"

"Me?" said Mr. Hargreaves. "Well, I travel. I mean I'm a traveller, a business man. I'm in the rag trade really, I suppose. As to life-saving, I could kill myself for being so slow. I meant to get out after you before the other three, but they beat me to it."

Helen had sat bolt upright. "The rag trade?" she asked. "You mean dresses and things?"

"That's right," said Mr. Hargreaves, "general millinery, wholesale dresses, haberdashery. That's a very, very nice suit you've got on, by the way. Nearly got properly mucked up!" and he gave a little chuckle.

Helen felt breathless. She gasped a little as she asked,

47

"Whom do you work for, if you don't mind my asking?"

"Rather an old-fashioned concern, in a way, but big, very big, and surprisingly up-to-date on some things." He was looking at Helen with a queer little smile, primly encouraging, like a teacher with a bright pupil. There was a pause. Helen said, just loudly enough to be heard:

"334, Strand, W.C.2. And at Cheapside."

"Over a hundred branches throughout the United Kingdom," said Mr. Hargreaves with a triumphant wink.

At the Austrian frontier it was snowing hard. Helen gazed entranced from her window at the crisp, crowding flakes, so thick in their falling that distance was annihilated. To look at, there was only this changing curtain of snow and the white crust piling on the sleepers of the track. Stationary wagons in sidings were thickly frosted, and the small cabins dotted about marshalling yards seemed foresters' cottages deeply eaved with snow. Seasonable or not, this was the weather she would have chosen and now, still a little drunk with brandy and shock, she began again to dream a little, to prepare for contact with a world whose fascination had always moved her. When, at school, her unimaginative teachers had touched on certain histories, certain geographies, Helen had learned and studied with a will. Finding all Scandinavia tame, the Low Countries dull, she could see even France as only on the way to the dark, exciting places—Austria and Rumania, Hungary and Poland—Czechoslovakia alone seeming to have opted out, to have become a kind of Low Country in itself. These were her childish views, and though she had since learned to find much that was admirable, pragmatically, in other countries—Sweden, for instance, and Switzerland—it was still to the frontier lands of the Orient that Helen's temperament inclined her to turn. No doubt that this was known to Mr. Sanders. If he had wanted her to go to Stockholm, he would have "sold" it in a different way, but if he had simply said "I want you to go to Senj for a certain time," and nothing more, Helen would not have complained.

Mr. Hargreaves fell silent, and eventually slept; but even in sleep relaxed very little, looking as skeptical, orderly and alert, almost, as when he was awake. Helen studied him with new eyes, wondering a little at the impersonal devotion which had made him her preserver, and disliking herself for certain small, snobbish conclusions she had come to about him before the attempt on her life. She had been in some strange relations with men in her time, but never one of this kind. This must be that very rare thing, a really grown-up man. She marvelled at his ability to refuse even a word of gratitude, let alone requital. Helen felt that if he were to ask for anything, even for her body, she must comply; but knew quite certainly that he would never ask. For this, although she would feel gratitude and respect and even, in a certain sense, love for Mr. Hargreaves all her life, she could not help being glad.

At Vienna it was snowing as hard as ever. The attendant knocked and Mr. Hargreaves was instantly awake. The two men spoke together in French and Helen was obliged to recognize that Mr. Hargreaves' French was even better than her own. Then the attendant pulled up the blind of the window, smiled encouragingly at Helen, and left, locking the door.

Mr. Hargreaves stretched, and he too smiled encouragingly.

"Small precautions," he said. "We'll just sit tight for a little while, and then your troubles will be over. For the time being, anyway," he added in a neutral tone.

Helen hesitated for a second before asking him: "Do you know what I'm doing, where I'm going? Do you know why I'm here?"

"Haven't the faintest," said Mr. Hargreaves cheerfully. "*And* I don't want to know. None of my business. My job was for this train journey and—well, I'm not too proud of myself, to tell you the truth. Damn nearly muffed it, which would have been a pity, on several counts," and he smiled with a shade more warmth than usual.

The train came to a halt with a gentle jerk, and the noises of a great station mingled with the bumping jostle and the cries of passengers pressing like startled sheep, to get out. Along the platform hoarse voices shouted: "Wien—Westbahnhof! Wien—Westbahnhof," porters called out for custom and, as a kind of ground-bass, a loudspeaker system delivered what sounded like a long lecture in a guttural monotone. Mr. Hargreaves lifted down Helen's luggage and stacked it neatly. After a while the carriage became silent. The shouting on the platform ceased and even the loudspeaker became quiet. Only the vast breathing echo, the hiss and grinding of a terminus continued outside.

The sleeping-car attendant unlocked the door and began to pick up the bags. In silence they followed him to the end of the corridor and down the steps to where a porter waited with a trolley. At the sight of the steps Helen felt a wave of nausea. The attendant put his hand on her arm and looked at her kindly.

"Au revoir, Mademoiselle. Bonne chance!"

They hurried behind the trolley along the now deserted platform. Helen found her legs a little unsteady, but enjoyed with every movement the feeling of solid ground. She felt light and empty and somewhat detached from what was going on. She no longer felt tired and was even, to her surprise, rather hungry.

They passed a row of administrative offices on the main platform and barged serenely through a double door marked "Eingang verboten!" Three officials in tall peaked caps, working at a table under a green-shaded light in a narrow hallway, did not so much as glance at them as they passed through and out again by a door at the other side. A car was waiting, with a young chauffeur who saluted Mr. Hargreaves, stowed the bags away and tucked them both into the back under a thick rug with amazing speed. There was no question of tipping the porter; he had disappeared.

The car, powerful and very quiet, and of a make unknown to Helen, nosed out of the small goods-yard in

50

which it had been standing, and set off down a broad street glazed with new-fallen snow.

"Where are you staying?" asked Mr. Hargreaves.

"The Hotel Elisabeth."

"I thought as much," he said, "the best possible place after a day like you've had. Driver, the Elisabeth, please," he added in German.

Helen opened her window an inch or two and leaned back to feel the dry, cold air on her forehead. A flake of snow spun in and settled on her cheek, a frosty kiss. Dark and tall, rendered insubstantial by the white veils blowing past them, great buildings loomed and vanished in Helen's eye. Rococo streetlamps, archways, an arcade of brilliant shops, an equestrian statue riding high in the snowstorm, the glimpse of a fountain, its basin white-rimmed, long lines of yellow lights running to vanishing point and haloed with dancing flakes—all came together to lull Helen, to hypnotize her a little. Mr. Hargreaves remained silent but sympathetic. She would have liked to drive like this for a long time, to drive and drive and postpone for a while, perhaps forever, the encounter she so dreaded. There was little daylight left. It was half-past five on Tuesday, 21st October. The first stage of her journey was done.

Blue-white light filled the bedroom where Helen still lay sleeping at nine o'clock the next morning. The snow had stopped, but the sky over the quiet little street outside hung heavy and low, promising more to come. A maid, whose gentle rapping at the door had gone unanswered, wheeled in a trolley loaded with steaming dishes and white damask, and then stood a moment looking down at the sleeper with the frankest admiration. In the steady warmth of the room, Helen had let slip the covers a little while she slept, and now lay on her back, her cheek to the pillow, with one bare arm thrown up, fingers curled like a child's beside her head. Her brown hair fanned over the pillow beside her face. The little maid, who was perhaps seventeen, said, "Beautiful" very decidedly, and out loud. Helen, hearing through sleep the sharp monosyllable "Schön," frowned suddenly, touched with nightmare, seeing descending steps, the roaring rails, feeling a blast of air. She struggled awake and opened bewildered eyes on a young, high-colored face smiling down at her, on maize-colored velvet curtains, grey-blue walls, and a painted baroque wardrobe like a frivolous confession-box—her room at the Hotel Elisabeth. Helen sighed, smiled and, sitting up, said, "Grüss Gott!"

While the little maid presented her breakfast with flourishes, pointing to all the good things one by one, and Helen responded with smiles and a severely limited stock of German, she was setting her mind to work piecing together the hours since she had got off the train in Vienna. Luminal had made a white fog in her mind but, as she drank coffee and ate rolls which were both as good as she would have expected in this city, little by little events came back to her and settled into place.

Mr. Hargreaves had simply, and with customary lack of fuss, gone out of her life—possibly, he had soberly implied, forever. Helen had entered the hotel alone, to be given at once a most extraordinary sense of having come home. She had heard a great deal about Austrian charm; she also knew a great deal of what Austrians had been through since charm had been, in any sense, part of their daily lives. Something about the Hotel Elisabeth was, in any case, beyond mere charm. In every particular of decoration and appointment, and in the concertedness and alert benevolence of its staff, it was scarcely, in any way that Helen could recognize, a hotel at all. Mr. Sanders' words came back to her, at the moment of signing the register: "You are to be as comfortable as possible. A little holiday."

Mr. Sanders never did anything without reason. He must have had his reasons for sending her by that particular train, a three-cornered journey via Paris, rather than by the faster service through Ostend. He must have had his reasons for giving her a day and two nights in Vienna. Somewhere in all this organization, the particular order in which impressions were to come to her, and the quality of those impressions, must—Helen was sure of it—be deliberately planned. Henry Sanders was a man of immense kindness, in more than simply a personal sense, but he was not one to waste the powers of his organization, or to risk anyone's life, simply to give Helen a good time. He probably had a very much clearer idea than she could have what might be awaiting Helen in Senj. Time being short, he would wish her to be fortified as much as possible before the ordeal began. If this was a fortifying process, Helen smiled to herself, it was certainly wonderfully comfortable, and just about as far removed as it could possibly be from life in S.W.7. Her head still felt a little wooly from the sleeping-pills. She remembered that she had an appointment at eleven. Helen put aside, for the present, further consideration of why and wherefore and addressed herself to the strange new day.

The hall porter, like the rest of the staff at the Elisabeth, was courteous with a courtesy that was curiously positive. He bent his great height over Helen and looked, with his large, sad eyes and lean face, like a baroque saint brooding over a mortal in error.

"Of course," he said, "of course. Madame Violette. Her shop, Fräulein, is only a little distance, a few streets away, just off the Ringstrasse. But in case you should have any difficulty, any difficulty at all, in finding it, I shall send the boy with you, to show you the way. Also, it may begin to snow again at any time and you have no umbrella!"

So Helen, divided between pleasure and a slight embarrassment, set out for her rendezvous with a tall page in gilt buttons and crimson livery, who carried a green umbrella of enormous size. I could scarcely be more conspicuous, she thought, but if *they* think it's all right. . . .

They came presently to a small square, simply, the widening, for a short space, of a narrow street, and the boy stopped and pointed at a low arcade on the far side.

53

"Madame Violette—there," he said, and stayed to watch Helen solicitously as she crossed the square.

Smiling, she turned to wave to the boy, and then was lost to his sight in the chilly dusk of the arcade.

There were four shops in all, each one in its way a model of discretion. One, a posticheur, had nothing but a ginger wig surrounded by mauve velvet curtains; another had six medals in a mahogany frame, and nothing else at all; the third, a confectioner's, had a single glass jar with a tall spike to its lid, containing sugared almonds; and the fourth, which was Madame Violette's, had a mink stole, a pair of white gloves, and a pearl bracelet before a background of grey satin screens.

Helen, who had three minutes in hand, examined this reserved display for a while, then turned, feeling that something had altered. Snow was falling again, falling as though to smother the world. Helen could only just make out the wavering black outline of buildings at the street corner where she had left the boy. The city's sounds had receded and what had been a roar spiked with the sharp sound of horns, was now a muffled throbbing, and the horn notes mellow as a spinet. The short arcade in which she stood was suddenly isolated, secret, like a boat moored in backwater. Nobody was in sight.

Helen glanced at her watch and pushed the bright brass handle of Madame Violette's door which had its owner's name scripted in gold with a thick flourish.

Warmth, soft carpet, a light and pleasing scent, the sound of voices talking quietly, greeted Helen as she went in. The shop was long and narrow, with grey-painted cupboards the length of one wall. Cheval glasses stood here, and there. At the far end, at a small counter, under a skylight, a woman dressed to the chin in tight black satin, with a fuzz of wiry white hair, was talking to another, in black furs with a wide black hat, who was sitting with her back to Helen. For a moment, no one appeared to notice her entry; then the white-haired one— who might be Madame Violette herself—excused herself to the other and came forward lurching slightly on very high heels. Helen had caught the word "Prinzessin," addressed to the woman in the black hat, but Madame Violette (if this were she) spoke to her at once in English.

"Good morning, Miss Clark," she said, in a pleasant, scarcely accented voice, and with a wide, crooked smile from a thin, scarlet mouth. "You are good to be so punctual. Will you come over here and sit down? I have some things to show you." ("They have something for you which may interest you; and you may meet someone who will help you.")

Helen settled into a chair in a corner near the window and waited a little tensely while Madame Violette fetched from a cupboard a deep cardboard box. Helen wished strongly that she could see the face of the woman in the black hat, but she remained firmly planted with her back to the proceedings, turning over patterns on the counter without once turning her head.

Madame Violette pushed a low table in front of Helen and opened the cardboard box. Helen, who had made many guesses as to what the "something" might be which she was to receive—papers, an important message, even firearms—could only gasp at the sable muff and the small round sable hat which emerged from a froth of tissue paper in Madame Violette's hands. She came round behind her chair and settled the hat forward on Helen's bare head, then handed her a glass to see the result for herself. From the glass a darker, wilder Helen looked out. The glossy fur curved lightly over her forehead, which was high and very white, and with its rich darkness accentuated that whiteness. Beneath it her eyes, reflecting the cold daylight, were piercingly blue. Between the sable and the tall, black velvet collar of her travelling coat, Helen's face—she could not find words to express to herself so rare a feeling of satisfaction, for she was not given to admiring her own looks—had an amazing purity of line. The image was timeless. It really does make me look like someone out of Tolstoy! she thought with wonder and gratitude.

"Where you are going," said Madame Violette, pursing her mouth, "there is little elegance and less beauty. You will certainly do them good. I am to ask you if you will accept this hat and muff?"

"Accept!" Helen almost whispered. "How could I not?" She guessed that this was Henry Sanders' last gesture, the symbolic equivalent of his anxious look at parting. It was a way—but what a way!—of saying: "From now on, you are on your own."

"That is good, then. These things shall be sent round to your hotel this afternoon, and now—"

"And now I shall introduce myself." The woman in the black hat had silently moved and was standing supported by an ebony stick, a little to Helen's left, smiling a smile which was only just not a grimace of pain. Helen felt her own glance caught up and held by a pair of large, ravaged, but bright and intensely intelligent eyes.

"Miss Clark, I am Mrs. Sidney. We have friends in common." The voice was deep, a little harsh, and full of authority.

"How do you do." Helen was on her feet, feeling as awkward as a child before the experience these two seemed to represent.

"I do very well, thank you. And so, I know, will you. Now, we shall say au revoir to our friend, and then we shall go somewhere for a little talk," and she moved stiffly but rapidly towards the door.

Madame Violette opened the door, said, puzzlingly, "Guten Tag, Prinzessin!" and then, with a sharp nod and her crooked smile, "Good day, Miss Clark." Helen followed the heavy black figure of Mrs. Sidney out into the arcade. The door closed behind them with a click.

Mrs. Sidney stopped and smiled her painful smile.

"It is not very far, my dear, that we have to go!" she said, and pushed open the door of the confectioner's shop two feet away.

A fat woman in a white overall beamed delightedly at them from behind a counter loaded with boxes and jars of sweets.

"Here," said Mrs. Sidney over her shoulder, "is the best coffee in Austria, which is saying, I hope you will agree, quite a great deal."

56

With many chuckling sounds, and "Na! Meine Prinzessin"—here it was again—the fat woman showed them
to the only table, at the far end of the shop. The table
was of white marble on gilded cast-iron legs and was set
in front of a red plush sofa, on which Mrs. Sidney settled
herself comfortably, resting her stick and throwing back
her voluminous furs. Helen took off her heavy coat, the
little shop was so hot, and sat down beside her, but at a
respectful distance. She had not yet made up her mind
whether she liked Mrs. Sidney, but she certainly found
her impressive.

For a little while there was a silence which Helen did
not attempt to break. Her companion was busy, with long
bony hands from which a crust of heavy rings gave out a
soft fire, organizing a quantity of scarves and chains
which had become entangled beneath her coat of
shabby, long-haired fur. Helen had a chance to study the
face of Mrs. Sidney cautiously, to make a preliminary
sketch in her mind, while this was going on. After a second she thought: I wish I could paint! and then: she's
seen everything, and she doesn't care any more. . . .

The old woman—and perhaps she's not as old as she
looks, but her life has taken it out of her—had a forehead
broad and rather high and a long, pointed face which,
yellowish, deeply creased, and flecked with small brown
patches like freckles, still spoke of beauty of a high-bred,
a now antique kind. The bones of beauty were there and,
between the great oriental eyes, leaf-shaped under their
wrinkled lids, came strongly her curved nose, thin now
and pinched but, in shape, the Persian poet's "scimitar"
to perfection. The mouth told much. In a lifetime a
mouth may take many shapes according to its uses, where
harder material must stay the same. Mrs. Sidney's mouth,
puckered now in concentration on something which was
caught among her ornaments, showed suffering, pride,
a fluency which her authoritative manner seemed to con-
tradict.

Mrs. Sidney looked up and her eyes, of an almost am-
ber lightness, met Helen's from their darkened sockets,
calm and brilliant and amused.

"My dear, I am clumsy and rather blind. Something here is caught. Will you help me?"

Helen leaned across and freed a black woollen scarf which had caught on the pin of a brooch. Mrs. Sidney sighed, straightened the scarf and revealed the brooch, a large oval miniature, set in old grey diamonds, of a young man in a tie-wig with a scarlet coat, epaulettes and many sashes and stars. Helen sat back, her nose pricking with the mixed odors of camphor and a dry, spicy scent like pot-pourri. She had made up her mind. Mrs. Sidney might be formidable, but she was someone whom it might not be difficult to love.

Large white-and-gold cups of coffee, crested with whipped cream, were put before them, with brioches and Sachertorte, by the fat woman, who seemed to draw enormous pleasure from their presence in her shop.

"Now tell me," said Mrs. Sidney, "how is my old friend Henry Sanders?"

Helen began to glow. This was, all of a sudden, the purest delight, to be able to speak of H.T.S. without fear, and to someone who knew him well.

"He's wonderful," she said. "Wonderfully like himself!"

The old woman chuckled. "He's wonderfully unlike anybody else, I am quite sure! Now I look at you I am, all the same, not certain that I am pleased with Henry for sending you to do this work. You were younger, almost a child when I saw you last, and still—"

"When you *saw* me? Mrs. Sidney, where *can* you have seen me?"

The old woman seemed to be enjoying the sensation she had created. She looked sideways at Helen over the rim of her cup. "Do you not, then, remember Owlsey Towers?" she asked.

"Of course. But . . . I knew everyone there always, all the time. I knew the whole place inside out. If you had come there I must have seen you."

"And the South Lodge, the far-away one on the road to—was it?—Tow-cester. Did you always know who was there?"

58

Helen had to admit that she could only remember an unusually dour and disagreeable lodge-keeper, with a face stiff-starched as her apron, who had not encouraged visitors.

"The South Lodge!" she murmured, and thought that soon she would be numbed against all surprise.

"So," said Mrs. Sidney, "I was in that nasty little house for three months, and I must tell you that it is my ambition never to go back to Northamptonshire! Well, I saw you then. Henry thinks the world of you, you know. In fact, I think he loves you very much." She looked sharply at Helen, to see the effect of this.

Helen felt color climb into her cheeks. "I suppose," she said slowly, "perhaps, in a way, he does. He is a great man. . . ."

"He is a great *man*," replied Mrs. Sidney with firmness, "and that is more important. But do not look so anxious. Love, with Henry, has grown beyond the jangling of the bedsprings. This does not mean that he does not see what God has made of you. Henry, in his time, has been in every sense a man. . . ." A flicker of simple naughtiness crossed Mrs. Sidney's face as she made this remark. "But he is tired now, and ill, and he has great burdens. No man, perhaps, has such burdens. So you are a little his daughter, too. And now, because he loves you, he sends you away in a small fur hat and a muff, like a little *backfisch* of my young days, to do a work which would frighten the wisest man in the world. Men!" she added, with a smile which was at once indulgent and reminiscent. "They are, at bottom, of a frivolity!"

She was to repeat this sentiment a few minutes later, but in opposite terms and on a grimmer tone, when Helen told her the story of her experiences in the train. Then her hawk's profile hardened into something which was almost cruel, and her eyes showed that, though she might have accepted much about this world, she would die, as she had certainly lived, a fighter.

"It is as I have said," she remarked in an even, contemptuous voice. "Men are frivolous—careless, in a truly dangerous way. And this they have to be, I suppose.

For, if it was left to women, they would preserve and preserve, and care so for life that soon they would cuddle it to death. It is our duty, yours and mine—and, now, more yours than mine—to teach our men to care enough, to look and to think twice, to build where their instinct is to destroy, to destroy only where this would bring good."

"I think," said Helen wryly, "that destroying me must have seemed good to those men at that time."

Mrs. Sidney exclaimed: "But, my child, you are right! *At that time.* But perhaps never, now, at another time. They are like that. I think I know who they are, your four men, and I am certain that you will meet them again where you are going. But this time you will drink with them, and they will make you compliments, and they will not even remember that, once, they wanted to kill you."

Helen laughed a little sadly. "I'm going to find meeting them socially a trifle awkward!"

"Ah, that is the difference. I suppose that, yesterday, they may have had a piece of information, perhaps quite wrong, which implicated you, and just there, on the spur of the moment, they decided to get rid of you. They failed. By now they will have thought of other things. It is our strength that we know this better than they do; it is theirs that the taking of life, destruction, means nothing to them, where it means so much in a more—what can we say?—feminine civilization."

"But who are they, if they're not an innocent Trade Mission, as they pretend?"

"I think—and, by tomorrow, I shall know for certain —that they are high members of INGRA, which is the secret police. They have an immense power and, for some measures, they speak directly to Soviet Russia. They are also peasants—highly trained and cleverly taught, but still peasants. Now my family *made* the peasants of that country over eleven centuries, and the peasants made us. It is part of my usefulness that I have it in my blood to understand them. My usefulness will not last forever, as the young ones grow who are trained from birth in the new things—but it will do for the present. And I, thank God, shall not last forever, either!" For a moment the old woman's face became wooden, a mask of remembered agony, the lips calm and resigned. Then Mrs. Sidney gave a small, explosive laugh.

"One still amuses oneself sometimes, just the same. And this—" she waved her hand round the shop, "*this* is decidedly pleasant!"

The old woman, Helen noted, had not once expressed commiseration with her, or remarked on the bizarre nature of such an occurrence on an international train. She's probably seen too much altogether, Helen thought. I think she really is past surprise. But if I'm ever in a tight corner again, I hope to have her with me.

"Do you live here, in Vienna?" Helen asked.

"No," said Mrs. Sidney. "I have no house here now. The last of my Austrian properties happens to be where we are sitting—this little row of shops. But I shall be on the aeroplane with you tomorrow. You see, I live in Senj."

Helen lunched alone at the Elisabeth, where she was welcomed back with a touch of solicitude, as though she had been much in the thoughts of the staff while out on her own.

Her luncheon was delicious and she lingered over it, drinking several cups of the unforgettable coffee, watching the people in the street, purposeful, anxious, drably clothed, moving against the still undamaged whiteness of the snow. How different, she had already found, the reality was from the Gay Vienna of lampshade and chocolate box. Now, Helen found, the city rang hollow. She realized that her schoolgirl's ideas of Vienna, of Austria, were wrong even at the time when she formed them. Whatever happened in the future to the people of this town and country, the Austria she had dreamed of would never be again. One thing, however, remained true. Austria lay now, as formerly, on the frontier of Christendom. The Turks would have had Vienna once, but for the arms of John Sobieski. The pagan hordes had often been

61

at the city gates and now, in the guise of the Russian army, they were here again. So the city, if hollow, was also electric, and as important in many ways as it had ever been.

A chasseur made his way towards Helen's table, bowed, and told her that she was wanted on the telephone. Helen's heart gave a little jump. She had spent her morning in such intimate seclusion, lost in that quiet corner of the city and double-locked by snow, that she had come to think of herself as nearly invisible. Was this friend or enemy, waiting on the line?

"Miss Clark?" A girl's voice, eager, youthful, very English, rang down the wire. "This is the British Embassy, Patricia Heber speaking. We've got some things for you to take to the Legation at Senj, and I wondered—I've got a free afternoon—if you're doing nothing else, whether you'd like to come round Vienna with me? The nice bits, I mean? I could bring you the things to your hotel and then we could set forth—that is, if you don't mind snow?"

"I'd love it," Helen said, quite sincerely. "I've got an appointment at seven, but I'm free till then. And this is my first time in Vienna, and I like the snow. So do come, as soon as you like."

Helen sat in a little white-and-gold drawing-room, turning over illustrated papers until, presently, Miss Heber was shown in. Helen felt friendship at once for this girl, so like one of her own friends of the old days, so irreducibly English, uncomplicated and bright. Miss Heber had a large manila parcel with her, tied with tape and importantly sealed, and a packet of letters, which she dumped carelessly on a small table before collapsing into a chair. Helen smiled at her with shy kindness, suddenly realizing that she felt enormously much older, more worldly-wise than this girl of her own age. It was a pleasure, though, in the exotic ways she was now treading, to be near a character of such familiar openness, so clearly not possessed of any dark corners, of any morbid aspects at all. The high, bony forehead, the perfect skin (uncared for because not needing care), the wide mouth carefully, brilliantly painted, the unplucked eye-bows and gentle red hands—these with the camel-hair coat, head-scarf and fur-lined overshoes, made up a tak-ing picture of a thoroughly nice girl (her mother's clear, rather plaintive voice said this phrase for her in Helen's mind).

Patricia Heber looked Helen over with candid blue eyes. "Well," she said, "I wonder if they know what they're getting in Senj!" She swung in her chair and ex-amined the pretty room with childlike gasps. "What can have come over the F.O.?"

"How do you mean?"

"Well, my dear, *all this!* Such splendor. Most unlike them. Usually, even the Y.W.'s considered too grand for the likes of us."

"It's magically comfortable!" Helen said, laughing.

"And magically expensive. You must be the happy vic-tim of a *colossal* clerical error! Never mind, you *enjoy* it while you've got it. Particularly in view of where you're going. . . ."

"Have you ever been to Senj? Can you tell me about it?"

"I've never been, thank God, but I can tell you it's *legendary!* We call it the Black Hole. People *pray* not to be posted there! I must say I'd go, I'd cheerfully go to see the faces of the women when they see that suit. Or when they just see you," Patricia added, with sudden shyness.

"The women—aren't they very gay?"

"Well, from all I've heard, the ones in the streets are perfectly tragic, poor lambs, and the government offi-cials' wives—the ones you'll be seeing—are all quite square, like boxes, and wear *loose covers* in various taste-ful stuffs, such as hessian and uncut moquette."

Helen laughed outright. "It's just how I've always imagined them," she said. "Oh dear—well, I don't sup-pose I'll see much of them, anyway. This job's to look after Victoria Ogilvy and, at her age, I expect she's a handful!"

"A poppet of the first water, by all accounts. Gosh,

you'll be a joy in that Legation, the poor loves, have *such* a gloomy life."

"Go on," said Helen, "cheer me up!"

"Oh, they're not gloomy *people*. Please don't think that. To begin with, the Minister's an absolute knock-out, in a remote kind of way; and the Counsellor, Charles Sweet, never was a man better named. Really my favorite man, and a bachelor, too—but confirmed, I fear, confirmed. Trouble is, they're shockingly under-staffed. There's no First Secretary till they get a new one; the Second's a boy called Martin Wright that I haven't met, but he's supposed to be a poet or something. No Military Attaché at present. *No Air Attaché!*" Patricia made it sound as though not to have an Air Attaché was the worst thing in the world. "There's a couple of secre-taries—Miss Hubbard and Mrs. Clothier," Patricia looked sideways at Helen, "sterling characters, years of service. Jolly good but just a *trifle* dragonish, you may find. Not that I really know them," she added hastily. "There's an Austrian cook who's said to be a genius, and some odd sort of local help, and finally a perfectly splen-did character called Tubb—without whom! He's every-thing—Chancery guard and major domo and Mark Ogil-vy's chauffeur, and general fixer—he keeps the whole place together, it seems. I wish I'd met him, he sounds fun. . . ."

This was all a great deal more informative than Mr. Harland's report, which had not told Helen much be-yond the fact that permission seemed to be needed for almost any activity outside the Legation grounds.

"It's something that the people are nice. I don't think I mind about there not being many of them." (All to the good, in fact.) "I expect it will be all right. After all, I've a job to do, and it's all new to me anyway."

"Yes, there's that." Patricia looked doubtful. "It is most fearfully restricted, though. We seem to go on and off the boil with that government a good deal, about diplomatic relations. One minute there's a thaw, and the next abso-lute non-speaks. We're rowing just at present, I believe. I *have* heard people say, who know the others, that it's not like the rest of the Iron Curtain countries at all. But then it's small—"

"And it's had an odd history," Helen said, "odder than most."

"Which is saying something in the Balkans. Or isn't it the Balkans? It's a toss-up which I'm worst at, history or geography."

Patricia looked at Helen reflectively.

"Of course," she said, "the Minister, Mark Ogilvy—he's a *widower*. And furiously attractive. That might take a lot of the black holiness out of the place. It would for a lot of us, I'm certain." And she looked sideways at Helen again, clearly doubtful whether her remark had been in good taste.

"A pretty recent widower," Helen said gently. "He's probably still absolutely miserable about it."

"He may be," Patricia answered. She sounded skeptical. "But if all one's *heard*—no," she sat up straight and began looking for her gloves, "my offering you chunks of gossip is not going to help at this stage. You really must stop me nattering. Mrs. Ogilvy was killed in a very nasty accident near Salzburg, a year ago. And the famously dashing Austrian count she was riding with will never dash again. He's only just finished with the plastic surgeons. Come on, let's go and see the sights. I know a divine place we'll drink chocolate in when we're quite frozen."

Helen confided the packages to the manager himself and, feeling suddenly carefree, followed Patricia into the snowy street.

When Helen came down at a few minutes to seven, the snow had stopped. While the head porter opened the door of her taxi she looked up into a black sky alight with white stars. In the main streets the snow had melted or been swept away, but it lay thick on cornices and eaves, and was still a white carpet in the less frequented places. Lights—of shops, of trams, of street-lamps—flowed past Helen in a golden blur. Her taxi stopped and the driver said, "Windsor Hotel, Fräulein."

Helen entered one set of glass doors, mounted what seemed an almost vertical flight of steps, red-carpeted and brilliant with brass, to a revolving door which swung her into a vast and busy hall. There were so many desks and counters and so many tall palms in Chinese pots, interfering with her vision, that it was a moment before she could locate the reception desk.

Helen had to wait for several minutes before she could get the attention of the reception clerk, who was politely trying to persuade a young British officer that no one called Colonel Todhunter was staying, or even expected, in the hotel. Pieces and ends of conversation—English, French, American—drifted to Helen on the general flood of noise. The air was the air of any large hotel, compounded of scent, carpet, hot paintwork and the cabbage smell of dead cigars.

When Helen's turn came to give her name, the reception clerk looked discreet as an owl. He covertly indicated a small door in the nearby wall, half-hidden by spraying palms, and motioned her to go through it. This Helen did, feeling furtive, wondering how many eyes were on her, to find herself facing a small, bald man in a morning coat, who bowed graciously across a large and littered desk.

"Heidegger!" said the man. "I am manager of the Windsor Hotel. It is a pleasure to meet you, Miss Clark."

"You have some instructions for me, I think," said Helen, looking gravely down on Herr Heidegger from her five foot, six.

Mrs. Sidney had not, it appeared, been so indifferent to Helen's unpleasant adventures as Helen had thought. Towards the end of their meeting she had let the vigorous flow of her talk thin to a trickle, and had then, for a time, fallen silent, thinking and twisting her rings. Finally she had said in a low voice, as though to herself:

"Quand même—we must not have you frightened again, if it can be avoided, and I think we can make sure of that, now, today."

She had then spoken for a while, and with a noticeable lack of warmth, of a certain Stoyan Anzip. This man, it seemed, stood high in the Party in her country, a situation where, in Mrs. Sidney's opinion, he had no business to be.

"He is an arriviste. He is also a renegade. He is, I regret to say, my cousin and the last male of my family, although he bears another name. He is—" here the old woman had made an odd, hawking sound of scorn— "one who thinks himself born to survive, to carry into the new world what he has got from the old. A little Philippe Egalité, making friends with revolution, understanding the new things, contributing a stabilizing influence to the difficult period of transition. Et cetera, et cetera!" The contempt in her tone was razor-edged. "Well, so far he does all right. So far! He is wholly without scruples and as calculating as a moneylender. I would kill him—I mean this—myself, if he were not, sometimes, useful. You see, he is not *quite* severed from the old world. Not quite as much as he thinks. And he is still, for various reasons, a little scared of me!"

"And he's in Vienna?"

"He is in Vienna."

Mr. Heidegger fussed Helen into a chair.

"We have a few minutes," he said, "and then *I myself* will go out with you and install you at a table!" He managed to make this sound such an honor that Helen's anxiety lifted for a moment and she almost laughed.

"The party in question," Mr. Heidegger continued, "will arrive at seven-twenty or thereabouts. After that, I believe you know what you are to do."

The manager was evidently rather enjoying this, Helen thought resentfully. For herself, she felt nervous, uncertain, on the edge of being out of her depth.

I'm tired, she said to herself. It's been a day, and she thought with longing of the Hotel Elisabeth, of sleep in her quiet room.

In a noncommittal voice, and studying his nails as he spoke, Mr. Heidegger said: "You are comfortable at the Elisabeth?"

"Wonderfully."

"It is a wonderful hotel." There was more than a hint of wistfulness in the manager's voice. With a brave effort at loyalty he went on, "Of course, here, we cater for—oh, many different kinds of people. We are most busy, really, all the time. It is not easy, I can tell you, to fill a hotel this size, even with so many military about. We were built in days when money was a real thing, when it flowed strongly in a narrower stream. Now! Well, we keep going."

"It seems a delightful place," Helen said, with less truth than kindliness.

The round, white face of Mr. Heidegger began to wag and twitch a little. His mouth seemed to be repressing a great smile, and his eyes sparkled.

"You should know, Miss Clark!" he said archly. "You are staying here! . . . Did you not know? You are registered with us. You have a room—everything! I ask no questions. I understand that these are necessary precautions. Perhaps, all the same, one day you will *really* stay with us." He looked at his watch.

"Now, Miss Clark, let me take you to your table." Mr. Heidegger bowed Helen out to the hall, then forged past her rapidly, but with portly dignity. Helen followed him to a small table at the far edge of a rank of pillars, and was settled with many attentions into a gilded wicker chair.

"I shall send you something to drink," the manager said and, with a final bow, ploughed away across the hall to speak to the concierge.

Helen looked at her watch. It was nearly twenty past. She tried not to fiddle with her gloves, resisted a restless impulse to cross and uncross her legs. A waiter brought her a drink in a tall glass, and went immediately away again.

Suddenly her stomach contracted. She had been told to watch for a party of three men, one short with a small beard, one slightly taller with thick glasses and a bald head, and one very tall man with dark, curly hair. Now, here they were to the left of her, almost beside her table, talking animatedly. Helen had been watching the door,

68

but the three men must have come from behind the pillars near which she was sitting.

The men paid Helen no attention and she, after one quick look, which she hoped had not been as startled as she felt it, leaned forward and picked up her drink, pretending to take a sip and then idly study the glass. She then let her glance travel slowly round to her right, and as slowly back again. When her eyes again reached the group of three, Helen received a distinct shock.

The tall man had half-turned from his companions and was standing in a relaxed pose, staring straight at Helen with an insulting, blazing intensity she had never encountered before. Her own eyes were caught, skewered, by the hard beam of these black ones, so that it needed all her will to move them slowly away, rest them absently for a second on the other two men, and bring them back to her drink. Giddiness ran all over her, and a sweet pain struck her bowels for a moment. She found it difficult to breathe.

Helen picked up her bag and began to ferret at random inside it, turning over familiar personal things—lipstick, comb, keys—several times, to give herself countenance. Then she leaned back, half closing her eyes, and looked straight in front of her. As though an electric charge were playing on her skin she knew, she could feel, that the stranger was still looking her over.

Never in my life, thought Helen, confusedly. Not even with . . . Stoyan Anzip's stare had been positive as a sword thrust, instinct with a savage arrogance and will to possess. She had an extraordinary sense of seeing herself as he saw her, naked and powerless, as though he had invaded her body in fact as well as wish.

Mrs. Sidney's blunt words came back to Helen:

"He is handsome—tall and slim and strong. He talks well. He would be irresistible to women even if his power in the Party did not make all possible." She had added: "I would not wish you to be mixed up with Stoyan, very much not. But I think your position at the Legation will protect you, even from him. What I want is for him to see you, knowing who you are. After that—I know him very well—his thoughts in your regard will not, at any rate, be of *murder*."

Helen looked at her watch, according to plan, drank a third of her drink at a gulp and got up from her table. Her legs felt heavy; the distance to the revolving door seemed immense. According to plan, she stopped to greet the concierge in grey frock coat who had moved forward a little to meet her.

"Your car is waiting, Miss Clark," he said quietly.

Out of the corner of her eye Helen saw the tall figure of Stoyan Anzip, in its sophisticated light grey suit, move easily across to the reception desk. He seemed to ask a brief question, for the clerk nodded emphatically.

Helen went through the revolving door. The concierge steadied it for her and then stood with his back to it for the time that it took her to go down the steps and into the waiting car.

Lying back in the car on the short drive between hotels, Helen tried to calm in herself a variety of insistent feelings. She was angry, and—she had to admit it—more than a little frightened. She told herself that she was being absurd, that what she had been subjected to was nothing unusual, that Anzip was ridiculous, a humorless passion-monger, a hero of the silent films. But there was no real use denying the sense of his power which she had experienced. She knew now that Stoyan Anzip was a dangerous person in more ways than one.

Helen dined in her room, bathed and repacked her bags. Then, suddenly, unwilling to sleep, she wandered about in her dressing-gown for a while, going over the day's events, the great crowd of impressions she had gained, trying to think in an orderly and constructive way. But something seemed to have shaken loose inside her. Irrelevant thoughts, wishes, memories long carefully buried, came back into her mind. She felt strung-up, deeply disturbed in all her being.

Helen was without defenses now, and soon, inevitably, she began to uncover in her mind the details of that love affair which had so shaken her life, details which she had ruthlessly, and successfully, suppressed for many months.

70

Of the affair itself there were no tangible memorials. Love itself apart, she had nothing to remember her lover by but a few meals in dark corners of cheap "amusing" restaurants, a few haunted, huffy telephone calls, and some flat words on very expensive writing paper, long since destroyed. She had, in any case, wanted nothing: no thing. She had had, and had believed secure, an extraordinary bounty of love—physical love of deep force and strangeness—which she had believed not possible save between the two that they were. Apparently she had been wrong. One day, quite without warning (she had not looked for warnings) this marvelous, world-filling exhilaration was removed. The other pole of her perfect polarity went out. Communication ended. The girl who had bloomed so splendidly, had grown with each day more confident, more graceful, more grandly and entrancingly herself, was flung back into her corner and, in a few hours, had almost withered away.

Shrunk in on herself, Helen for a while had had, literally, nothing to live for. She wilted in her high rooms, smoked endlessly, ate little, dozed or stared into corners. The saddest thing, she thought now, bemusedly, . . that for months she had even hidden her body from her own eyes—scrambling through her dressing and undressing, snatching hasty, unluxurious baths. . . .

Helen shivered. She could hear herself telling Henry Sanders: "I'm over it, you know. Quite settled down again."

"Oh Lord," she thought, "must this happen to me *now?*"

After leaving Vienna, the aircraft flew for a long time above cloud. Helen, whose previous flights had all been made at night, was, for a while, entranced with the rippling waves at cloud-top, the infinite milk-white sea flat-calm beneath them.

The manager of the Elisabeth had said, "Bonne chance!" to Helen in much the same accents as had H.T.S. The tall head porter had tucked her into the hotel car with mournful love. She had driven to the airport down ugly, shapeless streets, through raw developments of wire and concrete, past hurrying workers looking starved and miserable, in traffic crowded with official cars.

At the airport she had had contact with something truly foreign to her experience. The loud but calming tones of the public address system called, in four languages, for passengers on Sinavia Flight Number Two-Three-Three to report to the airline desk. Helen joined a queue of about twenty people already waiting, and immediately felt extremely conspicuous. Out of loyalty, and a kind of superstition, she was wearing her sable hat. This, with her wide-swinging travelling coat of fine black cloth lined with fur, would have looked distinguished, expensive in any gathering. Here, they were sensational. Admittedly the other passengers, with one exception, were men and therefore most likely to pay attention, but Helen was almost put off balance by the way in which they turned and lengthily stared. Themselves were so different from the other passengers in the assembly hall as to be positively exotic. Their effect in color was ashen, wholly without life. The men, mostly middle-aged, were grey in the face. Each wore a raincoat, grey or khaki-brown, thick boots, and a soft hat which did not look soft at all, which looked as if made of grey cardboard, with scarcely any brim to speak of. All carried paper-leather brief cases of uniform pattern, perfunctorily grained and noduled to imitate leather. Some had grey gloves, and some grey woollen scarves. The single note of color in the gathering was in the muddy green coat of the only woman passenger so far present; but what this lady lacked in color she made up for in drama. Seeing Helen approach, she swung sharply round, put her hands on her hips and fixed on the girl a long stare of burning, theatrical contempt, varied every so often by a round of complicitous, sneering smiles to her fellow-countrymen. She had the face of a middle-aged toad, with a receding forehead, pouchy cheeks and four gold teeth. Her hair, a wiry, neutral-colored substance, was pushed into a small bun under a hat like a doughnut.

Helen guessed that she must be fairly important, to be travelling in this manner at all.

After the first shock of receiving this blast of curiosity, incredulity and active dislike, Helen felt obliged to turn round and look elsewhere. Also she was on the lookout for Mrs. Sidney, although the old woman had forbidden her to make any sign of recognition.

"We will meet again soon, never fear," she had said as they parted.

Mrs. Sidney must have arrived almost last of all the passengers. Helen, patiently waiting while a wooden-faced young man went slowly through her tickets and passport with the aid of two glowering colleagues, suddenly caught a whiff of camphor and spicy scent and knew that Mrs. Sidney was behind her. It was hard to remember instructions and resist turning to greet her. Helen had just begun to realize how far she was travelling from the familiar; how lonely, in fact, she might be going to be.

Passenger comfort was clearly far from the thoughts of those running the Sinavia airline. At take-off, the pilot had held his machine down to a point where Helen, at least, wondered if he would ever get it off at all; and had then jerked it clean off the ground into a rocketing climb. There was nothing gentle about his turns and course-corrections, either. Sharp in—sharp out, seemed to be his motto. His human cargo reeled under this treatment, but remained calm. Helen alone, convinced that she was green in the face already, faced four hours and a half of this with no light heart.

The steward, a sour-looking man with a squint, had addressed them in his own language just before take-off, his high, throaty, stadium voice making his remarks sound like a political speech. After two hours this remained his sole contribution to their welfare. Since then he had been busy in a back seat with papers and a rubber stamp.

The calm cloudscape and clear autumnal blue gave place to towering black-edged cumulus and an unpleasant twenty minutes in cloud, where the aircraft bucked and wallowed, rose sharply or fell like an express lift. After this the cloud began to fray away and Helen's interest was again engaged, this time with a complex conjunction of mountain ranges, the higher peaks snow-crested, forests like green-black rugs slipping off the hillsides, and a broad gleaming river flowing in rhythmic curves.

Then, once again they flew into cloud, and stayed there for a long time, but with less turbulence. Helen closed her eyes and eventually achieved sleep. When she awoke, she had gone deaf, and knew that they were losing height. The aircraft was still in cloud but, for once, perfectly steady. Her watch showed that, if they were not behind time, they should be at Senj in half an hour. The time was a few minutes past midday.

Valley succeeded valley and, looking from her own porthole, and catching an occasional glimpse through one on the other side, Helen could make out that they were crossing at right angles a mountain chain which curved to the horizon in either direction. They were flying in a gap between high peaks. On these, where the forest ended, the rock was reddish-grey and black, and on many of them snow was already thick. There was no sunlight in the scene and, although visibility was good, the sky hung yellow-white and flat above the mountain tops. Helen wondered if she would find snow in Senj.

The land was falling away rapidly now and, at the wing's edge, Helen could see an ocean of varying browns and yellows which must be the great plain of Senj. Quite suddenly there was a village, set into pine woods, a little to the left of them, on Helen's side. After hours of blank cloud and wild mountains, to see houses again gave Helen pleasure. Her spirits lifted. It seemed all the same an odd sort of village to find in hilly country such as this. Several very large, gabled buildings with red-brown roofs, turrets and ornamental ironwork, stood apart from one another in clearings of the pine woods and, as the aircraft lumbered on, a strange edifice appeared, all of one story, but covering a large space, with a dome in the center clothed in fish-scale tiles, and long colonnaded wings. They were flying low enough for Helen to see that the roads leading to this building were grassy from disuse, and to discern in the even green parkland around it the traces of terraces and gardens that had been.

This, she immediately decided, was a disused resort of some kind, and then she remembered what it must be. Henry Sanders had taken her through the map of the country once again before she left him. He had pointed to a spot fairly high in the first range of hills to the northwest of Senj and had said: "Since the eighteen-nineties this was perhaps the biggest attraction of all for foreign visitors of a certain kind—Ostrány, one of the best and most expensive spas in the world, for I forget what. Run by a Swiss-German syndicate, and an absolute gold mine in its day. The syndicate's expropriated, of course. Part of the spa—one of the old hotels—is still used as a rest home for some particularly virtuous type of worker, but most of it's shut up and falling down. The railway still works but it's altogether too much of a job to get to Ostrány now. I doubt if anyone takes the waters there any more."

They were past the place now, but Helen could see the narrow railway, its rails dulled with rust, running like a brown zip-fastener down through the close green stuff of the woods. Even from above, the little group of buildings had looked forlorn and lifeless; but Helen thought that she would like to visit Ostrány one day, if only for its height and remoteness, if she were ever allowed to visit anything; if she dared take her eye, for one moment, off her job.

The pilot made one of his drastic steep banks and, when they were on an even keel again, Helen sat staring with wide eyes in front of her, hands tightly clasped in her lap.

Senj was nearly beneath them. She could see the wide, beautifully-rounded loops of a river which must be the Tvar on which Senj was built. In minutes now she would be in Senj and on her way to take up the post of nursery governess to Victoria Ogilvy. She was not worried that she had so little experience of children; she had, at least, a little. Victoria was no great problem. She could make Victoria happy, or if not that, then she could at least perform all the duties which the phrase "look after" is meant to cover. The child was in no danger, nor would she know or, in any ordinary sense, care for some years to come, that Mark Ogilvy, her father, was in very grave danger indeed.

For more than seventy-two hours Helen had been moving across Europe towards this moment. Now there would be no more luxuries, no more beguilements, no more terrors even, nothing at all to distract her from her real task. With no formal training, with nothing but her own beliefs, which were so instinctive that she never felt the need of formulating them, she was setting out to attack a position which its occupant supposed to be impregnable—and all because she could not bring herself to believe that H.T.S. could be wrong. As the aircraft sank towards Senj, Helen's heart sank with it.

The door clanged open, showing a yellow sky over the pleated steel doors of a hangar. The depressing steward stood stiffly at the top of the steps, neither smiling nor looking at the passengers as they filed past him. Helen took care to let the woman in green get well in front of her before moving herself. She had no wish to be pushed down the steps. As it was, the woman turned at the door and fired back at her a look of malign inquisitiveness before disappearing with the tide of grey-clothed men.

Helen walked slowly to the hangar, knowing that Mrs. Sidney was somewhere behind her. The man who had sat next to her throughout the trip, and who had slept without waking the entire way, suddenly surprised her greatly by taking off his hat, revealing a bristly grey head and smiling a brief, gilt smile. He gestured towards Helen, perhaps to indicate her general appearance, and said, "Good!" quite enthusiastically. Then he put his hat on again, turned his eyes to the front, rearranged his face into a conformable blankness, and trudged on towards the airport buildings without another word.

Oh, but it's cold! thought Helen. A steady wind, sting-
ing with iron cold, was sweeping across the airfield from
the north. How right Miss Martineau had been about
furs! If it's as cold as this in October, we're in for a long,
grim winter. Goodness, I hope the Legation's warm.

Far away to her left, beyond the runways, beyond
fields of purple roots and the blind, unfriendly walls of
a factory, Helen could see the mountains, the white
crenellation of the peaks over which she had just flown.
In front, the airport buildings were wide concrete boxes,
somewhat dilapidated-looking, with rails like a ship and
disproportionate windows of sheet glass, conventionally
functional. Long rusty stains ran down the concrete,
there were cracks and patches of sweat in the walls.
Striped black-and-white sentry boxes stood beside the
glass main doors, each with its armed guard in long grey
overcoat and short-peaked cap. Airport staff bustled about
the tarmac, on foot or in small, grey cars. Beyond the
hangars a number of large military aeroplanes, all of a
dull green color, were drawn up in line; beyond these,
squatting with their noses in the air, came a line of fight-
ers. An anemometer, spinning merrily on the roof,
seemed suddenly a symbol of innocence to Helen, she
could not have told why.

Inside the main building the warmth was almost suf-
focating. Even so, it was welcome, after the tearing, biting, grit-laden air outside. Helen took in a vague impression of a great many potted palms, huge, heavy mahogany counters like an old-fashioned draper's shop, frosted-
glass cubicles, rhetorical posters, and a vast mural showing men and women marching joyously through shocks
of gamboge corn on a remarkably fine day. Then a gentle, slightly hesitant voice said: "Welcome, Miss Clark!"
Standing before her was a young man in a blue overcoat
with a velvet collar, holding a black-braided homburg
hat, and looking at her with such sparkling pleasure as to
give his words more than their usual meaning.

"Welcome again. No need to ask you if you *are* Miss
Clark! You couldn't possibly be anyone else. What a
dismal party to send you flying with!" and he turned to

throw an amused but not unfriendly glance at Helen's travelling companions, now herding into the customs hall. "I am Martin Wright," he added, "and this—" he turned to indicate a tall, thickset man in chauffeur's uniform, with a long ironical face, a red-brown complexion and very sharp, amused-looking light brown eyes— "is Sergeant Tubb. He will see to it that the Glumbas don't make off with your luggage." Sergeant Tubb said, "Pleased to see you, Miss," and he, too, really looked pleased.

Helen felt exhilarated. Somehow she had not expected any kind of a welcome. She had sat in the aircraft so appalled by the prospect before her that it would not have surprised her to be met by a posse of lantern-jawed diplomatists nine feet tall. Wright and Tubb, with simple straightforwardness, had altered a whole perspective. She realized, however, that she must not allow herself to abandon all reserve. Her double game, worse luck, must continue to be played alone. It was for this reason that she watched Martin Wright for a moment, narrowly, as Mrs. Sidney went past, to see if he would make any sign of recognition. The young man did vaguely follow the black hat and shapeless furs a short distance with his eyes, looking mildly puzzled, but he did not refer to the old woman. Helen knew that, besides Mrs. Sidney, there were two people in Senj to whom she could talk without reservation; but she had no idea who they were, and it was in her instructions that she should wait until they revealed themselves.

Martin Wright wrung a clearance for Helen's luggage from a grudging customs officer, and waved Helen's passport under the control official's nose, without letting go of it, in a way which made that personage look like a dog being teased with a bone. Wright had already taken charge of the package Patricia Heber had given to Helen in Vienna.

When they were settled into the large black Humber, wrapped in fur rugs, and Martin Wright had fiddled with the heating, only to turn it off, and had been reproved by Tubb for this, he said:

"They don't mean half as much harm, you know, as you might think. They're just fascinated by *things*. That's why I hung on to your passport. It isn't that they're efficient—they aren't, in the least—or that they want to subject it to all sorts of sinister checks. It's simply that a strange passport, or a strange anything, is a tremendous treat, and everybody has to look, and feel, and say his say about it. That is why it takes such aeons to get the least little thing done. . . . I say," he added, looking at Helen with warm friendliness and candid admiration, "wait till Victoria sees what she's got!"

"Will she like me, do you think?" Helen asked, meaning her question, and hoping she did not sound coquettish. "What do you think she expects?"

"Oh, she expects another Mrs. Simpkin, and I think she already thinks one's enough."

"Mrs. Simpkin?" Helen asked curiously. This name had not been in Miss Heber's catalogue.

"Well, she's really called something like Sinkiewicz. She's a local who's allowed to work for us, probably for whatever she can report about us—I can't think what! Victoria calls her Mrs. Simpkin after a cat in a book. And we follow Victoria, as we do in most things."

"But what does Mrs. Simpkin do for Victoria?"

"She's a sort of Nanny-figure. She bathes her and feeds her and stays near her at night—all that sort of thing. But she's a fearfully gloomy old character, and she doesn't know much English, and I'm afraid Victoria gets rather fed up with her. On the other hand I think that, in a sort of dim, Glumba way, Mrs. S. is quite devoted. I must say I'd love to see her reports to the Ministry of the Interior! As far as I know she's never left the nursery floor in eighteen months. She must be a *mine!*"

"That's twice you've used that word—Glumba. What does it mean?"

"Oh, that's Tubb's word, of course. He's the other important person in our Mission. Sergeant Tubb took to using the word to describe the inhabitants of this interesting country. They really wrung his heart, I think, from the minute he arrived, they looked so depressed

79

and seemed so hell-bent after things he saw no point in. One day H.E. asked him why he called them Glumbas, and Tubb said, 'They're such a glum-looking lot of poor bastards, Sir, aren't they, if you'll excuse me,' and Glumbas they've been to all of us ever since."

They laughed together. The air in the car felt suddenly full of gaiety, full enough to dispel, for a while, Helen's recent sense of threat. She realized that she owed a more cheerful feeling to the skill and quickness to please, to be pleased, of her companion. No doubt Martin Wright had been trained to break ice and make propitious atmospheres, but he appeared perfectly sincere and completely light-hearted as well. Sergeant Tubb's broad back, his smooth and skillful driving, also contributed to a sense of safety and ease.

The car was travelling along a broad concrete road between acres of small cultivated plots which might have been allotments. The road was lined with poplars, whose yellowed leaves were spinning off in clouds in the harsh wind. On either hand, flat as the word itself and stretching into infinity lay the great plain of Senj. So wide was it that all sense of distance was distorted, big factories looking no more significant than small cabins under the huge yellow sky. To their left lay the railway line, with a child's idea of a train, all box-like brown carriages with a small, hump-backed engine, puffing slowly along it. Straight ahead of them, dark-colored and compact, lay the city of Senj, its domes and onion-crowned steeples dramatically restated by the clear-cut snowline beyond.

With a good deal of impatient hooting, a large black car driven by a stiff-faced soldier pulled out and passed them. From the side window, and leaning right round to stare harder, the woman in green thrust her toad's face towards them as her car went past. Martin made a small sound like "Ouf!"

"Tell me," Helen said, "who *is* that? She's been giving me terrible looks ever since Vienna. She rather gives me the creeps."

"You are right to be given the creeps. That is Luba Kassin, Minister of Culture and Education. A vintage revolutionary, held in high esteem you know where. Also a murderess and an absolutely full-time nymphomaniac. I'm sure she hated *you* on sight!"

"If all the government officials are like that, you must have a life!" Helen said.

"They're not, thank goodness. Some are pretty grim, in that they're clever and enjoy *playing* clever, if you get me. There are two or three really big stinkers, of which your friend is one; the rest are simply the most stupefying bores and yes-men. Except one man, who is really so nice that I cannot imagine why he hasn't been bumped off long ago!"

They were running now beside the river Tvar which divides the city of Senj. When an economy is wrenched from one set of objects and put to quite different ones, there must always be a sad dilapidation and neglect of once-valued things. Sooner or later these relics would be obliterated, but Senj had only known its new masters for seven years and still, along the river's banks, were broken evidences of a riparian life which, Helen could see, had once meant much to those who lived it. Low, pleasant-looking stone houses, formerly plastered and color-washed, and still bearing traces of color, stood shuttered in gardens already choked with weeds. What had evidently been riverside cafés and restaurants hung broken balconies over the green-white, snow-swollen waters.

"I notice one thing," Helen said. "It's been bothering me since we left the airport. I haven't seen a single shop or a single advertisement. Not that I want to see advertisements particularly, and there are any number of signs and posters—only they all look so anxious and dramatic. I'm beginning to long for a frightful great hoarding saying soap or tea!"

"Hortatory is the word for the posters, I believe," Martin said. "They're all exhorting people to *do* something —to do without something as often as not. As to soap and tea, those are rationed and obtainable only at the

81

government co-operative against the production of cou-
pons." He made his voice sound pinched and official as he
said this.

"Sounds familiar. How long's it going on for?"

"Ever, I should think. Poor old Glumbas! They used,
I'm told, to be a lively and independent lot, full of jokes
and songs and not badly off, economically, in a simple
sort of way, with this great rich plain to dig about in,
and the ore in the mountains. They had customs and
traditions and a king, and all sorts of old-fashioned
things, and they enjoyed the protection of Austria while
that was any use; when it ceased to be they got on quite
well without it. Diplomatically, they were always pretty
bright, which is more than can be said of them now. Although, of course, it isn't *them* any longer; it's the other
Them, if you know what I mean."

"And it's for the other Them's sake that they go without, and have to have all this good advice on posters?"

"Mm. They've been promised all sorts of wonderful
things in the future, of course, provided they tighten
their belts now. But—I dunno. Five-year plans, ten-year
plans—that sort of thing could go on forever. . . .
Meanwhile, they're hell's delight to deal with in our sort
of work. We're having a little rest at the moment, as a
matter of fact, owing to a nicely-engineered misunder-
standing, but usually we're kept pretty hard at it. The
Minister's in London, reporting."

"He's not here? Sorry! That's what you said! When
will he be back again?"

"Let's see—it's Thursday today. Probably Saturday, or
it might be Monday. In time for Victoria's birthday
on Tuesday, I do hope. Carlo's Chargé at the moment,
studiously avoiding any action. You'll like him, I think.
He's a very good chap."

"Charles Sweet, is that? Do you call him Carlo?"

"Oh yes." Martin's tone was sheepish. "Carlo Dolce,
you see. That's the kind of terrible joke some of us
are driven to making; and like the Glumbas, it's stuck."

Martin Wright confirmed Patricia Heber's comment
about the Legation's being understaffed.

"It's a travesty, just at present," he said. "Liberians would turn up their noses at it. We bleat continuously. Signals fly about all the time. The Office is very sorry; it says it is doing its best. We keep on being promised people of great talent and charm, to bring us up to strength, and always, at the last moment, something goes wrong. They break their legs, or are desperately needed in Washington, or put up terrible blacks and get fired. We're short of a First and a Third Secretary, two service attachés, about three clerks, and someone to help Sergeant Tubb. But I must tell you," he went on, smiling at Helen a little shyly, "that, except when I think I'm being worked too hard, I find the situation perfect. I'm with people I like and admire, in a place which, in spite of all restrictions, interests me, and I have a bit of elbow-room. Which is why I don't write to *The Times* under an assumed name, calling attention, etc."

Helen smiled, but said nothing. She turned her head away to look out at the crowding houses which were the beginning of Senj. The Legation's staff troubles might be, as Martin suggested, simply a matter of chance. If, on the other hand, H.T.S. was right about Mark Ogilvy, then the fewer people in the game at the game's end the better; and those only people who could be trusted to help to the last inch and beyond. The uncertain diplomatic situation in this country could explain unorthodoxy, if questions were publicly asked. The more Helen thought, the more sure she became. Those now surrounding Mark Ogilvy were all experienced, especially trusted people: even the clerks were old hands. Tubb was evidently an exceptional person. Any addition that might now be made in the staff would be of the same quality. Only Martin was young, in years and service, but Helen could feel that he might have strength, steadiness, a capacity for loyalty, with all his sensitiveness and fluency. His next words seemed to confirm this:

"Anyway, Mark Ogilvy could run any show with no staff at all and both hands tied behind him. He's miles the brightest of the younger men. We're jolly lucky to have him."

They were off the concrete now and on to cobbles; old cobbles, Helen thought, and could trace in a jumble of scaffolding and hoardings the lines of once handsome buildings lining a broad street with an arch at one end. The hoardings carried bigger-than-lifesize pictures of grim-faced men—Stalin, and others not yet known to Helen—all wearing the constipated expression common to people who suppose themselves the instruments of Destiny.

The car slid under the fine Renaissance arch, whose positive elegance, shells and swags of fruit and pedimented niches, looked theatrical, over-dressed amid the latter-day squalor surrounding it. This was regrettable, thought Helen, since, for the authors of that squalor, a point might seem to be proved.

"The South Gate of Senj," said Martin. "It will not be with us much longer, I'm afraid. They plan to drive a thumping great boulevard through here all the way from Maria-Theresa Square which is now called the Square of the 15th of October. Carlo says it equals the sum of the squares on the other two sides."

Helen giggled. Martin had managed very well to convey to her the Legation atmosphere—friendship and foolish family jokes, small human glosses on a basically intractable situation. It was typically British, she supposed, and probably none the worse for that, this slightly dotty, seemingly careless, public attitude concealing a lot of private anxiety and hard work. Each nation had its own way of managing such problems. For the present, Helen was glad to be allowed to slip into a pattern familiar to her and by no means despised.

Once through the arch the car swung right, and left again, and Helen exclaimed with pleasure at the view in front of them. They were running along a cobbled quay, with the Tvar rushing greenly past them, its water almost level with the stone coping a few yards away. Tall, stately houses, all differentiated but all bearing an organic resemblance to each other, ran up and over a steep slope ahead of them in a racing curve.

"Don't look too closely," Martin said. "Nothing is

84

what it seems. Look, there's the Alexander Bridge." A solid stone bridge with three arches spanned the river ahead of them. It looked older than anything else, as if designed, with its great bolsters of stone, for the traffic of heavily-armed men, but its superstructure was of a charming late nineteenth-century frivolity, with clusters of lanterns on elaborate bronze standards, bronze dolphins and a parapet of fretted iron.

To the right, across the river, tall gabled buildings were separated by narrow passages, dark even in daylight. Leading from the bridge on that side, a street dived sharply and burrowed into an irregular mass much older, less consciously organized, than the buildings on the river banks.

"The Old Town," Martin said, and Helen, remembering Mr. Sanders' box, looked for and found, at a great height above their surroundings, the twin onion steeples of the Cathedral of Senj.

"Because there are houses on both sides of the river, and because they're all more or less all of a piece architecturally, some ass, at some time, called Senj 'The Florence of the Balkans,'" said Martin. "Well, there you are. That's what so many people used to come such miles to see. Oh, the acres of water-color, the reams of prose! And how I wish it still went on. There's a book in the Legation Library called *Off the Beaten Track in Senj*, by Catherine Tidmarsh Brown, which I turn to whenever the present day gets too much."

The first, tentative flakes of snow starred the windshield and melted. Beyond the graceful quays and the vista of bridges, where the mountains should have completed the perspective, was now only a darkening haze. The light was prison-light, filtered painfully from a long way off, and in it Martin's hands and face were colorless, almost luminous. "We're going over the Old Bridge," he said, "and then we'll be home in no time."

The Old Bridge, roughhewn, strong and without ornament except for two flat-capped, pepper-pot turrets at each end, was the bridge in the other picture Helen had seen. She recognized the turrets and the palace-like buildings opposite, on the other bank. This proved now to be only one wing of an immense, elaborate eighteenth-century structure, with a fine, pillared portico and carved pediment to its centre block, which enclosed a stone-paved square on three sides. This, Martin told her, had been the royal palace. It was now the home of three ministries—Interior, Foreign Affairs, and War. The courtyard was full of dull-green and black cars, and many dark-clothed people climbed or descended a great bank of steps. They swung to the left and, as they passed a small park, Helen saw the top of a bandstand and, beyond it, large houses spaced among thick trees. She asked where the Ministry of Culture was. "Just so that I can avoid it!"

"I couldn't show it to you as we came, because it's not on the waterfront. I'm sorry to say it's far and away the loveliest building in the town, the old palace of the Sideini princes in what's now called Karl Marx Square."

Helen sat up suddenly, without meaning to. She said to herself: Sideini. Mrs. Sidney. Prinzessin.

"Who were the Sideini?" she asked, with careful neutrality, but Martin had no time to answer. Sergeant Tubb had swung them in a smooth curve out of the cobbled street and in at tall iron gates set in a twelve-foot wall. Dark shrubs enclosed them for a moment, and then they were at a halt under a deep stone portico.

"His Britannic Majesty's Legation," said Martin, smiling with a touch of solicitude, "and welcome once again. Here comes Victoria."

The glass doors of the Legation were opened by a man-servant in a white coat, and the child came slowly out on to the steps. Victoria's eyes looked very large in a face pinched by shyness. Her straight, smooth hair was sleek and shining. She stopped at the top of the steps and stood still in her blue corduroy skirt and white Jersey, her feet in red shoes placed together neatly.

"Victoria," said Martin, "look! Here's Miss Clark, all the way from home."

The little girl frowned. "Home is here," she said. She

had the clear articulation of children who live much with their elders. There was a pause. Help! thought Helen, she is not going to like me! Suddenly Victoria dashed down the steps and leapt at Martin, who caught her in his arms. "Wright! Wright!" she said into his chest, and then wriggled to sit on his arm with her head turned towards Helen, looking wild but a little reassured, and inquisitive, like a small monkey.

"Say how do you do," Martin prompted.

"How do you do?" The red lips formed the words like pearls, showing straight white teeth. Victoria's eyes were almost violently blue.

"Can you sing 'Pa Pa Pleckship'?" the child asked.

Helen looked blank for a second. Martin laughed. "If I tell you," he said to Helen, "that the next line is 'Hiff you inny vool?' you will recognize it, at once, in Mrs. Simpkin's rendering."

"Oh," Helen cried, "of course I can, Victoria! 'Baa, baa, black sheep.' Shall I sing it now?"

"Not *now!*" Victoria was shocked. "Bedtime!"

"Bedtime, then." Helen came closer. The child put out a hand and stroked the sable hat. "Soft," she said. "Pussy-soft," and then, with a look of cheerful wickedness: "Hullo, Miss Clark!"

"Please say Helen."

"Helen."

Martin gave a loud sigh of relief. "Dieu merci, cela c'est passé très bien!" he murmured. "Come on, both of you, it's snowing like a paper-chase. We'll have some sherry before stirring hand or foot. After that Victoria will show you your room. All right, Victoria?"

Victoria began to dance. She slipped a warm hand into Helen's and began to catalogue the splendors of Helen's bedroom for her as they went up the steps and into the house.

The British Legation had once belonged to a millionaire, an industrialist and financier who had pioneered, amongst other things, sugar-beet cultivation and the city's first department store. He had built his house in 1900, in a style that was cautiously palatial. Being a good businessman, and mindful of the uncertainties of politics in Central Europe, he had taken care not to overreach himself; on the other hand, he had not been niggardly. The result was a well-built dwelling of manageable proportions, with some palatial features, such as a green marble staircase cunningly arranged to soar and return steeply within a shallow well; a great deal of inlaid wooden flooring; and, in the three communicating salons on the ground floor, a wealth of rococo plasterwork on cornices and coved ceilings of quite pleasing design.

The building had housed the British mission since 1920. After the occupation of Senj by the Germans in 1940 it had suffered, thanks to the energetic caretaking of the Swiss Minister, nothing worse than occupation by a clerical branch of the military government.

Upstairs the bedrooms were arranged on two floors. Low-ceilinged, with thick, unpainted wooden cornices and window frames, and tiled stoves like china castles built into the walls, they were almost conventually simple and entirely charming. The contrast, after leaving the restless gold and green upward rush of the staircase, was striking. Martin Wright thought that the original owner probably never went to bed, but slept in his boots amongst the debris of a perpetual party in his splendid drawing-room downstairs.

The Office of Works, whose duty it is to look after British official properties abroad, had contributed its own correct if unadventurous taste to the general furnishing. There was a good deal of chintz on immense armchairs, and a quantity of small rosewood tables. Portraits of the King and Queen looked down on them as they drank sherry before a bright fire in a grey-and-gold morning-room made pale as marble by the light from falling snow.

". . . and a little bed at the end of the big bed, and a bear on the floor!" concluded Victoria.

"It sounds lovely," said Helen. "I can't wait to go to bed in it."

She recognized this as a precious moment, and savored

it deliberately. Large as florins, the snowflakes chased each other across the tall windows; beyond was white haze and a shadow which must be trees. Perfect quiet made the swift flutter and crack of the fire sound loud and comforting as the morning fire in a sick room. Victoria's voice had a wintry clarity of its own. Her foot still on the threshold of a life, a world, herself not yet wholly engaged, Helen tasted the milder fire of her sherry and let her mind relax in peace.

Presently Victoria led her up the steep, deceptive staircase to its narrow half-landing, turned smartly right and continued upwards, puffing slightly and counting to herself: "One, two, three, four, five, nine, eleven, SIXTEEN."

"Nine, *ten*, eleven, *twelve*, Victoria," Helen said, trying her new rôle.

Victoria shot her a look of amusement, as though Helen had missed a joke. "There are *sixteen* steps!" she said. "One, two, three . . ." Helen felt a shade discomfited. "There must be sixty, at least," she thought. "I suppose Victoria has favorite numbers. After all, she won't even be five till Tuesday." Clearly, there was more to being a nursery governess than simply knowing best.

"There!" said Victoria, who had capably opened a door at the head of the staircase by pulling on its gilded latch with both hands. "Look! A big bed, and a little bed, and . . ." she took a running jump into the middle of a large polar bear skin which took up a third of the floor, and sat there regarding Helen with brilliant eyes.

The broad, low-ceilinged room was warm and shadowless in the aching snowlight, its bareness and muted colors welcome to the eye after the complicated magnificence downstairs. The floor was shining, honey-colored parquet, which creaked slightly underfoot. The wide, low bed had indeed, as Victoria had proclaimed, a narrow chaise longue at its foot. Bedcover and curtains, the chaise longue and the valance of the dressing table, were all of the same glazed cotton, innocently patterned with moss-rosebuds. A tall stove set into the right-hand wall

89

was covered with tiles painted in pale pink lustre, showing hunting scenes. There were two heavy carved ward-
robes in dark wood, on either side of the stove, and, on
the white walls, a number of unemphatic English colored prints. At the end of the left-hand wall, next the
window, a door stood open on a corner of what must be
Victoria's day nursery. Helen could see the grey tail of a
rocking-horse, and pink carpet reaching to the wall.

Victoria was up again, pulling at Helen's hand. "Come
on, Helen, come and see my nursery. Come and see Mrs.
Simpkin!"

Helen went where Victoria pulled her, taking in the
clear-lit, cluttered familiarity of an English nursery, and
saw, standing motionless in yet another doorway opposite her, a short, stiff-backed figure in a white overall.

"Mrs. Simpkin, Mrs. Simpkin!" Victoria was bounding
across the floor, talking excitedly at the top of her voice.
". . . and she can sing 'Baa, baa, black sheep'!" she
rounded off her jumbled commentary, pulling Mrs.
Simpkin across the room.

Mrs. Simpkin moved reluctantly some paces forward
and then stopped. To Helen's greeting she replied with
an odd bow, neither gracious nor self-abasing, merely
the grudging recognition of another person's existence.

Victoria looked from one to the other, flushed, her
eyes black with excitement, and repeated her last remark.

"So!" was Mrs. Simpkin's only comment.

Something in the broad-browed, square-edged face,
the stocky figure, the unrevealing black eyes hit a chord
in Helen's mind. Something about Mrs. Simpkin was not
unfamiliar, although Helen knew she could never have
seen this yellowish, immobile face, this neat, skimpy grey
hair with its door-knob bun. Her feeling, all the same,
was so strong that for a moment she could not find anything to say.

Mrs. Simpkin, perhaps from shyness (or sheer dislike,
thought Helen anxiously) seemed unable or unwilling to
speak. She looked down at Victoria, however, with a per-
ceptible softening of her expression and said:

"You come now and *vosh*, Victoria! For you is dinner downstairs today!"

With many backward looks, and injunctions to Helen to wait for her, Victoria allowed herself to be led away through the farther room to wash. Noting idly that the nursery had no door of its own to the corridor, but must be approached either through her own room or the night nursery, Helen went back to her bedroom and washed her hands in a brown marble basin whose hot water—a steaming trickle—came out of a shell-shaped spout over the legend "Hofheimer, Wien."

"Just at present our movements are a bit restricted. We're in slight disgrace, you see. Not that we've *done* anything! It's just that old Whiskers is on again about the Wicked West. So there's a chilly breeze from the East, politically, and we're being made to shiver. As if this snow weren't enough! It's really settled in, I'm afraid. We're going to have a long, white winter!"

Charles Sweet had pushed his chair back and was half-reclining now, his head on one side, legs crossed, one foot jerking rhythmically. His brown face, yellow-brown from years of strong sunlight, was benign. He looked kindly at Helen from pale blue eyes, much creased and puckered at their corners. His worn brown tweeds, bow tie and heavy shoes made him look not much like Helen's idea of a diplomatist; more like a country doctor or auctioneer.

Cigarette smoke tapered upwards, scurried thinly and melted in white light. Tall windows, netted with snow, lit a small white-and-gold dining-room, hung with official pictures, full of reproduction Chippendale, close-carpeted, warm.

"I don't think I mind," Helen said. "We seem pretty cozy here. And if the food's always like that—!"

Martin Wright laughed. "I think Madame Elvire's pulled out all the stops for your first day. But I must say she's a genius—she almost never fails."

"She makes everything bearable," Charles said. "Although how she does it on NAAFI groceries and what little she can wring from the Glumbas, none of us will ever know!"

They were sitting over coffee, after a luncheon as surprising as anything else on this surprising day. The two clerks, Mrs. Clothier and Miss Hubbard, had left them to go back to the Chancery. Victoria had consented to rest upstairs only on condition that she might, later, help Helen unpack. Now Martin Wright was excusing himself.

"Got to do my stint on that something wireless," he said in explanation. "How I hate Marconi. How I should prefer mud-spattered horses for my messages. Or even cleft sticks!"

Helen, seeing that Charles Sweet made no move, realized with pleasure and a touch of apprehension that she was to be left alone with him. She suddenly felt tired, remembering her early start, the uncomfortable flight, the haunting oddity of Senj. To postpone what might be momentous she said:

"Do you always eat all together, like this?"

"Well, as I expect Martin's told you, we're rather an unorthodox Legation at the moment. We all have to do about nine different jobs, and we're pretty cut off most of the time. So, yes, this is a sort of common room. The Minister joins us sometimes, when he hasn't got a guest. Sometimes he and I lunch or dine alone together. We're far too thin on the ground for much protocol. And we're all, in a sense, bachelors. Personally, I greatly prefer it."

"It's . . . extraordinary," Helen said, "after those empty streets, and the shabbiness, the shut-upness of everything . . . and the snow . . . to come into this. It's not 'homelike'—but it's like home!"

"Corner of a foreign field," Charles Sweet smiled at her. "It's the same in most places. British embassies and legations are all much the same inside. Seldom beautiful, you understand, frequently most uncomfortable—but dependable, reassuring. . . . I suppose they might be worse."

"It's amazingly comfortable. And warm! I did worry rather, at the airport, whether it would be warm!"

Charles laughed. "And well you might! But, you see, we have Sergeant Tubb." He said this as though no further explanation were necessary, but went on: "Tubb and I arrived together, two years ago: that was before Mark was appointed." Charles frowned slightly, looking at his cigarette. "Tubb's first battle was with the central heating. We got fuel, somehow, but more than fuel was needed. The radiators were really alarming. They used to honk and whistle and make pools like large dogs." He smiled at Helen, she thought a little pleadingly. She had a feeling that here was someone badly in need of light relief, of another person to joke with about small, farcical, everyday things. The tired lines about the eyes, the deep, vertical furrows in Charles's face, indicated present strain as well as the effect of past years and climates.

"What did Sergeant Tubb do, in the end?" she asked, to keep him going.

"Oh, one of his usual miracles. I'm used to them now. But, then, I was astounded—simply held my breath! Don't ask me how, but he actually got hold of a team from the Ministry of Reconstruction, about six absolutely silent men with monkey-wrenches. There was a lot of hammering, pretty well day and night, for a long time, and then, one day, the place was warm as toast— and we haven't had a peep out of the hot-water system since. It simply purrs. And so do we. Or would, if we were let. . . ." Charles Sweet looked suddenly much older, almost cast down. He leaned rather abruptly forward and stubbed out his cigarette with a decided motion, as though he were affixing a seal. Without looking at Helen he said, in a lower voice, slowly:

"I am sorry, truly sorry, that you had that beastly experience on the train. Thank God that H.T.S. never *does* miss a trick, that he had somebody there—"

Relief and curiosity struggled in Helen with an odd feeling of anger. The fear, the mystification, the anxiety of the past weeks were suddenly a sour discord, struck anyhow across her nerves.

"So you're another of them!" she said, with what sounded in her own ears like sharp resentfulness.

Charles Sweet's tired blue eyes met hers, puzzled, solicitous. He went on rather quickly:

"Yes, I'm another! Please believe we'd all have given anything to . . . H.T.S. has a very high regard for you, and I think I begin to see why."

Helen said furiously, "What happened on the train was only part of the game. *I* know that. Irrelevant, perhaps, but something that always can happen. Why should you all *mind* so about it? You . . . Mrs. Sidney . . . H.T.S. himself, it seems. And why do you all say you can see what he sees in me? When I can't in the least? It's perfectly maddening! How can I do any sort of a job—how can I even make a shot at this . . . this impossible thing, if I'm treated like a sacrificial lamb and told every other minute what a good girl I'm being? Oh," she looked at Charles Sweet, appalled. "I'm sorry! I must be tired. But it's all so . . . nothing's been like anything I've ever seen or dreamed of, for weeks!"

Charles Sweet had opened his eyes, wrinkled his forehead in mock-comic surprise.

"Well, bless you, Helen," he said in a tone warm with amusement. "I don't think I could answer all those questions. And," he added slowly, while he fished for a cigarette case, "if I *could*, I don't believe I *would!* I'm just very glad you're here, safe and sound, that's all. And that is something you can't stop me being. As to your seeing what H.T.S.—or anybody—sees in you, why, the fact that you don't may easily be about sixty per cent of the whole point! Tell me, did you read fairy stories, when you were younger?"

"Of course!" Helen was impatient.

"Well, there is one—or rather, there are several—about a beautiful princess who was never allowed to look in the glass, never let near a mirror, all her young life. She was never to know how beautiful she was, never to know her power, until, one day, that knowledge became crucial for her."

Helen gave a cry of exasperation.

"But my looks! What in the world can they really mean in a situation like this? If some girl's looks could do the trick, surely, *surely* everything would have been simple? Idiotically simple?"

Charles Sweet put his head a little on one side and considered Helen gravely.

"My dear," he said, and his tone was ironical, "I think you really must be tired. Since no one led me to suppose that you were obtuse. . . . Your physical appearance is not in question—although," and here he blinked shyly, in what seemed to Helen an old-fashioned bachelor's way, "I should award it pretty high marks, myself. No, there are other aspects of a personality which may be the better, may indeed be really priceless, just because of their owner's ignorance of their value in the eyes of others. . . . No, that's enough!" Charles spoke with authority, was suddenly brisk. "Mark Ogilvy returns on Sunday afternoon. Between now and then we must talk —circumspectly. Meanwhile, you are to rest—as well as Victoria will allow you to. You'd better let her do your unpacking for you, and put your feet up yourself!"

He got up from the table and Helen, feeling weary, extended, rose as well.

"I'd just like to know," she said tiredly, with a little outward gesture of both hands in bewilderment, "I'd just like to know what earthly good I'm supposed to be good *for!*"

Charles, looking very tall and thin now he was standing, patted her shoulder with an unpracticed hand.

"Look," he said, "we both trust H.T.S. You certainly, and I probably, wouldn't be here if that were not the case. You know he doesn't believe in fighting this kind of thing by direct action. He despises blood-and-thunder, any drastic effort to attack a symptom rather than a cause. I know that he believes that certain people have power, consciously or otherwise, to alter the situations which confront them by being rather than doing—that certain sets of circumstances will make them behave in such a way as to change radically the nature of those circumstances. And that if they're the right people, it will

95

be a right change. Oh Lord, I'm being obscure. . . ."

"I can see what you mean," Helen said, "and I've no doubt that H.T.S. knows what he's talking about, too. What I cannot believe is that it could be me!"

"I don't think it's going to matter whether you believe it or not. Anyway, for heaven's sake don't worry about it now. We have time. Not a tremendous lot—but, I hope and think, enough. And you're not alone in all this, not all the time anyway. Forget it for the moment, if you can. Go and see Victoria! She's certainly a clue. . . ."

It was Martin Wright's idea that Helen and Victoria should go with Sergeant Tubb to meet the Minister that Sunday afternoon.

"For all the diplomatic business he could transact with you or me, Carlo, between the airport and here, he'd be much better off seeing Victoria's face since Helen took over!"

Certainly, Helen reflected, after only two days at least that part of her assignment seemed to be going well. She and Victoria had taken to each other at once and, if looks were anything to go by, the child was benefiting. Of this Helen was glad, not merely for comfort's sake, but because a strong feeling for Victoria would help keep in focus her resolution where Victoria's father was concerned.

Now she was driving back towards the airport, seeing once more the river, the sad suburbs, the beginning of the plain of Senj, already looking for remembered landmarks, already part of a world which could never be quite foreign again. Below her heart lay apprehension; she was in no hurry to reach the airport, to have to compose her manner and her mind for this encounter with her employer.

Victoria bounced and scrambled over the broad seat beside her. From time to time Tubb spoke to them over the lowered interior window. Small jokes, comfortable questions and answers made a safe, miniature world inside the car. Victoria's vivid restlessness, Tubb's solidity,

96

the unity of all three as strangers in a strange land, were qualities known before, loved, appreciated, part of Helen's stock of securities in life. Mark Ogilvy, when he joined them, would bring with him something problematical, dangerous, a calculated threat to all such securities. She was going to the airport to meet a man whom—if all that she loved in life were not to be proved worthless—she must think of as mortally sick. Yet she knew that, to him, her own health must be a sickness, his sickness the only possible health.

Helen shivered. Victoria who, she had already discovered, was uncomfortably sensitive to moods, flung herself across the seat to snuggle at her side.

"Cold Helen! I'll warm you."

Two small hands in woollen gloves clasped one of hers. The child crouched against her, laughing, vibrating like a small dynamo. Helen stared over her head at the immensity of the plain, sepia and white under its first snow covering. She was trying with all her might not to prejudge this issue, not to meet Mark Ogilvy with her mind in a crippling condition of dislike.

Yet, when Mark was suddenly there, before her eyes, striding easily from the airport building in brisk talk with Tubb; when he had jumped lightly into the car, hugged Victoria, taken her hand in the positive warmth of his own—then Helen found that she could look directly at him, talk to him, answer questions without constraint. Here was the face she had seen on Mr. Sanders' glass screen; she would, she felt, have recognized it under any disguise; but, in the reality of living movement, this face was less portentous, handsome undoubtedly, past question intelligent and marked by thought, but still no more than the face of a man.

Helen was struck by the fact that Victoria, who had been almost uncontainable with excitement on the drive out, had become, at sight of her father, tongue-tied and still. After a brief hug, she had settled herself quietly between the two of them and now sat, as they sped towards the city, looking straight in front of her, playing with her gloves. Is she afraid of him, Helen wondered. Or has she

97

some instinct of doubt about her father, some sense that all is not well?

"How was London, Sir?" Helen asked. It seemed so long since she had seen the place, she would really have liked a detailed description of it, gossip, some notes taken by another hand.

Mark Ogilvy smiled briefly, and gave a small shrug. "Very much as usual," was his only reply, before leaning sideways to look out at the factory-dotted white waste slipping by them to the left. His look was intent, eager, as though it were here, and not in London, that reality was to be found. He continued to talk easily, telling Helen details of the industrial establishments they passed, touching on collective farming, the development of production in various directions. Helen had nothing to do but make interested noises and watch, try to apprehend with all her senses this being who was to be so deeply her concern.

When Mark turned towards her again it was with a very shrewd and comprehensive look, a look which seemed to take in completely what Helen was; a look not without kindness, a hint of amusement, even a sort of remote admiration. Helen could see how these eyes, gazing now so directly at her, might in childhood have had the same black-blue glitter as Victoria's.

Whatever she might feel—or know—all that Helen could see at present in this man were fineness and strength. Fineness in the thin, long-fingered hands, the delicate mouth and chin, the broad care-marked forehead; strength in the slim body lounging at ease in its good clothes, the vigorous unruly hair, the live concentration of the eyes. Purely subjective, purely feminine, regret welled up in her, for here was a man that no woman could disregard, one who, unfathomably, had placed his allegiances beyond any woman's reach.

Mark Ogilvy—at thirty-seven the youngest head of mission of the service—must be extravagantly able in his chosen field. Helen remembered some words of H.T.S.: "His entry papers were, I believe, of a frightening brilliance. The F.O. was—and why not?—delighted

98

to have him. His service, no more than any other, has any really valid way of telling whether someone, at some date, will go round the bend . . ."

They were passing the South Gate of Senj. Helen said, "That's so lovely . . . and I hear it's going to be pulled down!"

Mark Ogilvy gave the great arch a quick, indifferent glance.

"A bit trumpery, don't you think?" was all he said.

Irritation flared in Helen. No, I don't think, she said to herself crossly. How dare he be so prodigal? And again, looking at her employer for a moment coldly, without sentiment: what a stupid waste!

With the coming of November, winter began in earnest. At first the snow, falling so straight and with such soft persistence, had seemed a blessing to Helen. She and Victoria had trudged happily through the deepening drifts, forging their way down the little-trodden pavement beside the tramlines to the park, where the bandstand now carried a conical cap of snow. They had played hide-and-seek round dark, snow-plastered shrubs, patterned small lawns with their footprints, smiled from glowing faces at the rare passer-by. They had ventured as far as the Old Bridge and the palace of the three ministries, and had watched the miniature icebergs spin slowly past in the malachite waters of the Tvar.

Then came the wind from the northeast. It began to blow in the night, driving the snow in horizontal streaks across windows, or against the glass with minute, irregular, moth-like thuds, urgent and menacing. The central heating in the Legation was stepped up but, even with this, and all windows doubled, the solid warmth of a room could be disconcertingly flawed sometimes with veins of cold. First one person, then another, would shiver; conversation would dry up, or change direction. Personal comfort became a preoccupation and a topic.

With the blizzards, walks with Victoria became impracticable, and Victoria herself lost zest for them. Helen now found herself glad that she could share a part of the

99

child's day with Mrs. Simpkin, so formidable was the job of entertaining a restless, intelligent child who was still too young to read, or even to play with much concentration.

Victoria had the run of the Legation. She was welcome everywhere, from the hot and stormy kitchen of Madame Elvire, to the calm office of Mrs. Clothier and Miss Hubbard in the Chancery. In theory she was not allowed to visit either her father, or Carlo, or the wireless room during working hours, without invitation. In practice, her father's was the only door she never seemed to want to try.

There were days when neither Helen nor Mrs. Simpkin could make anything go right for Victoria; and what was felt in the nursery was felt all over the house.

"I'll say this," Martin Wright said one day, when Victoria had upset an inkpot all over his desk, wept, run headlong from the room, tripped on the stairs and bruised herself and had to be comforted at length, with sweet biscuits, by the two lady clerks, to the detriment of much urgent work—"I'll say this: since *you* came, Victoria's been a different child. This sort of thing used to happen every day! There were times when we absolutely dreaded the sight of her, like a tiny Lady Macbeth, advancing with great hollow eyes, sucking her thumb, and pouting murderously. We all did, and do, adore her, but —it was heartbreaking—it didn't seem to be enough!"

"It never is," Helen answered gloomily. "Not if you can't bring yourself to believe it. It's her mother, I suppose. Running out on her—that's how Victoria must see it. It's—I imagine—an upset at any age. But only four!"

Martin gave her a curious look.

"Does Victoria ever speak of her, Helen?"

"Never. Not even obliquely. And I wouldn't dare—"

"Of course not." He looked thoughtful, absently mopping pools of ink from a ruined draft. "It's a hell of a life for her here, anyway. Or was, at all events. As I say, I think you've made things miles better, even in this short time."

"I'm not her mother, though."

Martin gave her a sharp glance. His expression was unusually cold, remote for a moment, and then changed to his normal look, which was warm, interested, even affectionate.

"A very fair exchange, in my view," he said shortly. "Go away, Helen. Leave me to what the Foreign Service calls drafting, and I call writing. You and Victoria! Women!"

As the days passed, Helen settled easily enough into the Legation's rather eccentric routine. Superficially she had, she realized, only exchanged one kind of limited existence for another. From the hurrying, hard-up, working girl's world in London to this beleaguered little community in Senj—the change was a change of annoyances; frustration wore a different face. The Legation staff were not, at present, allowed to travel more than six miles beyond the city limits without a pass from the Minister of the Interior. Official entertaining, such as it might be, no longer included them. Their telephones were tapped with insulting obviousness. The simplest facilities—such as getting the snow cleared from the drive—were only obtained laboriously, patiently, through a maze of official cross-references.

Supplies from Vienna were held up at the customs on various pretexts, and then arrived damaged or incomplete. Members of the Legation staff were liable to personal visits from the police, at which incomprehensible conversations were begun which had to be settled by appeal to the Minister or Carlo. "Uniformed police in really laughable hats," H.T.S. had said. But Victoria did not find them laughable. At sight of a pair of long-coated policemen in jackboots crunching up the drive, with belts and bandoliers and caps of a forgotten pattern, with square flat tops, she would run whimpering to hide her face against the nearest adult, preferably Helen or the always reassuring Tubb.

This kind of treatment had the effect of drawing the missions of countries friendly to one another into a kind

101

of mutual-aid society. There was a free exchange of supplies between the British, French and American legations, and as much coming and going as pressure of work and manifold anxieties would permit.

Once a week, on Thursdays, Helen and Victoria would set off with Sergeant Tubb for the American Legation, to attend a dancing class organized by Mrs. Preston Chalk, the Minister's vague and hospitable wife. The class was attended by five other children and was really the prelude to a tea party where the shortcomings of Senj as a post were discussed more amply, and in different accents, but fundamentally in the same sense as by Mrs. Clothier and Miss Hubbard at home.

Helen would have enjoyed these occasions more if her heart had not been wrung by Victoria's obvious misery. Whatever happens in the end, she said to herself on the third occasion, and whatever sort of a mess I make of this, one thing I will see to, if it kills me—and that's to get Victoria home to something more like real life; and then her breath had stopped for a moment as the thought came to her that Mark Ogilvy's supposed plans for the future almost certainly included Victoria as well.

She could hardly blame Victoria for acting at the dancing class in ways which made her another person from the bright and eager, or crotchety and demanding, but always positive child she was at home.

The other children were hardly attractive and, in addition, were all just sufficiently older than Victoria to be bored and callous with her, not old enough to be amused or kind. In particular, Wayne Landow, eight-year-old son of Morton Landow, Counsellor of the U.S. Legation, seemed to Helen a singularly disagreeable child. For Victoria he was almost worse than the civil police.

"Wait till you see his Pa!" had been Martin Wright's comment, when Helen first spoke of Wayne. "He's little Wayne to the life, only more so, naturally. I suspect that Mort Landow's great-grandparents, in whatever dank Central European marsh it was, ought never to have met, let alone married. *That* was no way to improve the human race."

Morton Landow was at Mrs. Chalk's tea party on the last Thurdsay in November. He had come in to collect Wayne but, without glancing at his child, and with scarcely a word to his hostess, had at once lurched across the room to where Helen was standing by a window, for the moment alone.

"Hi!" said Mort Landow, with the boyish grin he kept for pretty women.

Helen looked up with unfocussed eyes, momentarily unable to place this heavy-shouldered man with the spiky hair and curiously unreal air of joviality.

"Oh—hullo!" she said, without encouragement.

"What're you staring at?" She silently indicated the pavement opposite, the battened doorways crossed with wooden bars, the former shop-windows sealed with corrugated iron, the insistent posters, the cold, crawling, untalkative queue.

"Geez! The poor bastards!" said Mort. Something in his tone seemed to Helen excessively superior. Although she had been thinking much the same thing, she felt obliged to say:

"The trouble is—we don't know whether they are or not."

"Are or are not what?"

"As much to be pitied as we think they are. It's claimed that they *chose* their way of life. Perhaps they do find it preferable?" She did not believe this, but something overbearing in Mort Landow's manner seemed always to provoke argument.

"For God's sake!" he said contemptuously, his grin fading. "You Britishers are all alike! Always seeing shades of grey in black-and-white situations. These poor idiots backed the wrong horse, that's all. Now they're half-starved and run ragged by the people they trusted. You'll be telling me you believe in 'free elections' next."

"I really don't know what I believe in," replied Helen flatly, realizing with sorrow that this was true.

Morton Landow gave her a hostile look from small black eyes: "Then your security people ought to know about it!" he snapped. "Not that I'd give much for their

103

powers of observation," he added disagreeably. "How's that Minister of yours, by the way? Seems to me he sees a lot too many sides of a question, too."

"He's brains, that's all," Helen answered lightly. "A terrible affliction, of course—but *we* still believe in them."

Mort Landow's expression, which had again become wolfishly sociable, now underwent a slow change. He blinked, put up his chin as though at a challenge, sharply wriggled one shoulder inside his padded tweed jacket. Then he turned on his heel and called loudly: "Hey, Wayne! Get your coat on. We're going home."

Victoria came running from a corner where she had been playing with some chessmen, absorbed and happily unregarded. The small figure trotting so eagerly across the gleaming floor, although stout and unco-ordinated, was not without a kind of gracefulness. The round little face had, already, in the structure of the brow and the placing of the eyes, a gravity and meaning rare in so young a child. The wild blue glance, the perfect skin, the candid outwardness of Victoria's personality in this mood, drew from Helen a movement of love and concern.

"They've both got it," she thought, thinking too of Mark Ogilvy. "Inescapably distinguished—they'd stick out a mile anywhere. Whatever *his* fantasies may be. . . ."

She let Victoria jump into her arms and turned with her to look down again into the street, feeling the child's cheek against her own, supporting the confiding dead weight with joy.

Victoria gazed at the line of bowed, inward-looking people. They were mostly women—mostly elderly, Helen thought, although, muffled as they were against the cold, it was hard to tell. Their breath went up in a thin smoke against the scaling, iron-barred wall.

"Tubb says," said Victoria carefully, " 'Poor Glumbas! They're either not there at all or else they're in queue!' "

"Sergeant Tubb's about right, as usual, Victoria. Poor Glumbas!"

"Where are they when they're not there at all?"

"They work very hard. In factories, in the fields. You've seen them helping the trams."

"That's ladies! Where are the men?"

"In factories, mostly, I think. And being soldiers—and policemen."

Victoria clutched her.

" 'sgusting policemen!"

Helen gave her a small hug. "They're all right really, Victoria. They won't hurt *you*."

"Not horrible? Not 'sgusting?"

"Even if they were, we wouldn't let them hurt you."

"You, and Carlo, and Wright, and Tubb and Mrs. Simpkin?"

"And Daddy."

"And Daddy . . ." Victoria's tone was doubtful. She turned to look back into the room, stiffened suddenly and began to squirm out of Helen's arms. "There *is* Daddy!" she breathed.

Mark Ogilvy was bending over Mrs. Preston Chalk, who had risen in a pleased flurry to greet him and was holding his hand in both of her own. Victoria, slowly at first, and then at a quick trot, made for her father and clasped his knees. He disengaged his right hand to stroke her hair, looking down at her with the expression Helen had come to know, of a pleasure which seemed not far from anguish. Looking up, he smiled shyly at Helen. Helen moved slowly across the room to join him.

With the very slight stammer which sometimes came to him in public, Mark Ogilvy said: "It seems to be F-fathers Day at the dancing class! Sorry to appear unannounced, but I thought you and Victoria might come with me for a few minutes to the Ministry of Culture— they've got a dancing display there, too."

His glance was level, his forehead no more than usually troubled. It was perhaps the contrast between his smile, so curiously sweet and uncomplicated, and the near-torment above, which made the smile so attractive. Why then did Helen feel, as she so often felt, that his words were loaded, that there was a world of meaning concealed beneath the obvious one?

105

"Oh no!" Mrs. Preston Chalk was wailing. "You can't take them there! Poor Victoria! Poor Helen! Why, that Madame Kassin will just scare them silly!"

"I don't think they're as easily scared as that!"

"Easily! Well! of all the . . . Still, I mustn't say it, or Preston will be mad at me. It's hard, though, to be diplomatic *all* the time! This means there's a Thaw, I suppose? We're being asked out again?"

"Yes." Mark Ogilvy's tone was remote. "I think some misunderstandings have been cleared up."

"Well, for Heaven's sake, Mr. Ogilvy! You're the most diplomatic diplomat I've ever met in twenty years. Misunderstandings!" She put a small hand on Helen's arm. "You look after him, my dear. Watch so's that Madame Minister doesn't gobble him up!"

Helen looked down at a pair of round eyes gazing fearfully up at Mrs. Chalk.

"Who's going to gobble Daddy up?"

"Nobody, Victoria," Mark said, "nobody at all. We're going to see some little girls dancing. You'll like that."

"Mmm . . ." said Victoria.

The Landows, father and son, tramped past them on their way out. Mort raised a hand and dropped it in a lateral arc. His face was split by a wide, politician's grin. His little eyes were cold and jeering.

" 'Bye, Clara," he said to his hostess. " 'Bye, Ogilvy. 'Bye Miss Clark!"

"Dear Mort," said Mrs. Chalk vaguely and without conviction.

Mark Ogilvy had a formal word with Monsieur Hunziger, of the French Legation, was caught in conversation for a moment by the Military Attaché's wife, said goodbye in a general sense with nervous cordiality. Then Helen was following Victoria, who followed her father, down the long stairs to the car.

Sergeant Tubb was standing beside the car gazing, as Helen had done, at the slowly shuffling line of people at the other side of the street. His face expressed a kind of irritated sympathy. As they approached, he stepped smartly to open the door for the Minister and Helen.

Then he bent and made an arm for Victoria to climb on.

"May she come in front with me, Sir?"

He settled Victoria beside him on cushions evidently brought for the purpose, and the car slid cautiously away, its motion gravelly from the chains on the wheels. Three or four heads turned in the patient queue, three or four pairs of eyes looked dully at the car, without interest, perhaps without belief.

An extreme of nervous embarrassment possessed Helen for a moment. She rearranged her gloves, her bag, leaned forward and pretended to look for something on the floor, settled the rug about her knees, all without turning her eyes to the haunting question-mark of a face on her right. This is Carlo's doing, she thought, and about high time, too. I suppose. They turned into the great Square of the 15th of October, where military parades were held. The car slipped and swerved on tram-tracks. She thought: the first time I've been alone with him. Only the twelfth time that I've even see him. And: he knew there was a thaw on, when the American Minister's wife didn't. . . .

"Well, Helen." Mark Ogilvy's voice was friendly, the stammer had gone. "How do you find life in Senj? I've meant to say, before this, that I think you have made it quite a different thing for Victoria. I'm really grateful to you."

He sounds grateful, too. Helen forced herself to look round at her employer. She smiled at Mark.

"It's . . . very much more another world, even, than I thought it would be," she said slowly. No word must go unweighed, she thought desperately, yet which word will weigh the most?

"Oh?" Mark Ogilvy's tone was neutral, polite, his delivery careful. "Are the differences so very great?"

"So great that they're—well, hardly even relevant. I don't mean life in the Legation: that's got a tie, a pipe-line to things I know. It's what one sees in the streets, the look of the town itself. For instance—no shops."

"Co-operatives, surely?"

"Oh yes, *those*. But no little, individual shops all sell-ing, *saying* something different. No big shops like circuses tempting people in. No meeting-places—cafés or pubs. No idlers. No loitering."

"Perhaps these people feel they have no room for idlers. That, in our time, it is not safe to loiter."

He makes every statement sound like a question. He would never be easily caught. A little spurt of excitement went through Helen. At least, we're in some kind of communication—at last! Then, unregenerately: I wonder if he's any idea how attractive he is? There was no mistaking the warmth, the physical kindliness coming from the man at her side. Glancing at the controlled, overwrought face again, Helen saw it suddenly as cut-off, out of communication with the rest. She guessed that whatever Mark Ogilvy's heart—his body—might have to say, his head would have none of it.

Helen said slowly: "Six weeks ago I was in London. There, everybody's flying in all directions—building up, combining, setting to partners. Complaining like mad, too, about restrictions of one kind and another. The Government says one thing, and nearly everyone thinks something else." She laughed a little sharply.

"Why do you laugh?" Mark Ogilvy's tone was curious. He looked at her, seeing her all right, Helen thought, but as if from the other side of some barrier—a fence, a river, a world?

"I was just thinking that, six weeks ago, I thought people in London the drabbest things on earth. I thought I couldn't bear any longer the dull colors, the shabbiness, the look of worry and grievance. I was enchanted to get away. And now—well, since I've seen something of Tubb's Glumbas, and this town, London and the people in it seem positively glittering."

There was a short silence. Then Mark said, more deliberately than ever:

"You haven't had much chance to get about yet, have you? We must see if we can't rectify that. You say the people in London are building things up. Perhaps the same old things, with the same inherent disadvantages? Here, they are building something quite—quite—new." The finality of his tone carried, to Helen's sharpened hearing, a note of menace.

"Whatever people are doing at home," Helen said—and tried to sound dispassionate, not disputatious, "they mostly had a long war to think about it in. They must have wanted whatever they want really badly. And things aren't entirely the same, anyway. There've been huge changes. We've had a revolution, all right, in our own way."

Mark Ogilvy laughed softly. "I suppose you could call it that. . . ." The disbelief in his voice was not stressed enough to be discourteous, but it was plain to hear.

Dusk was falling, and street lamps were coming on, yellow-white in the bitter blue haze. Beyond Tubb's straight back and Victoria's round, smooth head tilted confidentially up to her companion, beyond the Union Jack fluttering rhythmically on the hood, Helen could see the clusters of lights on the Alexander Bridge.

"We're going to the Sideini Palace, aren't we?" she asked, thinking her voice sounded falsely bright.

"To the Ministry of Culture, yes."

"I'm glad. Martin says it's the finest thing in Senj."

"It is—very interesting, of its kind and of its period. They have adapted it very well, I think."

How noncommittal can you be? Helen felt a kind of admiration.

"What happened to the Sideini family?" she asked, with an odd sense that she was probing, being inquisitive instead of simply inquiring; but this might have been guilt, since she knew the answer already.

Mark Ogilvy's hands moved for the first time. He reached for his cigarette case from an inner pocket.

"The last male Sideini died before the war," he said, and boredom yawned from his voice. "There is, I believe, a widow—she was also his cousin. The Government allows her to live in the country—somewhere, I've no idea where." His voice was now vaguely indulgent.

And is that little rabbit coming out of the hat as a proof of the Government's enormous benevolence,

Helen wondered; and I wonder, does he know a great deal more than he lets on?

A hollow rumble mixed with the click of the chains and the dry whisper of snow, as they took the Alexander Bridge. Clusters of lanterns made yellow pools of light, picking out ironwork, dolphins, the elaborations of a forgotten idea of elegance. The Alexander Bridge had never been good, æsthetically, but it had been, perhaps, a happy expression of pride and prosperity, a florid phase of confidence at a time when life had, for some reason, seemed less dangerous than usual. In an obsure way it still gave Helen comfort. She risked saying something of this.

"It's like an impossible old aunt, incurably gay, always humming Strauss waltzes and talking about love to a lot of serious nephews and nieces who only care for biochemistry and social reform!"

Mark Ogilvy gave a snort of laughter which sounded quite genuine.

"Helen," he said, shaking his head, but looking at her with interest and amusement, "I'm afraid you may be incurably subjective! I don't suppose anybody in Senj notices that bridge except as a means of getting from one side of the river to the other. Still, I can see why Victoria likes your company."

"Do you mean that we are the same mental age, Sir?" (I'll be challenging, flirtatious, anything idiotic at all, to keep his attention. . . .)

Mark snorted again. His face was youthful, suddenly, smoothed-out, his look almost teasing.

"No, I do not. And you needn't call me Sir. There's everything in the situation to excuse formality."

Sergeant Tubb did not appear to think so. As they slid under one of the plain Roman arches at a corner of Karl Marx Square, he sat up very straight, grasping the wheel firmly, and looking severely to the front. Victoria, taking her cue, also sat straight on her cushions and stopped talking. The car slowed to a stately glide as Tubb brought it round the square, half-lit, half-shadowy and full of snow, in an even curve.

110

The Sideini Palace was alight at all its windows which, uncurtained, gave glimpses of blazing chandeliers, painted ceilings, a shifting crush of people on every floor. Flag fluttering stiffly, speed smoothly decreasing, the big car in Tubb's hands came to berth beside the delicate perron like a ship. He was out and standing rigid, cap in hand, beside the open door before the two sentries at the perron's foot were halfway through presenting arms.

Looking up at the authoritative curve of the steps to the towering doorway, to the slim, long windows, their pediments mantled in snow, to the lavish light and the darkly seething throng, Helen felt a twinge of nervousness, an excited sense that now, at last, she was coming nearer the reality she sought. Victoria put a hand in hers and pressed it quickly three or four times, a sign that she too was nervous.

Mark was being greeted by two dark, eager young men who had run down the steps the moment the car appeared. They turned, talking excitedly, and went up with him, one on either side. Mark glanced back to smile encouragement at Helen and Victoria who followed up the shallow steps at Victoria's pace, one step at a time.

Light and sound broke over Helen and Victoria like a wave, as soon as they entered the Ministry of Culture. The great hall seemed packed with people, mostly men, all square-built, alert-looking, serious, all clothed in black or grey. Waves of sound, chatter, a burst of clapping rolled down the splendid staircase. Music was resumed, a steady thud and tinkle; the chandeliers blinked, and leaves shook on the many palms in hammered brass pots which were stuck at random about the floor.

Heads turned to follow Mark Ogilvy and his party as they started up the broad stone staircase below grisaille panels of trophied musical instruments, and gilded wall lights shaped as hunting horns. Looks of amusement and pleasure were cast at Victoria, trudging upwards with an intent, pink face, holding tightly to Helen's hand. Looks more searching, ambiguous, followed Helen: people stood aside on the staircase, breaking earnest conversa-

111

tions, to let her pass, gazing at girl and child with passionate curiosity, but without hostility. At the head of the staircase, squat, confident, hideous, but with a large air of triumphant hospitality, and looking, Helen thought, every inch a usurper, stood Madame Luba Kassin herself.

She welcomed Mark with empressement, clasping his hand, turning with him to present one or two sallow women in black, some stiff-backed, broad-shouldered men—members, no doubt, of her staff. Then she turned and stood looking at Helen and Victoria with a kind of ogreish geniality.

"Aha! So here is the little one!" exclaimed Madame Kassin harshly, showing her gold teeth in a wide smile. Victoria's clasp on Helen's hand tightened. Looking down at the curve of a very pink cheek, Helen knew that her charge wasn't going to be able to stand much of this. Helen said quickly, in French:

"Victoria is so looking forward to seeing the dancing. She has just come from her own dancing class."

Madame Kassin's French was accurate, but strained, thick-sounding as her English. At Helen's words the smile went abruptly and the wrinkled top lip, lightly mustached, came down over the lower one like a hand. When she spoke, her voice was high, cracked, carrying:

"Bourgeois ideas of dancing have no place in the curriculum of our children," she announced. "What you will see here is not foolishness, narcissism, pleasure-seeking, but part of a training for life!"

I should like to tell her that I am not a public meeting, thought Helen rebelliously, but contented herself with saying: "Then it will be most interesting."

Madame Kassin shot a look of scorn and suspicion at Helen from light-colored irises set in yellow whites.

" 'Interesting,' she says! Yes, it will be *interesting*, my young friend. Many things in Senj will be *interesting*, you will find. Perhaps you may wish you had never set off from your backward, bourgeois England in your little fur hat!"

112

Victoria tugged at Helen's hand and whispered: "What is the lady saying?"

Helen had bent her head to give the child a reassuring smile. Before she could answer, a man's voice, strong and speaking French with a precise elegance, said:

"What are you saying to Miss Clark, Luba? She looks quite bewildered."

Helen looked up into the formidable eyes of Stoyan Anzip.

At this moment someone claimed Madame Kassin's attention, and Helen was left with Victoria to make the best she could of this new development. She hoped that none of her feelings showed in her face. Victoria said indignantly: "Ow! Helen, you're hurting my hand!"

Stoyan Anzip laughed, not unpleasantly, and said in English: "You are two babes in the wood! No one is going to eat you. We are pleased that you have come. Now, we will go into the salon and I will find you seats so that you can watch the dancing in comfort. Follow me, please."

Victoria hung back. "I want to go home," she said. "I want Tubb."

"Oh, hush darling. We're going to see the dancing. That's what we came for. I'm sure we'll love it!" Helen had never felt so false. They followed the tall figure of Stoyan Anzip, whose clothes were so different from the normal in this place as to seem an unwisdom, a rash expression of confidence. He bowed to right and left, answering other bows, which were solemnly respectful. He certainly counts for something, Helen thought. She had lost sight of Mark and realized, with resignation, that there was nothing she could do about the situation, for the time being, but accept it.

As they entered a long drawing-room whose curtainless windows were pillars of blue night, Helen saw an expanse of polished floor shining like water under the light of five towering rock-crystal chandeliers. A piano plucked and grumbled Chopin and a young girl in tutu and satin bodice, a chaplet of flowers on her smooth, dark head, was completing a ballet figure in the center of the floor. The audience, ranged on benches and bentwood chairs round all four sides of the room, were still as stones. This child (she was perhaps thirteen years old) was more than good, Helen could see. She watched, captivated, while they waited for the figure to end, with Victoria quiet and breathless in her arms. *This may not be bourgeois, but it's certainly traditional. Can this be what we came to see?*

On an almost inaudible dying chord the girl sank to the floor, head bowed, her tutu frothing round her. Applause came with a concerted crash, like a firing squad. Stoyan Anzip moved forward again and, with a little more than a glance, dispossessed four obsequious young men of chairs in the front row. Helen sat down demurely, looking straight ahead of her. Someone brought a cushion for Victoria.

Anzip's hot eyes followed the dancer as, after curtseying shyly to the company, she ran out of the room, her tutu rocking above delicate long legs.

"She is our star," he said simply. "The country is proud of her. Tomorrow she is to go to Moscow to complete her training!" His voice dropped a little, piously, on the word Moscow. Victoria wriggled and plucked at Helen's sleeve, her eyes jewel-bright.

"I want to be a ballet dancer," she whispered.

Helen looked down at her fondly, then turned to look squarely at the man on her left.

Often, in thinking about the brief incident in Vienna, Helen had called herself all kinds of a fool for being, even momentarily, upset. No man, she had later told herself, could possibly be as effective as all that: unless, of course—and here she had had to laugh ironically—one were in love with him. At first sight. The idea was ridiculous; but what about hate at first sight? Might that not be equally powerful, equally shattering? And was it not taught, nowadays, that the two came to the same thing? She had known, at any rate, that she was nervous of another meeting with Anzip, and had not been able to jeer herself out of this.

114

Now she forced herself to examine her companion coolly, and found, to her relief, that this seemed to humanize him. Even on a hard chair which reminded Helen of parish halls at home, Anzip somehow mananged to sprawl. He had that kind of positive elegance of proportion and movement which tells best in relaxation. Now he was leaning back, with one leg crossed over the other, one hand in a waistcoat pocket, the other dangling a cigarette. His shepherd's plaid suit, which would have been dull enough in London, looked here, among so much subfusc, almost startling. Helen noted the shining black waves of hair, worn rather long, the wide, low forehead, the pale skin, the long, pointed nose and narrow cleft chin. It was perhaps the deep, bony hollows of the eyes which gave them part of their effect—these and the high cheekbones beneath. The whole face was unquestionably arrogant, instinct with self-regard, but not—she had to admit—without a certain Pied Piperish charm. Only the mouth was unsympathetic; not ugly, but too wide, too mobile, the lower lip inclined to pout, and never quite closed over large, square, brilliantly white teeth. He needs a shave, Helen thought, but then he's the type that would, and thought, five-o'clock shadow, wondering if the phrase might not also be a description of the man.

Stoyan Anzip leaned towards Helen with a smile that was playful, amost arch.

"Do you know," he said, "I saw your picture before I ever saw you? I must say it did you less than justice!"

Helen raised her eyebrows politely. "It was only a snapshot, wasn't it?" she said calmly. "Taken on spec, I suppose—and under a misapprehension. A persistent misapprehension," she added meaningly.

"Ah, *that,*" Anzip's face became solemn, ". . . *That* I very much regret. What happened afterwards, I mean. Some people exceeded their instructions."

"You might call it that," said Helen drily. "Tell me—do you often make mistakes on that scale?"

Anzip's smile went out. His brows came together in a frown which was nearly a scowl.

"We do not often make mistakes at all," he said.

115

In some way goaded by his complacency, Helen said: "Tell me, then, what would you have done if I'd kicked up a fuss, complained—about the train thing?" As she spoke, she realized with a jolt at the heart the size of the error she had made.

Anzip turned towards her and his eyes were now less hot for her as a woman than coldly glittering for an enemy.

"Nothing whatever! There were no other witnesses. But how is it that you did *not* complain, Miss Clark? It would have been more normal, surely? How was it that there was someone so close at hand to help you? No, no, Miss Clark. I suggest that we regard that incident as closed. There is, in any case, no possible way in which you could cause us worry—now."

The word "now" fell coldly between them. It raised a dozen questions in Helen's mind, none of which was comforting. Victoria made a welcome diversion by wanting to go to the lavatory. This was not found without difficulty and several false starts—"I'm bursting, Helen," Victoria wailed as they tried the third wrong door—but, eventually, all was well. As they made their way back into the salon, Helen saw that Stoyan Anzip had been joined by Mark Ogilvy, and that they were sitting together like old friends, deep in confidential talk.

The dance floor shook to the tread of twenty-four adolescent girls in black pants and white singlets who were performing some kind of gymnastic excersise. Martial thumping came from the piano, the crystal plaques on the chandeliers spun and spat fire, the audience shifted, grinned, looked uplifted, talked and hummed. This was familiar stuff in their lives: they were pleased, or reassured, or dutiful, but no longer rapt.

Mark turned as Helen settled Victoria beside him.

"Sorry to lose you," he said. "I didn't want you to miss this."

Miss *this*, thought Helen with amusement. I wouldn't have missed the other for worlds, but . . . She tried to give serious attention to the marching and counter-marching, the wheeling, semaphoring and toe-touching

116

of the healthy young creatures before her. She could only
think that the gym mistress at her own beloved school
would have awarded few marks to such a performance.
Thump went the piano, whack-whack went the plim-
solled feet on the golden floor. Mottled thighs shook,
plump breasts bounced under singlets, sweat streaked the
round, red, devoted faces under spiked fringes of black
hair. Someone produced a banner, the girls began to sing.
Round and round they went, wheeling and interlacing,
until at last they were all in line, with the banner in the
middle, and the thudding feet were still. Helen felt embarrassed for them, she knew quite unnecessarily. They
were touching young things, standing there grinning and
heaving while the audience applauded lengthily. Helen
wondered sadly what intricate ribboned riot of a country
dance they had been weaned from, to perform this instead.

Mark looked down at Victoria, who seemed more than
a little alarmed.

"There!" he said. "Did you like that? Wasn't it exciting?"

"No," said Victoria.

"Why ever not?" Mark's voice had an edge of irritation.
(He doesn't know his child—doesn't even know how to
speak to her, Helen thought.)

"Too loud. Too big," said Victoria with finality.
"I want to be a ballet dancer!" she added.

Glancing at Mark's face Helen was struck by his look
of disappointment—serious, surely quite out of proportion to any possible reaction of Victoria's? Quite suddenly the truth came to Helen with the sense of a light
going on behind her eyes. Mark was not merely wrong-
headed, he was mad—or, at least, mentally disordered in
a particular and exclusive way. Helen knew, positively
knew, now, the reason for that look of disappointment.
He must be cherishing a dream, not only for himself, but
for Victoria too. This pathetic charade of young females,
with all its stale political and social overtones, meant
something precious to Mark. He sees her growing up à la
Soviet, like a girl in a poster, playing netball, short-haired,

117

shiny—as he must see it, *free!* she thought. Helen nursed her discovery for a momen.., her eyes vague. If she was right, then she might yet save the day on the plane of emotion alone. This was more, and less, than an intellectual matter. This came from a deep, perhaps an old and deep-buried pain.

Some words of Mark's mother came back to her, from the interview she had had on her last day in London.

"Mark's . . . danger has called everything in my life in question. You see, what I feel I did to his father, both of us did to Mark. It seems to me now that we drove him and neglected him by turns. He responded by doing very well—in the way we wanted; and if he had difficulties, well, we were not always there to see. And, I think, never there to help. . . ."

Shortly afterwards, they left the Ministry of Culture. Madame Kassin, to Helen's relief, was not in evidence; it was Anzip who accompanied them to their car. After he had pressed his lips to her hand with an odd little rocking motion of his head, Anzip said to her:

"We shall meet again shortly. I shall so much look forward to that." He let go her hand with reluctance, stabbing at her with his extraordinary eyes.

As they drove away Helen said lightly, to cover a certain disquiet, "I'm glad to get my hand back. I thought he was going to eat it! I thought hand-kissing was *out* nowadays—bourgeois, reactionary, an insult to socialist realism?"

She had hoped to make him laugh, but Mark Ogilvy did not even smile. He simply said, in his most controlled, least inflected tone:

"Stoyan Anzip is very much a law unto himself. His standing here is high. I think that, perhaps, his cosmopolitanism is thought valuable—as a corrective to . . . a certain quite natural provincialism."

"Well, I hope it lasts, for his sake! Being *allowed* to be a law unto himself."

"Allowed?" Mark's voice was chilly, far from encouraging.

"Well, I suppose even he can put a foot wrong. Others

118

have, who were just as well-entrenched as he seems to be. He gets bowed to, now. . . . He can chew up people's hands, and it's just cosmopolitanism. But one day, surely, he might fall? Why should he be immune? From prison, and the last walk from the cell, and a bullet in the back of his head?"

She had a vivid inner view of the straight, elegant back, of clumping, grey-coated guards, of a steel tube jabbed into shining black hair.

"My *dear* Helen!" (Bored and reasonable: he's not liking this.) "You really mustn't believe all you hear."

She had heard enough—from Carlo, with weary distaste; from Martin, with more youthful, angrier compassion; in oblique, contemptuous references by Tubb.

Something in Mark Ogilvy's manner stung Helen. She hesitated a moment, remembering wisdom, prudence, the delicate balance of the situation. Then with a small shrug which meant "to Hell with prudence," she answered warmly: "If even one tenth of one per cent of what I've heard is true, then I wouldn't give a penny for Mr. Anzip's future. Nor for any of their futures. Not even Madame Kassin's! I don't know much about this dreadful world. They may be, as you say, building something quite new. . . . They may be doing it well. . . . They may make sense some day. But I've been here long enough to know that they're enormously incompetent about a lot of things. I'd say that the one thing they *do* do well—the one objective they pursue with insane logic and faultless efficiency is—death."

I've done it this time, she thought. He can't not react to that. She waited, her nerves burning, looking straight in front of her at the child's head, the proud flag, the dark and looming town.

"So what *did* he say?"

Carlo was mixing one of his powerful drinks. He turned, with a bottle of gin in one hand, to look at Helen searchingly.

"Absolutely not what I was expecting. He gave a little sigh and half turned towards me. For a moment I

119

thought he was going to take my hand. Then he said, quite gently: 'It may be that we mind too much about death. It may be that there are worse things.' "

"Lord!" Carlo said. He had spilt some vermouth and was mopping the foot of a glass with his handkerchief. He gave Helen her drink.

"*How* did he say it?"

"Gently, as I said. He sounded faraway, and awfully tired, like someone who suddenly sees there's any amount more work to do, when he'd thought he'd finished working. He wasn't cross and he wasn't anything like as frosty and definite as when we started. . . ."

Helen, after putting Victoria to bed, had come to Charles Sweet's rooms for a drink. Martin was expected later, when he had finished dealing with some urgent telegrams.

Charles Sweet sat down, crossed his legs, and sipped his drink, twitching his free foot rhythmically from side to side. He thought for a while, staring into the fire which played brightly under a low marble chimney piece.

Presently he said: "Helen, are you discouraged?"

Helen considered this for a moment. "No," she said. "I *was*. Or rather, not so much discouraged as completely at sea. Life went on here, and I never seemed to come nearer the chance to—to take a grip, do anything—except what I'm paid to do. Now, this evening, for the first time, I feel I've moved. I think, now, I could begin to know him. I believe, at last, he's noticed me."

"He's noticed you, all right, from the beginning, make no mistake. I've seen him look at you very oddly on one or two occasions."

"What sort of a look?"

"Well, as you know, he's got a way of shooting glances at one, suddenly—very shrewd glances, usually when one thinks he's not attending. He looks at *you*—sometimes—with something very like regret. Like someone who wished he had time for one more cast over the big pool before his train went!"

Helen laughed. Carlo made no secret of his preference for the world, the way of living, in which he had been

120

brought up; nor of his intention to return to it on retirement, if he could find a fragment still intact. His metaphors were colored by this.

"Elegantly put," she said, "but I suppose I see what you mean. I think I was more pleased than I've ever been about anything, with that touch of uncertainty he showed this evening. As though, just possibly, there might be another side to the story. . . . Carlo, have you ever tackled him directly?"

Carlo shook his head vigorously. "Impossible," he said. "I know him well. I've known him a long time. He simply wouldn't have admitted a thing; and we'd probably have had some stupid, pumped-up row, and any chance I might have had of being some use would have gone for good."

Silence fell between them. Helen, feeling bruised and still strung-up from the afternoon's events, made herself relax, slowly drinking and watching the dancing flames.

"*You* fixed it, this afternoon, I suppose?" she asked at length. "That we should be taken on to the Min. of Culture?"

Charles nodded. "Yes," he said, "I've had to bide my time, as I told you at the beginning I would have to, until the freeze-up wore off. Now we shall be able to do several things without being noticed. And I think, now, we must be prepared to move fast. The next thing I want you to do is have tea with me, tomorrow, at the Olimpia."

"The Olimpia!" Helen's tone was wondering. Six weeks of diplomatic life in Senji and the thought of an outing was already quite strange, exciting. She remembered the post-report: "The only hotel for foreigners is the Olimpia, now owned by the Government, and it cannot, in any particular, be recommended. . . . Officers will find that they will be obliged to make their own entertainment on the post." She had discovered the truth of the second sentence. Now, nothing would have kept her from finding out about the Olimpia Hotel.

"We are going to have tea—if that's the word for it," said Carlo, "and then we are going to visit an old friend of yours."

121

Helen looked up sharply. "Mrs. Sidney?" she asked.

"Mrs. Sidney. Or—as she is known in this town—Panja Sidnic. Or, as she properly is: Ilena Princess Sideini. We should have gone before this, but there was the freeze-up—and anyway, I wanted you to get the feel of things here, first."

Helen now recognized, with astonishment, that she had scarcely thought of Mrs. Sidney since the flight from Vienna—and yet the old woman had made a powerful impression. Simply, she supposed, life had been so full, for all its apparent emptiness; she had so thrown herself into learning her ostensible job, and trying to apprehend the situation of Mark Ogilvy; she had, with Victoria being so loving and demanding, and the other members of the staff so friendly and so hard-pressed, simply never got around to learning all she wanted to know of Mrs. Sidney and the family to which (Helen had correctly guessed) she belonged.

Carlo chuckled. "She is a fantastic character, and a magnificent one! It's so like her to insist on being called Sidnic which, in this country, is a joke name—insofar as anything is a joke any longer. It's one of the paradoxes of our time that she's allowed to go on living here, even under her present name. Her family virtually *were* this this country for centuries. They are infinitely ancient. They descend from Michael Sideini—Michael the Beautiful—through a line of chamberlains at the court of Byzantium. When they thought this country needed a king, they just made one—and not one of their own family either, or only indirectly. They made the king and they kept him there through the troubles of the ages, until 1940, when the last one was murdered by the Germans—as part of a deal with Kassin and her friends, who were biding their time to make the Revolution which has landed us where we are."

"Were they popular?"

Carlo frowned. "They were *there*," he answered, "like the mountains and the forests and the great, rich plain of Senj. I don't think popularity came into it. They certainly lived like princes—you've seen one of their palaces. They certainly did themselves well. But they did the country well, too: kept it safe and moderately wealthy, controlled the rest of the nobility, clipped the merchants if they got uppish. They moved with the times. They had damned shrewd ideas about agriculture, and a good deal of general intelligence which seems to have been hereditary. Diplomatically, given the context of any particular time, their activities were a model."

"Why *do* they let her live here?"

"Scared stiff of her, I really believe. Don't forget, the Revolution's still new. The young are not yet quite indoctrinated; the middle-aged and elderly remember quite other things. Ilena is for them a reminder of those things, and a last hope that times might get better. As far as the Government's concerned, they'd probably rather have her here than outside, doing all kinds of mischief. Ilena herself feels it is her duty to be here. They curtail her life as best they can, but she manages to be remarkably—active, just the same."

When Martin Wright came in with some papers he seemed tired and put out. He looked frowningly from Helen to Carlo and said in a morose voice, "Bad news. Trouble in Paradise."

Carlo gave a loud, theatrical groan. "I don't want to know," he said. "I simply don't want to know!"

"Wait till I tell you, and you'll want to know still less. This is not diplomatic, Carlo, it's domestic. Our peace is about to be shattered. Our beautiful enclave is to be invaded. For months and months we might have been dead, as far as the F.O. was concerned, and now—wham! Please give me a drink."

Carlo mixed a swinging drink and gave it to Martin in a large glass. "Go on," he said, "go on! I see I can't stop you."

Martin silently handed over the telegrams and drank his drink standing, like a disgruntled schoolboy, kicking one foot with the other and staring into the fire.

"No!" said Carlo under his breath. "Oh *no!*"

He looked so grim, suddenly, and fatigued, that even Martin seemed surprised.

"Don't take it too hard, old Carlo," he said. "It will pass. Tout passe, la légation reste!"

"What's happening?" Helen asked, "—if I may know?"

"You *must* know! Forewarned, etc. Our staff is being temporarily augmented by a Mr. Leslie Maidment and a Mr. Nigel Orde-Gibbon as from November 30th. They are coming in by RAF plane from Vienna. November 30th is this Sunday, in case you'd forgotten—three days from now. And on Monday the 15th of December, all the way from England, no fewer than six Members of Parliament, ironically described as an "all-party delegation,' descend on Senj to see for themselves—something. Whatever it's thought suitable for them to see, I suppose."

Helen could sense Carlo's disquiet, although by now he had resumed his usual manner and was drinking thoughtfully. It could hardly be the parliamentary delegation which was worrying him. That would certainly mean work, annoyances, but hardly danger. Yet Carlo had looked for an instant, just now, as though some deep fear had been realized.

"Who are they, Carlo?" Martin asked.

"Security," said Carlo in a neutral voice.

"Cripes! They'll turn us upside down. Will they be here for Christmas?"

"I don't know."

"Do you know them?"

"Orde-Gibbon, slightly."

"Nigel and Leslie. Two pretty men. They should be nice friends for Mort Landow. Security's his favorite thing."

"Well, it's not mine," said Carlo with sudden fury. "As though we hadn't got enough to do, without giving explanations to these louts all day about why we haven't changed the locks on the Chancery doors since breakfast, and why we don't eat all the secret waste instead of burning it!"

"You sound embittered, Carlo," said Martin who, his bombshell delivered, had cheered up remarkably.

"I've had some, that's all."

Helen could see that Carlo had made a great, and successful, effort to adapt his attitude to Martin's. He was treating the prospect solely as a domestic nuisance. Only she could still sense a more serious anxiety underneath.

"Well, Tubb will be more than a match for them, anyway," Martin said comfortably, "and I daresay we can enlist Victoria to harry and confuse them. We might make a deal with the Ministry of the Interior to have them arrested every time they go out. We could saw through the legs of their beds. We could . . ." and he continued for a while in ever more extravagant variations on this theme, till laughter had almost driven anxiety from Carlo's face.

"They may be very nice," Helen said primly, when Martin's extravaganza had finally run down.

"Go away, Miss Clark," said Martin. "You are subversive. How *could* they be nice? And what difference would it make if they were?"

The Hotel Olimpia smelled of dust and stale soup. It was dusky inside, lit by some daylight coming through stained glass, and a few weak, frosted bulbs in art-nouveau electroliers. Lethargy pervaded it. Two clerks behind their vast, brown-varnished counter were stiff as cataleptics, no doubt half-suffocated by the savory fug. Occasionally the hot twilight would be cloven by a draft like a sword, as someone pushed open the glass doors from the street. But there were few to push. Charles Sweet and Helen had the place pretty much to themselves.

They sat on a threadbare plush sofa under a flat dome, through the dirty stained glass of which daylight struggled, to strike no reflecting surface, but only absorbent, dark-colored stuffs, a chocolate carpet, the dulled leaves of many palms.

They sat for a long time in churchlike silence, gazing about them with wonder and distaste, before a bent and dirty old waiter brought them two glasses of tea and a plate of biscuits.

"Don't touch those biscuits," Charles warned her, "I

know them well. They're sawdust! This tea's only a token, anyway, just to show those who are interested—and they are many—that we are enjoying the pleasures generously restored to us. You'll get something much better in a little while. Now, just throw me a sentence or two from time to time, to look like conversation, and keep your eyes skinned. There's more going on than would appear."

Helen did as she was told. Clasping her glass of tea, which was by no means too hot, between her palms, she let her gaze wander round the vast, sprawling hall, noting the many corridors, screens and doors, the dark corners and small staircases, which it contained or adjoined.

Little by little she became aware of a good deal of activity at once hesitant and purposeful. There were never more than five other people in the hall at the same time, and they were never the same five for long. People came in, at long intervals, from the street, generally alone, paused, looked round with an air of idle appreciation, hesitated again—over the choice of a seat, to examine a notice board, to remove a glove—and then moved without haste but with absolute precision towards a door, a staircase, a corridor, and disappeared. Those who sat seldom ordered anything. They simply sat, like children in a game of hide-and-seek, as though counting slowly to a hundred, and then they, too, made off with perfect certainty to one or another of the possible ways out.

"Rum, isn't it?" said Carlo.

"It's more than rum—it's dreamlike! It's a little how I imagine one's subconscious mind."

Carlo laughed, a surprising sound in that place. "You're right," he said, "you are perhaps as right as it's possible to be. This hotel is, amongst other things, the headquarters of their counterespionage. Which is just double-talk for straight espionage, as I'm sure you know. It is also where they entertain valuable foreigners in a way far more lavish than we're seeing at this moment. Do you know where we are, Helen—geographically, I mean?"

"We're almost in Karl Marx Square, aren't we? I saw one of the arches as we were stopping."

"Quite right. As a matter of fact we are just behind the Ministry of Culture. This hotel was built on land belonging to the last Prince Sideini but one. There's a little lane between it and the old palace. That particular Sideini was a tremendous dog in his day but, like most of them, he had a high regard for appearances, so he made rather special arrangements not to be observed. . . ."

Helen was beginning to feel a touch of the old excitement, of childish fear and pleasure at a secret, adventurous thing. She gave Charles Sweet all her attention, forgetting, for a moment, the drab, uncomfortable place they were in.

Carlo looked at his watch. "Well," he said in a low voice, "you shall see for yourself." He placed some coins on the table and rose slowly to his feet. He stretched, then helped Helen on with her coat very deliberately, talking in an ordinary voice about the impending visit of parliamentarians. Then he took her arm and paced her across the floor, gave a nod to the clerks, motionless as fish behind their counter, propelled her gently through the double glass doors and down the steps to the street.

Sergeant Tubb snapped open his door and sprang out, making as if to open the rear door of the car.

"It's all right, Tubb," Carlo called in a loud, carrying voice. "We're going to walk a little way. Will you pick us up at the Ministry of Culture?"

"Very good, Sir." Tubb saluted smartly, with a slight narrowing of one eye which could have been a wink. They walked away from the lit portico of the Olimpia, along a pavement crowded with workers hurrying home. The cold, like a knife, pared at their faces; random fingertips of snow touched forehead and cheek. But it was too cold, now, for much snow. They were going down to the iron depth of winter, when the world is all snow, frozen solid as stone, and the brief days and endless nights seem fixed forever. Their footsteps rang, with those of the hurrying crowd, on the uneven pavement, scraped clean of snow between furrows of dirty white. This had once been the most luxurious shopping street of Senj, but now, between boards and sheet iron, and hoardings shouting political slogans, only four windows were alight.

"Are we being followed?" Helen asked, feeling suddenly awed by the darkness, the foreignness, the unguessable workings of this strange city. She had both hands in her muff; Carlo was holding one of her arms. He gave it a little squeeze.

"I should be surprised if we weren't," he said cheerfully. "But that'll be taken care of. Now—*slow!*" He slowed his own pace almost to a halt and, at the same moment, Helen became aware that the hurrying people had paused, come together, in some way clotted, both behind and in front of them. With a quick spin to her arm Charles guided her into a passage—narrow, little more than a crevice between two high buildings. "Hurry," he whispered. As they moved rapidly in single file, Helen could not resist turning her head to look back. Against the lighted street there seemed to be someone standing, blocking the narrow passage. No one else was behind them.

The passage widened a little, and Charles Sweet again took the lead, his heavy overcoat, scarf and braided hat looking sober, reassuring in this unlikely situation. Helen's heart was pounding.

"Rather an undiplomatic way of going on!" Carlo murmured between rapid breaths. "But then I'm not only a diplomat—thanks to our mutual friend. . . . Here we are. In you go, quick!" and he pushed Helen through a low doorway into a dimly-lighted shop.

"Straight on and up the stairs," said Carlo. "Don't stop to admire the view." He was close behind her.

Feeling, this time, really as though she were dreaming, Helen raced up a sharply-angled staircase, narrow and carpetless, which led from the shop. She had just had time to review an astonishing collection of junk of every description—bedsteads, mattresses, marble clocks, a samovar, a double-bass—and to smell the sweet-sour smell of poverty and dirt. She had seen an old man in a skullcap reading under a weak paraffin lamp, who did not so much as turn a page as they passed. She was on a narrow landing facing a large, old-fashioned carved press. There were doors in the wall on either side of it. The staircase twisted away from her upwards, out of sight.

Carlo was beside her now. Without another word he opened both doors of the press, and motioned to Helen to step inside. As she did so, the back of the press opened away from her and Helen walked from the bare, musty-smelling interior, from the dejection of the house and shop behind, into warmth and a soft light glowing on old gilding and many quiet colors; to the sound of a crackling fire and the smell of china tea; to the sight of Mr. H. Tenby Sanders in tweeds, and of Mrs. Sidney in a magnificent belted coat embroidered with scarlet flowers advancing towards her with outstretched hands.

Helen heard Mrs. Sidney saying: "So nice of you both to come to tea!" in a voice of humorous gravity. With her hands in the old woman's warm, bony clasp, she looked across at Henry Sanders, looming beside the fire. His eyes were watchful, his smile full of affection and a little diffidence.

"Hullo, Helen," he said. "How is the winter of our discontent?"

Helen moved quickly across to him, and returned him a frown for his smile.

"I'm wretched," she said in a low voice. "I feel I've failed before I've even begun. . . ."

Sanders' expression altered immediately. He frowned back at her, looking hard into her eyes.

"That you most certainly haven't!" he said sharply. "So don't think it, and don't say it! I have no complaint whatever about what you've done so far, by simply *being*, as much as anything. And now, I think, things are beginning to move. Fast."

Helen was never to remember much of Mrs. Sidney's room, except that it was long and low-ceilinged, white and warm, and blooming with antique shapes and colors: ikons, embroideries, dark-shaded lamps, and the comforting stable point of a wood fire. Her whole attention was caught between the old woman and the two men, who were weaving between them, by brief question and answer, an extraordinary impressive-seeming web of power.

An old manservant with a heavy white mustache, wearing a black silk jacket, handed glasses of tea, and petits fours which must have come from Vienna. Cigarette smoke hung in layers of blue above the lamps. No noise of any kind came into the room from outside.

For a while Helen was left to look and listen. Carlo had launched into a concise, almost telegraphic report to which the others listened with concentration. Helen watched his face, confirming to herself a thought she had had before—that varied experience had left, here, every conventional mark: lines, crows' feet, a tautening and down-drawing of the skin from prominent bones; but that all this was so much make-up. The basic face (if she could only, somehow, sponge away anxiety, fill out the hollows, put health back into the parchment skin) was that of the boy Charles still was, intelligent, indolent, eager to be pleased, sensitive and profoundly kind. At present his face expressed weariness, regret, and an acid distaste.

"So it looks," Charles concluded, "as if the whole thing's been put forward. This Parliamentary Delegation stunt's for *before* Christmas now. They're dashing over straight after their recess. Couldn't possibly stage *that* again in a few months. So we've got even less time than we thought." There was a pause, during which neither of the others moved or spoke. Charles went on more slowly:

"I suppose it was all fixed up on that last trip to London. . . . He's certainly buttoned himself up tight since he got back. I've hardly had a word with him that wasn't the purest routine. He's just—not with us any more."

Helen thought of Mark Ogilvy, of the charming presence growing daily more remote, elusive, speaking fewer words, making ever less demands upon his staff—causing the lady clerks to flutter and be loquacious, and Victoria to show off ferociously in a desperate, unsmiling bid for attention. And the charm remaining, the almost apologetic sweetness of smile and manner, the courteous and pointed listening, the sudden, candid brilliance of look; remaining, but dimming appreciably, perhaps to linger like the Cheshire Cat's grin, some while after the Minister's personality had vanished for ever. Was it true, then, this charm? Was it of the heart, a real clue to the nature of Mark Ogilvy? Or was it a trick, a piece of conjuring so well-learned, so often tried so successfully, as to be worth using, for tactical reasons, to the very last?

They had parted in silence, last evening after the dancing display. Mark Ogilvy had sketched a gesture towards Helen and Victoria and made off, with his long stride, head down, frowning, towards his study. Victoria, tired, had made heavy weather of the staircase, but had refused to be carried. Helen had dismissed Mrs. Simpkin and, conscious of the need to repair damage, to reassure, had given Victoria a lavish supper, read her twice the usual number of stories, and lent her some treasured bath essence for her bath.

Mark's own eyes, but of an unfatigued and piercing brightness, gazed up at her from the pillow as she sang, in Victoria's chosen order, four favorite bedtime songs. She was halfway through Luther's cradle song, which always came last, when the blue unblinking stare was deflected sharply beyond her shoulder. A troubled look came into the small face already half-stilled with sleep. Helen was conscious of a male presence towering beside her as she sat. Her voice faltered. She was about to look up when a firm hand pressed her shoulder and Mark's voice said, "Don't stop!" Quite astounded, and more than a little embarrassed, Helen continued her song, a trifle off key. Her thoughts scattered like confetti, she wondered brokenly if so much electricity—she had shivered violently—had gone out to Mark from her, or had come to her from him. Or whether it had worked both ways. The song ended. Helen had looked up into Mark's face and found it smiling gravely, calm, for an instant unravaged, and seeming almost as youthful as his child's.

Carlo's voice broke into her thoughts. He said to Henry Sanders: "Who's for the long hop this time?"

"Haven't you seen the names?"

"Not confirmed, so far. I *guess* Mr. Alexander Gloag-Jones. . . ."

"Correct. Helen. . . ." H.T.S. turned on the wide sofa he was sharing with the still, glittering figure of Mrs. Sidney and spoke across to her where she sat with Carlo at the other side of the fire. "There's something here needs explaining, unless Carlo's explained it already? No, I see he hasn't. About this Parliamentary Delegation. Do you know why this is so important?"

Helen shook her head.

"Well, as you probably know, there is—apart from the normal work of the House of Commons—a certain amount of to-ing and fro-ing of Members, at home and abroad, all the time. Fact-finding missions, good-will missions, delegations to this or that. Some are official party matters; others semi-official, mixed efforts, subscribed to by both major parties with the odd Liberal thrown in. Now, we've known for some time that these junkets, provided they are in certain geographical directions, have a strong appeal for one or two M.P.'s whose sympathies are rather more definite than they let on. There are a few members of the party now in power who are, secretly, fanatical and inconvertible Communists. I say secretly, because their own people would persecute them even more bitterly than their opponents would, if the truth ever got out. There may be one or two in the Conservative party as well—I'm pretty sure there are. Every Parliament contains a proportion of band-wagoners who are loyal only to their own ambition. If thwarted they're capable, often, of going to any extreme to make themselves felt. . . . But the point is that we have definite evidence about at least three men, and your expected visitor, Alexander Gloag-Jones, is one of them. Do you know Gloag-Jones?"

"No, I've never met him. I've only just heard of him. Is he really so important?"

"As a man, no. As an intellect, no. As representing a dangerous principle, yes. The Russians, who never miss a trick, however boring and futile, are very interested in him."

"But what harm can he do? Coming here with five others, three of them Conservatives? Beyond being nice to Madame Kassin, and whispering a few words of comfort to the Glumba comrades at an official party—words which they could invent, if they wanted to, without any assistance from him . . ."

There was silence for a moment. Mrs. Sidney looked at Helen with half-hooded eyes and a slight, expectant smile. Carlo's expression was almost comically disapproving. Henry Sanders' level gaze seemed to hold compassion, as though he might have bad news for her.

"The comrades in Senj," he said slowly, "are not in question. The day after his arrival here Mr. Gloag-Jones will be taken ill at the Hotel Olimpia, where the delegation will be staying. The British Minister will visit him and report well on the treatment he is receiving. The doctors will order a stay in bed for the patient some days longer than the sceduled stay of the delegation. The Minister will undertake to ship him home, when fully recovered. Do you see now?"

"I'm afraid I don't!" Helen felt mortified, almost ready to weep. She longed suddenly for the nursery and Victoria, for a child's clear perceptions and an end to riddles.

"Moscow is four hours' fl_ing from Senj," H.T.S. said gently. "The Hotel Olimpia—you've just seen for yourself—is a place of secrets and a centre of power. Your man is in bed with a bellyache at the Hotel Olimpia. Your man is in Moscow, spilling the beans. Who's to know? In good time, out he comes from the hotel, pale but evidently restored. He is whisked to Vienna in an RAF plane specially requested by HBM's Legation, and he's back for Christmas in the snake's nest he calls his home. There's only one thing, of course. He needs . . ."

"An accomplice?" Helen's voice was low.

"An impeccable accomplice," Henry Sanders gravely

133

agreed. Carlo made an odd, angry sound—of denial, of rejection—such as a sleeper might make in the course of a bad dream.

"And . . . when it's all over," Helen asked, "what becomes of the accomplice?"

Her voice sounded distant in her own ears. The proud and tragic mask of Princess Sideini was no longer smiling. Henry Sanders looked as old as the world.

"One evening he attends a party at the Ministry of Culture which, as Ilena knows, has many back doors. Then he, too, leaves Senj by air—flying eastwards."

"And his child?"

"She flies with him."

"Not over my dead body she doesn't!" Helen cried, and was surprised at the passionate force of her own voice.

She saw the others laughing, relaxing from their tense and doom-laden attitudes, glad—no doubt—of a chance to laugh. It was a moment, however, before she could join them, so shaken was she by this revelation of her feeling for Victoria, her anger against Mark.

"Sorry about my grammar!" she said a little stiffly, but beginning to smile. Carlo, who loved to laugh, was still chuckling.

"Perfectly good grammar," he said. "The double negative. Gives extra emphasis, especially in Slav languages. That's so, isn't it, Ilena?"

"Quite so. And Helen is a good girl. She is *there*. What this situation needs is a double negative. A treble one. No, no, and no again."

"Sable and snowflakes," said Martin Wright, brushing the dark fur tenderly with his fingertips. "What more poetical? And where less likely to be appreciated?"

They were standing under the rainbow light of a chandelier in the black-and-white marble hall of the American Legation. Tubb had driven them there at a slithering, clicking crawl through the worst blizzard of the winter. To this formally festive pre-Christmas party Mark

134

Ogilvy and Carlo would be coming later on. Meanwhile Helen and Martin who had been plastered with thick snow even in the three-yard scamper from the car to the Legation door, were stamping their feet and brushing at themselves to get rid of some of it before yielding their outdoor things to an unsmiling servant in a striped coat.

"How you glow and sparkle," Martin said, "and how undyingly grateful I shall always be to you for coming off that aeroplane looking like Anna Karenina! This should be St. Petersburg, Helen. And there should be something better waiting for you upstairs than Morton Landow and his boot-button eyes!"

Helen laughed. She was indeed radiant, from cold and the brief assault of the snowstorm, her color high and her eyes frostily bright. Martin observed that crystals of snow still hung unmelted on her long lashes.

"You are unfair to the Chalks," she said, "they are elegance itself. They probably know all about poetry too. And one Landow doesn't make a bear-garden!"

"Two would," said Martin gloomily. "Depend upon it. Just wait till little Wayne grows up!"

"Oh, I agree there. But by that time, thank goodness, I shall be far away. . . ."

"To my very great regret," said Martin, on so low and serious a tone that Helen stopped for an instant, poised on a step of the broad, curving staircase, to look at him searchingly. Martin gave her a wide smile in which his eyes did not share.

"Don't worry, Helen. I nearly always mean what I say, even if I don't always say what I mean. But I'm not—I promise—stepping out of line. Just formulating, with my usual simple vulgarity, what is in many hearts where you're concerned. And why not, is what I ask?" He put his hand lightly under her elbow as they approached the top of the stairs. "Beauty doesn't *have* to be a 'dono infelice'—to its owner or anyone else. In this place, at this time, with these people—I believe you bring us all the luck in the world."

"Do you think you need luck, then, so badly?" Helen

135

asked this question with a deliberate edge to her voice; but "Who doesn't?" was all that Martin, with a small shrug, would reply.

The party was nearly at its height and all the high, square rooms were comfortably crowded. The clash of the social chaff-cutter, varied by chinking sounds and sporadic volleys of laughter, enveloped Helen as she offered her hand to Mr. Preston Chalk. The Minister took her hand in both his own, and bent a narrow, handsome, patrician head to twinkle down at her.

"Miss Clark, as a representative of a decaying, bourgeois culture, I'd say you're a sight for sore eyes!"

"She's pretty enough to melt any old iron curtain," chimed in his wife, with enthusiasm.

Helen said to her companion, as they tried to drift into a human current which would wash them up at the buffet: "If I get any more compliments, my head will spin right off!"

"You won't for a little while. We are being ineluctably driven towards Mort!"

Sure enough, straddled across their path and blocking with his untidy bulk the way to the refreshments, Morton Landow observed their approach with a fixed, white smile. His eyes, black as currants in the dough of his face, were intelligent and unfriendly. His voice when he exclaimed, "Hi!" had a curious juicy harshness like a frog's.

"Hi!" echoed Martin courteously. It was remarkable how much scholarly solemnity he managed to put into the exclamation, as thought it were an important syllable in Chinese, to mispronounce which would be to alter the sense disastrously. Mort Landow gave him a stabbing glance of dislike and turned ostentatiously to Helen.

Helen sought Martin's eyes with her own, to discourage him. Mort Landow was an enemy already, of this she was sure. Whatever Martin Wright did or did not know about present dangers, Mort might be dangerously well-informed. It was safer not to goad him.

Accordingly she felt forced to smile warmly at Mort,

and even, in doing so, to imply a hint of dissociating herself from Martin Wright. This worked rather too well. Helen became subject to Mort Landow's pretty-woman manner, a variety of sub-suggestive ribbing too perfunctory to disguise an elemental sexual greed. If anyone is going over to the other side, it should be he, she thought. All his life he must have wanted a world where the master-slave relationship could be satisfactorily established. He must fear this tendency in himself, else why the passion for diplomatic witch-hunting? I hope poor Mr. Chalk can hold him . . . yet, in Mort Landow's America, the Chalks are as much foreigners as I should be myself.

Helen looked casually round her, to avoid having to look at Landow, and saw that Martin was engaged with Mrs. Mort. This lady was as elegant, fine drawn, beautiful and discreet as her husband was the opposite of these things. Mort Landow had married above him, if such a phrase were allowable in his world. "She is much more of a lady than he is," Martin Wright had once said. Now Martin was bending with real attention and sympathy towards her neat, fair head, trying to coax with his best conversation one or two more of the slow, gentle smiles which were Jane Landow's most violent expressions of amusement. When, once, Helen had said: "I can't think what made her marry him," Martin had answered quite sharply, almost with rage: "Simple mudhunger. Nostalgie de la boue. The brighter the feminine product, the darker that particular corner." And Helen had not pursued the matter, feeling momentarily shaken, her mind suddenly invaded by the image of Stoyan Anzip.

One of the young Secretaries brought Helen an Old fashioned. Mort said: "Christ, you don't want all that garbage! Lemme get you a bourbon-on-the-rocks."

"No, thank you. It's the garbage I like it for." And she thought, that is true—I like flowers and fruit in my drinks, and decoration of all kinds, and if people I don't like must make passes at me, then I want them with blue ribbons on. . . .

137

Martin was back at her side.

"Look over there," his voice was quiet. "Rosencrantz and Guildenstern."

Helen followed the direction of his nod and saw, tall and short, burly and thin, and eyeing the assembly restlessly over the tops of their drinks, the two unwanted guests, the security men, Maidment and Orde-Gibbon.

"Mr. Landow . . ." Martin was all diplomatic affability, "I'd be very happy to have you meet our two interesting new colleagues. Won't you come over and say a word to them? You too, Helen. We mustn't let them feel left out at this festive season!"

Mort Landow looked puzzled, on one foot between annoyance and suspicion, as he generally was with Martin Wright; but he lurched after Helen docilely enough and had his big politician's grin ready for the two Englishmen, just as though he did not already know exactly who they were.

Helen performed the introductions. Leslie Maidment said, "Pleased to meet you, Counsellor," and Nigel Orde-Gibbon said, "How do you do, Sir? What a *fascinating* house!" (Discussing this afterwards, Martin said: 'R. and G. are really splendid. One couldn't have invented them. Leslie made it all sound like the Mayor's parlor, but Nigel, with his little interior decorator's eyes, made Mort into an improverished country squire.")

Maidment and Orde-Gibbon—now "R. and G." forever to the British Legation staff—had arrived from Vienna two Sundays ago. It was now Thursday evening nearly a fortnight later and Helen doubted whether they had yet managed to carry out many of their instructions, whatever those might be. It was not that anyone had been deliberately uncooperative. The Legation was understaffed, and everyone quite genuinely too busy to have much time for matters outside the daily routine. Carlo, after being subjected to an all-out assault of charm from Orde-Gibbon, had decided to prefer Maidment. He had made it his business to see that neither of them got anywhere near Mark Ogilvy, but he did occasionally give ear to Maidment's worries about pay and allowances which seemed to be preying on his mind. Orde-Gibbon, who had recently been at the Embassy in Paris, was ready to talk by the hour about that sumptuous post. Carlo, who disliked smart people in general, and Paris in particular, was a poor audience for tales of the Duff Coopers, but Martin, for his own reasons, could never have enough. He spent so much of his limited spare time encouraging Nigel Orde-Gibbon to talk—"Go on, my dear fellow, tell about the Vicomtesse de Cabrol—I'm sorry, the *Baronne* . . . you *must* correct me if I get it wrong!"—that although it was quite obvious what was Nigel's weakness, Helen was sure that Martin would overdo the teasing and end by turning his victim savage.

For farcical though they might be in some ways, R. and G. were also dangerous, at least from Helen's and Carlo's point of view. The two men had been clamoring for a security conference since their arrival, to examine present practice in the Legation and to introduce new ideas. This event had so far been successfully put off. Helen suspected that Carlo was trying to irritate them into showing something of their true hand which, it had to be admitted, they were playing remarkably close to the chest. No, they were not to be taken lightly. Oddly assorted as they seemed to be, they yet were perfectly comfortable with each other, and this must argue an identity of past training and present aim. It was possible that to appear as commonplace, even as ridiculous, as they usually did was not the least intelligent of the tricks at their command.

Helen was as sure as she was of anything that there must be an ulterior purpose to the visit of Maidment and Orde-Gibbon. Something uneasy, stilted, overpolite in their demeanor to Morton Landow, and in his to them, made her certain of their complicity, if not yet in fact, then in intention. Mort Landow had, on more than one occasion, made edged remarks in her hearing about Mark Ogilvy, usually coupled with a jeering aside about the state of British security where the Russians were concerned. Landow might have followed a hunch and succeeded in stirring up the Foreign Office—certainly much

139

against its will—to take precautions. Or he might himself have hit on the real truth, or a sizable clue to it. One thing, however, was certain. Morton Landow simply was not equipped to judge Mark Ogilvy as a person, nor, probably, to interpret correctly the intentions of Great Britain in this uneasy world. Eyeing his profile as he spoke loudly, authoritatively, to the group surrounding him, Helen felt a cold dizziness, suddenly seeing this baying, wet-lipped mouth as that of the pack's leader, and Mark as the beautiful trapped stag, wild for freedom and struggling with every convulsion, more deeply into the trap. The friendly sounds of a party swelled and rang harshly in her ears, growing louder and more menacing, gathering to them all the cruelty of the crowd: the voice of the many in pursuit of the unconforming few. Unable to bear it a moment longer, Helen turned rather wildly and made for the nearest door.

She found at once that, at this party, another room was another world. The very quality of the sound was different, colors were darker, the air heavier and more solemn. She threaded her way through a dense crowd, mostly of men, all with their backs turned to the door at which she had entered, as though listening to a speech. People made way for her courteously, but with no more than a moment's glance her way before turning back to stare respectfully towards the centre of the room. Here, in a clear space under the crystal rain of a great chandelier, was a short, broad-shouldered man in a suit of purplish blue, with a bald bony cranium hedged with bristling grey, small pig's eyes, perfectly round, under jutting but almost hairless brows, and a long-lipped mouth now wide as a letterbox and flashing gold in a huge laugh. Helen stopped in her tracks, feeling a little afraid. This face she knew well, from giant posters in the squares of Senj, from newspaper photographs, from cartoons in the press at home. This was the Prime Minister, "The Guv," as the British in Senj called him—to distinguish him from "The Old Man," the President who, ancient and stunted and inarticulate, was paraded only twice yearly or so, at the great rallies, to show the senile bristles, the stiff white collar, the poor square boots of a battered Mr. Chips to blank-eyed boys and girls who saluted but did not see him at all. The American Minister and Mrs. Chalk, recipients of the Guv's latest joke, were smiling down at him with expressions of mingled anxiety and indulgence, like grownups trying to be nice to the delinquent child of an old friend.

Helen had fetched up beside Dick Phillips, one of the junior American Secretaries, an agreeable boy to whom Victoria was much attached.

"That was one in the ribs for Uncle Sam, I guess," he murmured in her ear. "Mr. Chalk's got his martyred look on, and all the Glumbas are looking smug as Hell!"

Helen felt steadied by Dick's carefree appearance, his cheerful freckled face and shock of red hair.

"Do you call them Glumbas too?" she asked.

"Oh, sure. I do, anyway. I got it from Victoria. How *is* my best girl?"

"She's very well—only furious at not being allowed to come this evening. She howled when I went to say good night to her. "You're—leaving me—all alone—with this old black Simpkin—*and you're taking Tubb too!*""

Dick Phillips' youthful and undiplomatic guffaw turned many heads in their direction. A movement in the crush suddenly brought into Helen's line of vision the pouchy profile of Madame Kassin and, bending attentively towards her, in a pose of exaggerated receptivity which somehow managed to appear ironic, the long back of Stoyan Anzip.

Helen's momentary breathing space was over. She turned her eyes quickly to Dick, to lose in the sight of his nice ordinariness the vision of a narrow waist and shining black hair. She felt choked again. The atmosphere had grown sinister. Too many square-shouldered men in stiff, dark suits, too much falsity, too much danger. She stammered to Dick Phillips:

"I must get out of here for a little. Help me get through, will you?"

"Sure, Helen, if you want. . . . Helen, you're not sick or anything?"

141

"No, no . . . no . . . I just want the bathroom!"

"Excuse me, Sir, would you mind letting this lady by?"

The square backs seemed to stretch to infinity, solid, immovable like standing stones. But, at Dick's words, first one, then two, three, four of them spun slowly on their axes and Helen, with a sharply contracting heart, found herself looking into a black and blue eye under a thatch of inky hair, and then into faces of Charlie and his two companions: all four members of INGRA, her enemies from the train.

Helen prayed that she looked less shaken than she felt. The bruise marks from the iron fingers of the black-haired man had not long faded from her arms, and here he was offering her his hand, in the bright light of the American Legation, and there was nothing she could do but accept it. She shook hands solemnly with all four in turn, managing a sort of smile for each of them. For their part, they simply appeared pleased to see her, as though for no other reason than that she was a pretty girl and this was a party. Only the black-haired man remained serious, putting away his party smile as soon as used, and gazing at her with a beetling insistence from his variegated eyes. Feeling ill with dislike, her knees trembling till she thought it must be noticed, Helen continued to smile and smile, while Dick Phillips stood hesitant, looking concerned, a doubtful grin on his face. The black-haired man spoke:

"You are liking Senj?" His voice was flat and rather high; his lips scarcely moved. Helen had to swallow before replying.

"Very much. I find it most interesting." (I am talking like a foreigner myself. . . .)

"And zis—zis infant . . . zis little gorl, you are liking her too?"

"But of course!" Thinking suddenly of Victoria, asleep in her narrow bed, Helen could smile more easily. But this conversation was like the most cloying and pointless of dreams. She must end it and get away. The four men were all nodding gravely. Their eyes flickered to each other and then back to Helen.

142

"If you will excuse me," Helen said, "Mr. Phillips and I have to—to meet someone." She gave them a smile of brilliant vagueness, laid her hand on Dick's sleeve, and together they forged on towards the farther door.

"Well!" Dick said, "I've seen some queer ducks. . . . That guy with the two-tone eyes—I'd know him anywhere again!" They were at the door now, and to right and left stretched a wide, red-carpeted corridor, for the time being empty and quiet.

"Let's hope you never have to see him again," Helen said. "Thank you, Dick, I'm all right now. I know my way. Go back and enjoy yourself!" Dick rolled his eyes.

"Enjoy myself! I have to tell you, Helen, that, as far as our official guests are concerned, I'm a total flop. I just can't seem to get through. . . . Don't stay away too long. I'm heading for the bar. Come and look for me there. 'Bye now!" She saw him edge circumspectly back into the crowded room.

Halfway along the corridor to Helen's left a small staircase ran up to the bedroom floors above. From dancing class days Helen knew where to find a bathroom. Suddenly feeling deathly tired she set off down the corridor, her feet dragging through the soft pile. She yawned across the back of her hand, smeared a lock of hair carelessly to one side, rubbed her eyes. She felt at once shocked and depressed, as though she had seen a street accident. The bright salon she had just left was full of murderers, habitual takers of human life, unsanctioned by a state of war. The Guv, Madame Kassin, the INGRA men, were all in blood up to their elbows; yet there they were, bobbing and beaming in their best clothes, firing off their flat, malicious jokes, hideous and complacent and firmly in the saddle, beggars on horseback riding high. Not corrupted by power, these, but powerful because of their corruption. All corruption empowers, thought Helen as she climbed the stairs. And Mark Ogilvy, born and made, if anyone ever was, to be on the side of the angels—Mark Ogilvy wanted to throw in his lot with these abortions of the human spirit. Well, thought Helen, if some women have a dark spot in their natures, a nostalgia for the

143

mud, so too do some men, and none the better for rationalizing it and building systems round it.

What awful deprivation was Mark trying to make good? Helen sat on a bathroom stool, her elbows on the rim of a black marble wash basin, gazing into her own eyes which looked at her despairingly from the toneless depths of a looking-glass. What loss, what crying, unanswered need had so unbalanced him that utter ruin should come to look like rebirth? His wife? From all the evidence, Helen could not think her so important. Caroline Ogilvy had simply got out from under. Her death had merely interrupted a fugal movement which would eventually have taken her out of Mark's life for good. Helen's inner ear caught the weary, beautifully controlled tones of his mother's voice: "I think that Caroline, in her heart, quite crucially *disagreed* with Mark, with what he was and what she thought he wanted. I think that, by the time they got to Senj, some part of her had also become frightened—frightened of a greater discomfort yet, mental or spiritual, which she had the intuition to guess might be coming to him. I think that, some time before her death, she had dropped her side of what they were both carrying. She had *unwished* him and was getting ready to go." And Caroline's infidelities, even Caroline's death, would have seemed to Mark no more than the last pieces of proof on which to rest his case.

"I suppose I can't sit in this bathroom forever!" Helen's limbs were leaden. Half-hypnotized by her own reflection she felt that to move a finger would be like the struggle to awake from one of those dreams of paralysis she occasionally had. She let slip the thought of Mark, to allow something else to come to the surface which had been obscurely troubling her. The black-haired man . . . it had been shock enough to come face to face, to have to shake hands, with someone who had sincerely tried to kill her barely six weeks ago. But there was more to haunt and puzzle her at this meeting. This time, there was something in his face, in the way his hair grew and the placing of the strange eyes, and the structure of brow and

144

jaw, to remind her not just of himself, but of someone else. Of whom? Helen leaned her weight on her arms, stared down into the hollow of the wash basin, and thought. . . . Suddenly she was on her feet, snatching up bag and gloves, her fatigue completely gone, wildly impatient to get back to the Legation, to Victoria. If Mrs. Simkin, at their first meeting, had reminded her of somebody, then she knew now who that somebody was. The eyes apart, by every line and molding, by the tone of his voice, even by the tight, disappearing smile, the black-haired man was the image of Mrs. Simpkin.

Helen came out of the bathroom on a swirling movement, banging the door and set off for the head of the stairs, heart beating hard, almost at a run. Then she stopped dead, half turned in profile, in a frozen moment of flight, her stomach twisting in pain from fear and excitement. Stoyan Anzip disengaged himself from the angle of the staircase where he had been leaning and came swiftly towards her, holding out his hand.

"Miss Clark, I must speak to you." Less silky than usual, more abrupt, Stoyan looked anxious, serious, almost diffident. Helen who had felt, for a moment, that all the blood in her body had rushed to her head, now felt drained of blood altogether, cold and completely at a loss. Anzip's eyes seemed to plead with her. The arrogance was no longer there, and he looked self-forgetful, almost untidy, a long strand of hair loose on his forehead, one wing of his soft collar cocked up over the edge of his waistcoat.

Through stiff lips Helen said: "We can't talk here. Anybody might come. . . . You must go back to the party. We could—we could meet downstairs."

Anzip shook his head vigorously. "We can't talk here, in this house, at all. We could not have three words together down there. No, but I must see you, and soon. This is truly important . . . and it is not what you think!" he added, smiling suddenly with great sweetness, a touch of complicity, bringing the sketch for an answering smile to Helen's own lips.

"That's a relief!" she said, in what sounded to her a decidedly governess-like voice. "But where can we possibly talk without everybody knowing at once, *my* people as well as yours? Or doesn't it matter about my people?"

Stoyan Anzip had been absently holding her hand during this exchange, shaking it a little to emphasize what he was saying. Now Helen withdrew it with gentle firmness. Self-command was coming back to her. She was even a little amused to see how lost the impeccable Stoyan was without her hand for contact. She saw him glance down at his own with a touch of doubt before plunging it into his coat pocket.

"Nobody at all must know," he replied slowly and with great gravity. "Not my people nor yours."

With rapidly returning confidence, now that the situation had proved to be this one rather than another, Helen said gravely:

"Am I, then, to trust you?"

Anzip gave a brief, dismissing smile and shake of the head. "You are afraid of a trap, Miss Clark? Well, I could hardly blame you if you were. But no . . . if anyone is to be trapped, it will more likely be myself. . . ." His thoughts seemed, for that moment, far away. "Now listen, please. Tomorrow your Legation will receive a message that, since you have expressed a wish to visit Ostrány, you are to be included in a party of foreign mineralogists who are going on a special visit. A car from the Ministry of Culture will call for you on Saturday, that is the day after tomorrow, at nine o'clock. After that, you will have to trust me. And I beg that you will, for what I have to discuss with you is of the first importance. I promise that you will be delivered, safe and sound, back at your Legation in time for dinner!"

Ostrány! And I wanted to go there, because it looked high and quiet. I've been wanting to go ever since I got here. And now I may be going with *him!* Am I mad? This could be worse than the train thing. I must speak to Carlo. . . . I must get back to Victoria. . . . With

146

a sense of too many things happening at once, Helen said:

"All right. I'll come." She looked hard in Anzip's face as she spoke, searching for a gleam of triumph, cruelty, satisfaction. But Anzip only looked relieved.

"That is good, then," he said. He drew his heels together and bowed quickly from the shoulders. "I think that you and I will do a good work, and that you will be thankful to me!"

"We shall see," replied Helen, and was amazed at her own coolness. "Now—I must go. My employers should be here now, and I need to get back to the Legation at once."

Stoyan Anzip stood back to let her pass.

"Till Saturday!" he said quietly. Helen went on alone down the short, curving stairway, to be confronted at its foot by Madame Luba Kassin, standing by herself, planted squarely in the middle of the corridor, her yellow-white eyes incandescent with rage. So violent was the feeling possessing her squat body that the Minister of Culture looked positively inhuman, as though fixed by a paralytic stroke in a posture as stiff and twisted as that of some Byzantine saint. So bitter and exclusive was the hatred she was nursing that her toad's face seemed almost ecstatic, its slack folds and lines and blotches transfigured by an annihilating orgasm of fury. In spite of herself Helen wavered, paused—almost, from instinct, ready to run back and claim the protection of Stoyan Anzip. But the pale eyes, to her amazement, barely turned her way. They remained fixed with demoniac anticipation on the entrance to the flight of stairs.

Pretending to have stopped only to change her bag and gloves from one hand to the other, Helen bowed slightly, murmured, "Bonsoir, Excellence!" and walked on towards the head of the main staircase trying hard not to hurry. She drew an audible, sharp in-breath of relief when she saw, just entering the first drawing-room, two well-known heads above the moving crowd. Mark Ogilvy and Charles Sweet had, at last, arrived.

147

Before allowing herself to be sucked into the drawing-room Helen glanced briefly down the corridor behind her, half expecting to see Stoyan Anzip stretched at Madame Kassin's feet. But that lady was now ploughing back towards the party like an overloaded scow. She had been joined by two obsequious-looking men in black clothes, who appeared to be trying to placate her. Of Stoyan Anzip there was no sign. He's either hiding out in the lav. like me—or he's found the backstairs! A kind of sympathetic amusement sparkled in Helen. She entered the drawing-room, head well up, a small smile on her lips.

She could see Martin Wright at one corner of the buffet, talking to a tall, thin man with a stoop. Helen made straight for them. Martin gave her a smile of welcome with a touch of questioning to it, as though she had been away from him many days and might have changed in the meantime.

"Helen, this is Monsieur Pribitek. He is Deputy Minister of Reconstruction and makes very good jokes."

Monsieur Pribitek's eyes were of an extraordinary innocence and gaiety, set in a long, narrow face which seemed marked by a lifetime of pain. When he smiled it was as if every bone in his body were being broken and he still, somehow, found it amusing. Helen remembered Martin saying: ". . . one man who is really so nice that I cannot imagine why he hasn't been bumped off long ago!" Monsieur Pribitek gazed at Helen for a long moment with searching kindness. Then his face crumbled in a look of almost unbearable torment, and with a slight lifting of both hands as though in blessing, he said:

"It is not of jokes that Mademoiselle makes me think. . . . Rather, of the music of Mozart!"

"Rather an anxious bit of Mozart, at present," said Martin, whose perceptions where Helen was concerned were painfully sharp. "What's up, Helen? Anything I can do?"

Before Helen could answer, someone touched her arm and she looked round to see Charles Sweet, unusually smart in black coat and striped trousers, at her side. He bowed to the Deputy Minister, nodded to Martin Wright, without managing much of a smile. Helen could feel the sense of tension and fatigue he had brought with him.

"Good evening, Monsieur Pribitek . . . Martin. Will you both excuse us for a moment?" and he drew Helen towards the middle of the room.

"You're to go back, now," Carlo said in a low voice. "Tubb's waiting to take you. Please sit in front, with him. And when you get to the Legation, go straight to my room, where you'll find someone you know."

"I've absolutely got to see you this evening—or tomorrow morning at the latest. Something very odd is happening."

"You're right about that!" Carlo sounded tired and displeased. "Yes, we'll talk later on. There's a cold supper and drinks in my room. I'll be along in an hour or so. Off you go. Don't say good night to anyone. Just wander away and get your coat."

I'm going straight to Victoria, Helen said to herself as she made a leisurely progress through the room and down the staircase. I wonder who's in Charles' room? H.T.S.? Mrs. Sidney? Perhaps both of them. She found her coat and her overshoes, and, without glancing back, went out into the swirling snow.

Snug in Sergeant Tubb's warm cabin, they slid and jerked their way through the white, silent town. Sometimes the wheels spun in drifts, and the car slewed and then straightened again to resume its rhythmically clicking way, on chains, over the glimmering close-packed snow. The windshield heaters kept a fan of crystal clear before each of them. The wipers, with a long soft squeak and a short thud, skimmed off the crowding snow feathers as they blew. Dipped headlights lit a receding cave of shadows and diamonds where nothing seemed familiar and distance had no end.

"You're not having much of an evening," Helen said. "This is your third trip in all this, and then you've got to come back!"

"I don't mind, Miss. One thing I can never get tired
149

of—snow. Don't know why, but I've always liked it, ever since I was a kid. And this stuff's the real thing; better than the sort of sprinkle we get at home."

Tubb is one of the most comforting people to be with I have ever known, she thought. Solid, competent—and quick. No chips on his shoulder, no apparent anxieties. Easy, tactful, and perfectly certain of himself. Another grown-up person. I am lucky to know so many. Helen said: "Have you always been in this sort of job—since the war, I mean?"

Tubb let a little time elapse before answering, then spoke with an odd deliberation.

"Two years," he said. "I came out here with Mr. Sweet, to start things up again; that's before the Minister was appointed. Before that I was in the haberdashery business in London. Cheapside and . . ."

"Three hundred and thirty-four, The Strand!" interrupted Helen on one breath, with a lifting heart. Here was her third ally—and she might have guessed!

There was a chuckle in Sergeant Tubb's voice as he answered: "That's quite correct, Miss. So now we can all get along together. I'd have let you know, myself, before this, only Mr. Sweet said not. He said: 'One thing at a time,' and I daresay he was right. Apart from anything else—and there's plenty else—you've got a full day's work, most days, with Miss Victoria."

"Oh, I love her!"

"We all do. She's a lovely little thing. But she's too bright by half and so she needs a lot of helping along. . . ." Helen felt that Tubb had only just refrained from adding: "Like her father!" Instead he looked at the clock on the dashboard and said: "We'll just be in nice time. Another five minutes and *he'll* be there, if all's gone as it should, and five minutes after that so shall we."

"I must go up and see Victoria first," Helen said, and went on to tell Sergeant Tubb about the man with black hair. He was silent for a while after she had finished.

"It may be a coincidence," he said at length. "People

150

do sometimes look the image of each other until you get them together, and then they don't. Still, you'd every good reason to remember *him*. And you see Mrs. Simpkin every day. So you may be right. Son, perhaps, or a brother much younger than her. . . . I can see why you're worried. It's another possible bit of trouble we could well do without. Only I don't think the people organizing this would want to harm Victoria. Left to themselves, I think they'd forget all about her. It's *he* that wants her included in the outing, when it comes. . . ."

Nevertheless, Helen made straight for her room the moment she got home, still feeling a core of anxiety for Victoria at the center of her thoughts. She threw down her coat, skimmed past Mrs. Simpkin, dourly knitting in the day nursery, and stood for a long time beside Victoria's small bed in the room beyond. Victoria looked, in sleep, as robust, positive, engaged with living, as she did awake. She slept with concentration, frowning slightly, one hand beneath her cheek. Little by little, Helen's apprehension died down. She kissed Victoria slightly, looked searchingly at Mrs. Simpkin (I am not mistaken. The likeness is very strong), and went back to tidy up before going to the other side of the house, to Carlo's rooms.

"Helen! I *am* pleased to see you." Henry Sanders was struggling with the wire guard on a champagne cork as Helen entered Carlo's sitting-room. In the light of the fire and one reading lamp he looked very large, tranquil and aboveboard; yet he must have been living in concealment, in continual danger, for at least three weeks.

"I was saying to myself: there they all are, enjoying themselves at Legations, so I will have a lonely little party on my own. . . . With this bottle of fizzy wine. . . . Which doesn't want to come uncorked. . . ."

Helen said: "I don't know about enjoying ourselves! It's been a fairly nerve-racking evening. This looks much more fun. . . ." There was a loud pop and H.T.S. dived for a low table where he managed to get a certain amount of the froth into a waiting glass.

"What they call a lively bottle," he said, mopping it and his sleeve with a large, clean handkerchief. "Have some."

"Will it go with Old fashioneds?"

"It had better," said H.T.S., "because we have a long evening ahead of us and no Bourbon whisky."

Helen took the glasses he offered her, and moved over to the fire. She looked at her old friend closely and with concern.

"Have you been all right?" she asked. "It must have been grim, hiding out all this time." Mr. Sanders looked shocked.

"Helen, please! I don't 'hide out.' I come and go . . . here . . . there . . . and—er—stay with friends. I keep pretty busy, really."

"But how can you? Ninety per cent of the people in this town are spying on each other."

"That's just it!" His voice was triumphant. "It's just that which makes it possible. Same principle as some kinds of conjuring trick—all worked out according to blind spots in the audience. We rather specialize in conjuring in my department."

"I wish I knew what your department really was."

Mr. Sanders had joined her by the fire, and together they looked down into the flames leaping yellow, blue and white from thin logs of birch. He looked across at Helen and lifted his glass.

"Good luck, my dear. I think the showdown is very close now. . . ." Helen's heart stopped, shook and went on again with a lurch, like a ship in a heavy sea. She could not reply.

"You want to know about my department? Well, the first thing is that it does not exist at all—on paper at any rate. Never has. Yet it's always been there, and always will be, if the whole world isn't blown entirely to bits. You might say it represents the conservative principle— and that has nothing to do with Tory politics, any more than patriotism has anything to do with Nationalism. We are a band of against-timers and putters of fingers in dykes. We go where we're needed. And we know that,

152

whereas failure can sometimes be permanent, success can only ever be temporary. In addition to which, by our very nature or lack of nature, we are outside the organized scheme of things, and so as likely as not to be hampered or unwittingly opposed by people on our own side. What it boils down to is that we are allowed to have first crack at certain very special problems—but we can never have the field to ourselves for long. For example, I fear that we are no longer the only people interested in the question of Mark Ogilvy."

Helen looked up sharply.

"You mean Rosencrantz and Guildenstern?"

"Yes. Their presence here would make me say that time was short, even if I hadn't other reasons for saying so. I've held the safety valve down for as long as I could, but I'm afraid that other eyes than mine have opened. Mark's been spotted. Something—I don't yet know what —has made someone else see him as a risk."

"Mort Landow!" Helen's voice was a whisper.

"Could be," said H.T.S.

Helen moved slowly across to the sofa and sat down close to the fire. Henry Sanders continued to stand, looking into his champagne glass, frowning. Clearly he was worried, but now no more than at any time in her experience of him did he appear uncertain. Whatever the outcome of the present troubles, whatever the nature of the showdown which, he had said, was near at hand, Helen could believe that H.T.S. would have foreseen it, that he would have plans ready to deal with it. Her own mind was giving her no comfort at this juncture. As in a house thrown out of gear by preparations for some great event, doors opened continually, lights went on and off; her thoughts scurried from place to place, searching, and not finding what they sought. One name kept recurring, Stoyan Anzip's. Helen remembered suddenly Mrs. Sidney's words: "He is wholly without scruples and as calculating as a money-lender. . . ." She made a litttle, involuntary gesture of bewilderment. Henry Sanders looked up.

"Tell me about Anzip," he said.

Helen gave him a frown and a smile at the same time.

"I'll need some more champagne first! H.T.S., I don't know how you do it! How did you know that I had something to tell you about Anzip?"

Sanders brought the champagne bottle and refilled both their glasses. The rings round his eyes were very dark this evening, the down-driving lines of his face deeply incised. His boxer look was pronounced, and there was a touch of guilt about it as well.

"Oh, Helen . . . you know how I like to keep an eye! And anyway, Stoyan Anzip is a key figure in all this, as you must have realized early on. But before we talk about him, let me go back to the beginning for a moment; to the time when you began to help, I mean. You didn't know it at the time, but Mark Ogilvy was then in London. That's how your picture came to be taken, by the way. I expect you've wondered how the INGRA people came to be interested in you so early on. They knew you were due at the F.O. that morning since—unlike myself, of course—" (and here he looked particularly guilty) "it did not occur to them that you might refuse to go to Senj. Taking your picture was sheer routine, part of their passion for fingerprints and files and checks and double-checks. Only, a little later, they must have got word that you were, or might be, something more than a nursery governess. Hence the snap decision to suppress you. Quite typical of them. Highly unpleasant for you. . . . By the way, you'll be sorry to hear we've lost Hargreaves." Henry Sanders' tone was gruff.

Helen felt a pang of misery, thinking of the quiet, brown man who had saved her life. Her throat swelled and she could only gasp, "Dead? No, *no!*"

"Afraid so. In Berlin. Doing something magnificent. . . . One of our best and bravest men."

Sanders always spoke telegraphically when he was moved. Helen, feeling the air run cold round her, could not say a word. H.T.S. shook his shoulders, a slow shrugging movement, and continued:

"Well, there you are. It happens from time to time, worse luck, our world being the stupid place it is. . . ."

154

He broke off and stood for a long time looking down at the toe of one of his large square shoes where it rested on the low steel fender. Then he quoted softly:

" 'For no one believes in joys,
    And Peace on Earth is a joke,
    Which, anyhow, telling destroys. . . .'

Humanity is afraid of joy, Helen. Offers it back to the scourge. Sticks out its neck for the halter. It's easier like that. . . . Joy takes guts, and experience, and a special kind of intelligence. It's so much simpler to break things than build them: to do without, to limit, to deny, than to receive and embrace and affirm. However, I'm wandering. We must get back to Stoyan Anzip. You saw him this evening? Then tell me everything that happened from the moment you arrived at that party."

Helen told, slowly and carefully, of her meetings with Landow and the INGRA men; described the fury of Luba Kassin; and gave, as nearly as she could manage, word for word her brief conversation with Stoyan. When she had finished, Sanders said:

"I must get word to Ilena tonight. This—this all fits in. I believe we are having some luck at last. Only, we must make sure that you are protected. Ilena will see to that."

"I am to go to Ostrány, then?" Helen's voice was level.

Henry Sanders looked at her for a long moment without speaking. His eyes were gentle. They seemed to be seeing far beyond that point in time, as though he were considering a Helen older by twenty years. He appeared to find satisfaction in this, for he smiled at her with a reassuringness so compelling that she at once felt safe.

"Yes, Helen. We ask you to go."

At this a strange lightness came over Helen till she felt she might float free of the sofa altogether. With it a vibrating thread of excitement laced her blood. Questions tumbled into her mind, too rapidly for her to formulate, so that she sat with her lips parted but did not immediately speak.

H.T.S. came and sat heavily, companionably on the

sofa beside her, and continued to speak looking across her at the fire.

"Anzip has been the principal contact between the various interested parties and Mark Ogilvy all along. It was to Anzip that Mark first disclosed his thoughts; and it was Anzip who made the preliminary soundings with the other side, and showed Mark how his intentions might be accomplished. Mark Ogilvy and Stoyan Anzip have been very close in this matter—probably closer than either has ever been to another individual in his life. For Anzip, too, is a lone wolf. . . . And not an entirely unsympathetic character, either, by any means—as you may have divined." Henry Sanders' voice, now, was neutral, almost monotonous, studiedly without inflection. "Ilena, of course, hasn't a good word for him, but that is largely a family matter. Anzip's mother was a Sideini, Ilena's first cousin, and Ilena regards him, primarily, as a traitor to the name. Also, being so uncompromising herself, she cannot forgive him his compromises, without which, of course, he wouldn't be where he is at present. For myself, I would say he is, principally, a gambler; and also a man determined to survive. I would say he is quite intelligent enough to know in good time if the game is going against him, cut his losses and go. What neither he nor any of them is proof against, of course, is the violent action performed on impulse, as the result of no process. It's this that's made Balkan and Russian politics such absolute gibberish to all of us for years. The incidence of sheer whim. The gratuitous act. Well, *you* know about that!"

Helen smiled a little wanly, remembering the Orient Express. Remembering also Stoyan as she had first seen him in Vienna, and trying to balance that image with the almost opposite picture he had presented this evening, she could find no intelligible middle point. Something ambiguous about her own feelings, something she could not bring herself to examine at present, made her take the offensive. Turning on the sofa to look squarely at H.T.S., she asked with irony:

"I wouldn't be being thrown to the wolves, would I?"

She was unprepared for his reply. With a small snort

156

of laughter Henry Sanders said: "No, Helen, you wouldn't. Quite the other way about. The wolves are being thrown to you! By which I mean," he added hastily, for fear she should have misunderstood him, "that I honestly believe Anzip's communications will be entirely political, and of very great importance to us at this moment. And if he should go beyond politics—why then, Helen, I know that, however you handled the situation, your handling would be right." He looked so pleased with himself that Helen burst out laughing.

"You'd have made a first-class Delphic oracle!" she said.

Helen's spirits had risen. She was beginning, in spite of herself, to look forward to Saturday. (And at least I shall see Ostrány, and it will be wonderful in the snow.) She felt hungry, and happy to be spending this time— secret time, not to be measured by ordinary clocks—with H.T.S.

They filled white-and-gilt plates from Madame Elvire's superb cold table and came back to eat by the fire. Another bottle was opened from the tub of ice where half a dozen were cooling, and Helen watched the leap and fall of the flames through the endlessly aspiring bubbles in her glass. Presently Henry Sanders said:

"There's one thing, Helen, we ought to talk about. I've never explained, and you've never asked, why anybody should go to any trouble to prevent Mark Ogilvy from committing the idiocy he has in mind. Oh, I know you know the obvious reasons—the vast propaganda value to the other side, their acquisition of secrets, the joy given to enemies at home, the shaking even further of American confidence in our security, and so on. But there are other agencies than mine which could take care of those things, given adequate warning. And, quite soon, those effects would wear off. . . . No, what matters here is that Mark Ogilvy is a really valuable human being, or could be in the right circumstances. . . . What he is contemplating is a form of suicide, only his is not a suicidal temperament. So he can't just take his own life. Nor can he cheerfully (or miserably) commit some misdemeanor, get involved in some scandal, which would get him flung out of the Foreign Service. Being who he is, he has to intellectualize his desire *to come to an end*—his instinct for disgrace. His sense of style (his conceit too, if you like) demands that what we see as his suicide shall be a step in a long process of reasoning which cannot be faulted on logical grounds."

"His mother gave me some clues—some of them without entirely meaning to, I think. He seems to have been unusually stupidly treated as a boy. Puffed up and let down with monotonous regularity."

"You are right. I know a little about Mark's upbringing. His mother was—still is—very beautiful, and had always been encouraged to think herself cleverer than she was. Mark was her only child, and I don't think she'd much wanted even one. Interfered with her being such a tremendous hostess. Such things existed then. His father was a brilliant fool, in the sense that he'd swept up every academic honor but, for lack of some essential common sense a duller man might have in plenty, never reached any height in the one career he'd set his heart on—politics. Well, being so clever and such an ass, he merely decided that he hadn't been, academically, quite brilliant enough—so Mark must do better. What a prospect for a boy!"

Helen's thoughts flicked back momentarily to Campden Hill, the calm rooms full of distinguished things, the harrowed, beautiful woman who was Mark's mother. She remembered a snatch of conversation when she had asked about Mark's father. She could hear again the pretty, precise voice saying: "They are so very much alike in some ways—more alike than Mark would wish to admit, I daresay. You know, if they had not been so striking-looking, and so good at things generally—my husband was a quite first-rate tennis player, and Mark is an excellent shot, although I think, now, he despises shooting—no, if they had not been so *unavoidable,* I believe they would have been tremendously unpopular—instead of only rather so!"

Helen felt an unexpected, maternal pang for the

pathos of a lonely, frowning, industrious Mark distorting his gifts to square quite futile circles. She said, vehemently:

"She's shattered now, his mother, and I can't say I'm sorry. She's much too intelligent, with all the self-deception, not to see what part she played in all this. But I strongly got the impression that the worldly side of it still matters most! Not what Mark's been through, or is going through, but what people will say. . . ."

"I'm afraid you're right. Well, there you have a general idea of the picture. Debating points in the nursery; every possible encouragement to win prizes, score off people, be precocious; and the kind of forcing treatment which will work wonders with a good intelligence coupled to an instinct for discipline. Purpose, but no pleasure. Wit, but never a joke. Approval, admiration—and no love. One doesn't have to be much of a psychologist to see what's lacking, has always lacked, for Mark Ogilvy."

"An inch or two either way and he could have been a monk, or a terrific delinquent."

"The latter, of course, is what he's been saving up to be. Now, there's one thing—I think he loves Victoria. At least he doesn't reject her. And the proof is that he's rationalized her into his schemes. She is to be saved from the horrors of growing up in the Western world. She is to be made heiress to historical inevitability. Do you agree?"

"I'd had the same idea myself. The day we went to the dancing display at the Ministry of Culture, I suddenly saw . . . But what I still don't quite see is why Mark has to go to this extreme. Could he not just have been one more disillusioned diplomat, famous for his dispatches and his command of French? He wouldn't have been happy, obviously, but he'd have been successful, and he seems to have been brought up to be that. Why, at an early stage of a rocketing career, does he have to pull the whole thing down on his head? After all, however bogus his parents' values were, I don't suppose betraying one's country was one of them."

159

"No, certainly not. And here, if we're going to start laying blame, we must partly blame the war. Mark, or a quite natural, boyish side of him, would have liked to be in the war as a combatant. This couldn't be, of course, so —like everyone else in that sort of situation—he overworked like mad. When peace came, or what we agreed to call peace, Mark's vision was squiffy with overwork, and he was already feeling done out of something—the chance to muck in with his generation, I suppose, to lose himself in the vast, friendly triviality of a war. Then you remember what a mess everything was for the first two or three years afterwards. Confusion, shortage, widespread bloody-mindedness, threats, screaming hysterics— no calm, no order, no pulling-together, no sense of having won anything, of having progressed an inch. Well, I suppose that Mark, with a terrific moral astigmatism, took what he thought was a long cold look at everything and found it hopeless, past improvement in its own terms. I imagine, also, that (being proud anyway, and accustomed to being right for far too much of his life) he didn't at all like the position he found himself in as a diplomatist. Foreign services in every country by then had come to loathe public diplomacy—politicians megaphoning at one another over the heads of the people who were trained and paid to do this sort of thing in private. This reduced their professional status and seriously hampered their work. I suspect that Mark was inclined to take this personally. After so much labor and discipline and deprivation, he did not take kindly to seeing his chosen career thus reduced, nor to hearing it slanged continually in public by every kind of axe-grinding ignoramus. . . . Helen, I'm sorry, I talk and talk, and you've probably thought it all out for yourself already. But there's so much to say!"

He got up and helped himself to another piece of chicken pie. Champagne, Helen found, was producing a high clarity in her thought. She felt wide awake, eager to continue for as long as might be necessary to understand everything. Tout comprendre, c'est tout pardonner; but

160

before Mark could be pardoned he had to be prevented. And there was so little time.

"It's a well-known thing," Helen said, "that people who are short of love in their own lives often have a great need to give love to others, if only as a way of getting some back. The late Mrs. Ogilvy—I suppose she wasn't much help?"

"None at all." Henry Sanders was emphatic. "Mark's love for her which, at the beginning (I saw for myself) was touching, transfiguring, simply didn't *take* on her. Victoria's birth made no difference either, although I think Mark liked the child from the first. Well, poor devil, she's all he's got."

"So now, I suppose," Helen said, pursuing her thought, "it's the human race in general that's going to come in for it. That's why Mr. Ogilvy is travelling eastwards. With his flair for discipline, and his rejection of his own world, he's off to sink himself in the one society which means to organize human happiness if it kills it in the attempt. And the—the treachery?"

"That will not have been difficult to rationalize. Don't forget that, with Mark, only the head is operating. The heart, if it isn't dead, is frozen stiff. Or . . . Helen, do you know Hans Anderson? 'The Snow Queen'?"

"Yes—and I know what you're going to say. Little Kay with a splinter of glass in his eye, and another in his heart." Helen began to laugh and, catching a gleam of slight apprehension in the limpid velvet-rimmed eyes, could only laugh the harder. She took a mouthful of champagne, choked, and went on laughing. Eventually she was able to say:

"And who, I wonder, is going to be Gerda? As if I didn't know!"

At this Henry Sanders began to smile, and shortly to shake with large, silent laughter. When Carlo came in, a minute later, cold, hungry, and far from cheerful, they were still laughing and, for a long time, could not tell him why.

161

Friday the 19th of December passed in a calm radiance, a musical spirit of relaxation which Helen was to think back on with longing more than once during the next few days. The blizzard had blown itself out and, beneath a delicate blue sky, a fresh covering of snow domed, eaved, gemmed and ruffled all solid objects, to make shining new and entrancing prospects under a white-gold sun.

Helen woke to the familiar hollow bang and scraping clash of shovels from the front drive and lay for a while considering the innocent appointments of her bedroom now lit with a blue-and-gold lucency which left no room for dark corners. She had gone to bed late, past one o'clock, after an exhaustive three-cornered conference with H.T.S. and Carlo. At the end of it, Henry Sanders had said:

"It's au revoir, again, Helen. This time I can't stay to see what happens. I'm off tomorrow. But you know what you're doing now and I know that, if we don't alter things for the better in the very near future, it will be through no fault of yours. So good luck to you! See you in London."

Carlo, although deeply interested in the most recent turn of events, did not disguise his anxiety on Helen's behalf. "Are you sure Ilena's people can keep her in sight all the time?"

H.T.S. had been a little impatient. "Look," he had said, "Anzip's not very likely—even being who he is and where he is—to pull out a gun and shoot Helen in cold blood, whenever they do happen to be alone together. At all times when they're moving about Ostrány, or travelling to and fro, someone of Ilena's will have them in view."

"Well, I think she ought to be armed."

"Don't be an ass, Charles. In all important respects she *is* armed!"

Helen had been, on the whole, relieved not to be saddled with the awkward potential of an automatic.

Friday morning was spent with Mrs. Clothier and Miss Hubbard, preparing lists of things needed from Vienna

162

for Christmas. The bulk of the things had some reference to Victoria, and it crossed Helen's mind that every outpost ought to be provided with a child for people to spoil and fuss over. Victoria makes a wonderful lightning conductor, she thought. I'm sure we get on each other's nerves so little, mainly because of her. . . .

At luncheon Carlo said: "Treat for you, Helen! You've been invited by the Ministry of Culture to go up to Ostrány tomorrow, with a party of Swedes and Finns, or Turks and Croats, or something. Mineralogists. Apparently, you'd expressed a wish?"

"Yes . . . yes I did, long ago. I can't remember to whom. . . ."

Martin said: "*I* can express wishes till I'm black in the face, but nobody thinks of granting them. Least of all the Fairy Luba! Well . . . you *are* lucky, Helen. Its a most lovely drive. . . ." His look was less pleasant than his words; there was anxiety there, and a touch of some sharp, restless emotion which might be jealousy.

"But what about the snow?" Miss Hubbard's voice was dramatic. "After last night, think of the drifts!"

"They'll get the road open pretty quickly; they always do, for their military stuff that's always moving up and down."

"No problem there," Martin said. "That's the great charm of a People's Democracy—always plenty of slaves."

"Well, bring us back some mineral water, dear—that's something we never seem to have." Mrs. Clothier was roundabout and vague in appearance, although not in fact vague at all. She was as untidy as Miss Hubbard was chic, seeming to trail knitting with her wherever she went; whereas Miss Hubbard was given to careful maquillage, earrings and a long cigarette holder and an air of being impatient to be gone. She was an eager listener, at all times, to Nigel Orde-Gibbon's tales of Paris.

Glancing down the table, to avoid looking at Carlo, Helen found both Maidment and Orde-Gibbon looking at her carefully, each in his different way. Maidment's mouth was slightly open and his eyes fixed in a frank stare. Orde-Gibbon, one arm hooked over the back of his chair, was gazing at Helen through the smoke of his cigarette from narrowed eyes. Something in the attitudes of both men proclaimed a more than usual interest in what was going on.

For some reason Helen was touched, all day, with a faintly valedictory feeling. This gave additional zest and point to everything she saw and did, sharpening her appetite for food, spurring her to write a few long-neglected letters, making her so good a companion for Victoria that the child's day was heightened, exciting, a kind of extra birthday, which found her at bedtime high-colored, sparkling, happily hysterical and unwilling to go to sleep.

Martin Wright's last words to her, as they said good night were: "Have a good time tomorrow, but do take care of your self. . . . We shall all be thinking of you. One of us won't sleep all day for worrying about you surrounded by mineralogists in all that snow. Desperate men they must be, to pursue their beastly science in the dead of winter!" He had also said: "Better be ready at dawn, Helen! Glumba ideas of punctuality . . . if they say they're coming at nine you may expect them at any time from five-thirty till noon."

In fact, a very large square-snouted grey car, almost a small bus, came crackling to a stop by the Legation steps at exactly eight-fifty on Saturday morning. From where Helen was waiting in the hall with Victoria, the car seemed to be quite full of men. Through the glass doors of the house and the car's steamy windows she could see the shapes of soft hats, with outlines of heavy spectacles and scarves. Victoria, earlier on, had shown signs of making a scene, of trying to restrain Helen from leaving her; but this mood had passed and, as the car snicked away from the steps Helen had a last glimpse of the small blue and white figure planted there, stoically waving, before Mrs. Simpkin darted like a black shadow out of the house to whisk her indoors. "Is too *cowld* out zere, Victoria!"— Helen framed in her own mind the guttural scolding, before turning to smile a little shyly at her travelling companions. Helen was in the front seat, beside the driver, and behind her on three rows of benches were eight men

164

all hatted, gloved and heavily wrapped against the cold. A number of friendly enough smiles came her way, and one voice said, "Good morning, Miss!"—but this was greeted with so many exclamations and gruff titters as to be evidently a lone sally, no part of a possible conversation. It seemed that the chauffeur had no English either; or, if he had, did not propose to sharpen it on Helen. With considerable relief she realized that she was going to be able to look ahead and enjoy the journey without interruption.

As they swung out of the Legation gates and took the snow-clogged tram-tracks with a swerve and wriggle, Helen was visited for a second with a most vivid, childish sense of holiday. The snowy world, the heavy warmth, the misted windows, the sound of foreign talk, the smell of mild cigars, all suddenly brought back her very first trip abroad, a visit to Switzerland with her parents when she was ten. That had been a time of pure rapture: success and failure in the ski-nursery, watched by her father; tobogannning, skating, long sleigh rides at night with lamplight and brisk bells, hot chocolate in warm, steamy tearooms—all with her father. Something, now, had brought back to her his physical warmth, his gaity and tolerance and delight in foreign things, his sensitive quick sympathy and compassionate kindness with herself. All this came back, but not in any way to make her sad; rather, Helen could feel, as she settled comfortably into her seat, prepared to miss nothing, that in a most positive and protective way he was with her; that, if he had ever been lost to her for a while, or mislaid, on this day he had returned, perhaps to stay.

It was the first time, since Helen came to Senj, that she had turned to the right, northwards, out of the Legation gates. Now they were bowling along at a fair speed with the Tvar to their left and on their other side, under snow-laden dark branches, the stone walls of villas beyond the Legation grounds. The city was beginning to come to an end, its older buildings petering out into high-walled wastes—some military dumps, some neglected industrial properties awaiting rehabilitation—and then into mar-

165

ket gardens, all black and white receding lines where live things were, under the snow. The tram-tracks finished abruptly with a terminus to one side of the road full of antique-looking small grey trams and knots of dark-colored people all, apparently, arguing fiercely. The straight road now curved away to the right, to the north-east, leaving the river which at the same time bent sharply westwards to hide its broken mirror-surface in the first wave of foothills.

Martin's information had been correct. As they jerked northwards again and the road began to wind up through thin pine woods Helen could see, from the high hedges of snow at the roadside, with their blocks and slabs tumbled one on another, that the road had been newly gone over with a snowplow. The surface was fairly even, with some fresh tire marks on it. At rare intervals they passed a big army lorry, dragging its dull green carcass up the unending hill in a cloud of oil fumes. Of human life there was nowhere any sign.

After an hour or so, they began to climb in earnest. The chauffeur shifted his position, sat slightly forward with a new alertness. The bends in the road were now sharper and more frequent, the intervals between them increasingly short and steep. The well-thinned woodland gave way to forest, something darker and more tangled, taller-seeming, which made its silence felt over the buzz and jingle of the car. Formalized, dramatic as a woodcut illustrating Grimm, long boughs of fir swooped low over the roadway and up again, each bearing a foot-high cornice, each flounced and scalloped with snow.

The talk at the back of the car continued with scarcely an interruption. It might have been technical, or political, or both, but whatever it was, it was intensely serious. Helen had no sense of a smile behind her head, and at no point did anybody laugh. Every so often some member of the party must have paid a small tribute to the scenery, for the discussion, so to speak, changed gear and there was a polite volley of grunting exclamations; after which the steady, low-pitched conference began again.

To Helen, listening with half an ear, the voices in the

car could as well have belonged to a party of bears, so heavy an undertone was there of growl and grunt. She had decided that these men must be Scandinavians, chiefly because of one who began all his sentences with "Unck," and she had once known a Swedish industrialist who had done the same. They could equally well have been Dutch, for the matter of that; and, again, equally well a body of local thugs, INGRA men, murderers, for all Helen could know to the contrary. The last thought, instead of depressing her, gave Helen a stab of exhilaration, and this obliged her to face the fact that she was greatly looking forward to seeing Anzip. And that, knowing very little about him, and nothing to his credit, she was serenely counting on him for protection.

At eleven o'clock they were still climbing under the frosted darkness of the fir trees but, by now, the high mountains were beginning to loom, to make themselves felt, like jailers beyond a closed cell-door. There was a touch of vertigo, now, in their progress as the car sped on upwards, more slowly, swinging a little to grip the snow surface with its chains. Helen had an impulse, which she resisted for form's sake, to grasp the handle of her door.

When they came out of the forest it was to follow the restless conformation of a mountain side above a sheer drop whose lower depths, dark as porphyry, showed the white vein of a river running through. Far back, far below, Helen could see, beyond black woods, the white plain of Senj, with the Tvar a pale blue snake across it. The mountains were crowding in now, towering into a sky of dirty sulphur. Distance had become deceptive, and the air seemed in some way to be thickening, acquiring a darker tone from the dark jade of the trees, the dull red and grey of the rocks still clear of snow. There was certainly going to be more snow, and plenty of it. Helen turned to the chauffeur, and back again to her corner, with irritation, realizing that it was useless to ask him how far they still had to go. She found herself suddenly impatient, nervously glancing at the sky, at the twisting road, sitting on the edge of her seat, willing the car to make Ostrány with all speed before the blizzard began.

They dived again into a pine forest, but now the road was level and straight as far as the eye could see, and now, at last, there were signs of human life. A lorry full of silent soldiers met and passed them on its way to Senj, the first vehicle going that way they had yet encountered. More soldiers were at work beside the road, repairing a telephone line which Thursday's blizzard must have brought down.

At once, and as if she had willed it into being, there appeared round a short bend, much battered and leaning sideways, but still largely legible, a blue-and-white enamelled sign of great size which said: "OSTRÁNY-LES-BAINS. HOTEL DU PARC 3 km." This message, so confidently bald—how had it escaped the zeal of the reformers which had thoroughly expunged all such cosmopolitan evidences from the city of Senj? Helen's heart was amazingly lightened, not only by the nostalgic charm of the notice itself, but by its mere existence as proof of an inefficiency which might yet leave room for hope. She was ready to sing for pleasure when, a minute later, round another corner, a second notice appeared, black and yellow this time, which, for all that it was patched with rust where the enamel had gone, said clearly enough: "HOTEL ZWINGLI PALACE 2.5 km. Près du Kursaal. Grand luxe. Golf—Tennis—Equitation—Piscine. R. Zwingli, Prop."

Helen hardly had time to savor the delicious implications of these notices, utterly incongruous with present time and place, banners of an ancient cult so proudly flying as scarcely to seem sad at all, when a military checkpost came in sight, its green-and-white diagonally striped barrier lowered to bar the road. If anyone wants to know who I am, we're going to have fun explaining! she thought. But, as the car slowed down, ready to halt and be challenged, the bar swung upwards to the vertical above a striped sentry box, and the sentry himself ran out to wave them on.

And now the whole character of the scene was altering. Wildness had gone, or at least been pushed to a safe distance. The pine woods still pressed close to the road, but

168

these were plantations, neatly spaced trees of equal height, showing light between their trunks. Although overgrown, in places tumble-down, open spaces, gates and once-white fences of post and rail still spoke of a passionate orderliness, a devotion to the spick and span which Helen found touching and reassuring. She realized how much of a castaway she had become in two months, that to stumble on this evidence of "human" habitation should move her so.

Hardly had the car got into top gear after the checkpost than the chauffeur changed down again and swung sharply across the road to the left. A lane of weedy gravel, scraped nearly clean of snow, gave a new sound to the chained wheels. They went into a shrub-crowded driveway through stone gate piers over which an arch of rusty iron still held, in cut-out letters, the name Hotel du Parc. The drive wound elaborately through close-grown shrubs, all dark and dolloped with snow, which magnified the noise of the engine. There was a feeling of expectancy, now, in the car, where Helen's travelling companions had fallen silent. They emerged with great suddenness onto a plateau of cleared gravel before what had once been the Hotel du Parc, and stopped, ungracefully, with a jerk.

The building which towered above them was of stone and wood, with jutting eaves and a gabled roof crowned with ornamental iron. It looked like an enormously overgrown chalet, and was much in need of a coat of paint. Helen had no difficulty in recognizing in it one of the strange, large buildings she had seen from the air that day which now seemed so very long ago. It could never have been beautiful, but its position was superb, with the ground dropping steeply away to a deep valley now swimming with dark vapor, with black forest climbing vertically to the iron outcrops and sheeted snow-slopes of a great triangular mountain on the other side; and away on either hand, other mountains of still stranger geometry diminishing like distorted icy echoes of the first as far as the eye could see.

The chauffeur was bustling the mineralogists out into the cold. With several shakes of his head and a stabbing

169

movement of his forefinger in the air, directed at Helen's lap, he had indicated that she was to stay where she was. Helen lit a cigarette and gazed at the view, noting how curdled and yellow the sky looked, pressed down on the great peaks in front of her. There it hung, heavy as destiny, the snow; but there was no wind, nothing to stir the mantled evergreens. Perhaps it would hold off long enough for her to get safely home.

The chauffeur, his face still completely wooden, and without so much as a glance at Helen, scrambled into his seat, started the engine, engaged gear, and slammed his door, almost all in the same movement. With a sharp spurting of gravel they were off. Helen looked at her watch, which showed a minute to half-past twelve. Clearly they were expected somewhere at the half-hour, or very soon after. They shot out of the gates and slid leftwards across the road in a long, controlled skid. The road ran straight before them for a kilometre: no vehicle, nobody was in sight. But Helen, from her glimpse of the Hotel du Parc, her knowledge of the presence of the car party and a few soldiers—and Stoyan—had constructed a tenantable Ostrány. Desolation lay behind her, her spirits had revived, and she was both curious and hungry.

A pair of tall gateposts, without gates, and topped with concrete finials made space in a thick wall of evergreens. The car went through, and immediately downwards in a series of sweeping curves through canyons of white and green, to emerge in a sullen amplitude of snow and lowering sky onto a terraced plateau where, seeming immensely long, the Kursaal stood shuttered to the iron day. In the centre of this low range of buildings—this stucco Trianon drawn out thin—a semi-octagonal bay, of great size, stood out, its tall windows rising from a surrounding flight of steps to a baroque cornice, above which hung, wetly gleaming in the neuter light, the dome of grey fish-scale tiles which Helen had remarked from the air. The driver, with a rapid succession of gear changes, put the car at the terraces of the Kursaal in a series of sharp, lurching turns. At the topmost level they ran straight along the garden front, so that Helen could see the windows frowsed with dirt, the starting wood-work, the paint in jagged flakes. Car tracks ran ahead of them through the deep-drifted snow. To their right were the shrouded tumuli of former gardens, the valley, the mountains rushing into cloud; to their left the dead palace of the wealthy ill; ahead the strange, dominating bay with its heavy, preposterous dome. At one of the tall French windows facing them, the shutters had been folded back, so that the glass was like black ice. The driver stopped near the steps and pointed upwards to this window. He remained seated, evidently expecting Helen to get out on her own.

After the dry fug of the car the mountain cold took Helen's breath away. She stood a moment, breathing fast, feeling the air, like iced water, numbing her lips and teeth. Cold stung her eyes, her ears, ached in her temples. She cast one rather desperate glance at the car, which was already turning to go, at the cold shoulders of the mountains, then climbed the steps, where they had been swept clean, noting the rough texture of their ochre stone.

Even when she reached the doors, and had her hand on one of the chased gilt handles, Helen still did not look up. Through the dark glasses she could see trousers moving towards her, square boots, the lower half of a grey-striped cotton coat. The door squeaked open, to let her in to a high, octagonal hall, floored with dusty boards, empty of furniture. Helen took in carved gilt pelmets with no curtains, a dirty chandelier of glass drops and china flowers, a ceiling painted with roses, fore-shortened urns and fuzzy clouds. The air was comfortably warm, and perfectly quiet. The short, burly manservant had a face of wood, deeply carved, with a fringe of black hair over eyes that seemed blind, they were so blankly ex-pressionless. He closed the door after Helen, with a quick, peering glance outside, then turned and, without saying anything, led the way across the hall to one of a number of high, narrow doors.

Stoyan Anzip was standing dead still beside an unshut-

171

tered window as Helen entered the small grey-painted room. He did not move at once, but bowed a little stiffly, his eyes direct and serious. Helen heard the door close behind her with unhurried finality and a sealing thud.

"Welcome!" said Anzip softly, barely opening his lips. He moved towards her without haste and put his hands on the back of a chair. Welcome to Vienna. . . . Welcome to Senj. . . . And now, Welcome to Ostrány. The clichés of tourism were not strong enough for their load of possibilities.

"I think it's going to snow again," was all that Helen could find to say.

Anzip nodded his agreement and, pulling out the chair he was holding, motioned to her to be seated. The room which had, perhaps, been designed as a morning-room, appeared to be in use as an office. Plain chairs were tucked round a baize-topped table; green baize notice-boards hung on either side of the low marble fireplace, where a bright fire burned. A gigantic hatstand stood just inside the door, and slime-green filing cabinets lined one wall. The room was very warm, and the quiet was absolute. Helen looked round her slowly as she pulled off her gloves, avoiding Anzip with her eyes, feeling hollow and strange and a little afraid. She noted, however, with approval, a table beside the fire loaded with plates and dishes, a brown earthern casserole over a spirit flame, two tall green bottles in a silver cooler. It had always taken a great deal to upset Helen's appetite.

Anzip's manner remained grave and watchful, his usually mobile face unsmiling. It was almost as though he were waiting for some sign from Helen. Not knowing what move, if any, to make, and suddenly vibrantly alert, Helen completed her movements with gloves and coat—throwing the latter back over her chair—while letting her eyes wander round the room with an appearance of mild curiosity. She was not going to be caught trying to force the pace. Anzip continued to stand with his hands on a chair-back, looking at her remotely, with a shadow of speculation, as though he were undecided as to what, or how much, to say.

172

When he did speak, it was only to say: "Let us, at least, eat!" After which, and as if glad of the chance to be busy, he shook out and threw neatly over the green baize a stiff white cloth, and went on to set the table with precise, economical movements. Of all the stages in Stoyan Anzip's metamorphosis since Vienna, this surprised Helen most, until she reflected that one in Anzip's position must be accustomed to looking after himself, and doing it well.

Helen repressed her instinct to be feminine, to take over the job of producing the lunch. Sitting still and regarding the proceedings gravely, she had Anzip at a slight, but possibly useful disadvantage. If he was aware of this, however, he gave no sign, and in a very few minutes was presenting the casserole to her with a slight swagger, stooping a little from his great height to hold it at the proper level on her left-hand side.

"Bourgeois tricks!" he murmured with a short, preoccupied chuckle. "How they come back to one!"

"Dare you admit that they come *back*? And don't you get terribly tired of that word 'bourgeois'?"

"Terribly!" he replied simply, helping himself and looking up at her with a brief smile. "But . . . words. These are not of importance. And it's a useful sort of shorthand. Or a password, rather. One is safe with it; or safer, at any rate."

The food was very good. The casserole had contained a salmi of game, and was followed by a cheese which, Stoyan said, was "a cheese of our mountains," in somewhat the same tone as he had used of the little dancer at the Ministry of Culture. We need to be loyal to something, Helen thought. It's just the terms of loyalty that get transmuted, not the thing itself. But she remained alert, behind an easy and uninsistent manner, for some revelation of the reason for all this. The metamorphosis of Stoyan, from the successful powermonger with a sideline in smash-and-grab sexuality, to this courteous, rather absent and sober gentleman, who could have belonged anywhere, to any settled situation, was fascinating and puzzling. Helen knew, or knew roughly at all events, why she was there, sharing a slightly old-fashioned upper-class

173

picnic in a deserted spa with this dark and, supposedly, dangerous man. But, from a touch of uncertainty in Stoyan's manner, and from his withdrawn look (as though in debate with himself), she could divine that there were more reasons than one for his presence. It must have been a long time since he could have allowed himself the luxury of ambivalence, of a divided wish. Or was he, simply, schizophrenic, whatever that might truly mean? If he were, though—if he managed his diffi- cult balancing act so brilliantly on the reciprocation of two totally different personalities—then, surely, the touch of doubt, of hesitancy, would not be there? Personality number two (reconstructed country gentleman taking his ease) would have been going full bat, without this gen- tle, thoughtful, almost anxious avoidance of putting a foot wrong.

The green bottles contained a wine pale green as birch- buds, with a just-ripe summery sourness less emphatic than Hock. Helen, after a couple of glasses, recognized that it was stronger than it seemed, but something, an ex- traordinary and unlooked-for *pleasantness* in the occasion. made her want to let go, enjoy herself, forget her mission and the really enormous danger she might be in. "Ilena's people," where were they at this moment, she wondered. She was pretty sure that the wooden manservant was not one of them. Supposing she were in a trap? Suppos- ing that all this—the quiet room, the warm fire, the good food, the agreeable and undoubtedly attractive man across the table—were just the preliminaries to her death? Whatever Ilena's people might do, they could in no circumstances prevent that. . . . And yet it was only in externals that the present scene differed from others in which Helen, in which every pretty girl since the begin- ning of the world had been a more or less willing partici- pant. The red flames sprang upwards, spent and renewed themselves in the marble fireplace. Cold wine stung the palate, combining elementally with the farmyard flavor of the cheese. Outside were snowdrifts, unregarding mountains, a world at odds with itself. Inside were warmth and quiet. The time was the present. It would have to be proved that political considerations had the power to override completely so much ancient, sure, unformulated magic.

Stoyan Anzip leaned gravely across to Helen and lit her cigarette from a heavy, old-fashioned gold lighter. Lighting his own, he lay far back in his chair, slipping forward a little on the seat and stretching his legs comfortably. The long cigarette, one-third cardboard tube, extended with its slim length the narrow length of his hand, so that the effect was of sensitivity refined almost to emaciation. Through a dissolving fan of smoke he caught Helen's eyes and held them, gazing at her gravely and still with an air of selecting in his own mind from a great mass of material something of especial weight and quality with which to begin. Helen, aware that this, at last, was "it," sat quite motionless, scarcely breathing at all.

When he spoke, in a low prosaic voice, a thin sword went through Helen. His use, for the first time, of her Christian name struck more sharply even than his first statement, which was startling enough.

"You are in bad company, Helen—you know that? There is blood on my hands, if you wish to think so. I have caused or, at least, I have not prevented, the deaths of many men." He paused, and Helen had to admit, simultaneously, shock and an extraordinary wish to excuse, to find justification for the fact, long suspected, now uttered by Stoyan as a truth. His eyes continued to hold hers, and she supposed he could read in them the starts and reversals of her thought. To her inward question: why does he have to tell me? Stoyan immediately gave an answer.

"I tell you this," he said, "so that you shall be under no doubt of the realities of a situation which is, I think, more foreign to you than it could ever be to one born, like myself, in the middle of Europe. And what is foreign to you is foreign also, whatever he may persuade himself, to Mark Ogilvy. And it is about him that we have come to talk." Helen noticed that Stoyan's English, under the stress perhaps of his sense of gravity, was becoming less polished. His face, she was cool enough to notice, had lost

175

the darting, animated look she associated with it, and had become sullen, brooding and marked by an almost pitiable fatigue. The dark eyes which looked into hers, looked also beyond her as if, in a rare moment of vision unconnected with action, Stoyan Anzip were indeed seeing far.

"You shall see me, Helen, put all my cards on the table, although I shall not ask to see yours. I know many things about you, apart from what my eyes and my blood have told me." Here he smiled, an oddly shy, apologetic smile, as if to beg her pardon for digressing. "I do not know quite who it was who sent you here, but whoever it was has all my admiration. He is very clever indeed, and clever in a way that makes the work of politicians and secret policemen seem a game of little children. Better than clever, in fact—for even monkeys are clever—really wise. . . . Helen, your side will not lose Mark Ogilvy. This I can tell you, although I do not think *he* could—not yet." Stoyan looked down at his hands, at the curving grey-black ash of his cigarette. His image wavered, receded in Helen's vision suddenly washed with tears. Relief, like a weight, dropped through her, leaving her empty and still. Stoyan's voice, level, reflective went on.

"There is still nothing to prevent him from going. The way lies open. At the other end they still have uses for him. The plan has not been cancelled. Only . . . he no longer wishes to do this thing with his life. His head, as I say, perhaps does not know about it yet. But the part of us that makes great decisions . . ." he offered the next word with diffidence, as though it were new to him, or half-forgotten . . . "the heart? This has decided for him—in the negative."

Helen swallowed twice and then said: "But what do you people care about that? Whose heart has ever been consulted in the world *you've* made?" Seeing his quick grimace of pain, she felt a vivid elation. He gave a bitter little grin, and said slowly:

"The heart, I admit, is a bourgeois organ. . . . It may be that, just the same, some of us are obliged to listen to it, however dangerous this may be—however inadvisable.

176

He—Mark—has listened. And now I, too . . . And this, Helen, is your doing."

A touch of an old irritation made Helen say sharply:

"That is ridiculous. Mark Ogilvy was found out, that's all—rumbled by his own people, long before it was time for the getaway. Somehow or other, he'd have been prevented. As for you, your circumstances are special. You've kept a footing very well, even I can see that, but it's probably been less difficult here than in other countries. You've probably still time to skip, start a new life somewhere else, if skipping seems a better idea than soldiering on. . . ."

Stoyan interrupted her. "You are wrong, Helen," he said gently. "I think that you believe what you say, but you are wrong just the same. Nobody, nothing in the world could have prevented Mark Ogilvy's flight, if he had continued to want it. The plan is foolproof, and depends upon no special circumstance. If he wanted it now, now this minute, he could be in the air within an hour. As is . . ." he looked at his watch, "your Mr. Gloag-Jones!" The mention of the politician's name made Helen blink, brought back to her the world of Senj, of the Legation and its problems, which had, in the intenser reality of this colloquy, become insubstantial, an airy back-drop to the action of her thoughts. In particular, the face of Gloag-Jones presented itself, pudgy, loquacious, with its elastic mouth, broad nose and black feathers of hair above owl-round, thick-rimmed spectacles; his perpetual "The point is . . ." and "I mean to say . . ." Mr. Gloag-Jones had been, as predicted by H.T.S., indisposed in the Hotel Olimpia for the past three days. Mr. Gloag-Jones, with his fears and flaws and hysterical sense of mission, was winging his way eastwards, a small traitorous frog near to the bursting-point of his self esteem.

"You can't speak of the two in the same breath!"

"As men, of course not. It was only of methods that I spoke. . . . No, there would never be a shortage of Gloag-Joneses. But they—the other side—are not, you know, so unsophisticated. They know very well the value of a Gloag-Jones—and of a Mark Ogilvy. No doubt which one would get the big welcome. It is still prepared. So that, when Mark does not go, there will be some very important angry people, both there and here. . . . Well, we shall see!"

Again a wave of relief which was like faintness went through Helen. It's all right! We've won! But (the thought saddened her, so that Stoyan, with an unpolitical pang, saw the corners of her mouth turn down) —it hasn't been my doing, after all. . . .

Curtains of heavy stuff, faded to the brownish crimson of old brick, caught some of the day's white glare and softened it as it fell. The fire muttered steadily, sometimes coughed and exploded gently in sparks as a log broke in two. The smoke of their cigarettes drifted upwards and dispersed above the comfortable disorder of the table, wooden plates pushed aside, piled with cheese rind and broken bread, white butter in a thick green crock. Three times since the day it all began, the same thing had happened. First in Mr. Sanders' office, then in Mrs. Sidney's fantastic hideout, and now here at Ostrány, the whole inchoate, menacing, incomprehensible situation had been brought to the sharpest focus, its complications narrowed to a single point of truth. And each place had had a quality in common with the others, in that all were comfortable, all concealed from the world's eyes, and all apparently empowered to abolish the normal sense of time. It was, Helen recognized, not really the places themselves which held this magic, but the personalities who had planned them. People were at work here who had the power to impose their own view of the truth and their own civilized preferences of the world in which they found themselves. Against a minority so intelligent and so sure of itself, the majority must always come off worst in the end: provided that the minority's members never lost touch with one another. This was their greatest danger, and this the area where their real battle lay.

Helen sat up very straight, tilted her chin and looked slantwise at Stoyan Anzip. He saw her hands clasped lightly on the table in front of her. She appeared to be seeing through him. Something in her extreme stillness, her listening look, made him restless. He leaned towards her, as if eagerly, in swift reaction from his former indolent pose. His eyes, full of black fire, were no longer the eyes of a conqueror, but almost boyish, dazzled, and with a hint of supplication in them. He sought to catch and hold her glance, to give strength and admit weakness, and to ask the same of her. But Helen, in a rapture of thought and insight, with brain and intuition for once hand in glove, saw him and saw beyond him, so that he was only one figure in a moving frieze, one element in a composition now rapidly building to its final form, to the shape in which history would know it.

"Helen. . . ." Stoyan's voice was low and without resonance. "Mark Ogilvy is not the only one to have changed his mind."

At this Helen looked directly at Stoyan, calmly and speculatively, as if she had known what he was going to say, and could guess what he would say next. She said nothing, and Stoyan continued, his voice growing flatter, with the very tone of exhaustion and defeat.

"I think we need not pretend any longer that you and my Cousin Ilena are not friends. Ilena—whom, strangely enough, I love—will not have spoken kindly of me to you. Which is not quite fair—although, why should she be fair? She is much older than I am, and a fighter at heart, and her whole life's work has been destroyed by the Revolution. Whereas, for me—well, if I wanted to have a life's work in my own country, then I had to accept the Revolution, stay with it as best I could, and see what might happen."

Helen, with a slight widening of her eyes, and a forward movement of her head, encouraged him to go on. Straining her inmost ear to catch the least flaw of insincerity or falsehood in his recital, she could detect nothing that did not seem to her true. She was amazed that pride could be so put off, like a coat, leaving a nakedness which might be a better kind of pride.

"I told you before that I had been responsible for the deaths of many people; and this is true. I am sorry. But I should like you to believe that I never planned or be-

179

gan a process against anyone, to lead to his death. Yet I have had to—to acquiesce in many deaths. This way I paid to survive. And I could not see that it would help if I did not survive; whereas it—just possibly—might help, if I did. Ilena, of course, would spit on me for this. She would say: honor. But . . ." he touched his eyes at their outer corners with thumb and second finger, a gentle pinching movement, "I don't know. Sometimes I think that honor is like the queen in the chess game: a valuable piece, a precious piece, but one which it is sometimes necessary to lose, because the checkmate can be better made with a few more ordinary, less glorious pieces, and the queen attracts danger. . . ."

Stoyan, whose glance had dropped to the tablecloth during this speech, looked up at Helen a little blindly, and with a small, sweet, hesitant smile like a child who asks reassurance. Helen could not afford the least movement towards him in return. All of her was listening. She had to get the sense, and the inner sense, of this—and get it right. Stoyan looked down again and went on:

"I knew, you see, that what had come, had come to stay. Oh, and we're very lucky still—in this country. Because it is small, and has its curious history and geography, and not many things of immediate value—no great industrial complexes, no urban proletariat to be remade and used—we have had not much more to contend with than a shift of power inside our own walls. With all the cruelties and stupidities that go with it—oh, yes, indeed—but on a smaller—" he laughed, a sound like a dry cough—"a more *human* scale. When one thinks of Hungary, or Rumania, or Poland, or the eastern side of Germany, then one is glad to have anything that is less than what they have; even though one knows that one day, before very long, we shall have that too. . . . *They* do not sleep. And they do not mean to fail." He was silent for some seconds, his hands a lathe turning an unlighted cigarette. When he spoke again his voice was quite dead, and the eyes which looked at Helen were seeing a precise and hideous future. "One day soon, they will begin with us in earnest. And then, from being still, a little bit, the comic-opera part of their empire, we shall not be comic at all. On that day, or on a day soon after, Ilena will lose her life."

Helen's indrawn breath made a small sob. "You mean they will shoot—kill her immediately?"

Stoyan frowned. "They will have to. She will go to war. It is like this, Helen. These mountains where we are now, with their good forests and rich valleys, belonged always in a very special way to Ilena's—why shouldn't I say it— to *our* family. Now, in all countries under foreign domination there is the possibility of a rising; and it is usually the first care of the invaders to prevent such a possibility. For some reason, partly because of me, I think, they have been, in this country, not so thorough, not—you would think—so afraid as usual. Almost careless. The people of these mountains, although ruined and without future, are still doing much what they have always done, farming and foresting, and they have kept their family feeling and, especially, the authority of the old over the young. Everywhere else, in the towns and villages, things are different. The young have their lives to lead. One must not expect too much. If there is to be a rising there, it will be a rising of the old, whose lives no longer matter. But in these mountains, if the old and the middle-aged decided to fight, very many of the young will fight with them. And the old and the middle-aged are Ilena's to a man."

"But it will be horrible! They cannot succeed, however many there are of them, however brave."

"However many there are could never be enough. Not to win. Not to decide anything. All the same . . ." Helen, with a sense of relief, saw that his eyes had come alive again, that he was considering a picture which he could admire. "All the same, this is difficult country, and it is their own, and they know it perfectly. They would hold on, skirmish, annoy for—oh, quite a long time. They would cost a colossal effort to smash, and perhaps, while this was being prepared, some little bit of luck might make it important to our masters what the world— *your* world—thought, and so some good might be done. One cannot see so far. But this is certain, this one thing.

181

Ilena will do this, if she sees the need, and nothing will prevent her. And she will be right. She will follow her own logic, and she will be right."

Helen flopped back into her chair. The lovely movement of abandon, from recording angel to inattentive child, made Stoyan clench both fists sharply, as if to catch something too quick for him, but Helen was not looking. She felt irradiated by a glowing sense of rightness, and peaceful with the peace of total surrender. Excitement ran right through her, sharp-edged and searching as the pleasure of love. It was as if her blood had turned to gold. Her surroundings became at once actual in the extreme, so that she could feel, she could almost *be,* the texture of the curtains, the worn, splintered wood of the floor, the streaking ribbons of heat in the fire, the locked-in savors of food and wine, the blue-white surgical delicacy of the light, the haunted, hunted integrity of the man who looked at her so curiously. In all this a thought struck her mind and glanced off into the bright haze of her revelation: he wants me, and he wants to live. . . .

Stoyan leaned forward. "What did you say, Helen? What was that you just said?"

Helen was unaware that she had spoken aloud. She raised her eyes to Stoyan's, which were brilliantly alive now, and murmured dreamily:

"I think . . . something his mother—Mark's mother—said to me before I left home. 'History is the sum of our private lives.' I do not know if she was quoting."

"I am beginning to believe that it is true. But," his voice was strong once more, and touched with an ironical inflection, warm and teasing. "I think we will have a little difficulty in persuading our friends in Moscow of this!"

With their shared laughter, the last hampering bonds were broken. Elbows on the table, they gazed at one another with the utmost friendliness, as people do who have lived through a testing experience. Stoyan opened a fresh bottle of wine, and they drank with a touch of solemnity, as though giving thanks. Helen said:

"I have no right to be so cheerful. From what you have

182

told me it looks as though the future contained nothing but death and disaster for Ilena, for many good people—perhaps for us as well."

"Well . . . death is perhaps not always the worst thing." Where had she heard that before? "Except as *they* practice it—" his look was heavy, embittered again for a moment. "For them it is expediency, a prescription, the routine treatment for certain symptoms, the last word in an argument they mean to win. . . . Et moi, j'ai été complice!"

His wretchedness, which rang true to Helen, threatened their communication. To turn his thoughts Helen said, "Stoyan, what did you mean when you said Mark Ogilvy wasn't the only one to have changed his mind?"

"Only that I have changed my own. I cannot continue here. I must give Ilena best, and admit that I never should have attempted, even, what I have tried to do."

Helen felt a throb of anxiety. She could hardly find breath for her next question, which seemed desperately important.

"You're not suspected yet? No one knows this they? What will you do? Will you just go away? Soon?"

Stoyan compressed his lips and narrowed his eyes in a smile of great gaiety.

"What a lot of questions, all at once! You almost make it sound as if you minded what became of me!"

"Don't fish!" Helen said childishly. "Please just tell me that it's all organized, that you'll be all right." Stoyan's look changed at once.

"I shall be all right. I promise you," he said gently, "but please—what is 'fish'?"

"Oh—you know!" Helen was impatient, "fish for compliments—make people say nice things about you."

Stoyan looked at her for a long moment. There was admiration in his eyes, and a kind of distant considering which reminded her of H.T.S., as though Stoyan too were looking into her future with approval. He gave a short sniff of amusement and said:

"One thing I feel certain you have never done, Helen.

183

Fish for compliments, I mean. And yet . . ." he paused, looking suddenly sad, "and yet, Mark Ogilvy's decision and my own are both, in their way, compliments to you. Not fished for . . . but earned!"

Here it was again. The something which others seemed to know about her, which she did not. The reason why Henry Sanders had sent her to Senj. Only, this time, Helen felt no exasperation. She looked briefly at this enigma which lay at the centre of her personality, like a stone in a pool—looked and let it lie. Her eyes were on Stoyan's face, and it would have been hard for her to look away. Not long before, she had watched this face with hostility, and had seen much to criticize. Now, drawn and preoccupied as it was, and rid of its presumptuous mask, every line and plane was satisfying. Her body dreamed of him as he sat there, slackly elegant, unselfconscious, deep in thought. A self of hers moved towards him, although Helen did not move; a projection of herself, proud and a little afraid, but ready—if things were right—to comfort and be comforted. Without any special intention, but because sitting still was suddenly impossible, Helen jumped up and, with a quick stumbling step walked past Stoyan to the window and stood looking out, one hand grasping a thick fold of the curtain. At once, and as if on a physical reaction of politeness, Stoyan sprang up and came over to stand close by, looking out at the terrace.

It could be seen that the weather was worsening. The sky seemed lower, more yellow in color, and a leaden haze began where the terraces ended at the valley's edge. To their left a thick wood was purple-black, dappled above with white, a white blur without life or glitter. Untrodden, smoothly contoured, the snowy terraces ran down and away from them. Shrubs stood still under their cusps and cornices of snow, looking sculptured and permanent as tombs. From the tumbling of her thoughts Helen brought out something to say. She quoted softly, in a voice that sounded choked to her own ears:

"Frozen, immobile the earth: the rocks are ice
And porcelain the flowers. . . ."

184

Stoyan turned to her the face of a dreamer, but with a look of hesitant, sleepy recognition. He said—and his English was suddenly, noticeably much worse:

"But—but this is a poem of *my* country! This that you say is a—what is it?—translation. . . . Say, then, some more!"

"The trees blown gems of glass:
No bird or beast that is not frozen stiff
Here where it hunted or made love or sang.
Over much ground broken or fouled by men
Lies deep the peace and pity of the snow."

Stoyan cried: "But that is it! Vasnović! Our national poet of last century. Vasnović!" And in a deep, steady voice he repeated the poem for her in his own language. The strict, lilting rhythm, the rushing gutturals and sharp vowels of the original made a musical completeness which Martin Wright's translation could not reproduce. When he had finished, Stoyan looked down at Helen with an expression of pleasure and gratitude, and wonder as if at a gift. It was as though two people had suddenly discovered that they had played together as children.

"Vasnović!" he said again, laughing. "Oh Helen, but I wish you could see him in a picture. He had—what is the word? My English is quite going—*huge* facial hair!"

At this, and before she had laughed even a little at his way of saying beard, they were in each other's arms, and the world had gone.

When Helen woke she said, "Victoria!" on a tone of such anguish that Stoyan who had been quietly watching her sleep, gathered her into his arms, and shook her gently, to dispel the clouds of a bad dream. . . . After their first kisses they had wandered, floated almost, full of elation, through the maze of the Kursaal. Sure of them both, and gleefully in command, Helen had insisted on a thorough exploration, teasing, procrastinating just this side of danger, her instinct making her put off a little the

185

conclusion they both so wished. At one point Stoyan had given a long and careful instruction to the expressionless manservant, who had then disappeared, looking unusually brisk, by one of the many identical doors.

Everywhere they went, the past sprang out at them or nudged them with gentle wistfulness; and the present lay untidily upon it, adding to the litter but producing no real change. Here and there they opened stiff-hinged shutters onto rooms and galleries still furnished and arranged as though no more than waiting through the winter for the season to begin. Elsewhere, the rooms had been stripped of carpets and curtains, and crowded with stacked chairs of a school-room pattern, or piled with crates and boxes bearing marks like military stores. Everywhere the chandeliers and wall-lights remained, their ormolu furred with dust, their lustres dull as dry pebbles, making aërial palaces for spiders. They found that, in some parts, the electricity was still working, and amused themselves illuminating one decaying vista after another with weak, watery radiance which turned the daylight at the shutters' edges white as ice. They peered into pantries, storerooms, wine-cupboards, fingered the dust on the great tomb-like reception desk in the pillared hall, discovered with exclamations of awe a whole range of bathrooms and massage-rooms, festooned with complex piping, wheel valves and dials. Through these they hurried, being both momentarily chilled by their associations. Clinical efficiency had been too lately, too foully, misused; the marble massage-slabs had too much a mortuary look. But nothing damped their spirits for long. They were contemplating a race down the garden gallery in bath chairs of high ingenuity which seemed to have been left standing just for this, when the small figure of the manservant appeared at a far door to announce their destiny. Helen's heart had struggled in her breast as Stoyan turned to look down at her gravely, and to take both her hands. "It is ready, Helen," he had said. "We may go up now. But Tadusz must lead us because, for me, I am quite, quite lost!"

Tadusz had led them immediately, and to Helen's gasping surprise, into the Grand Pump Room, the very heart and shrine of the whole place. An immense, circular hall, floored with black and white mosaic, with tall thin pillars of cast iron supporting a glass ceiling, held in its centre a solid circular counter of mahogany, carved at its edge, and panelled along the sides with yellow marble, encircled at its foot by a thick brass rail now black with dirt or green with verdigris. It was all like a splendid East End pub, even to the engraved glass panels of a kind of overmantel which towered up in the middle of the bar, each section with its spindly pillars still full—and this was curiously touching—of bottles of mineral water shaped like Indian clubs. Above these again a marble version of Ingres' "Source" stood among the leaves and tendrils, the water-lily heads and frilled glass shades of an electrolier in gilt wrought iron. A lowering tomb-light fell through the green-and-yellow lily-patterned glass of the roof, reminding Helen of the Hotel Olimpia. The floor was scattered with paper, shavings, untrodden dirt. An old bird's nest and a recently dead mouse lay near the door. Tadusz' footmarks could be seen clearly, a splayed leaf pattern leading to the opposite side of the hall. In her strung-up state, Helen had senses for everything and nothing. Later, she would be sure that on the breathless air there hung the faintest discernible ghosts of old patchouli, of once perfect cigars. From the down-turned marble pot held by the naked girl above the bottles, which had been so placed as to allow its waters to run down an artificial rock-formation which still showed the brown stubs of ferns, there fell a whispering trickle of water, so feeble it did no more than slime the rocks below. But in the total quiet of this forgotten place the stream, which had laid a crust of sulphur at the pot's rim, made a clear and musical small sound, as though glass were being rung with a stick some distance away.

They had shaken their heads, as if unwilling to consider the implications of so extraordinary a place; as though they had too much history on their hands to undertake an assessment of this machine-age Pompeii. Hand in hand, they followed the wooden figure of Tadusz through the farther door, and up a narrow winding staircase to an upper story. Here, once again, the manservant had shut them, sealed them in to a place where they could be quiet. They were in the dome itself. Two low-ceilinged white-panelled rooms had been rapidly, efficiently dusted. A new fire was just taking hold in a deep brick hearth. A great white bearskin beside a low, wide bed suddenly brought back the Legation to Helen—her room, her friends, Victoria. For an instant she stood doubtfully on the threshold, crumpled inside with fright, frozen with all the possibilities she had, till then, refused to consider. Stoyan, who had been stepping capably about, rearranging this and that, testing the bull's-eye windows for drafts, turned suddenly and seeing her standing so, had crossed the room in two strides to take her by the shoulders.

"Helen!" he said, and the strength from his hands was already calming her. "Helen, don't tremble so! Look—these were the director's rooms. He was such an important man, quite round like a cheese; I can just remember him. . . . Helen, you do not think—you are *not* to think—that I planned all this? That we are here is grace, and fortune, and my good Tadusz. Let us, then, be happy, for we have not long. . . ."

Now there was only the glow of firelight on the white walls. The small windows, curtainless, were ovals of darkness, but of a darkness which stirred continually. Every few seconds a white feather hit the pane. It was snowing again, and hard.

Blinking at Stoyan's dark, anxious face bent over her, Helen came slowly back to life. She did not know that she had cried out, only that waking was painful and that she would like to go to sleep again. She forced herself to stay awake, however, and smiled at Stoyan, reaching up to touch his shoulder. Something softly sharp tickled her bare arm, and she saw that the white bearskin had been spread over the bed while she slept. Following her glance Stoyan said:

"You have slept for two whole hours. When the snow

came it began to be very cold, so I put the old bear on top of you!"

"Two hours!" She saw that Stoyan was wearing shirt and trousers, but no shoes. "Did you sleep too?"

"I couldn't. I had things to think about. And I had to look at you to see what there was there which could explode my whole life. . . . But all I saw was a girl in her love-sleep, and so I was none the wiser. . . ."

Suddenly flooded with cheerfulness, Helen said saucily: "A sight you're perfectly used to, I have no doubt," and then, seeing Stoyan's expression, wished that she had held her tongue. She put out her hand again, swiftly, to touch him, reassure him, take the bitter regretful look from his face. She smiled at him and said, "Sorry!" Nevertheless when, a little later, they were sitting beside the fire, by the light of two candles, with a bottle of champagne which the admirable Tadusz had found for them somewhere, she could not help asking:

"Why did you look at me like that, the first time you saw me, in Vienna? Enough to scare any ordinary girl out of her wits!"

Stoyan made a grimace of impatience, perhaps of self-disgust. "Well," he said, "there are three answers to that, I think. In the first place, I have this curious and perhaps not very safe position to maintain, somehow, and such ways of behaving are a part, a useful part, of what you would call the 'build-up.' In the second place, my poor little Helen, you are not an ordinary girl. This may even not be a good thing for you, although I think it will, in the end, be very good. And, in the third place, paste and diamonds are indistinguishable at a distance. One has to have expert knowledge, and the chance of a closer look! . . . But it is useless, anyway, to speak of any time but now. This, now, is a high moment of my life—I do not say of yours. When I am with you I am better than myself. Voilà tout!"

Too full of well-being to be vulnerable, yet, to the future, Helen drank her cold, prickling drink, and looked from the fire to Stoyan's fire-shadowed face, to the reflection of the candle flames in the window's black mirror.

Her watch said six-thirty. They would have to be going soon.

On the heels of her thought, Stoyan said: "When we have had some food which Tadusz is inventing for us, we shall have to go back to Senj. . . . I tried to get a message to your Legation, to say the snow had delayed us, that we might not get through . . ." he looked diffident, rather guilty, as though he might have presumed too much, "but *of course* the lines are down. One little breath of wind, one little piece of snow, and piff, paff! down come the telephone lines! So now, we shall have to go back, or else your Minister will have the army out looking for you!"

"But shall we get back? When it snows in your country it really snows!"

"It's really snowing now, I can tell you. But yes, I think —I fear—that we shall get back. Tadusz has had a word with the locals"—Ilena's people? Helen wondered rather anxiously—"and they say this first storm will blow itself out about eight o'clock, and that there will then be two hours or so before it begins again in earnest. Men are waiting with a snowplow to make a way for us the moment the snow stops. Others will follow in case we should get stuck." He gave Helen a melancholy smile. "These, you see, are the advantages of my political position. . . . The first time that they have helped me to anything I really wanted. Well, one day quite soon I shall no longer care. It will be a new life. . . ." He turned his melancholy like a coin in the candlelight, and showed a shining side of it. His moods changed so swiftly, each seemed only an aspect of the other. Helen saw his face momentarily quite smooth, boyish, carefree. She felt immensely much older, and as if responsible for Stoyan's safety.

Partly for her own comfort Helen asked, hesitantly: "There's no danger of anyone knowing about this— about today, is there? It would hardly be safe for either of us." She was remembering the contorted toad's face of Luba Kassin on the night of the American party. Stoyan laughed.

"There is one who would work hard to see that I lost

my famous political advantages, and everything else too, in the most painful way possible, if she ever even suspected that you and I had loved each other." Helen, beneath the warmth of her contentment, felt the cold blade of fear. "But she will not know."

"You are sure, Stoyan? What about Tadusz, and the men who will go with us tonight? Don't forget I came up here in one of Madame Kassin's cars, on one of her cultural jaunts. She must know about that."

"Oh, she knows you're here, all right. But me—she thinks I am in Vienna. And as to your returning by another car, at a later hour: all that, I promise you, is taken care of. Don't forget I have nearly as much experience of secret movements as she has! As for Tadusz, he is *my* man; and the others, they are trained not to ask questions and to see as little as possible, where their party leaders are concerned. Please, Helen, do not be worried. There will be many *ennuis,* perhaps even dangers, for us both after this. But just now we have some hours that are all our own. And look! Here is Tadusz with our dinner."

It was just past one in the morning, and snowing hard, when the same blunt-nosed grey car with Helen alone beside the driver turned into the Legation drive. Stoyan's organization appeared to have been perfect. After a frequently hair-raising descent from Ostrány, with the snowplow sending up a whirlwind of gold sparks in their headlights, they had turned off into a narrow loop-road five miles from the city where this car had been waiting. At the end Stoyan had kissed her on the forehead. His kiss still burned there. He who was usually so articulate had not been able to find words. He had turned abruptly away to be lost in the darkness of his own car. The metallic slam of its door still sounded in her ears.

Light streamed widely from the Legation out into the glittering downpour. Every window in the building was alight. Panic seized Helen. Was there—could she have forgotten—a party, a reception, something arranged for the visiting delegation? Two cars, dull green staff cars with military chauffeurs, stood under the portico. Figures

191

moved across the upper windows where curtains had not been drawn. She crouched to squint upwards at the top floor. There were people moving in her room, in the nurseries beyond. Before the car had stopped, Helen knew that this was no reception; that something was seriously wrong.

She sprang up the steps, and was through the doors and into the hall in what seemed one bound. The house was full of the sounds of movement; voices buzzed in distant rooms, or came loudly in gusts of sound as doors were opened. Carlo was coming down the stairs with a stranger, a thick-set army officer in breeches and field-boots. Each was keeping as close as possible to his own side of the staircase, and speaking stiffly across the gap between.

When Carlo saw Helen burst through the doors and stand tense, staring up at him, his manner altered. Stiffness went from it, and he ran down the remaining stairs, leaving his guest to follow at a more stately pace. When he reached her he put his hand on her shoulder and gave her a tired smile. He looked anxious and ill.

"Helen!" he said, "thank goodness *you're* all right. I was beginning to think I should have to worry about you too. Helen, Victoria's gone. Kidnapped. Mrs. Simpkin's gone as well."

The patterned pavement of the hall, the green staircase, the clustered lights all began to slip sideways, sideways and round, up and over, faster and faster. Helen's stomach contracted viciously; cold vomit burned her throat. Carlo's voice reached her muffled and far-sounding, as through water. Then she felt his strong grip on her elbow, his arm round her waist. The scene steadied and came to rest, although now the light seemed leaden, all colors sullied and drab. She was looking into opaque small eyes, a pitted, bristling, confident soldier's face with a mustache like a strip of fur. If the face had any expression, it was one of slight contempt.

"Major Zradkin," Carlo was saying, "I must ask you to excuse us. This is Miss Clark, who looks after Victoria.

192

She has had a shock, and now she needs a drink. May I expect to hear from you in the morning?"

An unemphasized sneer lifted one edge of the strip of fur.

"So? Looks after, you say? And yet, you say the little girl is gone. Where was Miss Clark at the time?"

Helen could not even open her lips, which were stiff and trembling and cold with sweat, so perfectly had Major Zradkin expressed her own agony. Carlo's voice was sharp.

"No possible blame can attach to Miss Clark in this matter," he said with a stern finality Helen had never heard from him before. "Now, if you will excuse us? Or . . . may I offer you something before you go?"

"Thank you no. I, at least, have work to do. I shall telephone you in the morning, by which time, of course, a quite rational explanation will have been found for this . . . 'disappearance'!" A quick bow, a sharp concussion of the field-boots, a final glance of unveiled dislike, and Major Zradkin was gone. Helen heard his staff car go off like a rocket, roaring and jangling, as Carlo led her into the little morning-room beside the hall.

It was the same white-and-gold room where Helen had first talked to Victoria, and it was haunted, as was every room in the big house, by the child's presence. "A little bed and a big bed and a bear on the floor!" A bear on the floor . . . a bear on the bed . . . Oh, my baby, what have I done?

Carlo closed the door and gave Helen half a tumbler of neat brandy. She needed both hands to raise the glass to her lips; her teeth chattered on its edge. Carlo kicked the fire to a blaze and piled on logs, but for a long time Helen could feel no warmth.

He left her in peace for a few minutes, while he pretended to be busy with some papers at a desk in the corner. Finally, he came over and stood leaning an arm on the chimneypiece, looking down at her very kindly.

"There," he said at length, "you're thawing out. No sense in talking till you're ready."

Helen nodded quickly several times and whispered, "I'm ready. Please tell me what happened."

Carlo gave a great shrug, and frowned. "None of us knows, that's just the trouble. Victoria went out for a walk with Mrs. S. this morning, when it wasn't snowing. They went to her favorite place—you know—the little park with the bandstand. Came back all right. Victoria played all afternoon in the nursery, or so we thought. She was due for tea with Jean Hubbard and Dolly Clothier in their rooms at half-past four. By five, when she hadn't turned up, they began to wonder, and Jean went up to the nursery to see what had happened. Found the night nursery door locked, and couldn't get an answer, so went round through your room to the day nursery. That door was locked, too. No response to knocks and shouts. . . . Well, Jean's not one to panic, but she went and dug up Martin, who found Tubb, and together they went over the whole place, outside as well. There was just a possibility that Victoria, who has the strength of ten, might have persuaded Mrs. Simpkin into a hiding game. Not a sign of them anywhere. By now, it was about six o'clock. Martin came to me, and a state of panic was declared. I gave Tubb permission to force the nursery door. . . . God knows what ghastly thoughts were in all our heads. You can imagine—only don't! Whatever's happened is better than that. Must be. I'll explain why in a moment." He paused, and Helen cried, "Go on!" furiously. Carlo said, hurriedly, "The rooms were empty. Perfectly tidy. No one there. But Victoria's little travelling bag and a lot of her clothes were gone, including all her warm coats and leggings. . . . So it looks if, wherever she is, she'll still have Mrs. Simpkin. And that's about the only comfort in the whole bloody business."

Slowly at first, then in a blinding flood, Helen's tears ran down her cheeks, which felt not cold but paralyzed forever, incapable of further expression. Carlo watched them fall a little while, then slowly tendered a large white handkerchief. Helen dabbed, and blew her nose, snuffled and blew it again, dabbed and felt steadier.

"God!" she said, "I must look terrible." Carlo seemed relieved.

"That's a girl," he said, and added awkwardly, "Terrible—that you could never look. But shattered—yes. Now, Helen, listen. None of us is going to rest until Victoria is found, and that goes for Mark Ogilvy too, in a big way. He's absolutely distracted—thank God. I don't think I could have borne it otherwise. . . ."

"Where is he now?"

"On his way back from the Guv, I hope. He wrung an interview out of the old brute, got permission to break in on some frightful party he's giving in his house. That took doing, but—well, you should see Mark at this moment!"

"Shall I see him tonight?"

"I rather hope not. I made him promise to go straight to bed when he gets back. The rest of us can take care of anything that crops up between now and breakfast. But I don't fancy we shall hear anything much tonight."

"Is there nothing we can do—*now?*"

"Helen, we've done everything possible, I honestly believe. We've badgered the Ministry of the Interior. There are Security Guard people in the house now— Zradkin's boys. We've had ordinary police, and odd characters in overcoats and hats. We've kicked up the biggest stink possible on a non-diplomatic issue. Non-diplomatic at present, that is. . . . We've got just one clue, which may or may not be some good. When Victoria came in to luncheon she told Jean Hubbard about her walk, which was unusual, as she generally doesn't think it worth talking about. She said something like this: 'In the *park* we met Simpkin's *friend,* and do you *know,* Hubby, he's got one eye *black* and one eye *blue!*' Can you make anything of that?"

The room seemed to rock and clatter, a cold wind whipped round her, bright rails streaked past. Helen felt again the iron fingers gouging her flesh, felt them for Victoria, gripping fragile arms, and opened her mouth as if to scream.

Then Carlo did an odd thing, for him. He stepped quickly across to Helen, took her firmly by the shoulders, and shook her vigorously twice. Sheer surprise might have been enough to pull Helen together, but better was the substitution of Carlo's friendly hands for the nightmare ones holding her and Victoria. Helen subsided into her chair and smiled weakly up at him.

"I'm sorry, Carlo. It's just that I know the man Victoria saw. He was the one who grabbed me on the train. I was just seeing . . . never mind, it's all right now. It's better, in some ways, to know my enemy." She thought for a moment. "Carlo, who's the head of the INGRA?"

"Insofar as anyone in this country is head of it, it's General Krykula."

"Well, black-and-blue eyes is an INGRA man. He is also, I'm positive, related to Mrs. Simpkin. He may even be her son. Carlo, this thing may go back a long way. And I think it *is* a diplomatic issue."

Carlo passed a hand across his eyes. "Sorry if I'm stupid, Helen, but I can't see any sense in this. Why should INGRA go after Victoria? And what goes back a long way?" He looked at her searchingly. Then his face lost its look of exhaustion and became flooded with excitement.

"Helen, am I mad to have forgotten why you went up to Ostrány? Please tell me everything. What Anzip said. Everything."

I can't tell him everything, Helen thought sadly. After such joy, what a homecoming this has been. . . . She told him, however, all that it was necessary for him to know, and was rewarded by seeing his face grow younger under her eyes.

"I see," he said, "I see. And, of course, you're right. They seldom miss a trick; they check and double-check everything. Anzip may have done the organizing, but they weren't going to take his surety alone for Mark's going. They must have planted Mrs. Simpkin with exactly this end in view. In case they should ever need to use Victoria to persuade Mark. . . ."

"And I don't think that's the whole story. You see,

196

Anzip's getting out as well, which is going to give no pleasure to Madame Kassin. I think—I know—that the old horror's madly in love with him, and furiously jealous. She's shown what she thinks of me, once or twice, and pretty venomous she's been about it. I don't know, but I just have a sinking feeling. . . . About today. Anzip was quite confident that she didn't know he was there to meet me. He said she thought he was in Vienna. But I'd never dare be so sure. . . . Not with people like these, people like Kassin. It's just possible this may be a personal issue, nothing to do with General Krykula or the Guv or anyone. Because, at present, I'm quite sure that no one knows Mark Ogilvy's decision but Stoyan." The Christian name slipped past her guard. She hoped that her way of saying it had not given too much away. Carlo might not have noticed, in any case. He was walking up and down, thinking hard.

"If you're right—if this is a personal decision of Luba Kassin's—and she has all powers, she can even command Krykula—then that explains something that's been puzzling Martin and me since this thing started. We've been feeling that we were being met with a certain degree of genuine bewilderment. You know how these people are. If they're up to something, they either close their ranks and meet you with an absolutely ungraspable smoothness, all telling the same story, telling it perfectly. Or they just flatly refuse to see or speak to you. Clam up. Become completely inaccessible. Neither thing has happened this time. They've been flustered, and obviously bored stiff, but clearly there's been no time to declare a party line. They've even been quite co-operative in a grudging sort of way, like grown-ups pestered by children when they want to talk. I wonder. . . ."

"What?"

"If you're right about Luba Kassin. I'm going to assume that you are."

"What will you do?" Action, any action, was desirable. The more the wheels spun, the more she herself was engaged, the less, perhaps, the image of Victoria—lost, frightened, in pain—could come to torture her.

"Get Ilena on the job. I'll go up to the wireless room now, before the others get back. And you, Helen, take some more brandy and go to bed. At once, I mean it. The ladies have made up a bed for you in their sitting-room. They've taken all you'll need across. So don't go near your own bedroom tonight." Carlo took her hands and pulled her to her feet.

"You've done well today, Helen," he said. "I know nothing I can say will stop you reproaching yourself, so I'll just promise to get Victoria back for you, safe and sound. Ah, if only this hadn't happened, how pleased we should be tonight. . . ."

"It's funny. The whole object of my coming here has been achieved—I still don't know how. But now, there's only one thing in the world that can really please me."

"All will be well. I promise. Ilena's intelligence service is perfect. And Ilena has been waiting to deal with Madame Luba Kassin for a very long time."

They all breakfasted standing up next morning. Somehow, it seemed that no one could bear to sit down. Perpetual restlessness afflicted everybody, so that people were continually coming in and out of the dining-room, picking things up, putting things down, forgetting them, coming back for them. It was a kind of substitute for the action about Victoria which they all so badly needed. Mrs. Clothier and Miss Hubbard were red-eyed, Carlo and Martin untidy and badly-shaved, Helen white as death. Even Maidment and Orde-Gibbon seemed, in their detached way, mildly affected; but their eyes, discreet or direct, went continually from face to face and, Helen felt desperately, to hers most of all. The Minister breakfasted alone, waited on personally by Madame Elvire, whose reactions to the crisis had echoed through the Legation since dawn.

"I can't stop her," said Carlo helplessly. "She's in there, like Niobe, coaxing him to eat, and keening in Viennese argot. I feel she must do her bit, and it may be maddening for him, but at least it's a distraction."

"I hope H.M.G. doesn't declare war or anything this Sunday morning," Martin said, "because a more inattentive mission it would be hard to find."

No news had come from any quarter, but Carlo drew Helen aside, just as she was nerving herself to go up to the nursery, and murmured: "Ilena's at work. She's following your lead. She thinks she may be able to get us some news by midday. . . . Oh, and the Minister wants to see you in his room in half an hour." Helen was too numb, after some hours of dead, dreamless sleep, to have much feeling either way about an interview with Mark Ogilvy. She dragged her way up the long staircase, glanced absently round her room (which could, now, have been a stranger's), passed the shattered nursery door and made straight for Victoria's toy-cupboard. She searched for a while, looked in various other places—a doll's cot, a pram—then straightened and looked out into the falling snow with a slightly more cheerful expression. Oh, I'm being mawkish, I suppose. But I'm glad she's got him with her! There had been no sign of Tedder, Victoria's battered old plush bear.

Mark Ogilvy was standing looking out of the window behind his desk, when Helen entered. He did not immediately look round. The large official desk was bare of papers, rigidly tidy. Only the telephones were out of the straight, their cords twisted, as if they had been much in use. When Mark turned to greet her, his looks made Helen, who was moving towards a chair, stop still and stare at him anxiously.

Since yesterday, he seemed to have lost weight, to be all bones inside his well-made grey suit. His hair, which usually sprang so vigorously, which was hard to keep in order so that it soon became rather attractively untidy, looked dull and sick, lying close to the broad, intelligent head. In their deep sockets, under heavy brows, his eyes burned feverishly. But there was more to disquiet Helen. There was, in Mark's expression, something oddly hostile, yet embarrassed, and perhaps sulky as well. When he spoke to Helen, asking her to sit down, he did not meet her eye.

199

"Well, Helen, you know what's happened. I just wanted you to know that I don't hold you in any way to blame."

In other circumstances, from another employer, this might have been a kindly enough speech; in these, and with this one, it was intolerably false. Helen was astonished at the strength of her own reaction.

"If I had known this was going to happen, do you think I would have gone to Ostrány?" she asked angrily, and was even glad to have her anger to bite on. Mark's tone in reply was level, polite, but still touched with a controlled hostility.

"You returned to the Legation, I understand, at one in the morning?"

I must not be so angry I cannot speak. . . . Helen clasped her hands in her lap to stop them shaking.

"And Victoria disappeared some time in the afternoon, before I could possibly have got back. There was also a major blizzard in the mountains."

"Yet the party you travelled up with was back in Senj, I am informed, by seven o'clock."

"If I had travelled with them I should still not have been back in time to help poor Victoria."

There was a pause. Mark Ogilvy picked up a pencil and turned it round and round in his fingers. Once again Helen noted, even through rage and a growing alarm, that his hands seemed quieter, kinder than the rest of him. Somewhere in her mind light began to break. Mark was being unreasonable, in a manner quite out of character with what she knew of him. Just as children will seldom admit the real reason for a scene they are making, but allege some trivial, contingent cause, so men will, when they are jealous, do the same. Could Mark be jealous? She felt a wave of panic and, to break the silence, decided recklessly to carry the war into the enemy's camp.

"You seem to be uncommonly well-informed. But it seems to me that we are wasting time. All that matters, just now, is that Victoria should be found."

Mark gave a weary, unamused little laugh which Helen found extremely irritating. "You have my agreement about that, of course," he said. "And as to being well-informed, it is my duty so to be. And when—" a little heat crept into his voice; almost with relief Helen felt his control slipping, "when one of my staff enters into intimate relations with an important member of a government which is, largely, hostile to my own, then it is also my duty to take notice."

Oh God, this pomposity! How can we ever make sense out of this? By intuition, and into a hollow silence, Helen murmured: "Rosencrantz and Guildenstern!"

Mark Ogilvy straightened sharply in his chair, and looked, for the first time, really angry. "What my sources of information are is quite irrelevant. Do you admit that you went to Ostrány to meet—a certain person, by arrangement?"

"I am not, I think, bound to answer your questions; but I will. I did meet someone in Ostrány, yes."

"With whom you spent the afternoon in seclusion, and drove back with him later, in his own car?" With a strange feeling of elation, Helen saw Mark's real self emerging. His eyes were on hers now, angry, shocked— yes, even hurt. She was right, then. This was a personal matter, after all. Suddenly relieved, amost cheerful, she said:

"Let's make the 'certain person' quite certain. I had lunch with Stoyan Anzip, your old friend, and I drove back with him in his car. We also explored the Kursaal. Nothing else concerns you, unless I say it does."

Mark's face now was sulky, but nothing worse. "I suppose you know Anzip's reputation?" His voice was almost a growl. Helen, seeing her advantage, instinctively pressed it. With a swift movement she was on her feet, looking down at him.

"I know what I think about Stoyan Anzip, and that is entirely my own business. I also know that he is about to leave this wretched country forever, and I pray he gets out in time. And I know something else, something which matters to my own country far more than—I think—it should . . ." the scorn in her voice spoke for all her misery about Victoria, for all the anxieties and disquiets of the past eternity of weeks. "Your Excellency came very near accusing me of treachery a few minutes ago. Your Excellency should, perhaps, think again about treachery. Your Excellency would like to blame me, anybody, anybody but himself for Victoria's loss. . . . Oh, I can't keep this up! You're only ten years older than me. We might—we might—" She was gasping, to her intense disgust, almost in tears. "You've been saved, by the mercy of God, from something really horrible. . . . But, you flaming idiot, if you weren't the stupidest clever man in the world, and the most conceited, Victoria would never have been kidnapped at all!"

Mark felt her words, every one of them, and looking up, could only see her as wildly beautiful, standing so straight, head high, her arms pressed back, like a figurehead. He made no reply, but slowly put his head in his hands.

Feeling flat, concerned, no longer angry, Helen sat quietly down again. It was impossible for her to leave without seeing Mark's face, but this, for what seemed a long time, he continued to hide. Once or twice Helen was on the edge of speaking, of saying almost any banality, just to break this silence of taut wires, but refrained. Eventually, Mark Ogilvy looked up at her, calmly enough. He smiled tentatively.

"We don't know the size of the punishment yet, Helen," he said, and his voice was gentler, yet more direct, than she had ever known it. She realized that he had never quite spoken *to* her before. "It's a relief to me that you seem to know—about everything. We'll talk about that later—if you'll let me, that is. Will you tell me something now, though? What did you mean when you said I was only ten years older? You said, 'We might—we might—' What might we do?"

Helen sighed. She was not used to victory.

"I'm not sure. I was rather worked up. I meant anyway—be friends."

Mark Ogilvy nodded, as if the idea gave him pleasure. Helen took her leave. On her way back to find Carlo, she

202

accused herself of lack of candor. Since yesterday it was by no means certain that the actual blame for Victoria's disappearance lay with Mark. If Luba Kassin had known of yesterday's meeting, the blame might equally well lie with Helen.

Monday, December the twenty-second. In the freezing blackness before dawn, Tubb and Carlo were packing the big station-wagon, the Legation's second car, with stores for a long journey. They were in the stable yard at the back of the house, from which a gate gave onto the small lane that skirted the Legation grounds and joined the Tvar road a hundred yards to the right of the main entrance. Madame Elvire, who was in on the secret, had the sentry cozily settled in her deep kitchen, half asleep on spiked coffee. Helen was handing various items to the two men, from a pile in the kitchen passage. All were dressed in their warmest clothes, Helen in ski-trousers and anorak which were part of the outfit provided, it now seemed so long ago, by Miss Martineau.

They worked in silence, with an occasional muttered word. They worked fast, for it was necessary that they should be away, and well on their road, before first light. When all was ready, Helen climbed in the back of the car, arranged herself as comfortably as possible among the assembled gear, and Tubb closed the doors on her. She had just got herself wedged safely between a couple of cardboard boxes, on a pile of rugs, with another rug wrapped around her, Tubb was in the driver's seat and had softly closed his door, there was only Carlo to come, when Helen became aware of sounds in the darkness, voices whispering sharply; something was going on outside. Then a tall figure in dark greatcoat and fur cap ducked through the nearside door, pulled over the folding seat and half fell into the back of the car beside Helen. It was Mark Ogilvy.

He raised his hand in greeting to Helen, then busied himself, as she had just done, in making some room for his long legs amongst the awkward cargo on the floor.

Carlo got in, and at once turned towards Mark, as if to continue an argument. Helen could not see his face, but his words came cold and clear-cut, chiselled by anger.

"I damn well *do* protest. This was a perfectly adequate search party. We had a fair hope of success. Now you insist on coming along, and we've a fair chance of a major international incident. Haven't you done enough? Do you absolutely have to wreck everything?"

Mark's tone in response was almost cheerful.

"Protest away, Carlo! I've every right to join in, and not you nor anybody else could stop me. If there's an incident, I shall welcome it. My career's wrecked anyway. So cheer up, for heaven's sake. Carry on, Sergeant Tubb."

Carlo faced forward, with an angry uncharacteristic shrug which half buried his head in his collar. Without a word, Tubb took off the brake. They coasted silently down the slope of the yard to the gates; the engine started, sounding enormously loud between the stone walls of the lane. Within seconds they were skittering on the tram-tracks beside the river. Sergeant Tubb was getting his trip to Ostrány after all.

Luckily the blizzard of Saturday night had blown itself out by Sunday morning, and the snowplows must have been over the road again since then. Tubb was driving as fast as he dared, with a tail-heavy vehicle on a road he scarcely knew. Already the night was greying to a winter dawn. They must make the best time they could, to reach a particular spot in the mountains before the first army lorry came down on its day run to Senj.

For nearly an hour nobody spoke. Mark sat hunched in his heavy coat, never moving; Carlo did the same. Helen was beginning to long for a cigarette, but somehow did not wish to be the first to move. Finally Tubb lifted his head and spoke over his shoulder.

"If you'll forage round to your left there, Miss, you'll find a haversack with coffee and sandwiches. We can't stop—we'd never get started again; but we can have it as we go. Never do to get too cold." His voice was as quiet and equable as ever, but there might have been a note of humor in the last remark. With relief Helen stirred herself, found the haversack, and became busy with the difficult job of pouring coffee through a succession of sharply-corrected lateral skids.

This diversion had the effect which, probably, Tubb had intended. To get his coffee, Carlo had to turn round, and, while cups were passing sloppily about, there was the chance to talk, joke, rearrange the atmosphere between them all. Helen was relieved to see that Carlo's anger had not lasted. He gave her a great wink, and Mark a friendly grimace. In the growing light Helen could now see their faces. Carlo's was much as usual, perhaps a little more careworn, but not without a touch of eagerness, of excitement at what they were doing. Mark Ogilvy's seemed to have shed twenty years.

Mrs. Sidney's first message had reached Carlo early on Sunday afternoon. Her people in the mountains had reported the arrival at Ostrány, that morning, of a staff-car with drawn blinds, driven by a civilian, which had been waved through the check-post without formality. Those watching had expected the car to turn into the grounds of the Hotel du Parc, since this was the usual destination of military traffic. Instead, it had kept straight on, past the entrance to the Kursaal, along the seldom-used road which ran between the Kursaal park and the shut-up Zwingli Palace, towards what had once been the golf course. Here there were thick pine woods on both sides of the road. Just past the Kursaal, the car had turned left on to a woodland track which led to a small group of buildings, long disused, where once senior servants of the Kursaal had lived. No one, at that time, had been able to see the other occupants of the car, but a later message reported that a detail of soldiers from the Hotel du Parc had arrived in the wood, that smoke was coming from the chimneys of a cottage, and that the figure of a woman in black had been seen at an upper window.

They had waited in a trance of anxiety for the rest of the afternoon, for a further message. Carlo had insisted on waiting, although Mark was wild with impatience; and although Helen felt as if she was slowly bleeding to death, she had had to admit that he was right. They must not waste their efforts, and they could not afford to be mistaken. Through all the heavy minutes of waiting, while time sputtered like a slow fuse, and while she was drearily tidying Victoria's toy-cupboard, Helen could not get out of her head some words of Henry Sanders: "The incidence of sheer whim. . . . The gratuitous act."

At five o'clock the message came. An old woman had approached the guards saying she had noticed the activity in the deserted cottage, and offering to sell them eggs and cheese. The cottage stood at the corner of a small yard making, with other outbuildings, an enclosed square. The guard, consisting of two young soldiers, was posted at the entrance gate. There was no other exit from the yard. The old woman had got as close as she could to the gateway, even to the point of being threatened with a rifle, and had argued deafly with the soldiers for as long as possible before being rougly spun round and pushed on her way.

She had been able to see the cottage clearly. She had seen the door open and a child appear, a little girl in a blue coat, red in the face and scolding loudly. The child had been clumsily grabbed from behind by a soldier, whereupon she had twisted round and bitten him, hard enough to make him shake his hand in the air and curse. She had then kicked him for good measure, as hard as she could, on the shin and had immediately been gathered up and carried indoors again by an elderly woman in a black dress, who seemed to be trying to soothe her.

On hearing this news Tubb had said, with a brief smile: "That'll teach 'em to tangle with Miss Victoria! And I'll say this for that dismal old Simpkin—she may be up to her neck in the thing, but she's really fond of the little girl, and they'll have her to reckon with if they get nasty." Helen, in anguish, supposed she might take some reassurance from Tubb's words, but found it beyond her reach.

At five-thirty Tubb set off in the Humber towards the town. An hour later he was back again with Mrs. Sidney and, ten minutes after that, a council of war was in full swing in Carlo's room. Carlo and Tubb, Helen and Mark sat quietly while Mrs. Sidney outlined the general situation, and told them in detail the plan they must follow. Mark's rôle in all this had been curious. No longer in obvious command, he had, in some way, caused his personality to diminish. He had looked, simply, desperately anxious, a father whose child was in danger, and very much a new boy where the practical side of it all was concerned. At the end, when plans and their timing had been agreed between the four who trusted one another, Mrs. Sidney had raised her splendid head and looked at Mark from hooded eyes.

"So, Mr. Ogilvy. This is what I think must be done. Do you agree with the arrangements? Will you help us—this time?"

Mark had answered, very quietly: "Of course." He had shaken his head sharply twice and then, with a thin ghost of his old smile, had said: "It seems I know very little about what really goes on. At present, I just want to find Victoria. I cannot see beyond that. . . ."

This was not to be a day of sunshine. The blizzard might have stopped, but there was still snow in the air, and the daylight only seemed to grow, with the passing minutes, not so much stronger as a shade less feeble. They were in forest now, and the car's heater was not doing much to mitigate the grinding cold. The windows were steamed over at the back and sides, and all their faces looked waxen, pinched, in the steely light.

Through the clear spaces of the wind-shield Helen saw the forest break ahead of them, and they swept out into a whiter light with the mountainside on their right and the precipitous mist-filled valley to their left. Helen remembered that, soon, they would be in forest again and that it was there, on the straight road, that she had met the lorry full of soldiers, on that Saturday which was at once a lifetime and less than forty-eight hours ago. She looked at her watch, feeling a sudden fear, and saw that the time was eleven minutes past eight. A moment later she saw Carlo do the same thing. They were re-entering the forest. He turned his head.

"Slow, now, Tubb—it's somewhere in the next hundred yards. Two black posts." He spoke over his shoulder: "Touch wood—we've just about made it in time."

Helen gasped, and gripped the boxes on either side of her as Tubb spun his wheel to the right and they took off into the forest. Fir boughs whipped the windows, slapped and rang on the roof. Sheets of soft snow fell round them. Expecting a nosedive, a crash, Helen hung on with all her strength; but the ground below was firm, if bumpy, and, after a moment, Tubb pulled serenely to a stop.

"Just a minute," he said, and jumped from the car, taking with him a small shovel which had been stowed alongside the driving seat. Carlo took off his spectacles and turned round to smile at Helen and Mark.

"Too bad if there *hadn't* been a road! However, Ilena's never been wrong yet, and there's no reason why she should start now."

"Where's Sergeant Tubb gone?"

"To cover our tracks. Even Glumba soldiery could hardly fail to notice that someone had taken to the woods."

Tubb had switched off the engine. Utter quiet enveloped them. Carlo seemed to be listening, and neither of his companions spoke. Soon they heard a faint metallic mutter which became a hum and then a roar as a heavy vehicle went by on the road towards Senj. When its noise had died away, they could hear sticks breaking, a muffled tread, and Tubb came back to them, his face glowing.

"That was them," he said. "I wouldn't care to have cut it much finer! Brr, it's a bit chilly! Have you got any more of that coffee, Miss?"

Helen found another thermos of coffee, more sandwiches, and a flask of plum brandy. "Bless Madame Elvire! She never fails, either." They laced their coffee with the white spirit, because the temperature inside the car was falling fast.

"What do we do now, Carlo?" Mark looked eager, interested, completely in the moment. "Do we walk?"

"No. We wait for a guide. He should be along any minute. We'll be taken to the house Ilena spoke of, where we can sort ourselves out and get warm. Then we start on the next phase." He was wiping his window clear of moisture as he spoke. "Here we go," he said.

Helen leaned forward to peer through the nearside window. A dark figure was approaching through the trees a little to their left. It was heavily clothed, and muffled round the head, but she could see a square red face, a heavy mustache, and a smoke of breath in the freezing air.

"Your bird, Carlo," Mark said, "and I only hope it isn't some dialect even you don't know!"

Carlo grunted. He had been rewarded more than once by the Foreign Service for proficiency in languages, but admitted that this particular one was the toughest in his experience. "Lovely stuff," Martin Wright had said. "Like a large mouthful of broken glass."

Both Tubb and Carlo got out of the car, and Carlo went forward to greet the newcomer. They met some yards away, and were immediately deep in talk. Tubb, meanwhile, was collecting thin bundles of brushwood which must recently have been laid beside the track, since they had no covering of snow. The station-wagon had been stopped on a slight upward incline. Fifty yards farther on, insofar as it was distinguishable at all in the general whiteness, the track seemed to run gently away downhill, into the bewildering crowd of straight-boled trees. Tubb laid brushwood close under the wheels at both ends of the car, then climbed back into his seat and waited.

Carlo came back to the car and, as Mark had done, scrambled over the folded seat into the back, where he perched uncomfortably between Mark and Helen.

"No, don't bother," he said, when they tried to make more room for him. "It won't be long, and anyway I've got to interpret."

The stranger followed him into the car, sketching a wide, grave gesture of greeting, and sat beside Sergeant Tubb. The car started, rolled backwards a foot or so, slithered, gripped and bounded forward over the crackling brushwood. They breasted the incline, and dropped cautiously away down the other side.

For the next ten minutes there were sharp, guttural instructions from the guide, rapid translations from Carlo, swift responses from Tubb. A rhythm established itself, and the station-wagon crept on lurching and dipping, sometimes skidding, but always moving, always finding something to bite on under the interminable smooth coverlet of snow. At length, and when Helen's eyes were almost blind from staring at the patternless monotony of dark brown and white, what she had taken to be an extra-thick stand of trees showed suddenly as a tall, wooden barn, its doors wide open to embrace the track itself. Tub said: "Nothing if not convenient!" and ran the station-wagon neatly in beside a large object under a holland sheet. Their guide jumped out and ran to close the doors and fasten them with a heavy wooden bar. In the quiet brown dusk of the barn they all looked at each other. Phase one had been successfully completed.

At the other side of the barn, and reached through a low doorway, was a forester's house, which consisted chiefly of one large room, lined with unpainted wood, lit by small windows, hung with antlers and skins. A brilliant fire roared in a great stone hearth. Beside the fire a thin, long-haired hound, too perfectly trained even to twitch at their entry, lay nose-to-paw regarding them with an alert yellow eye.

After the constrictions of the car they all felt liberated, each one himself again. It was possible to be hopeful, optimistic about the outcome of their mission. Victoria, now, was only a couple of miles away from them. Themselves were well concealed, for the moment safely bestowed in the secret intricacy of the forest. They had time to think, plan, prepare carefully for the next move. Carlo, Mark and Tubb removed their heavy greatcoats, stretched and wandered about. Helen took off her blue anorak, and the bright coral red of her jersey shone vividly in the sober masculinity of the room. The for-

210

ester, who had been their guide, disappeared through another door, to return in a moment without his heavy coverings, in long loose jacket and cord breeches, like any gamekeeper at home. He was followed by an old woman, seeming small as a doll, and as neat in her long black dress, who, avoiding their eyes, but with many little bobs, offered the traditional welcome of the country, glasses of plum brandy and spoonfuls of sharp-sweet jam.

After they had made themselves comfortable, the forester cleared a few small objects—a pewter dish, a vase of plumed grasses, a half-dry bottle of ink—from an ancient, axe-hewn table, and they sat round it on tall chairs. Carlo nodded to his host who, at once, launched into a long discourse, emphasizing a point from time to time by pressing his fist onto the table top, as if setting a seal. After a while, Carlo pushed across to him some sheets of paper and a pencil, and the forester made a couple of tentative, unpracticed drawings, which he then explained in detail to Carlo, looking at him anxiously, for fear he should not be understood. Finally Carlo took over. He looked at each of his companions in turn and said:

"The situation does not appear to have changed, except that they have doubled the guard at the cottage, and now have men posted all round it at about two hundred and fifty yards. Our friend here is confident that the guards can be dealt with—scragged, decoyed or confused—but his instructions now are that we should hide up in the Kursaal and be ready to move at dawn tomorrow. No use going to the Kursaal until dark, so we may as well relax here. Tubb, you were dead right about the need for stores. I apologize for doubting it. They're to be off-loaded onto a sleigh. They can, apparently, be got across to the Kursaal in daylight, without much risk, disguised as a load of wood."

Mark said: "How do we get to the Kursaal?"

"On foot. The station-wagon stays here. There'll be another car for us tomorrow morning. In fact it's already in the Kursaal garage. One of those green, official things. Make our getaway easier. . . ." He chuckled. "That's the great thing about a thoroughly irregular situation. Once we've succeeded, they can't complain about anything at all, without admitting their own part in the proceedings."

Helen felt numb with disappointment. Since before dawn she had been nursing the hope, the almost certainty, of finding Victoria; had imagined the rescue over and themselves on the way back to Senj by tea time, and Victoria once more in her own bed at the Legation next morning. Now the morning would be strange indeed, and very likely dangerous. What if they failed? What, then, would become of Victoria, of them all?

Mrs. Sidney had been emphatic that Victoria's kidnapping was the work of Luba Kassin, a direct use of her enormous prestige for more than a political purpose. The Government might be, already, slightly embarrassed; might anticipate being very much more so; but there was little they could do. Luba Kassin had a head start on everybody, and one very powerful card in her hand. For as long as she could pretend that, holding Victoria, she could force Mark to do what they wished, they would not look further into her motives. Only Helen, and Stoyan, and—just possibly—Mrs. Sidney knew the more compelling reason for Madame Kassin's conduct. With a sinking heart Helen thought: she's capable of killing us all, and probably Stoyan as well. . . . And now they must hang about in the forester's house for more than six precious hours, before it would be safe to move.

She looked up to find Tubb's eyes on her. It was plain that he had guessed her thoughts, for he pushed back his chair and said: "Best to have something to do, Miss, since we're to be here for a while. Would you like to come and help me unload the car? You can tell me what we're likely to need for our night out!"

As if Tubb would ever need that kind of guidance from anyone; nevertheless, she rose eagerly, and followed him to the door. Mark and Carlo were re-drawing the forester's maps, and talking absorbedly. The forester himself was watching their lips, trying with a frown to follow their rapid foreign talk.

It was dusky and quiet in the barn, and very cold. The

sleigh they were to load was pulled up against the far wall, at the other side of the sheeted mass which had, somehow, so oddly elegant and incongruous an air in that place. The sleigh came squeaking over the rough stone floor, a little taller than a woodcutter's sled, its runners shod with steel.

"You get inside the car, Miss, and hand things out. It'll be warmer for you."

Helen went to work vigorously, easing and shoving the heavier boxes to the edge, where they toppled into Tubb's hands; clasping bundles of rugs and blankets; handing out smaller packages whose contents she could not guess.

"Well," she said at one point, "I *was* going to say 'everything but the kitchen stove'!" She held up a large primus, which Tubb took from her with a slightly sheepish grin.

"Doesn't do to be caught out! Or so they used to tell me. I must say, it's a long time since I've had to do anything along these lines. Overdone it a bit, perhaps?"

"I'm sure you haven't. We've got a long night in the Kursaal, and nothing much to do but eat and drink. I'm all for doing things in style." Her heart twisted at the thought of her last picnic.

"Good gracious! Sergeant Tubb, was this your idea too?"

Helen had opened the largest and heaviest of all the boxes, to see what it could contain to make so much weight. Inside she had found what looked like the bulk of the Legation dinner service, white china plates of all sizes, gold-rimmed and bearing gold crowns. There was silver too, of the familiar pattern, tied into neat bundles, and a silver chafing dish with a spirit lamp attached.

"Not guilty. That's Madame Elvire, you can be sure. Not going to have us letting ourselves down. I'd say 'leave it behind'—or most of it. We've got to eat off something, so let's take a plate apiece, and a set of irons. Then, if we have to get away in a hurry we shan't have so much of his Majesty's property to account for. There'll be a bit of explaining to do anyway, what with one thing and another. But I don't mind betting there'd be more fuss, in the end, about the crockery than anything else. If the army's anything to go by, that is."

"Do you think we're going to have—trouble?"

Tubb looked vague, bent his head to his work of loading the sleigh.

"Better to prepare for it. You never know with these monkeys. Someone might lose his head and do something silly. . . . Still, let's hope for the best. By the way, is there a small green haversack back there, right behind my seat?"

Helen, on whom many possibilities were beginning to impress themselves, handed the bag to him without a word. It, too, was remarkably heavy for its size. Tubb finished squaring up the various items on the sleigh. The load which had made for so much discomfort on the journey up seemed small enough when packed like this.

"I'll leave the cording and camouflaging to them." Tubb had laid the green haversack on the tailboard of the stationwagon. He now began to undo the straps. He talked as he worked, rather like a dentist before a tricky operation, Helen thought.

"Ever handled one of these? No? Well, I don't know. . . ." He looked round him at the lofty barn. "Mightn't hurt to have a few rounds practice in here. We'll ask the old chap. . . . There now, Miss. There's yours. And a lovely little job it is. Long barrel's better for accuracy, just in case you should need to be accurate." He produced three more heavy revolvers. They lay on an outspread chamois leather, giving off a faint blue glimmer in the scanty light, three inescapable facts. Helen's slim, long-barrelled .38 was cold, and surprisingly light, in her hand. It felt alien, an extension to herself as unwelcome as a steel claw.

"Right. I think I'll carry these and the ammo with me, in that haversack, till we get there. I can always dish them out if we hit any awkwardness." Tubb gave a short, dry laugh. "The armory at home's a bit depleted, I'm afraid. If they decide to rush the Legation tonight, Mr. Wright's going to have his hands full!"

Helen thought with compassion of Martin, holding the fort almost alone. "Never fear," he'd said, "I'll be the stoniest of walls. I'll keep R. and G. out of mischief, somehow, I promise. Only—I wish I were coming too!"

Tubb, after checking the ammunition, returned two of the weapons to the haversack. "Hang on here a minute," he said, "I'll go and get Mr. Sweet to ask the old chap if it's all right to loose off in here."

Helen stood on the tailboard looking, with wide eyes, at the revolver in her hand. She thought of bullets and their effects. She realized that she had never seen anyone shot, nor ever been shot at herself, although she had been in sufficient danger once or twice. It came to her suddenly that bullets could not be counted on to drill neat holes, nor to hit where they would scarcely hurt. She felt, all at once, vulnerable, wretchedly without protection. Her nerves tautened as she compared, in her mind's eye, the polite woundings of stage and cinema—simulated shock, hand clapped to a mentionable place—with the reality: a welter of bone-splinters and black arterial blood. When Tubb came back she was still staring, white-faced, at the gun in her hand.

Tubb, who had his own views about the probable realities of the situation, was not acting aimlessly. He had brought back with him a sheet of paper and a pin.

"It's all right," he said cheerfully. "The old chap says it's quite OK to fire off a few rounds. The place is nearly soundproof, and we're miles from anyone. *And* he's got chaps posted round about. He's gone out to warn the nearest scouts, that's all, in case they think we've gone mad and started shooting each other!"

He pinned up his sheet of paper on the door of the barn, came back and held out his hands to Helen.

"Jump down, then. That's right. Give me that and I'll load it for you. Clap your hands a bit; you look too cold to take aim." Helen did as she was told, knowing that her hands had never been so unwilling for any work in her life.

"Right, Miss. You have first go." Tubb showed her how to aim in a number of ways—free, over a raised arm,

215

over a steadying object. "Depends where you are, and how much time you've got. Try it each way. Take your time. We can't really spare more than six rounds each."

What surprised Helen was the relative mildness of the noise her pistol made. She had expected an enormous bang. A sharp crack, a light kick in her hand—that was all. She was on the target with four of her six shots, and in the center with one of them. Tubb walked over and ringed her shots with pencil.

When he came to fire, with a .45, Helen jumped. Where she stood, the noise was much louder. She was beginning to be interested, even a little regretful that they could not spend the morning at revolver practice. But if we haven't got very many bullets, she thought, I just hope we aren't besieged! Tubb brought the target back, and they examined it together.

"Well!" Helen said. "If there *is* going to be trouble, I'm going to stay close to you!"

They were about to leave the barn for the warmth of the house when Helen paused.

"I'm sorry," she said, "but I absolutely must see what's under that sheet!"

One at each end they lifted the coarse linen waist-high. Glossy, and gleaming richly even in that light, the body of a large black limousine came partly into view. Tubb whistled on two notes.

"A Rolls!" he exclaimed. "I'll bet you anything . . ." and he twitched his end of the holland cover up over the hood to prove himself right.

"It's in wonderful condition," Helen said, gazing into the mirror-depths of the paintwork, noting the unworn corrugations of the running board. "How old do you think it is?"

"Oh—about 1935. But a special body—a very special body!" He opened the rear door. A cold breath of fabric, varnish, and petrol came out of the interior. With it there was something hauntingly familiar to Helen: a dry spicy scent, faintly tinged with camphor. She closed the door again thoughtfully, and stood studying the elaborate coat of arms on the panel.

216

"Wonderful condition," Tubb was saying. "Look at those tires—pretty nearly perfect. Well, it won't do for what we want, so we'd better cover it up again, and get used to the idea of walking."

"You know whose it is?"

"I can make a good enough guess!"

It seemed to Helen that they had been trudging through soft snow, between identical bare trees, for the best part of her life. Dusk was thickening amongst the tree trunks, shortening distances, dusting the air with blue. Snow blindness made everything flicker, and sometimes the snow changed color strangely where she watched the toes of her ski-boots plod rhythmically on. Sometimes she missed her footing and righted herself slowly, feeling sick with fatigue. Yet—she kept saying to herself—it was only a short walk, really, only two or three miles, something to be made light of at home. But this was not home, and the going was harder, the forest more vast and unending, than anything she had ever known.

They moved in silence, save for an occasional low-voiced exchange between Carlo and their forester guide. Their path lay for the most part through a shallow ravine, which wound interminably between tree-lined banks on a course, Helen supposed, more or less parallel with the Ostràny road. Once or twice, as they went, a muffled figure stepped into their path and gave the guard a brief message or report. It was some comfort to Helen to know that they were, in this way, among friends; but there was little else to comfort her at that moment. She thought of Victoria imprisoned, with only the enigmatic Simpkin for protection, facing another night away from home. She thought of all that might have been done by their enemies during the long hours that they had had to spend in idleness in the forester's house. She thought of Martin stonewalling; and wondered whether, by a miracle, they had managed to get away to Ostràny that morning unnoticed. When, at the fall of darkness, they came to a black, regular mass more solid than the trees, and moved from the soft, deceitful forest ground onto the pavement of a yard, Helen was almost too miserable to feel relief.

"Where are we?" she whispered to Tubb, whose still reassuring presence was at her side.

"One of the big hotels. Zwingli Palace. All shut up and deserted. Not far to go now." Even his whisper managed to sound encouraging.

They halted for a few minutes in the hotel yard, to rest and to take stock. It would not do to halt for long: the night was bitter, and thin snow was already beginning to fall.

Carlo, in a loud whisper, called them together. "We're at the back of the Zwingli Palace, which is pretty well opposite the back of the Kursaal. We've only got to get through the gardens here, and across the road, then about fifty yards of driveway, and we're there. Ilena's people are dotted all along the way. All right? Everyone ready? Off we go! And for Heaven's sake, keep close!"

Helen felt a hand under her elbow. "On you go, Miss. I'll be behind you. One of them's behind me."

Very cautiously now, they moved forward, their footsteps softly thudding in the enclosed space. Helen was aware of door-jambs on either side of her, of a larger air, and the sense of the bulk of a great building on her right-hand side. Mark Ogilvy, next in front of her, turned to whisper: "Look out, steps . . . six of them." She said: "Watch it. Steps," over her shoulder to Tubb. So they proceeded, by fits and starts, going downhill all the time, and came at last to a halt.

"The road!" Mark breathed.

They waited for what seemed a long time, scarcely daring to shift their weight, although the cold soon struck through thick boots and heavy clothes. If the Kursaal lay ahead, then the cottage where Victoria was must be in line with it, about a quarter of a mile to the right. Helen turned her head, and thought she could see a light, but too much snow had made her eyes unreliable; she could not be sure. In her mind she told Victoria that it would be all right, that they were near to her now, that soon she

thin mattresses unrolled themselves. "If I'd known you were coming along, Sir . . ."

"Doesn't matter where I sleep, Tubb. Probably shan't sleep anyway—"

"Best have a try. Anyway, we've enough blankets to make another bed without worrying about a mattress."

So, rapidly and with the minimum of fuss, four sleeping places were arranged round the walls. Tubb then stood up, looking thoughtful and soon, without a word, disappeared through the nearest narrow door.

Carlo had made a corner for himself. He had thrown off his trappings of hat, scarf and topcoat and was busy, with spectacles on the end of his nose, comparing, collating maps with notes, oblivious of the activity around him.

Helen, who found herself curiously helpless in this world of masculine self-help, had set to to open the boxes of provisions. She lighted the primus and squatted for a while, trying to compose a menu in her mind which would satisfy them all without involving the use of more than two utensils—a frying-pan and a small saucepan—which were all she had to work with.

Tubb came back into the room, looking pleased.

"Through that door there, second on the right . . ." he murmured to Helen. "Best German plumbing, works like a dream! Now, which of these tins would you like me to open?"

Under the cold, impartial light of shadeless bulbs hung high in the echoing bare spaces of the Octagon, they settled like hunters to their evening meal. Coffee and plum-brandy were circulating. Each of them had made a more or less comfortable nest on one of the beds. Tubb had just suggested that all they needed was a campfire in the middle of the floor, when the door through which they had come swung sharply open. At once the three men were on their feet to welcome Mrs. Sidney, who stood looking at them with a kind of stern benignity as she shook the snow from her furs.

"My children," she said—and her voice, always compelling, had a new vibration in that empty air—"my children, our work is not yet finished. It is only begun. Much has happened, even since you left the forest. The Kursaal is surrounded by special forces of General Krykula. The General himself is here with his staff, and with him that animal, Kassin. We are going to have an interesting time getting you all away with Victoria. But never fear, it will be done."

For a moment no one spoke. Helen wondered if this news had knifed through anyone else's stomach with quite such a sharp pain of terror as it had through hers. She looked from one face to another and found reassurance. Charles had raised his eyebrows and turned down the corners of his mouth in a comic grimace of surprise. Tubb looked interested, polite, as though waiting for more, and more significant, details. Mark—well, she couldn't help thinking that Mark's face bore the eager anticipation of a schoolboy about to be awarded a prize. It was Helen who spoke first.

"How . . . how did you get in?"

"By the same means, Helen, as you will later use to get out!"

Mrs. Sidney turned to Charles Sweet.

"We shall try to get you away at dawn," she said. "It is ten o'clock now, so you will have to wait about eight hours. For the present I do not think Krykula will move. I think he will wait for the first light. But I must ask you to stand to here, in the Octagon, to spare my own men, who are few at present, for other parts of the Kursaal. One never knows. They might attempt to occupy the place while it is still dark."

"How are they armed?"

"Rifles and, I suppose, grenades. There may be mortars—we are not yet sure. Tear-gas, too, probably. But I do not think even Krykula, even with that animal screaming at him, will open a battle without formality. There will be an attempt at a parley, I am quite sure and this will give us a little more time. Also . . ." and here she turned to look directly, sternly, at Mark, "whatever Kassin's plans may be with regard to the rest of us, Krykula will want *you* alive."

It seemed to Helen that the old woman was on the

edge of saying something more, perhaps what was in all their minds about Mark's presence there. But the words were not spoken and, instead, Mrs. Sidney turned to Sergeant Tubb.

"Will you come with me?" she asked. "There are arms for all of you here, but the boxes must be broken. I shall need you for that. And Helen, you shall come too: it is necessary to do something, since we have to wait."

Without further words, Mrs. Sidney turned and strode to the door, looking taller now, more commanding than Helen remembered, her dark furs no longer seeming shabby but simply traditional, a suitable winter covering for this mountain world. Helen observed that she was wearing high boots of soft black leather, with strong, square heels.

Quietly Helen followed on through a pair of anterooms and into one of the cluttered salons she had first seen with Stoyan. Here Tadusz was before them, methodically attacking a big wooden case with a hammer and chisel. He handed Tubb a heavy case-opener, without looking up. The dust of the operation hung fuzzily in the air round the dirt-filmed bulbs of an electrolier.

Helen and Mrs. Sidney stood a little apart, watching the two men at work. Stealing a glance at the old woman's profile, Helen was struck by a stillness, a kind of radiant purposefulness it displayed. Whatever doubt or fear or sheer incongruity this situation might hold for others, for two people at least—for Ilena and for Mark—it was evidently the longed-for, worked-for point of no return.

One after another, the lids of the long, narrow cases came up, squeaking at first, and then with a sharp, splintering crack. In each lay six rifles, their polished brown wood and blued steel nested in wooden racks. Mrs. Sidney gave a little nod of approval which seemed to settle something in her thoughts. She turned abruptly to Helen and spoke in a low voice.

"My child," she said, and there was compassion in her tone, "you have come a long way to be embroiled in something not of your making, something with which you should, perhaps, not have had to do at all. Things will happen now which will not be amusing; and no one—least of all I myself—can tell where they will stop." She paused, biting her lip, and looking closely at Helen, as if doubtful whether or not to continue. "If I were such a fool to waste my time, I could be very angry with Mark Ogilvy. But . . ." she gave a short, gruff, but good-tempered laugh . . . "why trouble? He has moved history a little, this way, that way. That is all. He has put you and his child and his friends in great danger: and for this he will be very sorry . . . when he awakes. But he is not awake. You have seen his eyes. He is seeing action at last, the solution to so many problems—but only, at present, for himself. Helen, there is nothing I can do, now, about the danger. By coming with you Mark played into Kassin's hands. She had the right, then, not just only the wish, to call up Krykula, to make a fight. Now, I want you to look after Mark, to protect him as far as it is in your power. He must not be killed or captured for, if he is, I can hardly save any of you. With that look on his face, he is capable just now of all idiocies. So, I pray you, Helen, guard him well."

Helen, who had opened her mouth to protest, to suggest that things might not be so bad, closed it again, in cold realization of the truth. She shivered. Mrs. Sidney patted her cheek lightly.

"Courage, little one!" The strong voice was comforting. Helen managed a narrow smile.

"It's just . . . Victoria, really, that I'm frightened for. If only she could be got back to the Legation safe. . . . Then I think I could face anything."

Mrs. Sidney's sudden gaiety was a blaze of light, warmth, reassurance.

"There is no need to worry for Victoria, Helen," she cried. "Our plans for her are settled and will not miscarry. She will be sad and homesick and angry a short while longer, she will perhaps bite another soldier (and Heaven knows where a practice of biting soldiers may not, one day, lead her! They are terrified of her already!).

But she will be all right. It is only here that the situation is, well, a little problematical!"

As if to underline her words, Tubb came up beside them. Deceptively elegant, new-minted, shiny as toys, six short rifles gleamed in his arms under the tired light.

"I'm taking these through," he said quietly. "Could you bring one of those boxes of ammo, please, Miss?" and to Mrs. Sidney: "The rest are ready for your people when they want them." Helen saw that Tadusz was holding up for her a small wooden box.

"Go, then, Helen. Go on with your preparations. I shall leave you now for a while. We shall, however, meet again before long!" With a wide wave of her arm—part salute, it seemed, part benediction—the old woman strode to the farther door and disappeared.

Helen took from Tadusz the heavy black-painted box. Its thin rope handles bit into her fingers. Tadusz stood looking at her, as woodenly as ever but with a warmth, perhaps of respect, in his eyes. Helen cursed the language barrier which denied her the chance to question him, to wring from him news of his master. Nevertheless, and leaning a little forward, fixing his eyes, willing him to understand, she said breathlessly:

"Where is Stoyan Anzip?"

At the name Tadusz, too, bent forward, a small movement of eagerness. To Helen's pleasure he shyly put out a hand and touched the sleeve of her jersey. Then he nodded his head vigorously, up and down, several times, and finally pointed with a stiff arm to the wall at her right. From the way in which he moved his pointing finger upwards, Helen knew that Stoyan must be near, somewhere to the northeast of the roadway, somewhere in the snowy forest through which she herself had trudged that evening. Her hands full, she could only smile her gratitude to Stoyan's servant. She carried her burden, with care and loathing, back to her comrades in the Octagon, decidedly lighter of heart.

Mark and Carlo were bending over an improvised map. Somewhere a folding card-table had been found

225

and set up in the empty centre of the floor, directly below the chandelier with the snuffy glass drops and dusty china roses which, with the faded trompe-l'oeil of the painted ceiling, made the whole setting so inappropriate: as though a ballet, rather than a battle, were about to be staged here.

Helen set down her ammunition box near the rifles which Tubb had stacked between two windows. The five shuttered windows, each occupying one face of the projecting part of the Octagon, were separated from each other by an angled space of a few feet. To Helen's left, as she came back into the room from the main block of the Kursaal, the first window would look northeast, to the upper terraces and the small wood she had seen, from another window, with Stoyan. The shutters farthest on her right must conceal the glass doors which Tadusz had opened for her that same day. The three windows in between must command the falling terraces, the former gardens, and the driveway leading from the main road near the Hotel du Parc.

Tubb came past Helen, looking calm but preoccupied and vanished in the direction of the arms store. Helen, seeing that the two others were engrossed in drawing and annotating their map, wandered over to a window, and pressed her hands against the tall blankness of its shutters. The wood was stout and heavy, she could somehow feel this, and the iron bars and catches were heavy too, hand-forged, black and free from rust. Helen stood for a minute looking up at the forlorn festivity of the gilded pelmets, at the workmanlike strength of the bars and catches. She thought that, for a commanding position, a field of fire, the Octagon had much to recommend it. But the windows reached right to the floor, and if they could command they could also be commanded. She stood still, biting a fingernail, seeing the room now as a trap. Then she noticed something about the shutters. They not only were made to fold in upon themselves and so into a cavity in the window-casing at either side. They were also in three separate sections, so that the two higher pairs could be opened while the lowest remained closed. This,

226

about four feet high would, if reinforced in some way from within, make an adequate protection for anyone who wanted to see out and, if need be, fire.

"Sandbags," she said aloud.

"Well, it's an idea," said Tubb's voice behind her. She turned to find him examining the shutters. His look was sceptical.

"*If* it was to be a shooting matter, and *if* we had nowhere else to go, I'd say you were quite right. But I don't at all like the idea of having to hold this place. All right for kipping in, if we're not disturbed. Just possible if they'd nothing but rifles. We've got the drop on them there: if we fire first that is. . . . But, no; one grenade well aimed, still more one little mortar shell, a bit of machine-gun fire and you'd be surprised how exposed we'd feel! Also, have you thought of firing over sandbags, through a broken pane, all right, with all that mountain of wood and glass to come down on you?"

Helen, who had achieved, momentarily, a strategist's detachment, was crestfallen.

"Well, but what *are* we to do? Mrs. Sidney seems to think there'll be shooting."

"There may well be. But she thinks they'll parley first, and I think she's right. Also, and above all, we must not fire first. Our job's to get away from here on time, by the prescribed route, pick up Victoria and bolt for home, not hang round playing soldiers."

Helen looked closely at Tubb. His face was as composed, kindly and alert as ever, but the usual mild irony of his tone had sharpened to something within sound of contempt.

I believe he's angry, thought Helen. He's a professional, and we're amateurs, and one of us, Mark, isn't even yet touching reality. I believe Tubb's seeing farther than any of us at this moment. . . .

"She left me some instructions," Tubb went on, "Mrs. Sidney did. The escape route's the old underground supply-passage to the Pump Room. Comes up just beside that great round bar thing. Comes out in a shrubbery at the edge of the woods beside the stable yard. All the

227

pumps and stuff for the sulphur spring are down below, and they used to fetch and carry crates and bottles, and service the pumps, through this passage, out of sight of the paying patients. That's our objective, and that's where we're going without firing a shot, fun or no fun, if I've anything to do with it!"

Tubb's tone was severe. Helen felt nonplussed, almost guilty, as though she had been caught wanting a fight. Tubb said more gently:

"All the same, if nothing happens during the night, we'll have these shutters open a peep, at first light, just to see what we *are* up against."

Tadusz had joined the two men at the table and was answering questions from Carlo. Helen and Tubb joined them. After a while Carlo pushed his spectacles up onto his forehead and looked at Tadusz and his three companions with compassionate irony.

"Well," he said, "what a pickle! As Ilena says, we're surrounded. Pretty neatly too. Look, Helen!" and he leaned towards the map pointing with a pencil. The map showed a rough layout of the Kursaal which looked less complicated like this than Helen had found it in experience. Rough indications were given for the garden terraces and doubled arrow-shapes showed coppices and the edge of the thick forest. She saw that, in addition to the road to the kitchen yard which they had used that evening, and the winding main drive leading to the terrace front, there was also a continuation of the drive which ran past the Octagon, past the northeast end of the Kursaal and on up, in a series of loops, to join the upper road on the Senj side of the Zwingli Palace. Here and there on the map black rectangles had been drawn and filled in. Carlo pointed his pencil at each one in turn.

"Here's the largest concentration, at the edge of this wood, where the main drive comes out into the open. It's almost directly below us there—" he pointed to the centre window—"about a quarter of a mile away. There's half a company of men with rifles—we know they have rifles, they may have other things—a radio-truck and, till twenty minutes ago, a staff car with Krykula and Luba

228

Kassin on board. They've gone away temporarily, probably back to the Hotel du Parc. Here, by this small wood at the southwest end of the Kursaal, there's ten or a dozen of them, also with rifles and signalling equipment, and here, at the back, about a hundred yards from the kitchen door, another detail with radio and a portable searchlight. And the interesting thing about them—" Carlo shook his glasses down onto his nose and looked over them at Helen, "is that they're sitting right on top of our escape route!"

Helen for the moment could not face the implications of this news. She bent more closely over the map to hide her eyes from Carlo.

"There's a block on the road we crossed, isn't there?" she asked, a little thickly.

"There is. Set up just where the service road from the kitchen comes out. And finally," Carlo stabbed his pencil down at the northern edge of the wood she had seen with Stoyan, "just here, at the turn of this road that goes past us and up to the right, they've got a machine gun detachment nicely sited to fire right down on us. What beats me," he added crossly, "is why they don't trot up and settle down under the windows. They must be expecting us to make a fight of it."

"Well, they know there are more people in this building than just the four of us," Mark said.

Carlo gave him a steady look.

"That is one of the more regrettable features of the enterprise," he said evenly.

"I should have thought it was rather lucky for us!"

"Certainly it is lucky for us. Very lucky indeed. Only it's rather more than possible that, because of us, a sizeable civil war will now begin. Ahead of time. Probably at the wrong moment. Unquestionably with disastrous results. However," he shrugged his shoulders, his face heavy, "there's nothing to be done about that, unfortunately, except to try in every way not to make matters worse!"

Glancing at Mark she saw his chin go up, his forehead crease in a frown. This must be the first time he had ever listened to a lecture, even so oblique a lecture, from Carlo, perhaps from anyone.

Tubb broke in quickly. "I don't think Mrs. Sidney means to have any shooting if it can be helped," he said. "If all goes according to plan, we might, just possibly, get away without it. All of us: her lot as well."

Helen thought of Stoyan, hiding somewhere up there in the black forest. She thought of Luba Kassin, so near her quarry now, and free to make any number of "accidents" happen. She thought of the calm resolution of Mrs. Sidney's face, and shook her head slightly, feeling a sorrowful sense of fate. There will be fighting, she whispered to herself. There can't not be. This is it.

They stood silent, looking and not looking at one another, under the stale, sugary light of the chandelier. The vast building ached with silence. Outside the world, packed with patient hostility, was icily still.

"Listen!" Sergeant Tubb's sudden loud whisper stung like a lash. "Someone's coming." Helen strained her ears to catch the faint rhythmical thudding, which grew louder, of boots on the hard snow, the scrape of boots on the stone steps beyond the glass doors, the imperious rapping which rang like thunder in the room, the sound of doom itself. Mark started forward, towards the sound, and was seized at once by Tubb.

"No, Sir." There was little respect and some flat exasperation in Tubb's lowered voice. "Not you. You're not even here. Please go into the far room, the one where the guns are. Go quietly and take Miss Clark with you. Mr. Sweet will open the shutters to see who this is, and I'll stand by him."

Helen could see that Mark was on the edge of telling Tubb to go to Hell, to announce that he would take orders from no one; but Carlo turned on him a face of tired good sense, with a hint of amused sympathy. "Go on," he said. "There's a good chap. Don't make matters worse. We've got Victoria to think of, don't forget."

Mark bent his head, appeared to reflect for a moment, and then turned and set off, his shoulders hunched, in the

230

direction indicated. He looked angry, but did remember to tread carefully, to make as little sound as possible on the bare boards felted with dust. Helen followed him on tiptoe, feeling her feet heavy as ingots in their clumsy boots. As they went they heard the squealing cry and iron clang as the shutters were opened. A male voice, flattened by the glass between, said very loudly, in English: "We have come to talk to you. Please let us in."

In the poorly lit salon, amongst the packing cases, the stacked chairs, Helen and Mark faced one another, each seated on an empty box. Watching him directly, Helen saw that a struggle was going on inside Mark. His look was compounded of bad temper and, she was relieved to see, what might be the dawning of a sense of doubt. He looked angry and anxious and, after a few seconds, more anxious than angry. He blinked at Helen and smiled faintly, much as he had smiled at her at the close of their interview the day before. (Could it really only have been the day before?)

"I'm sorry!" he said, unexpectedly. "I'm only just getting used to standing on my head!"

"Your feet, you mean. You've been on your head for years!"

Mark laughed. "All right, all right. You're a bracing sort of girl, I'll say that. . . . But what do we do now?"

"Sit tight. Hope for the best. We've got more than seven hours still to go before anything can happen. Anything that we want to happen, that is . . ." her voice was hollow.

"Do you think they'll . . . shift Victoria? Move her somewhere else, now we're so near?"

"I don't know. I pray not. I don't see why they should —as long as they think they've got *us* trapped. As long as they don't know about Mrs. Sidney and the escape route."

Mark sat forward, hands clasped loosely between his knees, looking up at Helen from his deep-set eyes. Through the funnel of the intervening rooms, Helen could hear voices, but could not make out what was being said. Half her attention, half her nerves were ready to jump to some kind of violent action at the sound of breaking glass, an explosion, a shot.

Mark appeared to have resigned himself to a secondary rôle; to be most interested, at present, in studying Helen. She felt a small creeping sense of embarrassment beside her other preoccupations, a wish to efface herself or distract Mark's attention. But he continued to look, gravely and wonderingly, at her: inoffensively, she had to admit, but with insistence. Against her will she said with a slight nervous crack in her voice:

"What are you seeing?"

"You," he answered simply, "or as much of you as anyone can. I always thought you beautiful, but there is something more. What? Authority, perhaps. The authority that distinguishes a work of art. . . . Helen, what will you do when all this is over?"

"When it's all over!" her voice, pitched low, was vehement. "It's scarcely begun, and yet you seem . . . you seem able to concentrate on something which may not—even—survive. Can't you see? We'll be lucky if we have any future at all!"

Mark's slow headshake, his unusual calm, were maddening.

"We'll get through, all right," he said.

"How *dare* you be so sure?"

"Oh," he shrugged his shoulders, "we'll simply have to. We're not the sort of people to be . . . let off."

"I could hate you," Helen said, her voice husky, just above her breath. "You land us all—and Victoria—in this, and then you talk as if it were an exercise, something from a textbook. We're lost, miles from anywhere decent, surrounded by enemies who really know how to hate: maniacs, murderers. We depend for our safety, for Victoria's life, on an old woman and a handful of peasants. And you sit there talking about inevitability."

Mark gave a sudden, totally carefree grin.

"How am I ever to get into your good books?" he asked. "You're perfectly right, of course. But I may be

232

right, too. I can't be wrong all the time!" His touch of humorous pleading might have been infuriating, but he suddenly looked so like Victoria at her naughtiest that Helen softened a little towards him. She raised her head sharply.

"Sh! Listen!" The voices had stopped, and from the Octagon came the bang of closing shutters, the clank of an iron bar. Carlo came rapidly towards them over the bare boards, his footsteps sounding dangerously loud.

Mark rose quickly and stood waiting. Carlo gave them a worried smile. He seemed short of breath, as though he had run some distance.

"Sit down," he said, "may as well be comfortable. We've got some time yet—at least I think we have."

"Who was it?"

"Major Zradkin. Depressing man who came to the Legation the night Victoria disappeared. One of Krykula's right-hands, it seems."

"Anyone with him?"

"Couple of soldiers. Perfectly silent. Kept at a respectful distance, covering the door with automatic rifles."

"Well, what had he got to say?"

"He said . . ." Carlo seemed hard put to it to find breath. "What he said was quite simple. He said . . . deliver you and Helen up straight away. No quarrel with the rest of us. If I'd do that, then Victoria would be restored. Safe conduct back to Senj for her, Tubb and myself." Something of the horror Carlo must have felt at this suggestion showed in his face. "I told him—rather pompously, I suppose," he gave a thin, regretful smile, "that I hadn't the faintest idea what he was talking about. That Tubb and I had come to look for Victoria; that we'd been forced to spend the night in Ostrány because of the weather; that if he and his masters wished to avoid the most almighty international stink, they'd help instead of hindering. And, finally, that I'd have no further words with anyone but General Krykula, and preferably not with him; and that I proposed to continue my own course without reference to anyone; and that they

233

would have to settle with my Government if any harm came of it. . . . Not exactly playing from strength, as you might say, but the best I could do in the circs."

"What did he say to all that?"

"Nothing much. He's not a man of many words, I'll say that for him. Just repeated that they knew you and Helen were here and that *others* were helping us, who would be dealt with later. That the Kursaal was surrounded and that they would move in at dawn to get us. We had till then to think better of it. He was pretty angry. There was some curious heel-clicking and then they all marched off again, and we shut the shutters. It's snowing hard, by the way, which is good for us. Funny!" Carlo chuckled briefly. "It was all so deadly serious . . . and perishing cold, because I had to break a pane of glass with my elbow to hear what he was saying properly . . . but I couldn't take my eyes off that beastly square mustache of his, going up and down, stuck full of snow!"

Helen lay, fully dressed, under a blanket on one of Sergeant Tubb's mattresses. She lay on her back, staring wide-eyed at the preposterous ceiling. Her eyelids felt creased with strain, but she had found it useless to close them. Rest, of a sort, was possible: sleep was not. "Watered-down Tie-polo," Helen said to herself sneeringly. And then, in reference to the chandelier: "Pantomime birdcage." She had tried reciting poetry, remembering the plots of films, even humming music soundlessly. Now she was phrase-making to pass the time. She had rationed herself where looking at her watch was concerned; even so, the hands moved so slowly betweentimes, that she had to listen to make sure the watch was still going.

She had gone to bed, under orders, at twelve. It was now half-past three. Tubb was on watch, seated at the card-table which had been pulled up close to the shuttered glass doors, smoking and playing patience. The other two men were lying down, but whether asleep or not Helen could not tell, since both were turned away from her. The beds had been placed each in an angle be-

234

tween windows and the would-be sleepers had their feet pointing to the centre of the room.

There had been some discussion earlier on about abandoning the Octagon entirely and retreating to the salon so as to be nearer the Pump Room when the time came for escape. But by doing this they would have lost a listening-post (since the salon and ante-rooms gave only onto the glazed gallery enclosing a garden to the west of the building, and this was already held by Mrs. Sidney's men under the command of Tadusz). A more compelling reason lay in the fact that the Octagon—through some magic of Tadusz'—was heated, where the other rooms were not. So they had decided to stay, thereafter spending a laborious hour "sandbagging," the lower portions of the windows with an assortment of materials—curtains, filing cabinets, folded-up invalid chairs—collected from the adjacent rooms. "We mayn't need any of this," Tubb had said at the end when, sweating and dust-streaked, they had contemplated their work, "and it wouldn't stop everything they might think to throw at us. But it's certainly better than nothing and, whatever happens, the Glumbas will have to tidy it up!"

Helen gave up making phrases and lay rigid, miserably considering her unprotectedness. The thick blanket might have been so much air, for all the comfort it gave; the thin mattress pressed up at her hard and flat with the hardness of the boards below. She was warm enough, in fact, but the chill of doubt and anxiety made her cold in bowels and heart. Every so often she shivered uncontrollably and clenched her teeth to keep them from chattering. Somewhere, not far away, was Stoyan and she longed with the longing of a child, of an animal, to be lifted in his arms and borne away, far away from doubt and danger, to safety and pleasure and peace. But where? Doubt and danger must now, more than ever, be his portion. His presence nearby must mean that he had taken the plunge, outlawed himself, declared for Ilena and counter-revolution. Helen allowed herself a small hope, a prayer that Stoyan might also be moving nearer to protect, to help her.

Her thoughts slid to Victoria, sleeping or waking, perhaps fretting, perhaps feverish, ill. So highly strung a child could never accept, acquiesce in such a situation. Was Simpkin faithful, even under duress? Had they *time* for what they were doing? How hazardous, in fact, were their plans?

Dawn would break in two and a half hours, at six o'clock or so, later rather than sooner, probably, because of the thick snow. At first light, if all went according to Mrs. Sidney's plan, they would hear firing from beyond the kitchen quarters, from the stable cottages where Victoria was held. They were to expect more firing a moment later, from the main road where they had crossed it the night before. These were to be diversions covering the rescue of Victoria. Shortly afterwards they were to expect another diversion, not yet specified, on their own, the southern side, of the Kursaal; and at that, they were to be ready to follow Tadusz through the underground way from the Pump Room, and so into the third and last phase of their journey. All entrances to the Kursaal, saving the Octagon, were heavily barricaded, and Mrs. Sidney's men, few in number but, Tubb had reported, tough, competent-looking and well-armed, were posted in the garden gallery and at other points from which they could fight a delaying action if this became necessary.

Helen turned on her side, focussed her eyes on the dusty floorboards, dozed and fell suddenly asleep. Her dreams, a web of confusion, shook briefly into coherence and she found herself with Mark in the Legation garden. It was summer now. A sense of summer, of light and ease, pervaded her dream. Victoria was there, playing quietly, looking serious but contented. Helen spoke to her, but the child seemed not to hear her, only continued her game without looking up. Mark, younger and somehow bigger, more solid, seemed to say to her, urgently: "One more, Helen. There's still one more!" She woke, her dream world arcing, narrowing, turning faster and faster, rushing away like suds down a sink. Tubb's firm hand was on her shoulder.

"Don't panic, Miss. I'm going to put out the lights. We should be able to see something soon."

Desolate, cold and fearful Helen stammered:

"What's the time, Sergeant Tubb?"

"Eleven minutes to six."

The others were standing waiting, each beside a window. Mark smiled across at Helen.

"We let you sleep," he said. "I envied you!"

"Ready?" Tubb called from the doorway.

"Ready!" they answered, and darkness fell like a blow. Helen had struggled to her feet, and now stood holding a corner of the window-casing to steady herself, staring through the darkness at the place where the shutters would soon show a crack of light. There was no light at present.

"Dark as the inside of a cow!" came Tubb's voice from somewhere behind her. There was a clicking, metallic sound and weak light suddenly threw them all into dramatic relief, standing against their own shadows. "There! I thought this torch was bust!"

Tubb moved quickly across the room, looked briefly at the shutters of the northeast window, and extinguished the torch. They heard the catch move, the iron bar rise and descend, scraping along the wood, the dead thump it made at the end of its travel. The shutter squeaked. After a pause Tubb said:

"It's stopped snowing. The sky's clear. No one near the building on this side." The shutter squeaked again and the torch went on.

"Are you going to open the lot?" It was Carlo's voice.

"No, I don't think so. That one, because it'll give a view of the opposition up there at the edge of the wood and it commands the road that way. This one over here," and he swung the torch beam over to the window second on the right, next to the glass doors, "this one, I think: it looks right down on their main position and it commands the road all the way up. For the blind spots we'll have to depend on Tadusz and the others. . . ."

Again the torch went out, and they heard a shutter open.

"No one near on that side, either." There was a hint of relief in his tone. "Now, Mr. Sweet, if you'll take up a stand over there, you can tell us what goes on up the hill. Keep well back and don't open more of the shutter than you have to. Miss Clark, you stand just behind him, but so's you can see. We'll need your eyes on this. You, Sir, will stand here if you please," he indicated the other window. "I'll be just behind you. If there's any shooting everybody gets right down behind the barricades double-quick. And don't any of you fire back unless I say. All right?"

Carlo and Mark picked up their rifles from the stack. Their pockets bulged with spare clips.

"You stick to your pistol for the present, Miss," Tubb called. "I'll put a rifle in the corner there for you, with some cartridge-clips in case you need it."

Helen's .38 hung heavily from a short lanyard round her neck. It clung to her malevolently, like a growth. She felt better holding it; the butt, fitted into her hand, was, at least, something solid to grip. She followed Carlo across to their window, her feet heavy and unwilling. Tubb's torch went out. She felt a cold breath from the freezing glass as Carlo eased the shutter open.

Helen prayed, an undirected, incoherent prayer—that Victoria would be safe, that there need be no battle, that Stoyan would come to her. Carlo said: "It's getting lighter."

Above, the sky was polished black stippled with pale stars. High up in front of them, a black bar without luminescence must be the forest beyond the road. Helen, in the misty grey expanse of the snowy world before her, could just detect the line of the road, hairpinning upwards, could just make out the darker smudge of the small wood where the machine-gun post must be. There was no apparent movement anywhere. The scene was set: action alone was lacking.

Tubb said suddenly loudly: "They're off!" His trained ear had caught the first distant tap of gunfire from the northwest. Then spattering, ripping, its echoes slamming round the steep hillsides, the noise came to all of them,

238

muffled but very real. Tears sprang to Helen's eyes. "Don't be frightened, Victoria!" she said desperately— out loud, it seemed, for Carlo put back a hand to grip her shoulder. "She won't be, Helen. Victoria's as brave as a lion. She'll be all right. Just trust Ilena."

Helen thought she saw movement now at the edge of the little wood. Gobbets of darkness were detaching themselves from it, wavering to form a smaller clump on the now whitening snow-slope. As she gazed, another tearing burst of fire flung its echoes across the others, from nearer at hand this time, from the main road above them to their left. The second diversion was taking place according to plan. One big explosion made the windows rattle, and a silver flash blazed on the dusky landscape for an instant, lighting the heavy eaves, the blinded windows, of the Zwingli Palace where they showed above the towering snowy ridge.

Now Helen could see clearly the contours of the road, the shape of the small wood, the knot of human figures crouching in its lee. The stars were almost gone, and the patch of clear sky round which black towers of snow-cloud still stood waiting, was pewter-colored, cold and grim.

It seemed, to Helen's ear, that the fierce firing they had first heard, from the northwest, was petering out. From an almost continuous stammering roar, it had quieted to single shots, distant drum-taps behind the concerted racket going on at the road.

"I wish I had some field glasses," Carlo said. "I don't know, but I rather think our friends at the wood are looking the other way. Here, Helen," he stood back to give her a better view. "You've got good eyes. What can you see?" In the strengthening grey light Helen gazed up the snowy slope to the snow-crusted brown-black hump of the wood. She saw first one, then another, tiny dark figure break free from the group and run uphill to be hidden by a snowbank at the bend of the road.

"You're right," she said. "They must be more interested in what's happening outside the Zwingli Palace." She felt fear and anxiety suddenly lift, float free of her, to release an excitement that was almost gay.

239

"Hang on," she said, "I'm going to desert my post for a minute."

Helen ran to the corner where last night's cooking materials had been stowed. She had filled a thermos with coffee before going to bed, and then forgotten all about it. Helen handed Mark and Tubb their cups. Tubb stood back to let her see past Mark, down the ridged snowfield of the terraces, to the enemy camp at the edge of the woods. She caught her breath at the apparent size of the concentration there, the sense of power and purpose which came to her from the parked trucks, the groups of men standing easy as if waiting, at any moment, to move. She spoke over her shoulder to Tubb.

"Wasn't . . . wasn't Major Zradkin to come up again, to call on us to surrender?"

"He was. Only I rather think the diversions may have changed their minds. The staff-car's been and gone in a hurry—probably up the main road to see what's gone wrong."

"Well," Helen said bleakly, "it's back!" The long green staff-car had just shot out of the shrubs concealing the driveway and stopped in a flurry of snow. Helen saw the driver spring to open the rear door, saw a figure familiar, even at this distance, in its arrogant squatness, followed from the car by a very tall man in uniform. An officer approached, saluted. Luba Kassin seemed to be doing the talking. She pointed, first beyond the Kursaal towards the Zwingli Palace where the shooting had now died down, then directly at the Octagon: directly, Helen felt with a twist of the heart, at her. The officer saluted again and went at once to what must be the radio-truck. Helen wrenched her eyes from the spectacle of Luba Kassin enjoying vengeance, and took Carlo some coffee. As she put the cup into his hand a flight of crimson bees began to come slowly, in a long dropping curve, from the little wood above. Before Helen could do more than wonder what was happening Carlo, with a shout of "get down, everyone!" pulled her roughly down with him behind their barricade. At the same moment an immense clatter

240

broke out above them, glass smashed and fell tinkling from behind the closed upper shutters, slates and pieces of guttering thudded down outside.

"They're using tracer," Carlo shouted. "Get away from that window for a bit. Crawl, both of you, and get in by the wall to the right there. From where they're firing, they can't possibly hit you this side!"

"Go on, Helen! Hurry up!" She was still squirming across the floor, feeling horribly exposed, when a second burst of machine-gun fire sawed through the window at chest height where they had been standing thirty seconds before. From comparative safety in their corner, she and Carlo could see the loose shutters flung back by the hinges, most of the glazing-bars and all the glass gone from the window, and a drift of glass fragments, wood splinters and chips of stone on the floor inside. Bullets had ploughed long yellow furrows in the dirty boards of the floor. The air rang with violence and smelt evil. Helen felt sick.

"Well, really," said Carlo mildly. "It doesn't look as if there's going to be any more parleying! What do we do now, Sergeant Tubb?"

Mark and Tubb had moved up beside them and Tubb was standing to open the shutters of the central window.

"Unless diversion number three happens soon, this isn't going to be a very nice place any longer," he said. He had got a shutter open and was peering out. "Um. Just as I thought. General Dracula's on the move. They're just fanning out to come up the hill. We haven't much time. Stop still, while I have a look and see what's happening up above."

They watched him anxiously as he edged round the walls towards the shattered window. They saw him drop to his knees, then to all fours, at the near corner of the barricade and then with immense slowness, move his head up centimetre by centimetre to get a view. Helen held her breath, Carlo and Mark were still as stones. Slowly Tubb's head came up and, at each second, the watchers expected another hail of bullets to come streaking down.

The room was bitterly cold now, washed in dead, icy air. When the noise came, it came amplified by the great hollow frozen amphitheatre outside. The first explosion made Helen cry out, in fear for Tubb. But no bullets came their way. Two loud, reverberant crashes, faint shouts, the methodical barking of automatic rifles sounded down to them from the direction of the wood. Tubb straightened swiftly and peered round the window-frame. For a moment he stayed perfectly still, as if in stupefaction, then smacked a hand to his head.

"Christ!" he exclaimed. "Armor!"

Helen jumped up, on an impulse, and looked through the opened shutter of the central window. Krykula's men had indeed set off up hill towards the Octagon but now were halted, seeming undecided, all looking one way towards the machine-gun post. For the moment they appeared astonished, uncertain. Some men had turned back and were running for the headquarters vehicles, perhaps for the radio-truck.

Mark and Carlo had moved up beside Tubb. Something was riveting their attention, something which made them think it safe to stand half-exposed. Helen joined them and Tubb stood back to give her his place. The firing was continuous now. A blue cloud of cordite drifted towards them down the hill. At the upper bend of the road, beyond the little wood, a great black car was moving slowly forwards. Although half of it was still hidden by the snowbank, Helen recognized it at once. She could see flashes coming from the wind-shield, from the side windows, and a square red flag blowing stiffly from the roof.

"Couldn't see any use for that car, at the time," Tubb's voice was wondering. "Can now, though!"

"It's the Princess' car," said Helen, "but—why is it flying the red flag?"

"That is no red flag," said a well-known voice behind them. "That is the scarlet banner of the Sideini princes. It has not been raised in battle for two hundred years!"

242

In all the maze of Helen's preoccupations, one was dominant. She seized Mrs. Sidney's hand. "Did it go all right?" she begged. "Is Victoria safe?"

"Safe as safe, my dear. Safer than you are at present. She has been very good and soon she will be at home."

"Shall I see her?"

"Soon, Helen, soon—if all goes well. She is waiting for you. And now." Mrs. Sidney's tone was brisk. "We have very little time. That car is driven by my cousin Anzip, and it contains three of my men. They have silenced that machine-gun with grenades and now they are coming on down here. They are coming straight into heavy fire from Krykula so we must get them out of that car and into the Kursaal without any delay. Fortunately, some work has been done for us. There is no more window."

Without prompting, Tubb and Carlo bent and pulled away the components of the barricade. Tubb undid the lowest shutters, opened them, and kicked away the remnants of glass and wood at the foot of the window. As he did so firing broke out below them, to their right. Helen could hear the high swish and moan of the bullets as they went past towards the car, towards Stoyan. She could not move, could not take her eyes from the square black shape now coming very fast towards them, skidding, jinking, slewing on and off the road in a thick scatter of snow. Above the sound of the guns, she could hear the engine whining in low gear, the sweet clatter of glass as bullets found the windows. She saw a milk-white spider's web in front of the driver and prayed he had not been hit. She felt Mrs. Sidney's hand grip her arm.

"He must get through," she whispered through her teeth.

"We must hope," said the old woman. "I am glad he came back to us. Rather late, perhaps, but . . . I am glad: and a little proud."

There had been flashes coming from the car, on its way down the hill. She had seen the muzzles of rifles pointed from the windows, firing past her, but now, as the car drew nearer—now she could see the paintwork holed and scored silver by bullets, the smashed radiator, the starred windshield—there was no more firing. A hundred yards, seventy-five, fifty—and the noise of firing from the other side was more intense. The snow round the car splashed up in countless spurts of spray, like water under hail. Thirty yards, twenty-five, almost home, almost in the safety of the Octagon walls, out of the field of fire. The car skidded convulsively, swished round in a tail-skid and stopped, its hood pointing towards their window. It was now about fifteen yards away and still full in the sights of Krykula's soldiers.

All Helen's impulse was to run out into the murderous snow, to find Stoyan. She must have started forward, because Mrs. Sidney seized both her arms. Helen moaned, pulling against the strong hands which held her. Then she saw the rear door on the far side of the car open and, with relief that was like a pain, saw a man in dark-green jump, crouching, to the ground. He reached up, opened the driver's door, and pulled Stoyan Anzip out on top of him. They fell together in the snow, in the shelter of the car, which rocked and rang with the impact of bullets upon it. The man in green got to his knees, half dived forward and slung Stoyan over his shoulder. Then, pausing a moment to adjust his burden, he rose and stood crouching, nerving himself for his task, in the lee of the car.

Tubb swung on Mrs. Sidney.

"Yell at him to stay where he is. Don't let him come on till we've had a shot at drawing their fire. All of you—grab a rifle apiece and we'll try our luck."

Helen found herself with a rifle in her hand, bent double behind the barricade of the central window, beside Mark. She could hear the voice of Mrs. Sidney ringing imperiously out into the snow, the harsh syllables sounding sharp and distinct amidst the blurred chatter of the rifle-fire.

"Bust the glass with the muzzles," shouted Tubb, "and fire at the ones nearest, fire into the brown—anything to distract their attention." As he spoke he fired. Mark's rifle cracked ear-splittingly beside her. Helen aimed roughly at a dark advancing shape and pulled the trigger. The

244

dark shape stopped, as if reflecting, spun round once very slowly, and fell to the snowy ground, twitching. Horror froze Helen's fingers. Nausea rose in her. She put her head down for a moment thinking: It was for him! Faintly, as if through water, she heard Tubb's voice:

"How does it look now?" Bullets were smashing the glass, splitting the shutters of the Octagon as Krykula's men returned their fire. Mark's rifle and Carlo's were firing steadily; the air of the room was thick, acid with cordite fumes.

"Better." Mrs. Sidney called back to Tubb. "It cannot be perfect. I think he should come on. The others in the car must be dead, and Stoyan is hurt, perhaps badly. Also, we cannot wait. We have only minutes now."

Helen heard the commanding voice raised once more, and knew that the short, interminable journey had begun. She began to fire wildly at the advancing soldiers, now no more than a hundred yards away, scarcely troubling to keep her head down hoping to distract one or two bullets at least from Stoyan and the man in green.

"Ah God, he is down!" Mrs Sidney's voice rang with anguish. Helen heard feet rush by behind her on the boards and half turned in time to see a tall figure flying through the window.

"Come back, Sir! Wait—oh, bless his heart, the silly old bastard—" Tubb's voice was broken. Helen darted to Mrs. Sidney's side, to see Carlo, familiar peaceful Carlo, topcoat and hat and all, run swiftly across the snow, pick Stoyan's body from the lifeless arms of the man in green, turn and begin to drag him with great heaving jerks towards the window. They were so near that Helen could hear Carlo's breathing. Then they were nearer still. There were, perhaps, five yards left to go before the jutting Octagon would have given shelter, when Carlo stopped, patted with the familiar gesture the pocket over his heart, fell to his knees, fell forward and lay still. His brown hat rolled a little way and came to rest, brim upwards.

Through blinding tears Helen saw Tubb step forward, push past Mrs. Sidney, stride out of the window to Stoyan. With what seemed terrible slowness he looked once, closely, at Carlo's body, then with his arms under shoulders and knees, gathered up Stoyan and carried him easily into the Octagon. Helen did not look twice at the stony misery of his face. She could hear Mark swearing monotonously and somebody sobbing, which must be herself.

"Take him through to the salon." Mrs. Sidney's calm was bracing. "We must abandon this place and be on our way. "No." she said sternly, as Tubb turned mutinous eyes on her. "No—he must stay where he is. He was brave, and we loved him. He would wish us to complete our work. . . . Also, he is best there, in the snow. It is cleaner, and they—even they—will respect him."

For the moment the firing had ceased. White light glared in at the windows. The room, shabbier than ever in daylight, littered with glass and splinters, layered with cordite smoke, seemed suddenly deadly, a place to be left behind. The party, headed by Tubb with his burden—not dead, Stoyan, but somewhere badly shocked or wounded—edged through the door and on to the shuttered, ill-lit, comparative security of the salon.

It seemed to be understood that Helen should kneel by Stoyan, gently undo his fur-collared hunting coat, uncover the blood-soaked shirt and the black-centred welling red rent in his chest. Tubb had gone back to the Octagon, regardless of risk, for dressings. There was not much they could do beyond the most temporary cleaning and staunching. During their ministrations, Stoyan lay cold and still. His forehead, which had been masked in blood, was clean again, nicked all over with cuts from the splintered wind-shield. His pulse was weak, irregular. There was no question that, ideally, he should not be moved.

Tadusz appeared silently and stood beside Helen looking down at Stoyan, his face working slowly as though he were chewing. Firing had broken out again and now from points along the garden front and from the Kursaal roof, Tadusz' men were fighting to delay the enemy, to buy for them all a little more time. Working swiftly,

Tubb and Mark had filled wheelchairs with combustible materials, doused them with paraffin, lit them and rolled them blazing into the Octagon. They had then closed the doors and left them to do their work. Already the roar of flames taking hold was increasing in the narrow, sound-magnifying spaces of the rooms.

Mrs. Sidney spoke briefly with Tadusz, then turned to Helen. "My dear, he is badly—perhaps very badly—hurt. We cannot possibly carry him with us. It might well kill him, and it would quite certainly mean that we should fail to escape. Tadusz, who also loves him, will take care of him. He can be got away soon, quite easily, by another means. And then . . . why then, we shall see!"

"I seem to draw comfort from everybody, and give none myself. . . ." Helen warmed Stoyan's icy hand in hers, thinking he could not look more far away, even in death.

A great fatigue came over her. To her shocked annoyance, she yawned largely. Mrs. Sydney laughed.

"Will you trust him to Tadusz, then? More than anyone, more than anything in the world, you need your sleep." She turned at this, and went out through the door leading to the Pump Room, closing it behind her. There were faint sounds, just audible in the continuous noise, of activity beyond the door.

Helen looked up to find herself alone with Stoyan. Mark and Tubb must have gone off with Tadusz for a last-minute estimate of the defenses. She laid her head for a moment on Stoyan's limp arm. There was so much to mourn for, so many tears to shed, so much bruising pain and fear to be lived down. The future seemed flat and pointless at present. If Stoyan were to die . . . Helen shook the thought away, and tried to remember all the first-aid lectures she had ever heard. Stoyan's wound was deep and ragged—from a heavy-calibre bullet, Tubb had said. It might have touched, or missed a lung. He needed skilled attention, and soon. And she must leave him to Tadusz, to weeks of hiding in an area certain to be combed and combed again by Krykula's men. She clasped the cold hand a little tighter, and promised

247

foolishly a world of simplicities beyond the confines of time and pain.

Musing, and striving to communicate some of her strength to Stoyan through their hands, Helen had lost awareness of her situation. Her mind had only vaguely registered one or two extra-loud crashes, an alteration in the tempo of the firing, shouts and sound of breaking glass somewhere at the west end of the building. Absorbed with Stoyan, she had relinquished to others the task of protecting them both.

Where she knelt beside the silent Stoyan, Helen had, on her right, the doorway leading towards the Octagon, and on her left the closed door of the Pump Room. Directly behind her another door gave on to the glassed-in gallery which ran on all four sides of a small garden. On the far side, she vaguely knew, there was another entrance to the Kursaal, barricaded like all the rest. Less absorbed, more alert, she would have connected various recent sounds in her mind with their points of origin, and realized that, somehow, an entry had been forced through the side door; that fighting was going on in the Kursaal itself; and that not minutes, but seconds, might well decide the issue now. Fatigue and anxiety had made her careless. When a draft of colder air warned her that the door behind her had opened, she was still slow to turn her head.

When she did turn her head, Helen was on her feet in one movement, standing protectively in front of Stoyan, revolver in hand. Framed in the narrow doorway, neck thrust forward, her wide face split across by a leer of triumphant fury, was Luba Kassin. Behind her white smoke billowed down the gallery. Shouts and explosions volleyed at her back. She had a heavy automatic pointed at Helen's breast.

"Do not move," came the harsh, carrying voice. "You who find my country so interesting, you will find this interesting too. You meddlesome little bitch, I am going to kill you. Do you understand? I am going to shoot you—" she took a sucking breath, saliva and air at once— "not in the head, which is quick; not in the heart

248

you think so important; but low, low down, little Miss, where you think you are better than me. You will be quite a long time dying and I will watch you die. Now!" The point of the automatic descended slowly. "You will not have the courage to fire first . . . I said *don't move.* . . ."

Helen, who could not have brought herself to fire, half-hypnotized as she was by the yellow eyes, the blasting force of their hatred on her, had side-stepped hopelessly a foot or so, revealing, as she moved, the still head of Stoyan Anzip.

The automatic wavered, Luba Kassin's eyes changed direction. The fixed, theatrical grin dissolved, leaving her face lopsided, flabby, suddenly greatly aged. Her voice came thick, husky, no longer ringingly harsh.

"He is dead?"

"No, Luba, I am not dead!" Feeble, exhausted, a mere thread of a voice, but it was Stoyan's voice. Helen looked down to see his head turned towards her, his dark eyes open. He seemed to be trying to smile, for his lips stretched a little and his eyes widened.

"Then—traitor!" Force was coming back into Luba Kassin's voice. As though pulled together by a string, her features reassembled into their pattern of rage. She took a step forward, glaring down at Stoyan, and spoke through clenched teeth:

"I have you both. I shall kill you both."

A voice of high and piercing sweetness struck like a glass bell on the troubled air of the room:

"I think not, Your Excellency!" As Luba Kassin turned, automatic raised, to the sound of the voice, Mrs. Sidney shot her twice in the stomach. A hideous high squealing, suddenly choked to a gurgle, a deep retching cough, came from Luba Kassin, as she doubled up, clawing her stomach, and fell, and lay twitching on the floor. For perhaps half a minute she lay thus, her thick limbs thrashing more slowly until, with a dark gush of blood from one side of her mouth, her head lolled and was still. Quite paralyzed, ill with horror, Helen looked at Mrs. Sidney, standing proudly, her face pale and clear as a cameo, a priestess in her robe of furs. The old woman moved, very deliberately, from the doorway where she was standing, stood looking down at the dead, malevolent face for a long minute—then, with a swift movement, ground the strong heel of her boot into the yellow flesh, this way and that, until there were no features at all, only a scarlet smear. She turned a face of alabaster, a carved mask of sorrow, on Helen.

"You must believe" she said softly, "it was not for myself I did that. It was for my people. And for all the women she has murdered as, tonight, she would have murdered you."

Incapable, now, of taking in any more, Helen turned, her knees crumpling, to kneel beside Stoyan. But Stoyan, perhaps having saved her life, had gone from her again, this time forever.

"Heart failure!" Helen's voice was low but charged with scorn, with regret. She heard the old woman in the high chair move sharply, as if in sudden pain, but would not look at her, went on staring down at the winter trees, the palely lit, cossetted villas of Campden Hill. She slapped the broad sheets of *The Times* together and dropped the paper beside her chair. Mr. Charles Sweet, C.M.G., said his obituary, had died suddenly of heart failure at our Legation in Senj. . . .

"Tubb says my daddy fought like a tiger!" There was pride and a hint of warning in the clear voice. For this Helen could thaw.

"He did, Victoria, I promise!" and to Mark's mother: "There's no doubt that, but for him, we should never have got away at all. Things were very bad towards the last. We'd set half the Kursaal on fire; we still had access to the underground passage. But they—Kassin and her people—had forced a side door and there was fearful confusion. All the time she was . . . with me . . . Mark and Tubb and Tadusz were fighting hand to hand. They were getting back to the rest of us, step by step, and holding their own all right, when another wave of soldiers came through the door." She looked directly at the old
250

face—tired, beautiful, somehow touching in its rejection of pride—and said more warmly: "It was then that Mark went berserk. 'Bloody well went for them solo with a tommy gun,' Tubb says. How he escaped I'll never know, but he gave Tubb time to bundle me down into the passage, and was last in himself, still firing, when we were already scuttling up it."

Victoria scrambled to her feet and planked a sheet of paper in Helen's lap.

"Draw me a tiger, Helen."

"All right, darling. Let's see. I'll do the tiger and you do the stripes. . . . It was Mark who covered our rear as we floundered through the woods to the little railway station. By then, Tubb was taking *his* orders—glad to, as he told me later. We found Victoria waiting—it was fantastic—*waiting,* as good as gold, in the waiting room, with a bodyguard of foresters. . . ."

"They gave me some gingerbread," the child put in, without looking up. "They said Simpkin would be all right. Dismal old cow!" she added in a low voice, but not low enough for her grandmother not to hear.

"Victoria! you are not to say that, about anybody. Also, I have the impression that Mrs. Simpkin did well by you, according to her lights!" Amusement lightened the delicate features, thinned so by pain and fear since Helen had seen them last. Victoria changed the subject.

"What colors are tigers, Helen?"

"Yellow, with black stripes. Do the yellow first and put the stripes on afterwards. And the whiskers are black, too."

The old woman leaned towards Helen, lowering her voice again to say:

"He will be here at five. Will you stay?" Her look, her pose were pleading. Helen felt a jolt of panic, an almost violent wish to be gone.

"I have no right . . ." the other went on, and stopped.

Neither you nor he has any right, Helen thought. Am I to help you sing your Nunc Dimittis? And, at the same moment, knew that she would stay. She bent her head in acquiescence, and heard the faint sigh, the chink and rustle as Mark's mother sank back into her chair again.

"Go on, Helen," the old voice was stronger now. "The railway station. . . ."

"There were men behind us. Not far behind, they kept taking pot shots. I grabbed Victoria and we all piled on to one of those rail-car things, with a handle you pump up and down, which was waiting, and shot off, over the edge of the hill and down—at a terrifying lick, till Tubb found the brake. A few bullets came near us, quite near enough—" she shuddered slightly, looking at Victoria— "but no one was hit . . ."

"Whee-ee-ee, plosh!" said Victoria with relish. Her grandmother shook her head in wonder.

". . . When we got to the plain, there's a little station —and goodness, I felt as if I'd been away for years! There was a perfect crowd of people. Martin Wright with Mark's big car, and Dick Phillips from the American Legation, and even Monsieur Hunziger! He's usually so stiff—he was almost in tears. The most joyful reunion you can imagine, until they heard about Carlo. . . . After that, they sort of shook themselves and concentrated on Victoria, and we were all borne pretty well shoulder-high into Senj."

"Martin came to see me yesterday. Absurd boy, he says he's going to marry at once and have six children—simply to call them all Preston, boys *and* girls, after the American Minister, whom he seems to admire greatly!"

"Well he may! It seems that, after we'd set out, Mr. Preston Chalk discovered that Victoria had been . . ." she checked herself, "had gone away. The story is that he rounded on his wife and said: 'Ellie, after years and years of goddam diplomacy, here's my chance to do something useful!' He then called into being what Martin calls 'Chalk's Irregulars' —Martin and Dick Phillips—and waded straight into the Prime Minister without further ado. When Mort Landow, his Counsellor—who was quaking with the impropriety of everything and, oh, general ambivalence—tried to stop him, Mr. Chalk threatened him with an adverse report it'd take the State Department three days to read!"

252

The old woman laughed with real amusement. Her eyes were shining. "Go on," she said. "Oh, I do love this! Go on!"

"Well, Martin says Mr. Chalk was magnificent. Really grand. He towered and thundered over the Guv. Something, Martin says, that doesn't belong to diplomatic history, but to the record of great good deeds. It seems he pledged his country to every kind of action, by no means short of war, and very convincingly too. He had the Guv really worried. Things went into motion and, if Kassin hadn't taken the bit between her teeth, not a shot would have been fired. . . ." Her voice trailed away. The thought of Carlo was like a lump in her throat.

"Because of him," she said, more slowly, "our friends, Mrs. Sidney and her people are safe. For the time being, at any rate. . . ."

"The Kursaal was completely destroyed by fire?" The old woman's voice was hesitant. Conscious of a stiffening in her face, in her voice, Helen answered, "Completely."

There was a pause full of small sounds—an old spaniel snoozing by the fire which creaked and settled softly, the child's crayon scrubbing industriously in the dying light.

"When you are as old as I am, Helen, you will know—and you may be, as I am, impertinent enough to say—that the heart is not incinerated. . . . Please believe, child, that I would undo nothing, overlay nothing. What you have you have, in the way of memory, and I pray you keep it. But there is life to be got on with . . ." her voice was weary, "and there is always *need*."

Another voice, full of relief and pleasure, had said to Helen, that morning, in a quiet office in the Strand:

"For one who thought herself not needed, you have a remarkable lot on your hands!"

Helen turned over this idea of need in her mind, trying to isolate her own. Victoria, Mark, even Mark's mother; their need was evident. "We go where we're needed," Henry Sanders had said, so long ago, in Senj. Over a dying man's dark head she sighed and said, just out loud: "I need—"

Through the dusky room, a maze of small tables, Victoria pushed past them both to the door. Animals and children tell people by their footsteps. Still pulling on the door-handle she called, "Daddy."

The door opened and Mark came slowly into the room. He seemed to hesitate, one hand pressing Victoria's head against him as if for comfort, his eyes on Helen. Silence and hesitation lay between them, seeming fixed, unbreakable.

Helen's eyes searched the face of this man she knew so well, yet scarcely knew. She must have an answer, now, to the question which mattered to her most. Mark's eyes were direct, almost beseeching, but his forehead was calm at last. He looked younger than she had ever seen him, and deeply uncertain. She found herself moving towards him, giving him her hand which he raised to his cheek and held there for a moment.

"Helen—it's all over now: all, all over. . . ."

She smiled, looked down at Victoria's questioning eyes. "No, Mark—dear Mark—it's just beginning!"